ALONG THE NILE

Also by Lauren O. Thyme

Alternatives for Everyone, non-fiction
*Thymely Tales, Transformational Fairy Tales
for Adults and Children,* 2nd edition
Forgiveness Equals Fortune, non-fiction, co-written with
Liah Holtzman, 2nd edition
The Lemurian Way, Remembering your Essential Nature
Along the Nile, a novel on ancient Egypt
From the Depths of Thyme, a book of poetry
Strangers in Paradise, a novel of forgiveness
Cosmic Grandma Wisdom, non-fiction

Coming soon:
Catherine, A True Story

Along the Nile

Lauren O. Thyme

2017
Lauren O. Thyme Publishing
Santa Fe

First published by AuthorHouse 11/6/2009
Second edition: 2017

ISBN 978-0-9983446-3-8

Interior and Cover Design by Sue Stein

Lauren O. Thyme Publishing
www.laurenothymecreations.com
Santa Fe, New Mexico

This book is dedicated to my precious partner, Paul.

CONTENTS

FOREWORD

Forewords are not usually the norm in books of fiction, but most people would not describe the life path Lauren O. Thyme and I have chosen as normal. Throwing tradition to the wind, we followed our intuitive minds and hearts and answered the call of the wise and powerful Ancient Ones, or Neterw, the Egyptian Gods and Goddess of the land of Egypt, known as Kemet. No matter that we aren't of Middle Eastern ancestry. When one becomes aware you've been chosen by Sekhmet, Hathor, or Isis, your life's journey has been sealed for you and you are gifted with the courage, insight, and boons that come along with that great responsibility as their priestess, the vessels for their voice.

Anthropologists teach that throughout history, new people borrowed from the myths and material culture of a past people of more ancient times. Jews borrowed from Babylonians. Christians from Jews and Pagans. They cherrypicked their best ideas, adopted their wisdom, copied their imagery and motifs and repackaged the spirituality for the current culture of clergy and people. Together with Lauren, many of us called by the Egyptian Goddesses, Isis, Hathor, and Sekhmet, did just that, what people have done since the beginning of time.

Lauren was one of the first to establish within her home a temple dedicated to the Neterw, as she delved into ancient mysteries and practices.

There she guided us in performing ancient Egyptian ceremonies re-adapted for modern sensibilities, making relevant once again the energy of these most Wise Ones. She ran the Egypt Store, enabling people like me to have beautiful reproductions of artifacts to honor and represent the Ancient Ones in my home temple, The Isis Temple of Thanksgiving. She guided us in making sacred ritual objects and ceremonial garments, as well as in accessing these divine energies both on the inner planes and outside ourselves. She has been a trailblazer, mentor, and teacher to so many of us as she challenged us to open our minds beyond traditional thinking and established academic beliefs in learning about the most ancient days of Lemuria and Kemet. Following her heart, her spiritual guides and her intuition, she helped many of us reconstruct the spirituality of the Neterw in a contemporary context so that the ancient wisdom and guidance of the Ancient Ones might live once again and their voices be heard in our modern world.

Now Lauren does this again within the chapters of *Along the Nile*.

Having spent decades dedicated to the Neterw, there is no one better qualified to write *Along the Nile*, as Lauren uses her brilliant mind, imagination, and divine guidance to bring this ancient civilization alive. In *Along the Nile*, Lauren's integrity and dedication to Hathor and Sekhmet shine through. She weaves together history and mysticism, romance and action, along with unforgettable and endearing characters, to create this marvelous tapestry that brings ancient Egypt and the Neterw alive for twenty-first century readers. And through this fictional vehicle, she is not hampered as is the archaeologist. She is free to incorporate historical facts alongside what she has learned from personal pilgrimages to Egypt, from working for so long with the material culture of ancient times and the energies of the Neterw to again be the voice of the Ancient Ones.

In her love and admiration for Hathor and Sekhmet, two deities still very relevant and important to us today, whether viewed as deity or archetype, Lauren is their dutiful scribe. *Along the Nile* is her gift to readers as she allows and challenges us to re-imagine and re-think these ancient times, to begin to know these Goddesses, and to glean what we can for ourselves from those ancient teachings and mysteries still so important to people today.

—*In loving thanks and gratitude, Rev. Karen Tate, Priestess of Isis Mistress of Goddess Spirituality (MsGS), Author of Sacred Places of Goddess; 108 Destinations Walking An Ancient Path: Rebithing Goddess on Plant Earth. Radio Show Hostess of Voices of the Sacred Feminine* www.karentate.com

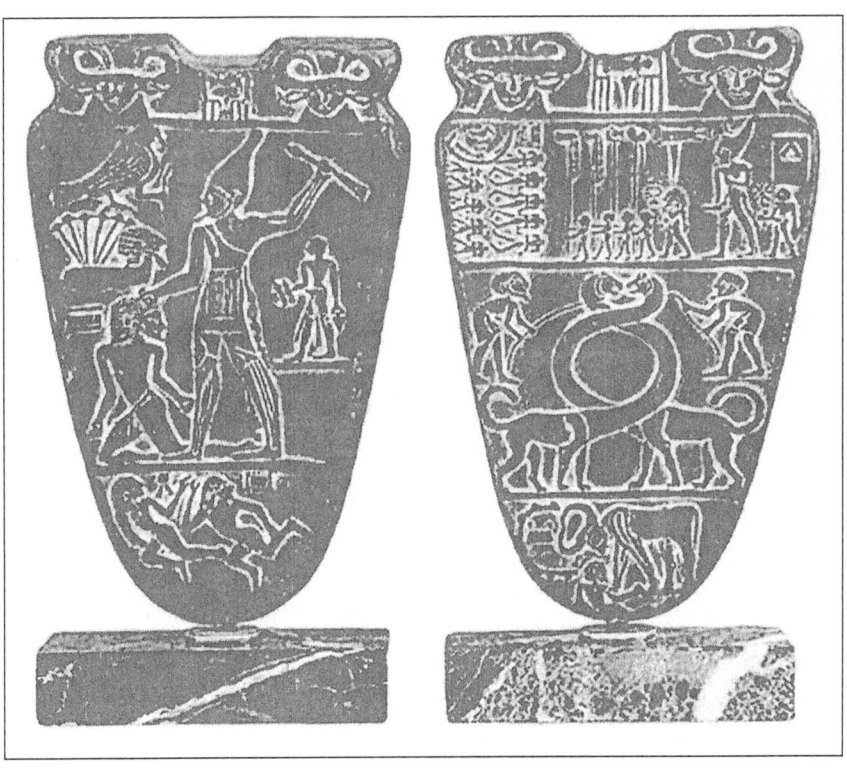

Narmer Palette, side 1 and 2
Image compliments of AncientTreasures.com

REVIEWS

It is a difficult task to weave history, story, and personal revelation, but Lauren Thyme has done it. Surely, as you read *Along the Nile* you can feel glare of the sun, the excitement of sisterhood in the temples, the devotion to the pharaoh and to the Divine, and, of course, the magic and intrigue that is part of any ancient Egyptian story. I can't think of a more exciting time to have written about than the beginnings of Egyptian civilization. Lauren Thyme is a true priestess, seer, and scribe. —*Normandi Ellis, author of* Awakening Osiris; Dreams of Osiris; *and* Feasts of Light.

Along the Nile will mystically weave its ancient magick upon you. Here is the "Moby Dick" of Egyptian historical romance, a novel in the old style that takes seriously the nineteenth century idea that such volumes should truly instruct as well as entertain. Although this book does not include an encyclopedic chapter about ancient Egypt within the body of the story, it does encompass so much information about Kemet that it includes appendices, among them a treatise on the ancient religion of the land of the pyramids, a survey of ancient Egyptian history, and a glossary of archaic terms and place names drawn from the hieroglyphs scribed by the ancients themselves. This book astonishingly turns out to be an entertainment of mystical hope for our own times, and a reminder of the importance of restoring the sacred balance and rightness of any society that has been shriven by the wretched excesses of unscrupulous and greedy schemers who serve only wealth and are drunk on power. This surprising novel of ancient Egypt assuredly will quickly find its way into your ba. So when you sit down to read this one, gird your Khabit. Hold onto your ka, your khat, your khu, and your Min member, too!—*Charles Elliott, Poet; Priest of Isis and Ra in the International Fellowship of Isis*

Lauren Thyme is obviously a person who knows her ancient Egypt profoundly. Her writing gives an almost hallucinatory impression of being there. *Along the Nile* is far and away the best novel about Ancient Egypt I have ever read.—*Colin Wilson, author of dozens of books including* The Outsider; From Atlantis to The Spinx; The Occult; *and many more*

"Blockbuster! Channeling/remembering ancient Egypt like Omm Sety did. Lauren really tapped into Egypt's past [with] important knowledge. I hated to finish *Along the Nile*. Cried a lot at the end. Loved loved loved this book." —*Phyllis Galde, editor of* Fate Magazine, *publisher, Galde Press Inc.,*

Image from Nefertari's Tomb (Het-Heru seated on throne; Winged Ma'at kneeling: Heru escorting Nefertari,High Priestess of Het-Heru

PROLOGUE

HET-HERU, THE GOLDEN ONE

In your modern time, no one believes in me and the other Neterw, those that you call gods. But we are not gods. We are forces of nature. No one can obtain scientific proof of the vast unseen world we are part of and inhabit, so we cannot possibly exist. But we do exist.

In the past we worked closely with human beings, as they could see us and hear us within their uncluttered minds. I am going to take you to a time in that ancient past when I was honored and even worshipped. A place you now know as pre-dynastic Egypt, before it became unified into one country. A young man lived there named Heb. He had such a strong affinity to me that there were times I could believe he was me in human form. I chose him to be my messenger, my helper in the construction of history. How else do you think history comes into being? By mysterious, intelligent forces of nature, me and my brethren, as we interacted with human consciousness.

By good fortune, Heb decided to keep a journal of his life. Thus, most of this story is told in his words. But remember it is I, Het-Heru, moving the action and creating a single reality out of infinite possibilities.

CHAPTER ONE

ATALANA AND HEB

I remember well the first day she came to live here, as if remembering a lovely dream.

I was standing on the precipitous cliff overlooking the Nile, with Abtu Palace to my right. It was a typically hot day of the season before the yearly inundation. Although I had applied black kohl around my eyes and on my eyebrows as well, my eyes were practically blinded by the incessant glare from the sparkling whitewashed walls.

Ra cast his noonday golden light upon the earth, delivering his blessings to the Royal Event that would shortly take place. Birds chirped and sang in the palm trees that swayed alongside Abtu Palace, securely built on the cliffs overlooking the southern Nile. The Sacred River lay far below me, her belly soon to be pregnant with floodwater, renewing life with her inundation. Fragrant lotus blossoms basked in the sunshine along her muddy banks.

From my vantage point outside, I could see the seemingly endless toil of water-bearers moving up and down the winding, steep path to the river. A steady stream of them, like busy worker ants, were lugging water from the river below to irrigate the plants and trees of the garden and to bring fresh water to the Palace for the Coronation/Wedding. A similar parade of those with empty jugs was descending the path down to the River to fill them up once more.

We servants had been preparing for weeks. I had hardly slept in many days, supervising and double-checking the innumerable details.

Nobles from every family in the Southern Kingdom, Ta-Meir Res, had been invited for the Royal Occasion. Guests had been arriving for days, including the Bride's family from Nekken. The isolated towns and cities of Ta-Meir Res were connected by the Nile, River of Life, separated by vast, virtually lifeless expanses of desert. Therefore, all of them had journeyed by boat to Abtu Palace.

Hoping to catch a glimpse of the Bride, the once-in-a-lifetime Royal Celebration, whole families of poor farmers and villagers, the rekkit, were arriving in their tiny fellucas. These common people camped out near the thriving village of Abtu outside the Palace walls, situated on the cliffs overlooking the river, their cooking fires twinkling at night. Women patted small lumps of dough into flat circles, cooking bread for their families. Happy children called to each other, running and playing with friends and strangers alike, while rivulets of sweat mixed with dust streamed unnoticed down their skinny arms and legs.

A few Noble late-comers were being assisted up the long, steep climb from the docks far below, or carried on litters, then crowding in through the two colossal gilded palace doors which stood open on their wooden hinges. The freshly polished marble floors of the corridors and Great Hall shone. Everywhere in the palace flowers from the garden were arranged in ornately carved stone vases, a legacy of generations of past stonemasons. Dozens of bedroom chambers had been prepared, while legions of bare-chested servant girls waited, each one assigned to serve a noble guest.

Abtu Palace rose magnificently before me. The resplendent palace complex was situated high up on a flat mesa overlooking the holy river, safe from the recurring floods of Sopdit. Its articulated walls, fifty cubits high, gleamed like an ephemeral mirage, shimmering in the heat. The squared arcades of the huge edifice stood tall and proud against the cloudless lapis sky.

Wood was scarce in our dry country, and only the holy Temples were built out of stone to last for eternity. Therefore the Palace masterpiece had been fashioned entirely out of dried mud bricks, over which gleaming white stucco had been plastered and then elaborately painted. The breeze toyed with the gauze curtains through many columns, which lined the open east and west portals of the Royal Apartments and Great Hall. These rectangular columns were painted green over the main trunks while the curved tops were colored Nile blue, symbolizing the ancient papyrus swamps of Rostau, the Sacred Mound of Creation. Ptah, God of Craftsmen and Masons, would have undoubtedly been proud of this achievement, accomplished after only ten years of labor. The Royal Palace had been built in the time of the current Pharaoh's grandfather Horem, but showed no signs of deterioration.

A tall Djed pillar, ten cubits tall, symbolizing the backbone of Ausar, Neter of new life, stood near the entryway to the Palace. This monumental wooden pillar, with its unusual shape, wider at top and bottom and narrower in the middle, had colorful green, red, black and gold stripes painted on the four levels, the lines parallel to the ground. Ausar's pillar had been raised at dawn by djedi-neter priests to commemorate this auspicious day. The raising of the Djed would ensure security and stability to the White Crown and to the people of Ta-Meir Res. I silently said a prayer of welcome to Ausar, whose ancient skull was reputed to be buried nearby at Abtu Temple.

The heat was intense and sweat dripped from my head onto my bare chest and linen kilt, making some of the kohl liquefy and run down my face in rivulets. I dabbed at my wet cheek. Then satisfied with the progress of the preparations, I walked through the entrance to the Great Hall at right angles to the front door, wiped my bare feet on the colorful rugs there, the smoke of myrrh heavy in the air. Priests had been up since before dawn, purifying themselves and the entire Palace. They were still chanting in the Great Hall, opening the sacred access to various Holy Emanations of Atum, to usher in the Divine Presence of the Neterw. In their chant, I detected the names of Ma'at and Heru, as well as the Divine Name of the protective sister of the Southern Kingdom, the vulture Nekhebet.

I proceeded down the main corridor, turning left through a narrower corridor, then outside to the back of the structure into the dazzling daylight, my feet making slapping noises on the stone walkway. Some guests were strolling along the walkways or sitting on marble benches in shady gazebos around the large man-made rectangular pond, 15 cubits long, which stretched the entire eastern length of the palace. Their jewelry sparkled like the water and was just as abundant. Blooming purple, pink and white water lilies floated on the thick green leaves, while papyrus soared strong and tall around its shallow edges. Jasmine perfumed the air. Encircling the pond were bushes, flowers, herbs and shrubs, while around them were hundreds of fruit and nut trees. Native figs, bananas, as well as date and coconut palms were laden with fruit, walnut trees were in flower, and a few more exotic varieties imported from the previous Pharaoh's travels were just beginning to fruit.

At the far edge of the garden stood the grapevines, Pharaoh's pride. Green vines hung like laundry on cords of rolled flax tied to trellises. The swelling grapes were maturing from green to purple and my mouth watered, thinking of the tasty fruit to come. Grapes would also be pressed into an intoxicating drink and some would be dried, preserving them for the cooler season. The greenery, coupled with concentrated sunlight glinting off the stonework, made me squint.

Beyond the lush garden, the endless desert stretched in every direction, hunched like a hungry jackal, waiting to suck dry the garden, pond and all the Palace inhabitants. The shimmering mirage of distant hills floated like a dream over the desolate sandy expanse.

Men had been up before dawn, hunting for wild birds to feed the new bride. Women had come from nearby villages to help prepare the feast. Hundreds of geese, pigeons and ducks had been force-fed to fatten them, then slaughtered, filled with raisins, coconut and dates, basted with honey, and were cooking a succulent golden brown. Huge haunches of beef and whole lambs roasted on spits. Tender vine leaves had been picked fresh, stuffed with grain, mint and chopped meat, rolled shut, then slowly cooked. Honeyed delicacies and dried fruits were arrayed on tables in the dining hall, awaiting the banquet. Jugs of freshly brewed barley beer, along with wine, stood on the long table, ready for hundreds of thirsty guests.

The familiar aroma of freshly baking bread wafted from the stone ovens and I was overwhelmed with happiness. Happy my beloved Pharaoh was wedding the woman of his dreams. Happy that now at last he would bear children to carry on his benevolent tradition. We, his people, were celebrating for him and for the sons who would surely come to continue the reign of peace and plenty throughout the land. We were confident, knowing that his new bride was young and strong, strong enough to bear him many healthy sons. This was not a beginning, but a continuation. His sons would continue a sacred heritage founded long ago.

I went to a carved water basin near the cooking area and washed my kohl-streaked face, letting the hot sun dry it, remembering the past with nostalgia.

I had been born in Abtu Palace in Pharaoh Ankhamun's twenty-seventh year and watched him as I made the steady trek to adulthood. When I was five, after the death, mummification, and final entombment of his father Menamen-Ra, Ankhamun was coronated with the White Crown of the South. Afterwards he wedded and bedded three wives over the next twenty years of his life. Two were daughters of the foreign kings of Urak and Mari, and one was the sister of Pharaoh of the Red Crown in Shmo, the Northern Kingdom. The women served to seal important treaties, bargained for like wheat in exchange for peace. But unfortunately none of the queens had borne him any children.

I often saw Pharaoh pace the corridors of the palace at midnight, when he thought everyone had retired, mumbling and talking out loud to himself about the lack of sons and the future of his kingdom. I yearned to bring him words of comfort, of reassurance. But I didn't dare approach him directly or speak to him before he spoke to me, free man though I was. I was not his son, advisor or friend. I was only his servant. At those times I would get out my Mother's talisman and pray to Het-Heru, Neter of fertility, to help my Master in his troubles.

Once during one of his nightly walks, he spotted me in the corridor, as I watched him and entreated Het-Heru to help him.

"Heb."

"Your Majesty."

"What are you doing here?"

Never having been a good liar, I fumbled with my words. "I, um, well, that is…"

Obviously the Pharaoh had family on his mind when he asked me the next question. It was an odd time and place to have a conversation. We stood in the chilly hall, in the middle of the night, while Ra was passing through the heavenly body of Nut, until She could give birth the next morning to Ra-as-Khepera, Neter of dawn and new beginnings.

"Why have you never married, Heb?"

I thought about the troubles with his wives and decided it was not a problem I wanted to share. "Sire," I told him, "I am bethrothed to serving you. Your smiles and happiness are my children. And I am content."

"Nevertheless," he replied sagely, "someday you must find a good woman to share your life with." "I have no need of a woman," I replied confidently, gazing at my feet in deference to him.

"We will see," he replied. Then he continued more urgently. "Heb, I must have a son, an heir. I must have a son very soon."

"I know, your Majesty."

"Time is running out. I am no longer young. What shall I do?"

I showed him my talisman of Het-Heru, Neter of women, fertility, children and childbirth. "I have been asking Her to help you."

"Will that work?"

I shrugged my shoulders. "I'm not sure. Perhaps it could not hurt to ask."

Soon after our late-night conversation, Pharaoh Ankhamun began to pray to various Neterw. In the Great Hall, he pleaded with the red granite statue of the falcon-headed Heru and Nekhebet, protectress of Res. In his private chamber he prayed to Min, the Neter of sexual prowess, and Heqet, frog Neter of fertility. Then he traveled to Abtu Temple, reputed to be the final resting-place of the skull of Ausar and home of the Neter of the underworld. The rectangular-columned temple wasn't located within the palace grounds but was far removed from the rest of the complex in the most sacred site in all of southern Ta-Meir Res. To get to the Temple of Ausar, one must walk down the steep incline to the river. Take a boat across the river. Then travel along its banks for about two hentis, where the ancient stone sanctuary stood back from the holy river. The Temple was so ancient no one knew who had built it or when.

The Pharaoh brought offerings, burned incense and chanted along with the Priests, asking Ausar to help. But still he remained childless.

Discouraged, he traveled throughout the Temples of Ta-Meir Res, his southern kingdom, making offerings to many deities, hoping to encourage the Neterw to send him just one son. Finally, in despair, he went to the holy temple at Enet-ta-Neter, where the Neter Het-Heru, Mistress of Heaven, Lady of Life, reigned supreme. I heard that mystical fertility rituals and ceremonies were performed there for the Pharaoh. I had faith that the Neter of Fertility, Spiritual Mother of Pharaohs, would intercede in his behalf. We, his people, prayed fervently, too. Without him and a son to follow him in smooth succession, chaos, disaster, even civil war could follow.

And then a joyful announcement was made. He had fallen in love with one of the young priestesses at Enet-ta-Neter, a noble woman in service to Het-Heru. Our beloved Pharaoh had found the woman of his heart and they would marry. Love, stronger than treaties and obligations, would surely bless him with sons.

Everyone celebrated for him. I, too, was exceedingly happy and whistled as I oversaw the progress of the immense and complicated preparations for the Royal Wedding to take place shortly. As I looked around the Great Hall for a final inspection, I found a small chunk of unburned incense on the floor and picked it up. Nothing must spoil this day. This was to be the Day of Days for my King. Everything must be perfect.

The King had been led in regal procession to the Great Hall. He readied himself on the heavy throne, constructed of precious hardwood that Pharaoh Menamen-Ra had brought from the forests of a distant eastern territory and had shaped into the royal throne. Imbedded into the throne's two sides were gold panels, depicting battle scenes the former warrior-king Menamen-Ra had won, illustrating the gods who had assisted him and hieroglyphics proclaiming the victories and the names of the vanquished. The massive throne stood on a raised dais, the ends of its four legs shaped like lions' paws. Semi-precious jewels were set into the sides of the royal chair while the back of the throne was surfaced with striped mosaic patterns in black marble and white alabaster.

Beside the throne stood a massive red granite statue of the falcon-headed god Heru, protector and embodiment of the living Neter - Pharaoh. On the wall hovering high behind Pharaoh was a carved painting of the vulture Nekhebet, patron and protectress of the King, wearing a feathered crown. The vulture sat perched on a double-headed royal dagger, clutching two ankhs in her talons, Her colorful wings were outstretched. Painted on the walls around the Great Hall were scenes of battle interspersed with ordinary life. Between colorful rectangular columns, the marble floor gleamed in readiness. Kings, princes, officials, and noble people gathered in front of King Ankhamun, patiently dignified, their hushed whispers echoing in the immense hall, waiting for the Bride.

Menamen-Ra's wife Miw-sher, Ptah and Shu's mother, was long dead, but hundreds of other wedding guests gathered in the Great Hall, except for King Ankhamun's three wives. Pharaoh's queens were embittered and angry, ensconced in the royal harem at Pharaoh's insistence. He hoped to avoid unpleasantness and to protect his new wife from their predictable jealousy at being usurped by another woman. Wedding guests were bare-footed in homage to Pharaoh, their sandals having been left at the entrance on the colorful rugs. The nobility glittered in dazzling elegance. Women's white gowns swept the floor, their arms and necks covered with gold; their wigs laden with jewels. Men were dressed in standard kilts or shentis, but their wigs were no less elaborate than the women's, circular collars around their necks. Or else they wore colorful nemes headdresses. All had their eyes outlined with mesd'emt, far costlier than kohl. Braziers smoked with the heady incense of myrrh while priests continued to chant sacred hymns along the back wall.

Ankhamun, the King of Ta-Meir Res, had earlier undergone elaborate and lengthy purification rituals of incense, natron and water with the Priests of Heru. Then he was dressed in his garments of office, pleated linen shenti, circular collar of beaten gold inlaid with turquoise, carnelian, and lapis, armlets and bracelets of gold encircling his arms, wrists and ankles. A leop-ard skin was draped around his torso proclaiming his position as High Priest of his southern Kingdom. With the heqa and nekhakha representing his temporal and spiritual position held ready, Pharaoh Ankhamun waited as breathlessly as the rest of us. His tall white crown, with the head of a vul-ture poised over his forehead, had been firmly placed upon his head. From my vantage across the room I saw he trembled.

I believe that often men are in awe, even a little afraid, of the women they love and I smiled to myself in arrogant, youthful self-confidence. I was secure in the knowledge that I would never be a slave to any woman. No one would be master over me except my beloved Pharaoh.

Slowly the Royal Barge had made its way down the Nile towards the palace. The oarsmen rowed in measured beat. All voices were now hushed as it drew alongside the quay with its precious cargo.

Because of my supervisory position, I was allowed to watch the pro-ceedings, but instructed to keep out of sight. I stayed hidden behind the curtains covering the columns facing west and peered out through the opening, looking down the hill towards the river.

The Royal Barque had come to a stop at the dock. Its gold and blue banners fluttered in the freshening wind, as if they were birds trying to alight. The young woman who was to become Queen was hidden behind a covered canopy. A signal was given and the rowers lifted their oars in salute and then dropped them gently to rest in the water, while the boat with its high curved prows woven of papyrus stems was secured to pylons with hemp ropes. I noticed that ten priestesses of Het-Heru, in elaborate temple garments, had accompanied her on the Barque, their cloaks blowing around them in the strong wind.

Pharaoh's Grand Vizier Ptah-un-Atum was on the dock to greet the queen-to-be and lead her to the Great Hall. The Custodian of the Crown, Pharaoh's youngest half-brother Shu-un-Atum, was also on hand to orchestrate the complex ceremonies. He scurried about the dock like a beetle, his skinny body in direct contrast to his lumbering older brother's obese figure. Ministers and other officials gathered for the solemn, yet joyful, procession.

The eldest and highest ranking Priestess on the barge, her wig blowing in the wind, pulled aside the curtain and a slim, delicate arm appeared from the innermost recesses behind the canopy. The slender arm was adorned with bracelets and armlets of turquoise, malachite, lapis, and carnelian stones, each woven together with gold thread. I surmised that Pharaoh had given her the jewelry as wedding gifts. She took the priestess's strong hand in her supple one and stepped out, anklets jingling on the tapering ankles, feet bare.

As she came forth into the sunlight, I gasped. For a moment I thought the Neter Het-Heru herself had emerged from the interior of the barque. Even from that great distance, the young woman's beauty shone like a thousand moons on a dark night. With effortless grace inborn and nurtured in a noble home, she stepped across the boat's ramp onto the pier and was thus handed over to the Pharaoh's half-brother.

Barely touching the long, slim hand and with great care, the Grand Vizier Ptah-un-Atum led the young woman over hundreds of carpets to a canopied chaise with four gilded carrying handles. He helped her to sit upon the carved and cushioned seat. Then a dozen strong young men, soldiers in Pharaoh's army, dressed in identical white kilts and simple collars, lifted the chair; daggers tucked into their waistbands to protect her with their lives. They carried the Bride over hundreds more of colorful thick silken carpets that lay between her and her new husband, where she would be crowned and married simultaneously.

Leading the way was Ptah-un-Atum, Grand Vizier of Pharaoh, panting and puffing up the long incline, his fat body unused to such exertion. Following her were Priestesses of Het-Heru rattling sacred sistrums; Custodian of the Crown skinny Shu-un-Atum; the rest of the officials; and other musicians. The procession made its way towards the Great Hall and the waiting bridegroom. I could hear the sound of flutes, drums and sistrums from a distance, as they proceeded up the long hill to the glittering Palace.

As the procession entered the Great Hall, Pharaoh eagerly stood up to receive his new bride. The soldiers carefully lowered the chaise in front of the raised dais and pressed their closed fists to their hearts, indicating their allegiance to the King. The young woman delicately stepped off and stood quietly, waiting for the appropriate signal.

An involuntary sigh rose from the congregation at her glowing presence. She wore an elaborately pleated wig headdress, which curled into two circlets just below her shoulders. Her vulture tiara was made of beaten gold, decorated with bits of green and blue faience glass. The floor-length ivory dress, which hugged her body like a caress, must have been spun of the finest linen, hung in whispering delicate folds at her feet. The form-fitting gown accented the lush womanly shape underneath.

The young woman's slanted brown eyes shone with pride and excitement, the cosmetic green eyeliner outlining them with feline obliqueness, the lids tinted a lighter shade of green. Malachite had been mined in the desert of Bakhet, transported over hundreds of hentis and pounded into a precious powder for the Queen's lids. Gold, ground into dust, delicately powdered her cheeks and arms. Her narrow aristocratic face with its high cheekbones was as beautiful as the Mistress of Beauty, Het-Heru herself.

Draped across the woman's young, full breasts hung a long necklace undoubtedly fashioned by a master craftsman. Draping around her neck, attached to five or more strands of lapis lazuli beads, was a solid gold image of Het-Heru, similar to the amulet I had played with since childhood! The carved white alabaster folds of the Neter's dress were intricately defined with inlays of turquoise and malachite. The golden disk and crescent moon above the Lady of Gold—Het-Heru's—head shimmered in solid gold, as did the finely-detailed sistrum and menat necklace she held.

I couldn't take my eyes off that necklace, nor the firm breasts on which it rested. I would like to be that splendid necklace, lying across my lady's breasts. I tingled hotly with the thought. My body began to take on a life unbidden by me. I wondered what the feel of those breasts would be in my hands, what womanly scent emanating from between their rounded flesh, as I buried my nose between them. My excited body responded with a huge lump that Min, the Neter of carnal appetites, would be proud of. Horrified and guilt-ridden, I blushed and quickly looked around, praying no one could see me and guess my thoughts, glad to be safely hidden in the curtains. But it seems I was not the only one entranced by our young queen-to-be. All eyes were upon her and no one moved or spoke.

Then the Grand Vizier, holding his ceremonial wooden staff, stepped in front of Pharaoh, facing him. On the top of the pole was a carved vulture's head, the Neter protector of Ta-Meir Res, Nekhebet, while Her vulture wings wrapped around the lower end of the wooden stick. Ptah-un-Atum turned to face the crowd, pounded his long staff loudly on the marble floor and introduced the Pharaoh.

"Ankhamun-Heru, Son of Ra, Speaker of Truth, Defender of Ma'at, Lord of the Diadem of Nekhebet, Protector of Life,

Beloved of Amun, King of Hedje and Lord of Upper Ta-Meir Res. Ankh. Uja. Senb."

All those present knelt and put their foreheads to the ground in obeisance to Pharaoh for a few moments. The regal clink of golden bracelets and anklets could be heard as the Nobility regained their collective feet. "Ankh. Uja. Senb," they repeated.

The sound of Ptah-un-Amun's ceremonial staff rang out again in the stilled Hall. "The Noble Lady Atalana, Priestess of Het-

Heru, Mistress of the Southern Sycamore. Ankh. Uja. Senb."

The assembly bowed as one body and repeated the words. "Ankh. Uja. Senb."

Fat Ptah-un-Atum moved aside with some effort and Atalana gracefully climbed the few steps to Pharaoh, standing in front of Ankhamun's throne, facing her husband-to-be.

As Atalana approached, the Supreme Master of Upper Ta-Meir Res held out his trembling hands like a shy schoolboy. She touched her carefully manicured hands to the heka and nekhekha, gazing reverently into his aging eyes, also outlined in green. Then she moved to his right side and, still standing, faced the congregation.

Pharaoh's youngest brother Shu-un-Atum, Custodian of the Crown, held the Hedjet - White Crown - in his skinny hands. He climbed up the steps to the dais and stood behind the royal couple. Priests and Priestesses proceeded to waft incense over the Royal Couple, then chanted long rhythmic invocations and recitations to the Neterw Ma'at, Heru, Ra, Amun, Het-Heru, and Nekhebet, while asking them to bring their wisdom, power, love, and protection to the new Queen.

When the long and complex oratory was finished, Atalana removed her vulture tiara, holding it in her right hand. Shu-un-Atum placed a White Crown similar to Pharaoh's own on the delicate feminine head, positioning it carefully over her wig. With the investiture completed, Atalana was now Queen. The Vizier backed down the steps and bowed low before the royal couple. The rest of the congregation followed suit.

Pharaoh Ankhamun moved the heqa and nekhakha to hold both in his left hand, took Atalana's small one and kissed it tenderly. At that moment they were married as well.

Priestesses rattled their sistrums while the drummers drummed. Sacred music for a joyous occasion.

Atalana smiled radiantly at my Master and the skin around her dark eyes crinkled with happiness. Her perfectly even, white teeth gleamed with rapture.

"She loves the Pharaoh," I thought to myself, at once happy for my master, yet filled with unfathomable, gut-wrenching grief. My manhood shrunk to a limp rag of skin as though I had dove into the cold river below.

Then Atalana turned and with the same joyful smile, bestowed her blessings on the congregation. With that gesture, she immediately endeared herself to all around her. A great shout of exaltation sprang simultaneously from all lips present, except mine. Wedding guests eagerly began to line up, maneuvering for position, to congratulate the newly married Royal couple. The harpists and flutists began to play a lovely song, while the noisy, excited chatter of the Nobility filled the Great Hall.

I abruptly left my position behind the curtain in the Great Hall, thinking I would inspect the vast quantities of food awaiting the wedding feast. But my eyes saw nothing and no one except the vision of Atalana's loveliness seared into my tormented brain. I passed unnoticed in the commotion as I hurried through the Great Hall to the main corridor. I stumbled like a blind man, agitated and confused, past interior rooms, out to the open courtyard, then to the cooking area behind the palace complex. I bumped into several women arranging food on large trays until I found a flat rock to collapse onto. My chest pained me terribly. As though a cobra was poisoning my body. Or a bird of prey was devouring my heart. At that moment I wished I had died before I had ever set eyes on her.

Yes, I remember that day. And my life would never again be the same.

CHAPTER TWO

ANKHAMUN AND HIS FAMILY

For many days and nights there was feasting and celebration and I assured myself that everything ran smoothly behind the scenes. I checked hourly that there was plenty to eat and comfortable accommodations for the many guests attending the wedding/coronation ritual and gala. Overseeing these details gave me time to ignore my conflicting emotions and try to calm my racing mind, although what I wanted most was to run far away from Abtu Palace. Since I had nowhere to go and no resources to feed, clothe and house myself, not to mention my undying loyalty to Pharaoh, this idea was out of the question. Yet I yearned for the freedom and tranquility of my former existence. Was it just days ago I had first seen the Queen? I thought perhaps several lifetimes had already passed. One by one the guests went home, the Djed pillar was taken down and stored, and the Royal household slowly returned to normal.

I didn't see Pharaoh and his new Queen again for almost a week. In fact, I tried my best to absolutely avoid them. Every time I thought of the scene of the coronation, I found my skin burning and my stomach was wound into a tight knot. If I was in a corridor and I heard their voices, I turned and fled the other direction. I felt guilty at my actions, but didn't know how else to protect myself – and them – from my feelings. I was an ungrateful cow-ard, turning my back on all the kindnesses I had received from the King.

As a young man, Pharaoh Ankhamun was benevolently disposed to-wards all his people. Unlike his father, the old Pharaoh

Menamen-Ra, who was a cold and ungenerous man, the new King de-voted his life to the inhabitants of Ta-Meir Res. The dead Pharaoh's lust for gold, semi-precious gemstones, slaves and other spoils of conquest, along with a warlike disposition towards neighboring tribes brought discontent and death to our land.

Menamen-Ra had several wives, three sons and two daughters, not in-cluding those children conceived in the slave quarters, although he tended to ignore or mistreat them all. Except for Ankhamun, his beloved eldest son, sa'a cherp, whom he adored and pampered, born of his First Royal Wife. When the old Pharaoh Menamen-Ra suddenly died of fever, the mourning was strictly formal. No one except Ankhamun was truly sad to see Mena-men-Ra journey in the Barque of the Dead to join Ausar. Although it was heresy, I privately doubted that Menamen-Ra could have passed the judg-ment of the forty-two divine Maati to reach Ra's sun barque as it traveled through the heavens. How could his cold heart be as light and pure as Ma'at's feather of truth and justice? I was an insignificant slave child and said nothing of my thoughts to anyone, for fear of punishment.

Possibly in reaction to his father's severity or maybe due to the love that was showered on him alone, Pharaoh Ankhamun was a kind and just monarch. He sought to make sure that no one went hungry, no one was without a home. He avoided war by maintaining solid truces with our de-vious, greedy neighbors, bargaining with the all-important commodity of food, so that his own people could sleep securely at night. He was a true servant and representative of the Neterw. And thus he was greatly loved by his people.

King Ankhamun's palace was the only home I had ever known. My un-happy Mother, Nyla, was brought as a slave from a distant land before my

conception and had died in my fifth year, just before Ankhamun's coronation. After her passing, women from the servant's quarters cared for me and
raised me to manhood.

One of them once told me, "Nyla was one of the most beautiful women
I have ever seen. Her eyes had a foreign slant to them, which made her face
very appealing. Like you, she was tall, very tall for a woman, with long,
graceful arms and legs, like a dancer. Although she had difficulty speaking
our language, her voice was melodious, while her singing inspired the court
musicians. There was a noble quality about her. She carried herself like a
princess, not a slave." The woman smiled in fond memory.

"Who was my father?"

She shrugged. "I do not know. Nyla never told me or anyone. She said
it was her secret. She took that secret to the afterworld with her."

My own memories of Mother were practically non-existent. I couldn't
even remember her face. But she had left me two items in remembrance of
her. The first was a carved, wooden charm, painted gold, about as long as
an adult hand span from thumb to small finger. This amulet depicted Het-
Heru, "Neter of love, joy, dancing, beauty, music, and spiritual nourishment." Het-Heru was carved as a beautiful woman wearing a cow horn
headdress with a sun disk, holding a sistrum in one hand and a menat necklace in the other. Het-Heru was a deity in keeping with a similar one from
my Mother's native land and she embraced the new Neter, "The Golden
One," as her own. Het-Heru was also Patroness of women and children. I'm
sure She was doubly appreciated by my lonely mother.

Mother's talisman had been carved and tinted by some local artist. The
statue was not made by a royal artist, thus lacking the quality found in temples and palaces. Yet it was a good likeness. Her statue faithfully represented
the cow horns and sun disk over Het-Heru, The Celestial Cow, holding the
sistrum, Her holy musical instrument, and the menat necklace, symbol of
health, one in each of Her two hands.

The second memento was a small seal carved onto a carnelian rod, about the length of my hand when I was grown, which fit perfectly in my Mother's delicate hand. The signet excised on the end was unknown to any of us. I stored my two keepsakes in a pliable drawstring pouch fashioned from the hide of an ass. When I was young, I often took out the two articles to look at them, fingering and playing with them as children do. Consequently the once-bright green and blue colors of "Het-Heru, Lady of Malachite and Turquoise" were wearing off.

I don't know if I was influenced by the hours of playing with the amulet or simply had an over-active imagination, but shortly after my ninth birthday I dreamt of the "Mistress of Dreams." Het-Heru appeared in my dream the way she looked on the amulet, but She sparkled and shimmered with a golden blinding light, making me squint. Then She spoke. I felt and heard Her unforgettable words.

"Heb, you will hold the future of Ta-Meir Res in your hands." Het-Heru smiled at me. Then She shook her Sistrum, the sacred musical instrument making a joyful, tinkling sound, and pointed her Menat necklace meaningfully towards my head. I was too young and ignorant to understand what that gesture meant, but I felt She was placing a divine responsibility upon me. I shivered.

Then, in the dream, the image of the Neter Het-Heru, "Mother of Pharaoh," disappeared to be replaced with what looked like a common scene at court. Pharaoh Ankhamun was preparing to seat his camel, readying himself for a trip. Normally a voyage by water would have been in order. But it was flood time and the Nile was rushing in torrential currents, unnavigable. Pharaoh's blue and gold nemes headdress covered his balding pate and he was dressed in a gala skirt with gold border, while a blue linen collar embroidered with golden ankhs along the edge covered his upper chest.

Woven rugs were piled on top of the camel's uncomfortable hump, which were then covered with silken cloth woven with gold thread and hung with tassels. Hundreds of people gathered around the Pharaoh on foot, to accompany him and serve him during the excursion. I was too young and inexperienced to travel. Wagons, filled with sacks of grain, drawn by oxen, stood ready. Several of his entourage were also astride camels. King Ankhamun's camel began screeching, its teeth bared, jerking at the leather reins, mouth frothing. Pharaoh mounted the seated camel and it rose to its feet, and began to walk unsteadily. Then it suddenly lurched and fell over. Before servants could run to help him, the Pharaoh's body was limp, broken and bloody, crushed under the heavy carcass.

I awoke from the dream, sweating and frightened. I loved my Pharaoh and the scene unnerved me. As days passed and nothing happened, I relaxed and slowly forgot about my dream, relegating it to an overactive imagination. But my dream proved to be prophetic.

After Menamen-Ra's death, Ankhamun freed all us slaves. I chose to remain in Pharaoh Ankhamun's service as he took control of the southern kingdom, Resu, the Red Land of desert and scorpions, the territory of Setekh. While a hundred of the newly-freed people left the Palace to make a life outside its Royal walls, I stayed to serve Pharaoh. After all, I was still a child and Abtu Palace was the only home I had ever known.

The King treated me with respect, though I was very young and of humble station, giving me important little tasks and watching how I performed. He knew he was a man, although coming from an unbroken line of noble succession derived from the falcon-headed Neter Heru. Pharaoh's ultimate responsibilities were to the people he protected and to the land which nurtured them all. Therefore, he appreciated others, even if they were lowly servants. And in return, he was greatly loved and worshipped by his subjects.

Just before my tenth birthday, the Pharaoh announced he would be making a long journey past the southern border into the land of Kush, the land upstream from the first cataract. He was traveling there to trade Ta-Meir Res's wheat for gold, the sacred metal of the Neterw. He would also bargain for precious ivory, incense, hides and carnelian. It would be a long and arduous expedition and dozens of people would accompany him. When I heard about the voyage, my dream came back into focus and I became uneasy.

When the time came for his leave-taking, I joined the crowd of happy well-wishers who were singing and chanting, along with a number of officials and viziers buzzing around him with last minute requests. It was still early morning, just a little after dawn, and the shadows were long in front of me. I rubbed my eyes sleepily. Bellowing oxen were tied together, to haul large wagons filled with grain, for the long trek south. Animal tenders traveled alongside the oxen, holding whips, to urge the animals forward. Palace servants had come to wish him a safe and prosperous trip. Pharaoh walked among his people, saying goodbye. I could tell by the look on the faces around me that he was a man who was greatly loved and respected.

A few of his entourage would have the luxury of riding astride a camel. The camels were noisily screeching, making their familiar but ungracious sounds of protest. They were irritable beasts and I was glad never to ride on one.

After saying his final goodbyes, Pharaoh climbed onto his reclining camel's back. The long-legged animal was kneeling on the ground, its legs tucked under its body.

The reins were made of burnished leather, carved with intricate hieroglyphic symbols for protection. Long red and gold tassels hung from the edges of the cushions. Ankhamun took up the reins, leaning far back in the saddle to counter-balance the forward motion when the camel stood up on its front legs. He waved to us, in a friendly gesture of farewell.

His camel's mouth was frothing. It caterwauled irritably as Pharaoh tried to make it stand. He kicked it several times to no avail. One of the camel tenders rushed over to us to find out what was wrong. One man pulled on the reins and whipped the camel's backside to get it to its feet, but without success. The froth from the camel's mouth turned blood-red and my nightmare from months before came into my mind, unbidden but clear.

I wanted to run to the King, to pull him to safety, but I was in a trance. I felt that slow-motion, agonizing movement one has in dreams. The sounds around me disappeared, as I had but one thought. With great difficulty, I pushed my way through the crowd, to his side. "Your Majesty!" I shouted loudly, trying to make myself heard over the din. Realizing he couldn't hear me, I clung tightly to the fringed seat, hoping he would at least notice my actions.

Vizier Shu-un-Atum, Ankhamun's youngest half-brother, hurried over to me, his narrow face shining with perspiration. He towered over me. "What are you doing, boy? Get away from there!" he ordered me belligerently, his kohl-outlined eyes flashing with anger.

His wig fell slightly askew. Unaccountably I wanted to laugh, but I refused to move, still yelling to get Pharaoh's attention.

Shu-un-Atum tried to pull me away with his bony, skeletal-like fingers but I held on with desperate strength. Out of the corner of my eye I could see Ankhamun's other half-brother, Ptah-un-Atum. He was watching our struggle with detached disinterest, the small eyes in his pudgy face casually taking in the scene.

"Sire, Sire!" I cried again, hoarse from my shouting. The camel was still screeching irritably. I shook the King's arm, the one closest to me. It was a daring action to take with the personage of the King, but I couldn't help myself. He was in danger. I knew it.

The Vizier shouted at me. "Do not touch the King!"

"But he ...."

Our argument alerted Ankhamun.

The kindly king looked down from his perch upon the camel's hump to see me cleaving to the saddle while his half-brother struggled angrily to loosen my fingers. "What is it, Heb?" Pharaoh recognized me.

"Please, sire," I said urgently, now that he was listening. "The camel. Something is wrong with the camel. You must get off," I blurted.

"Your Majesty. I am trying to dismiss this insulting servant, but without success," Shu-un-Atum shouted over the din of people and camels, frowning at me as though I was an insect needing to be squashed. "He is touching your royal personage without permission."

The Pharaoh observed the commotion I was causing to the dignity of the entire court. Pharaoh momentarily studied both our faces, then climbed off the camel's back. Fortunately, the animal was still reclining on its knees. Boldly I took Ankhamun's hand and pulled him a few steps away.

Suddenly the camel screamed and lurched over, dead.

I glanced up to see the Vizier Shu-un-Atum staring at me and his face darkened, his eyes narrowing, mouth set in a tight line. I had become his enemy.

Stunned, Pharaoh turned to me. "The animal must have been sick. You have sharp eyes, Heb."

"Yes, Sire," I replied, keeping those sharp eyes on the ground, while staying as far away from the angry Vizier as I could.

"I might have been hurt or even killed if it wasn't for your quick action, young Heb." He looked past me at Shu-un-Atum, who only moments before was trying to prevent my actions.

The Vizier's voice was icily calm, attempting to explain. "He was touching your Royal Personage, Sire," he repeated.

"Hmmp." Still puzzled, Pharaoh turned to me. "Thank you for your quick action," he said, putting his hand on my shoulder.

"It is my honor, Sire."

"Is there any way I can repay you? This sort of bravery must be rewarded."

"Nothing, Sire. I'm only glad I could help," I finished lamely. Then suddenly my prophetic dream became quite clear. My beloved Pharaoh could have died! My body lurched violently, and began to shake. My feet were on fire, suddenly blistered by the desert sand, and I felt my Ka leaving my body. Dizzy, I fell over, fortunately landing unhurt in the soft sand.

Pharaoh kneeled and touched my damp face. "Heb," he murmured.

I was immediately alert, responding to the King's marvelously compassionate act so characteristic his concern for even the lowly. Such a sympathy I now know was a special sign, an intervention by the powerful Het-Heru, The Mother Cow Neter, kind and nurturing.

I clumsily got to my feet, red-faced and suddenly shy. "I am all right," I mumbled.

"You had us frightened," Ankhamun said.

"I'm sorry."

Pharaoh Ankhamun nodded at me and patted me on the head. He turned unsteadily to his Vizier, the shock of his narrowly averted accident beginning to resonate within him. "Find me another camel. A healthy one this time," he said to his brother Shu-un-Atum and waited until a suitable camel had been prepared.

As the caravan was finally leaving, Ankhamun turned and waved to me from the back of his camel. My stomach knotted with apprehension. I lingered outside, observing his progress until the caravan had disappeared from sight. I sighed in relief when he was safely on his way. Although I didn't know it at the time, Pharaoh and I had begun a special and enduring relationship.

Months later, when Pharaoh returned from Kush, he summoned me into the Great Hall. Before an assemblage of viziers, priests and nobles, he announced, "Heb, you have saved my life. In return I want to reward you."

He bestowed a chamber of my very own to sleep in, although small, and special garments to wear, fit not for a servant, but in my eyes, a prince. He also ordered that I would be instructed in mathematics and taught to read and write the complicated hieroglyphic symbols. I felt I was the most blessed of servants in his household. Although there may have been jealousy from the others, no one ever said anything to me directly.

Years later, as I grew into manhood, Pharaoh honored me with a supervisory position, Custodian of the Palace, overseeing the army of palace servants and daily activities. Although I was only a young man, he recognized my deep loyalty and above average intelligence, and rewarded me accordingly.

I loved my Pharaoh like a father. I loved him as a dog loves his master. I would have gladly stood in front of a charging lioness, letting her tear me apart with her sharp claws and teeth instead of him.

I sought to protect Ankhamun from daily demands. When I noticed that my Master was weary, I informed the Grand Vizier, who would then close the doors to the flood of ambassadors, princes, kings, envoys, and other visitors. I knew his favorite foods, and advised the cooks to prepare them often. When I heard his three wives squabbling among themselves, I acted as a peacemaker. If any of them complained to Pharaoh (which they often did), I pretended that some urgent household business needed attending, thus removing him from the unpleasant situation. Whenever I heard good news about the realm, his subjects or crops, I hurried to tell him. And I made certain that his household ran smoothly.

I must have been extremely tired one blisteringly hot afternoon, as I became impatient with the Pharaoh's obese half-brother Ptah-un-Atum, the Grand Vizier. I usually could handle the most difficult situations, so I don't know what happened that day. I am still embarrassed just remembering the occasion.

Ptah-un-Atum had been insisting that he be given bigger quarters and more servants, although his was the largest suite of rooms except for Pharaoh's and he had six personal servants already. Pharaoh's half-brother had two major vocations in life – eating and sex. I suspected that he only wanted to house several new courtesans he had taken a fancy to recently. I saw no reason why the Palace should pander to these notorious women and in a moment's weakness I told him as much. I had never liked the Grand Vizier nor his skinny, devious brother, and I'm afraid my prejudices rose up to strike like a hooded cobra, against my better judgment. Vizier Ptah-un-Atum blustered, turned bright red, and haughtily strode from the area.

Moments later, the Pharaoh summoned me to join him in the quarters near his sleeping room where he conducted personal and Palace business. I always loved that room. The walls were plastered white, and the clean walls sparkled in the light. The east and west walls were open to the air, with slender lotus columns at harmonious intervals. The almost-transparent cloth covering the opening was made of the finest and sheerest material. One could tie the cloth back, to let in more sunshine, if one wished. The garden and the lotus pool were visible on the eastern side of the Palace. The golden Sun-as-Atum had set and the wind was blowing the curtains sensuously against the table and chairs, making the newly-lit oil lamps flicker.

The Pharaoh sat before a large writing table. The top was covered with a huge slab of yellow alabaster, with white streaks delicately enmeshed throughout it. It was so highly polished, you could almost see your reflection in it. Many scrolls were lying on the surface and an ink well made from half a coconut sat next to it, several writing quills stood ready nearby.

Standing next to the king was the Vizier Ptah-un-Atum, still trembling with rage, his beefy face mottled with red streaks.

"Heb," the king began, "Ptah-un-Atum has been to see me with a complaint about you."

"Yes, Sire, I know. It was my fault. I acted badly towards him." I turned towards the Grand Vizier and bowed as low as I was able in front of the sweating, corpulent man. He smelled bad, as though putrescence was oozing out of all his pores. He seemed to be decaying from the inside out. "Please forgive my transgression, Lord Vizier. It was wrong of me to have acted that way."

"Hmmmp," growled Ptah-un-Atum, adjusting his wide collar dotted with gemstones and pursing his sensuous lips petulantly. "Just see that it never happens again or I will make sure that you are removed from this Palace forever. Or worse," he suggested ominously.

"Yes, my Lord, I assure you that it will never happen again. Again, please forgive me," I bowed again, heat rising in my face from the confrontation.

The unpleasant man flounced from the room, rolls of fat swaying from side to side as he left.

"Oh, Sire, I am so ashamed," I told my King Ankhamun, hanging my head. "Can you ever forgive me?"

"Yes, I can and do, Heb," he replied gently. "It's hot and we are all irritable. I understand."

I fairly fainted with relief. I would hate to leave the Palace; it was the only home and family I had ever known. What would I do without it? I would starve to death or be eaten by jackals in the desert.

Ankhamun fanned himself with a small palm frond. Then the Royal King continued. "Yet the evening is cooling off. Perhaps we will have some cooler days. Yes, I hope so." Then he lowered his voice somewhat, in a conspiratorial tone. "In the future, if you have a problem with either of my brothers, please come to me first. I can smooth it over for you." Then he smiled broadly. "There are some things you must know about my brothers in order to serve them better." Ankhamun motioned to a chair next to the table. "And tolerate them as well," he murmured quietly.

I sat down on the edge of the chair, tucking my kilt modestly between my thighs, afraid to put my elbow on that glistening desk, listening intently. I would never be fully comfortable in his presence; I worshipped him too much.

The aging King took off his undecorated nemes headdress and wiped his sweaty, balding head with a cloth tucked in his waistband. "I'm sure you have heard stories of my father Menamen-Ra." I nodded.

The Pharaoh continued in a relaxed tone of voice. Intimacy with the King was most unusual and I wiggled uncomfortably. "He was not the easiest man to live with or be related to. He was often gone on war campaigns. When he was home, he had much business to tend to. Throughout his entire life he fought to make sure that Ta-Meir Res was safe from her enemies. But he had a temper, which could flare up at the slightest provocation, and many people felt the brunt of it."

His voice softened. "For some reason, though, he loved me dearly. I suspect I was the only one who occupied his heart. Perhaps it is because my mother Netikerty died when I was born. He loved Netikerty, his Royal First Wife, very much. My wet-nurse told me about their loving alliance. Netikerty was sweet and affectionate to my father and he adored her as much as she loved him. He called her Meruti Netikerty so often, that after a while it became her name. His beloved excellent wife."

I looked out the opening at the starlight, as the cool, evening breeze blew across my skin, raising the hairs on my arms. The jasmine was blooming. I could smell their fragrant aroma wafting into the chamber.

"After my mother died he became more and more ill-tempered, except to me. His other two sons, my half-brothers Ptah and Shu, were not as fortunate. I never saw my father speak to them except in his harsh voice or else did not notice them at all. He ignored them and almost shunned them."

The king paused momentarily, while a smile played on his thin lips. "Me, however, he lavished all the kindness that was in him, a legacy from my Mother I'm sure. He was, at heart, a good man—with huge responsibilities to hold our kingdom together. He made sure I had the best tutors, my favorite foods, the most talented musicians to play for me, the finest clothes to wear. I dearly loved him too, and often told him so. Until I became a grown man, he would give me bear hugs or wrestle with me until we both fell on the floor, laughing at our actions. I was the only one who cried for him after he died." Ankhamun stopped for a moment, remembering the unfortunate occasion.

I was surprised to see tears in his eyes and the King unexpectedly sighed at the memory.

"That was a long time ago," he said quietly. I could tell his father's death still affected him deeply.

I expected him to be finished with his narrative, but he continued. It was as though he wasn't talking to me, but to himself. I wondered if he had ever told another living soul what he was telling me.

Clearing his throat, the King went on. "The mother of Ptah and Shu— Miw-sher—was a noble woman, young and very pretty, with beautiful breasts the size of melons." He held his hands out from his chest to demonstrate their large lush shape.

I grinned in spite of myself.

"But she was prone to heaviness in her body as she got older, especially after Ptah was born. She loved honey cakes made with sesame seeds and raisins and ate too many of them I think. She lived for palace gossip and always knew everything that was going on. She wanted to be made First Royal Wife, but Menamen-Ra never appointed her thus." He became lost in thought. "I don't believe he ever made any other woman First Royal Wife after my mother died, preferring to run the Kingdom without help. Hmm."

I waited for him to continue. Being taken into the King's confidence was changing our relationship yet again. I felt as though an elder brother was confiding in me. I was pleased and yet anxious at the same time. I hoped I deserved his trust.

"I was about ten inundations when Ptah was born. I was in my father's office, this office, at this same table," he motioned around him, "He had been teaching me of Kingship, just as he did every day. I was privy to knowing most of the business that went on in the kingdom. So I saw what occurred that day. The newborn babe was brought to my father, but he just patted the tiny head without comment, then returned to his work. I thought it rather strange to ignore his son thus. Periodically Ptah's mother Miw-sher would officially request an audience of Pharaoh, but it was never granted. The only time I think she saw my father was late at night, in her chamber. Menamen-Ra often brought foreign women into the harem. Thus she was made to feel unworthy and shamed. That made Miw-sher very angry and she would take out her hurt feelings on those women, making their lives miserable. Miw-sher was noble born, and this treatment from her Royal Husband was unfair. She complained about it to everyone who would listen. I don't blame her for being upset." I leaned forward, fascinated by the King's story.

"As Ptah grew up, Miw-sher lavished all her attention on the boy. She nursed him until he was five or six years old, long after Shu was born. Ptah would come to her, seductively slip his hand inside, then remove her upper garment as though she was his lover, no matter where she was or who was around, and would begin to suck on her nipple. Odd, isn't it? She fed him her favorite honey cakes and allowed him to play in her chamber or the harem, instead of being relegated to the nursery. Ptah was a really handsome child, charming and friendly, always smiling, and the women in the harem fussed over him."

I was interested to hear about the innocent boy before the creation of the obese, obscene man that Ptah-un-Atum had become. Where was that charming, handsome child now? What had become of him? I listened intently.

"He preferred the harem to playing outside with boys of his own age. Of course, Ptah was allowed to listen to the women's gossip and court intrigue. I did not think that was healthy for a young boy. But I did not say anything to my father. Perhaps I was afraid Menamen-Ra would then treat me badly too, if I did. So instead I felt guilty that I was unfairly receiving the lion's share of the pharaoh's affection and kept silent. If only I had spoken up...."

The wind blew the curtains a little and he looked up for a moment, then continued once again.

"When Shu was born, Miw-sher was still nursing Ptah. When his mother wanted to nurse the baby, Ptah would often push the little one aside, and nurse until he had drunk his fill, leaving her breasts empty for the baby. His mother never protested, but allowed this unseemly behavior. Maybe that is why Shu is so skinny. He got colic, too, and could often be heard late at night, crying without letup."

The king stopped his narrative and looked thoughtful. "Is it possible the way my brothers were treated as children prophesized their characters as men?"

I couldn't help but feel that I was seeing Ptah and Shu for the first time through the compassionate eyes of Ankhamun.

Pharaoh continued. "As a baby Shu was unhappy and his tense, thin little face made me sad. Sometimes I saw Miw-sher pinch him to quiet his cries. Miw-sher was so frustrated at the baby's crying she gave Shu to a wet-nurse to care for him from that moment on, relinquishing her youngest son forever. I don't think she ever touched him or talked to him again."

"Yet, as he grew up, Shu adored his older brother, and never fought with him as children are prone to do, although Ptah teased him mercilessly. Maybe he wanted Ptah to be his father, since he didn't have one of his own. Sometimes he would sit at Ptah's feet like a dog, waiting to be noticed. Shu was a quiet and unobtrusive child, keeping to himself, but he had a thirst for knowledge and a keen mind for learning. He was given many scrolls to read from the time he was quite young and had learned to cipher. When he was older, he desired to go to Nubt Temple and become a Scribe Priest, but Menamen-Ra wouldn't allow it."

Pharaoh changed his voice, taking on an imperious tone, obviously imitating his father. "Your place is in the Palace. It isn't seemly for a Royal Prince to become a Scribe." He paused again, his voice returning to normal. "I wonder what might have happened if Shu had been allowed to become a Priest. Maybe he would have been happier." He played absent-mindedly with a fingertip to his lips as he mused about the possibilities. "By the time I was crowned as King, it was too late. He had become the man you know today."

"Unlike Ptah, no one fussed over Shu or even noticed he was alive, except his own older brother. By now, I was an adolescent and not much interested in playing with my youngest half-brother. I wished I had done so. Perhaps he would be happier today. Shu was not a handsome child nor charming, and was disparaged by the women in the harem, as well as his own mother and father. The few times I did go visit him in his room, he barely acknowledged my presence and seemed immersed in his scrolls."

His memory obviously became clearer.

"Once I went into his room late in the day, sometime after Ra-as-Atum had been swallowed by Nut, the sky neter. The room was dark as the oil lamps hadn't been lit yet. Shu sat in a corner, on the floor of his room, just sitting, not moving. I thought he seemed like a scorpion, waiting in the dark."

Then a look of pain crossed Pharaoh's face.

"I remember one terrible day when Shu was about three or four. I wasn't there to see but an aide who was in attendance told me afterwards what happened. Shu had found a baby frog in the lotus pond and wanted to show his prize to his father. Menamen-Ra was seated on his throne in the Great Hall, in full Pharaonic regalia, holding the heqa and nekhekha. He was unsuccessfully discussing peace with ambassadors from Assyria with whom the King had been having trouble. The three envoys were loudly complaining that Upper Egypt had been unfair to them. A recent trade agreement had promised them five hundred bushels of grain, but they claimed that they had never received the shipment. One of the envoys, an older man with a tall hat and pointed white beard, implied that not only had Menamen-Ra lied to them, but that he was trying to stall in order to build up troops to invade their country. White-Beard insisted Menamen-Ra had no intention of sending wheat, as he had promised.

"Do you say I am a liar?" the King had responded, his eyes narrowed in irritation.

"We have paid for the grain already with much copper from our mines and the wheat never arrived. What would you say if you were in our place?"

"I cannot believe that is the case. I sent the grain with my most trustworthy men and they returned empty-handed, assuring me that they had delivered it personally to your King."

"Perhaps they have cheated you and us as well."

"I cannot believe that."

"Untrustworthy men will ruin a Kingdom," a younger Envoy interrupted. He was Prince Uru-mu-ush on his first diplomatic mission. He acted in an arrogant and haughty manner, obviously trying to impress his delegation with his expertise.

Menamen-Ra turned to him. "Young man, I would trust my men with my life."

"My name is Uru-mu-ush," the young man retorted haughtily. "Your life must be very cheap, then, Sire," he retorted, "to trust disloyal men." It was as though he were taunting my father, wanting to bait him into undesirable action.

"Young man," the King repeated stubbornly, his ire rising, "You are speaking to Pharaoh, so mind your manners. What is it that your Father wants?"

"The promised grain, of course," the older man interrupted silkenly, trying to smooth over the open conflict. But he glanced at his two compatriots with a conspiratorial look.

"I have sent it!" Menamen-Ra stood up angrily, practically jumping off the dais towards his visitors. The Pharaoh lost patience with them. He knew instinctively that they were lying. Years of being a King made his senses very acute. The foreigners had received the grain and wanted more as well, or at least to get their copper back. Assyrians had a reputation of being deceitful traders and my father was caught in the web of their trickery.

"If you want war, then you shall have war," the Prince threatened. "We cannot play this game with you endlessly." The young and very inexperienced royal Ambassador was flexing his new diplomatic muscles.

Assyrians were fierce and bloody fighters, taking no prisoners and ravaging any country that they invaded. Naturally my father wanted to avoid war with them at all costs. "No, no. Of course not. We do not war any more than you," said the King, his lips thin with barely-restrained hostility, but he was cornered, and looked to his Grand Vizier for help.

Menamen-Ra's Grand Vizier had once been the wisest, most able diplomat in my father's kingdom, but he had passed the zenith of his ability. He was already quite advanced in years. His white gown was stained with food that had spilled from his lips at the morning meal and his hands shook with palsy. Besides he was losing his hearing and couldn't keep up with the conversation. "What did he say?" the old Vizier quavered.

Ordinarily the presence of the elderly Vizier would be appropriate in simple matters of diplomacy, but this was no simple matter. Pharaoh had no way of knowing in advance that the ambassadors' meeting was going to spiral out of control. My father was trapped without his other advisors and didn't want to repeat the discussion to the old man. It would only make matters worse.

"I will consult with my Council and we will continue this conversation later," King Menamen-Ra temporized. "I need more time."

"No! We have waited long enough and demand your answer now!" Prince Uru-mu-ush replied. He was toying with the older Pharaoh, feeling superior to him, trying to gain advantage over his elder, as young men are prone to do. The hostile Envoy was glaring at the King openly, standing in front of the throne with his arms folded over his chest, his mouth open in a sneer, like a young, menacing crocodile.

The two seasoned Ambassadors were embarrassed because of their Prince's overt threats, and were whispering together, attempting to figure out how to maneuver out of the corner the arrogant Prince had put them into.

It was at that pivotal moment that Shu ran into the throne room, to share the tiny frog with his father. Pharaoh, as I said, was desperately trying to avoid war when he was interrupted by his small son. Infuriated and enraged by the foreign ambassadors, particularly the cocky youth, the king turned on his son instead. Without thinking and at his wit's end, he began beating the boy with the heqa he was holding, until the child ran screaming and bloody from the chamber."

Ankhamun wiped his sweating forehead. I could see the telling of the story was upsetting to the kindly King.

"I was horrified when I heard my brother's cries ringing out throughout the Palace. I ran to find him in his room and tried to pick up the child to take him to the Senu, physician – priest, to bind his wounds. Shu's little body was trembling and bleeding, but he wouldn't allow me to touch him. Instead Ptah came in, picked up his brother and together we went to find the doctor. I tried to take Shu on my lap, to comfort him. But he pushed me away and bravely wiped the tears from his small face, gritting his teeth as the Senu rubbed healing salve on his raw wounds. From that moment on, Shu never approached our father again and became even more withdrawn than before."

Ankhamun looked at me. "Would you blame him?"

I shook my head no. Many minutes went by as we both sat quietly, each with our own thoughts. I, saddened by the story.

Ankhamun lost in his painful memories. I was curious and asked, "What happened with the Assyrians?"

"You will never believe it. They were terrified by Pharaoh's outburst and left the throne room immediately. Perhaps they believed they also would be beaten, or worse. In any event, the threat of war had passed and they returned to their own country without further discussion – and without any more grain. Ironically Shu helped avert a terrible war, but at such a cost to himself." Pharaoh Ankhamun shook his head sadly.

"So perhaps you can more fully understand my two brothers. I know I make allowances for both of them. But it is clear to me that they were wrongly treated by my father and I want to make it up to them. Once I was crowned, I gave them positions of power and influence. I allowed them to have whatever they wanted. They are my brothers and I love them. I would never hurt them or turn them away, as our father did. Can you comprehend what I tell you?" He looked to me to see my response.

"What a sad story," I sighed.

"Yes," he agreed.

At that point, I made an excuse to leave his presence. The confidence he had shared with me was more than he should have, given that I was a mere servant – not a relative or a confidant. I felt ill at ease because of that, and left to return to work. But it turned out that his remarkable conversation deepened the growing bond between us, more than I could have realized at the time. How could I repay his trust and kindness? Certainly not by my current behavior.

Early one hot morning, thirteen days after the coronation, I was summoned at Pharaoh's request to his small chamber. Carrying a platter of fruit, trembling and uncertain of myself, I took a deep breath and entered the room.

Ankhamun and Atalana were finishing their breakfast, facing the garden and the pond. They sat on the floor, lounging on cushions, while a gorgeous vista of nature – turquoise sky, silky wisps of clouds, the lily-clad pond and greenery around it -lay before them through the open-air portals. They sipped a refreshing drink made of water, lemons, mint leaves and honey in golden goblets set before them. An earthenware platter lay on the table next to small, almost empty, bowls of wheaten gruel.

Once again the Queen was wearing a sleeveless, delicate, floor-length white gown but of denser fabric. She no longer had on the incredible necklace of Het-Heru she had worn to her coronation, but a simpler one, consisting of many strands of turquoise and carnelian beads sewn together with gold links to make a collar. Her arms and feet were bare. A spicy, fragrant perfume of kapet wafted like an aromatic cloud around her. Pharaoh was without jewelry or collar. He wore only a simple linen kilt, while his bare head and wrinkled chest was beaded with perspiration.

As I approached, I could feel the heat rising on my face as I sought vainly to control a sudden surge of feelings. I placed the platter of figs and bananas on the low table in front of them, my hands shaking visibly.

"Thank you, Heb," said Pharaoh, taking no heed of me, his adoring eyes were focused on his new young Queen beside him.

"Majesty," I said formally, and bowed, not trusting myself to look into either of their faces.

"I don't believe you've met my wife," he said. Then he said to the Queen, "This is Heb, the man I've told you so much about."

I bowed again, still silent, hoping to make my escape as soon as possible.

She nodded politely in my direction, then casually reached for a banana.

"Atalana, my dear, let me," the King said tremulously. His hand shook with barely restrained emotion as he peeled the fruit.

"She affects him the same way she does me," I thought to myself. Then I murmured "Atalana," silently, repeating it over and over to myself in a sort of mental chant. Her name evoked the sound of a quiet eddy of mother Nile languidly flowing over smooth rocks on its journey north. In my mind's eye, I imagined her swimming naked, the water rippling over her smooth skin, sunlight sparkling on the drops. I instantly covered myself with crossed hands, afraid that either of them would see my burgeoning excitement evoked from my daydream.

"My husband tells me how valuable you are to him. How you saved him from being crushed to death under a camel."

Her quiet, assured voice made me blush. I could only hang my head in shame at my uncontrollable thoughts. I wordlessly begged the King to dismiss me.

"What is wrong, Heb?" the Pharaoh asked, suddenly solicitous.

"Nothing your Majesty," I hastened to reply. "I….I'm not feeling well this morning," I lied.

Instantly the young Queen rose and I could hear the pad, pad of her naked feet on the marble floor as she walked over to me and touched her cool hand to my hot forehead. "You're burning up!" she exclaimed.

"It is nothing," I murmured, while the sparks from her contact thrilled through my rebellious body. I rocked back and forth as if I would collapse, my head spun dizzily with fire, while huge beads of sweat coursed down my face and splashed on my neck.

She turned to her new husband. "Dearest, this man is quite ill." She clapped her hands together loudly and a servant appeared. "Get some more pillows," she instructed.

When pillows were brought in and arranged, the royal couple helped me to be seated upon them. As though I was in a trance, I numbly allowed myself to partially recline next to the Queen. It was all unthinkable, a dream, impossible that I was there seated in her presence, lounging also in the presence of the great King. I tried to rise but found I could not. My muscles refused to obey my commands. Dizzy, hot and flustered, my mind swirled in dismay and embarrassment.

"Is this why you have made yourself absent from my presence?" the Pharaoh demanded of me with concern in his voice.

"How long have you been unwell?"

"Please, your Majesty." I begged him with my eyes to spare me from talking and to allow me to depart in haste. Meanwhile my countenance reddened even more.

"Drink this," Atalana commanded me, and handed me her nectar-filled goblet.

I gulped it quickly, dribbling a few drops upon my chest, and set the goblet down again, having regained a little of my composure. I sat with my body turned so that they could not see the embarrassing lump of flesh rising like an unruly cobra beneath my kilt.

"That's better," offered the Pharaoh. "You always know what to do, my love." He took one of her slim hands and kissed the palm, his lips lingering there. "Did you know that she was a priestess trained in the healing arts?" he asked me, without looking up.

I shook my head "no."

"Can't you see that he should just rest now?" she asked her husband with a kindly tone but one that commanded respect.

"I'm sorry, my darling," the older man replied. "I'm simply shocked to see him in such a state." He turned to me. "Are you feeling a little better, Heb?"

"Yes, thank you." I struggled, unable to get to my feet.

"No, no. Just sit quietly for a while. The fever will soon pass." Atalana spoke as if she intuited my blackest secrets.

As I surreptitiously looked in her direction, searching her face for clues, I assured myself that she did not suspect anything. I breathed in relief and allowed myself to relax a little against the soft cushions. Atalana's glowing good health and vitality was obvious. Her youthful beauty eclipsed any lovely flower I had ever seen. My thoughts were interrupted by the King.

"Heb is my most loyal subject," Pharaoh said to Atalana. "He saved my life."

"Husband, you have told me the story a hundred times already," she joked, smiling, hugging him affectionately. Her face was radiant and even more beautiful when she smiled.

I sat mute, biting my lip, vastly unsure of myself, a new and terribly unpleasant sensation.

Then the young woman whispered loudly to Pharaoh, "I think Heb is afraid of me," in a teasing tone.

"No!" I replied adamantly and sat up, looking at her. She turned to me. Our eyes met for the first time and my heart skipped a beat or two. "No," I said again, softer this time. As I looked into her direct gaze, I could sense the wise intelligence behind the smiling eyes and saw she was serious. I examined the firm, soft skin, the sensuous lips, the arching eyebrows, "She is younger than me," I mused to myself, "yet seems so much older." I couldn't look away, but sat helplessly staring into her face, fascinated beyond my control, in spite of years of training to do otherwise.

The Pharaoh watched us with interest. "My dear, you have an enchanting effect on every man you meet," he chided her and squeezed her chin.

She laughed effortlessly, the tinkling of her laughter easing the uncomfortable, awkward situation. "I can't help it, dearest," she answered. "But I don't do it on purpose."

"I know, my sweet" replied the Pharaoh. "But you have that power, nonetheless," as he gazed rapturously at her. "It must be the effect of Het-Heru."

I felt I was an intruder in their private conversation and stood up, crossing my hands in front of me again, still wavering. "I must return to my work…" I started to say.

"No, Heb. I want you to go to your chamber. Rest. Sleep," the king interrupted. "I'm very concerned. I need for you to be healthy and strong, you know. I think all the work you did on behalf of our wedding celebration must have exhausted you."

I bowed, acquiescing to his command. "The wedding took a lot out of me," I agreed as I hurriedly left the chamber. "That is surely the truth," I mumbled to myself.

CHAPTER THREE

BASHTA AND THE QUEEN

The Queen's face, ephemeral as a desert mirage but unwavering as the star-filled Duat, refused to leave my mind. I spent the next several sleepless days and nights in the quiet of my room, my body hopelessly on fire. I wrestled with the growing conflict in my body and mind growing conflict and touched myself many times in order to bring release to my ravenous body, only to want more when I had done so. I tossed and turned on my pallet, unable to rest or sleep, unable to think except about her. The man that I had thought I was had vanished, to be replaced by an agitated devotee, unsure of himself, blinded with emotion and obsessed with physical longing.

On the third evening, still unable to sleep, I prowled the halls of the palace like a caged desert lion. I bumped into the serving girl, Bashta, who had been cleaning away the remains of the Royal supper. For years she had blushed and smiled at me in a way I now understood only too well. When she had finished tidying, I took her to my chamber, to find her not only willing, but eager to assuage my physical hunger. It wouldn't be the last time she would give herself to me. Whenever my distress became too severe, Bashta was there to soothe and caress me, and to bring temporary release to my body. Rather than alleviating my emotional and physical torture, Bashta would leave me longing for the object of my forbidden desire even more. Whenever I looked into Bashta's huge doe-like, simple eyes or ran my hands over her plump body, I imagined another woman in her place, a woman I could not and would not ever have. My mind screamed in silent agony.

Given enough time and Bashta's nightly pleasant ministrations, I found my body calming down in a week or so. Eventually I was able to handle my job once more, in a professional albeit aloof manner. The Pharaoh was too involved in his own blissful, married life to notice the change in me, for which I was grateful, and life went on.

I tried to avoid being alone with Atalana, however. Hearing her voice echo in the corridors was difficult enough, but to see her face, her body, would instantly bring back the love fever. I would replay her words and the sound of her voice many times before I went to sleep, only to dream of holding her in my arms and kissing her lips. Whenever she was with the Pharaoh, I kept my eyes downcast. I did not wish to recreate the aching turmoil within myself by the sight of her nor the growing jealousy I felt for my dear Master. Threads of guilt started to weave an uncomfortable cloth within me, as I secretly and involuntarily hoped the Pharaoh would soon die. The horror of my envy, my obsession, was unbearable. I got out my Mother's amulet and prayed fervently to Het-Heru, The Powerful One, to intervene, to release me from the dual bondage of desire and jealousy into more exalted and purer (and calmer) forms of emotion.

However, the Neter wasn't listening to my entreaties, while fate seemed determined to bring the Queen and me together often. Many times I would be hurrying through the halls on my daily tasks, only to find Atalana standing in a corridor without her maidservants. Our eyes would meet momentarily and she would search my face with an intense scrutiny. I always bowed quickly, blushing furiously, before I moved on. I sometimes had the sense that she had been waiting there for me to pass.

But of course I was a man desperately in love, subject to endless fantasies about the object of my affection.

One day I was sorting and arranging the Pharaoh's untidy mess of papyrus manuscripts and arranging them in leather trunks, elaborately carved with figures and hieroglyphics of Djehuti, God of Knowledge and Writing. One trunk for affairs of state. Another for correspondence. Yet another for the household ledgers. I was down on my hands and knees next to the Pharaoh's massive writing table with the huge alabaster top, organizing the dusty pile of papers when I smelled the fruity scent of kapet. I looked up to see the Queen watching me and got to my feet immediately. "Your Majesty," and I bowed quite low, moving my hand to my immediately-swollen groin as my body reacted to her presence.

"Please don't let me interrupt you, Heb," she said gently. "I've come for the weekly tally of expenses."

I felt the familiar rush of unmanageable sensations and knelt down on the floor to hide my embarrassment. I searched through a particular pile, found what she was looking for and handed it to her wordlessly.

She unrolled it and scanned the scrawled hieratic notations for a few minutes.

"I didn't know you could scribe." I spoke without thinking. I had meant to merely think the words.

"I can. A little. Mostly I can read and write simple ideas, names, and numbers. It must have been much easier for the ancient ones. They only had to deal with a few sacred symbols." She turned to leave.

As I knelt on the floor, I thought again how intelligent she was. The Pharaoh was wise in marrying her and taking her for his primary wife and co-regent. I wondered vaguely at her mention of ancient ones. Who were they? The hair on the back of my neck stood up and I glanced up to see her watching me again. "Is there anything else I can do for you, your Majesty?" "Um. No. I was just thinking that the Pharaoh is very fortunate to have such a loyal and devoted subject working for him." "Thank you, your Gracious Majesty." If only she knew my secret shame.

"You're welcome, Heb," and with that she turned and left, her slim naked feet noiseless on the cool marble floor.

On another day, I don't know how long after, I was summoned to the breakfast room again. When I arrived, I realized the Pharaoh was not in attendance, only the Queen. The heat from the brilliant, warming sun was pouring into the room. The curtains had been drawn to preserve the morning coolness. But it was the month of Ka Her Ka and although it was soon after Ra-as-Khepera's rising in the east, the room would soon be hotter than an oven. I could already feel perspiration drip down my neck. "Majesty." I stared at the table in front of her, unable to look up.

"Pharaoh has left for a few days on urgent business," she informed me. "I will take my meals in our private Chamber until his return," she continued. "There is no reason to sit in that vast dining room with nothing but three rancorous queens and their sly maidservants to offer me company. Please inform the stewards." "I will, my Lady," I replied and turned to leave.

"Heb?" she stopped me.

"Yes, my Queen."

"Are you happy here?"

The suddenly personal question took me by complete surprise and I paused for a few moments. "Why…yes, I am," I lied, not raising my eyes, but the coloring in my face changed to the color of ripe grapes, even though I tried desperately to remain self-controlled. How I longed to tell her how I really felt!

"Hmm," was her only response, yet I could feel her eyes boring deep into my soul.

I fidgeted, wishing that she would dismiss me, only too aware of the intensity of her unblinking gaze.

"Do you love the Pharaoh?" she then asked quietly.

"Of course," I replied without hesitation, looking up quickly. "I would give my life for him!" I continued adamantly.

She sighed then and relaxed her visual hold on me. "Thank you, Heb. You may go now."

"Thank you, your Majesty." I wondered about her questions, but was soon embroiled in a disagreement between a cook and his helper, and forgot about the incident. However, because of the short interlude with the Queen, my emotional distress and physical ardor tormented me that night worse than ever. Even Bashta was sorely troubled by my misery, although I could not discuss any of it with her, ashamed and embarrassed by my uncontrollable emotions and illicit passion.

I continued to pray daily to Het-Heru, with the aid of my Mother's amulet, to heal me. When the Pharaoh returned home, I breathed a little easier, knowing that his presence would sustain me somehow.

Many months later, I was lying with the amulet of the Neter clutched in my hand and Bashta curled up sleeping next to me. Her belly was filling with new life. I should have been happy with the coming child, my child, but I wasn't. Het-Heru was unfair, sending me a woman I didn't love and unable to be with the woman I did.

The moon was dark and the wind was violently blowing the sand outside into high drifts. I slept but fitfully. Then Het-Heru appeared to me in my dream, the first time since I was a boy. Her golden image glowed and I saw a withered, aged woman standing behind Her. My mother? "Heb," the Neter spoke. "You will hold the future of Ta-Meir Res in your hands." This was the same message She had given me when I was a young boy, although I didn't understand its meaning any more now than I had earlier.

Then I saw an image of the royal apartment. The Queen sat on a chair, with her head in her hands. Her face was blotchy and reddened from crying. The Pharaoh stood next to her, trying to console her. Behind them, an unseen menace was approaching. Crawling out from under the bedclothes, swarmed dozens of mature scorpions, lethal stingers poised above their heads to strike their targets.

I awakened with a start. My chamber was dark as a tomb. The oil lamp had burned out. Next to me, the slumbering Bashta moaned in her sleep. I wrapped my flaxen skirt around me, tucking the end in at the waist, then paused. If I were wrong, I would be disturbing the royal couple needlessly. But I felt a foreboding, an imminent sense of danger. I hurried through the darkened corridors, lit only by an occasional torch, until I got to the Royal Apartments. The inner sanctum, the palace servants called it. Rarely was anyone except personal servants and cleaning staff allowed in there. I put my ear to the closed thick door and could hear muted voices. They were awake. I mustered up my courage and knocked loudly, anxiously waiting until it opened. The King's eyes were red and puffy with lack of sleep and behind him I could see his wife, the Queen sitting on a chair, exactly as in my dream. Elbows on the arms of the chair, her head resting on her palms, eyes closed, tears drying on her face.

Now convinced of the danger and without further hesitation, I shouted, "Scorpions, your Majesty!" I strode to the bed and pulled down the cover. Fortunately, the Pharaoh and his wife had not yet retired, although it was extremely late. From under the silken material crawled a black army of deadly scorpions.

The Queen screamed in terror and clambered onto her chair.

For the first time since her arrival, I focused on the problem at hand and not with my uncomfortable feelings towards her.

"Get some men!" the Pharaoh ordered me. "And bring something to kill these."

Within moments I had awakened the guards sleeping in a chamber nearby, who brought sticks. We exterminated the vermin, smashing them flat. Their tough exoskeletons were difficult to break but finally we had killed more than twenty huge scorpions in all.

After the dead insects had been removed, the rest of the chamber was searched without finding more. I stood by the Royal Bed, aching with relief.

Ankhamun came over to me. His face was a study in emotions. "Heb," he said in a tremulous voice. "Once again I owe my life, and now my

Queen's, to you." He paused in confusion. "How did you know?" "I had a bad dream, your Majesty," trying to explain.

"No matter," the Pharaoh interjected. "I'm only glad you took such swift action." His mouth smiled in a grimace, yet his eyes expressed concern and anxiety. He went over to his wife, who had gotten down from the chair and was seated. Atalana was calmer now, and the King put his arms around her. She leaned into his shoulder and began to weep again. "Good night, Heb," he dismissed me abruptly.

"Good night, your Majesties," and I bowed and left. When I arrived in my small chamber, it was empty. Bashta had left for her own bed in the servant's quarters.

In the morning, all the inhabitants of the palace were questioned, but guilt was never laid on anyone's head. Obviously the scorpions had been concealed in the bed, ready for the royal occupants to retire. But by whom? Who was the traitor in the Palace? The mystery continued to confound us all but stubbornly remained unresolved. Fortunately the royal couple was unhurt. But trusted guards were now posted at the doorway to the royal apartments and outside all the openings as well.

Just after Sopdit disappeared from the sky, Bashta gave birth to a healthy daughter, our child. However, rather than move in with me, she remained with the child in the servant's dormitory. I didn't have the strength to turn her away, but couldn't ask her to permanently share my quarters either. I needed privacy to think, to dream of the woman I loved.

With Sopdit's annual return, the Nile flooded and receded, crops were planted and harvested, before I realized how much time had passed. Women in the palace gossiped that any day our new queen should announce a much-awaited pregnancy. The obvious and continuing happiness of our monarch made everyone certain of impending good news. But that announcement didn't come.

One night, the Queen's personal maidservant showed up at my chamber while I was sleeping.

"The Pharaoh wants to see you—now!" the maidservant whispered loudly as she shook me awake.

I nudged the sleeping Bashta. The baby was being cared for by another servant woman while the mother slept with me for a while. "Bashta, return to your room," I urged her. She got up sleepily and left. I hurriedly tied on my kilt and the maidservant led me to the Pharaoh's private living quarters. As I followed the woman, I wondered what urgent business would cause my master to summon me at such an unusual hour.

As I was ushered into the lavish apartment, I was in awe of the tranquil beauty of the Royal Apartment. I had only been there twice in my life, including the episode with the scorpions, but had never forgotten it. A large fountain bubbled in the middle of the spacious chamber. It flowed into a deep bath that had been dug into the foundation, its sides and bottom tiled with mosaics of variegated marble, while water flowed there from the fountain. The east and west walls were open to the outside, with the painted colonnades placed along their openings. Curtains were pulled across the openings, shutting out the darkness of the night, while the soothing sound of the splashing fountain pervaded the space. The two remaining north and south walls were solid and had been painted to mirror the garden and pond outside. Artful birds fluttered through the air or perched on the painted green trees. Every minute detail of the three-dimensional flowers and plants had been meticulously recaptured on the two dimensional surface. The unknown artist had so remarkably duplicated the aliveness of the garden that I half expected to hear the painted birds singing or the buzzing of bees.

Against one of the decorated walls stood the massive sleeping rack for the Pharaoh and his wife. Its four gilded posts must have been ten cubits tall. Lavish blue cloth spun with gold thread was draped over and around it. I mused to myself that it could have easily provided room for at least eight people to sleep comfortably, yet only the royal couple rested there.

In front of the bed, two solid wooden chairs were closely arranged next to each other, while a third chair was placed some distance away, facing them. Queen Atalana was seated on one of the two comfortable chairs, decorated in the same natural motif as the two walls. Her hands were calmly draped over lotus flowers carved into the arms. My Master stood near her, obviously eager to speak with me.

"Sire," I bowed deeply and waited awkwardly, my heart beating rapidly in the Queen's presence. I could feel the faint, familiar flush of color rising on my cheeks and the heat in my body.

He waved the maidservant out of the room. She bowed and left. All their other attendants had been dismissed as well, so only we three occupied the huge room. The two monarchs were fully awake and had been apparently waiting for me. They were each clothed in warm robes, the sleeves reached to their waists. My chest and arms were bare and I shivered in the chilly night air.

"My boy," Ankhamun said to me, in a manner even friendlier than his usual warm demeanor. "Sit here," and he indicated the third chair. Then he handed me a cloth wrap, which I put around my chilled shoulders.

I waited until he had positioned himself in the second chair before I sat down, perched on the edge of the seat in front of them, uncomfortable sitting in the royal presence. Neither of them spoke. "You wanted to see me, your Majesty?" I inquired after a long silence.

He raised a hand to indicate he had heard me but was not yet ready to talk.

I waited patiently, but was startled to notice that what hair he had left had gone almost completely white. Deep wrinkles were beginning to etch their way around his eyes and his mouth sagged. Why had I not noticed these before? How long had I been sleepwalking through the palace? One inundation? Two? More? Had I been so obsessed with my own personal demons that I had not been a faithful and caring servant to my King?

As I examined my monarch, I had to look at Atalana as well, seated close to him. I squirmed a little, feeling the familiar physical arousal I experienced whenever I was near her and forced my body to be still. She had a long dressing gown on, and was holding it closed with her hands. Her radiant beauty seemed to shine from a deep well inside her. A familiar ache in my chest throbbed at the sight of her glowing magnificence.

Pharaoh cleared his throat and began to talk slowly, carefully choosing his words. Atalana sat quietly next to him, seeming to encourage him by her mere presence.

"Heb," he began. "I summoned you here to discuss a most important matter. One that requires the greatest secrecy and discretion on your part. You must never disclose anything we talk about here tonight. Will you give me your solemn oath?" I nodded my head. "Yes, by Ma'at's feather, I swear it," even though I had no idea what I was agreeing to.

"Good. I knew I could trust you." He paused, a look of deep concern passed over his face.

Atalana reached over and held the aging hand with fond affection.

He seemed to gather strength from her touch and continued. "Heb," he started again. "You undoubtedly know…the whole palace knows…" he smiled grimly to himself. "That the queen and I…" he paused again. "That we…" He sighed deeply. "We are not destined to bear children together." His voice was heavy with emotion. He looked at Atalana and squeezed her hand in his. She smiled adoringly at him, yet with a tinge of sadness around her mouth and eyes.

I could see his eyes well up with water. A single tear escaped from the royal eye and made its slow passage down the wrinkled, aging cheek. The King wiped it away with the back of his hand and breathed deeply, rearranging his robe in front of him.

After a few moments he continued in a resigned tone. "As you know, I had hoped for sons to continue after I am gone." I nodded breathlessly. My own chest felt tight, empathetic to the king's sadness and despair.

"Without a son, I am gravely concerned about the future of our country." His voice had softened into a dream-like quality and his eyes seemed to look far away. "I had hoped to teach him, instruct him to be a good sovereign, to be a loving caretaker of the people and the land."

All of this I knew was no secret and wondered why he had called me. Did he need to speak these words out loud? Why was I sworn to solemn secrecy?

"Therefore, I have formulated a plan." He paused and scrupulously examined my face as though needing reassurance.

I leaned forward, hoping to convince him of my loyalty through my expression. The snaking tendrils of guilt and envy were forgotten in this moment, and I remembered only my love for my great Master.

He seemed content and continued again. "The plan that I have decided on…" He licked his dry lips, glancing nervously at his lovely young wife next to him. Her exotic face appeared serene and dignified far beyond her years.

I nodded for him to continue.

Instead he changed his approach. "Heb, you know I have always thought of you with great affection."

"Yes, sire," I replied.

"I have known your love, your unswerving loyalty and protection of me and my household. The incident with the camel, and then the scorpions prove to me what I know in my heart."

I blushed in embarrassment, not only at his praise, but also because of my conflict between my love for him on one hand – and secret desire and jealousy on the other.

"In some ways I feel that you are like my son, the son I never had. I saw your intelligence when you were a young lad and brought you teachers so that you could expand your mind. Your heart is kind and totally loyal. You are committed to the welfare of this country, the same as I. But I must have sons and soon. The episode with the scorpions has taught me that much." I bit my lips, knowing that his rhetoric was leading me to some important destination. But where?

"I know you love the Queen also."

My face immediately turned a bright shade of crimson, matching the red hues of the flowers on the wall behind the Pharaoh. I tried to think of a reply but my mind whirled in dismay.

He gazed at me fondly. "I know, Heb. I have always known." His voice was gentle. "I observed you when you first met Atalana. I could sense your feelings and the way you acted in her presence. I watched as you attempted to avoid us from that moment on. Remember, I have known you all your life. I know your expressions. I can read your actions like a scribe can read a papyrus."

I nodded, staring down at the marble floor, feeling both ashamed and relieved. Tears smarted in my eyes.

"It must have been very difficult for you." Atalana spoke for the first time, her voice and face full of compassion for me.

I looked at the two benevolent monarchs with appreciation and respect. "I tried to be very careful," I murmured.

"I appreciate that. But you couldn't hide what was in your heart – from me," replied Pharaoh Ankhamun.

"I am so sorry. Please forgive me!" I cried out. I jumped out of my chair and knelt on the floor in front of them, my forehead touching the cool stone, hiding my face from them, while salty tears wet the floor below me. My body shook with the sudden release of all my pent-up emotions.

"Now, now," said Pharaoh Ankhamun. "There's no need for that. In fact, your love has given birth to an idea. Please get up,

Heb. Sit here with us. I have more to say."

I rose and wiped my wet face with my arm, more bewildered than ever. I sat down nervously. "I'm so ashamed," I confessed.

"There is no need for shame. Love is never shameful," replied Atalana gently.

But I was unconvinced. They didn't know of my body's carnality or my mind's demented fantasies.

"We know it all, Heb," the young woman continued as if she could hear my thoughts. "There are no secrets between us." I gulped, shocked that I had left the portal to my life open for them to peer into. What else did they know?

The Pharaoh continued. "Of late, Atalana and I have discussed you behind these doors."

"You have discussed me?" The mere idea of them talking about me was beyond anything I could imagine.

"You may hold the answer to the fate of our country." He paused and smiled benignly. "You have saved our country on several occasions already."

"I, Master? But I'm just a lowly servant. How can I help you?" Yet in the recesses of my mind I remembered Het-Heru. What was it She had said to me?

"You will bring forth sons, whom I will adopt and raise as my own. Sons I can teach and guide and advise. Sons who will protect and nurture the land and all its people once I have gone to the Duat with Ausar."

"Sons, sire? But...I don't understand. I have no wife." My mind reeled with the impact of his words, while the full meaning of those words slowly seeped into my awareness. My forehead wrinkled; I was not able to or perhaps not wanting to comprehend.

"You and I will make sons for the Pharaoh, Heb" Atalana answered simply. She sounded out of breath. "You and I will create kings to lead our country, whom Pharaoh will adopt as his own children." She blinked and shyly looked at her husband beside her.

Could my ears be deceiving me? Atalana and I? The woman I desired above all women? The woman I had lusted for, fantasized in incessant monologues and dreamt of for so long? Endlessly replaying images of her beautiful face, her melodious voice, her soft womanly body while I comforted myself with the servant Bashta? My beloved Atalana? But what about Pharaoh? I shook myself and said, "I must be dreaming." "You are not dreaming, Heb," she said tenderly.

She glowed as though from some inner light, and once again I saw the visage of Het-Heru, Neter of love and joy, indelibly imprinted on her face.

"You and I will become lovers for the greater glory of our precious land. And from our blessed union will come sons. The Golden One has told me so."

At hearing her momentous words, I was stunned, excited, frightened, and elated all at the same time. My overwhelmed mind swirled as though I might collapse, but I remained conscious. I looked from one to the other, not believing, not trusting that I had heard correctly. Yet her words echoed inside, resonating to a deeper knowledge hidden within me, but only now surfacing. "I will raise the children as my own," continued Pharaoh. "No one but us three will ever know they are not mine." Outside the sky became tinged with pink.

"We haven't much time before the palace is awake," the Pharaoh said quickly. "I will announce that I have elevated you to the status of Personal Caretaker of Pharaoh. Thus, you must be housed close by to attend to all my needs – and wants."

"There is a chamber just beyond our apartment," Atalana spoke up. "It will be made ready for you to live there. A private door leads between here and there, so I can come and go without anyone noticing."

"You will come to my personal chamber?" I still could not entirely comprehend the idea they were proposing.

"Yes, of course." Her musical voice made my body quiver.

"Oh…" was all I could say in response. I was too overwhelmed to say more at the time. I glanced at my Master. His shoulders were sagging and he had put his arm around Atalana for support. How could he offer intimate access of his own beloved wife to a servant? How could I ever be worthy of his trust? I felt like a small child, found with my guilty hand in a bowl of sweet figs.

"Do you agree to all this?" asked the Pharaoh, sensing my hesitation.

"Yes, yes," I replied quickly. "Yes, I agree," and my body seemed as if it would explode with all the contradictory sensations I was feeling.

"And you will keep this a secret forever?"

"Yes, no one will ever know. I hope to pass into the West before that happens."

"Good," replied the Pharaoh standing up, leading me to the door to the hall outside. "You will be summoned when everything is ready. Remember to say nothing to anyone – not even upon your death," and the heavy door shut behind me.

I returned to my chamber, too overwhelmed to sleep. Every nerve in my body was intensely vibrating. I lay on my straw filled sleeping pad, trying to make sense of all that had been said. But the sad vision of the Pharaoh disturbed me and my head ached. He had asked me to be intimate with his wife, his Queen, in order to ensure safety for the country through the continuity of children. What misery would the Pharaoh have to endure? What jealousies of his own would he have to conquer? I empathized with his, while mine now felt like a minor disturbance in comparison. Would I have had the courage to do what he was doing? I could feel my selfishness returning again. "Atalana," I murmured to myself and my body responded as usual. My greatest torment would soon be relieved. The woman Bashta and our girl-child was forgotten. I clasped my hands together and closed my eyes. "Make me worthy of his trust, Het-Heru," I prayed fervently. "And thank you for intervening for me. Thank you!"

In the subterranean mists of my mind, I thought I heard the faint words of the Lady of Gold. "Be careful what you ask for,

Heb. You are likely to get it."

CHAPTER FOUR

PERSONAL CARETAKER OF LOVE

My Master relieved me immediately of my former Custodial duties, so I had nothing to do but wait. One day went by. Then another. Each passed like an inundation. On the third day, I couldn't sit still any longer. I walked the garden grounds, as my mind created new scenarios, ones that I could fulfill now. The water in the pond gleamed in the sunlight. The new green leaves on the trees and shrubs sparkled in the cool air. I also felt renewed, refreshed. My life had sharply turned down a new path and I hummed to myself with joyful expectation. I paced around the garden numerous times, but still no word was forthcoming. I sat on a marble bench then got up to pace again, the golden disk of Ra-as-Atum beginning to die on the western horizon. I saw a figure approaching me. Bashta. Waves of guilt flooded through me and my stomach tightened.

"I have been looking all over for you today," she said, smiling adoringly at me. She had ceased to blush in my presence some time ago. "You have not asked me to come to your chamber for several nights," she said with a faint tinge of accusation in her tone.

"Um, no," I fumbled for words. "I…I was going to tell you…"

"Tell me what?" she asked. Her smile disappeared and fear trembled in her voice.

"I've been appointed Personal Caretaker to Pharaoh, so I won't be able to spend time with you." "For how long?"

How long indeed? "I don't know," I said truthfully.

Water welled up in her full-moon eyes and plopped down her cheeks in large drops, which turned into a stream.

I held her shoulders to comfort her, full of remorse and ashamed at myself. I had been using her to relieve myself and now I was throwing her away without consideration of her feelings.

"Heb," she said, still weeping, "is it me?" she questioned carefully. "Have you grown tired of me now that I am no longer a girl but a mother with a child?"

"No," I replied. "Not exactly. I will be very busy with Pharaoh."

"But at night, too?"

"Perhaps. I must be ready to serve—any time of the day or night."

She seemed unconvinced of my explanation, but I was rescued from her misery and further discussion when a man-servant approached us.

"Come with me, Heb," he said without ceremony.

"I will see you again," I promised.

She stood silent as a stone without replying. Her grief-stricken eyes followed me into the Palace.

I followed the man-servant wordlessly to my new living quarters, my heart racing, clutching the pouch with the two mementos from my Mother, the only things in the world I owned. The chamber was much larger than my last, and decorated but not nearly as elaborately as the Royal Apartment. The walls had been freshly plastered and painted with images of the sacred couple, Het-Heru and Heru and hieroglyphics proclaiming their holy union and protection of our Land. This was to be, after all, a chamber to share with a Queen who was also a Priestess of Het-Heru.

A large bedstead stood in the center of the room. Next to it was placed an oil brazier but I had no need of heat. A round pedestal table was set with a white linen cloth. Two chairs, the seats and backs woven from the strong outer fiber of papyrus, stood next to the table near the single open portal, where curtains were hung, fastened back on wooden hooks to reveal the outside. From the opening, I could see Mother Nile below and I breathed in the clean, crisp air. New clothes for my use had been neatly folded and placed on another small round table nearest the bed. A pair of real leather sandals was placed next to them. The floor was made entirely of black marble with white swirled through it and I liked the feel of the coolness under my feet. Torches burned on brackets fastened to the walls, as the light was fading fast. On each table an oil lamp burned in a small, elongated, baked clay vessel with symbols of the Udjat Eye carved into each of them, also lit for me. For me! Was I awake or dreaming? I took off my old kilt and lay naked on the bed, the mattress filled with goose feathers, covered with a silken cloth, quite unlike the hard sleeping mat I was used to. I luxuriated in its softness, feeling as though I was floating on a cloud in Nut's sky. I rubbed my bare legs and arms against the silky cloth, softer than any I had ever known.

Quietly the adjoining door opened and Atalana stepped into my room, closing the door decisively behind her. "Does this satisfy you?" she asked, indicating my room, the bed and my new clothes.

"Oh!" I hastily pulled the coverlet over my nakedness, feeling awkward and vulnerable in her regal presence.

She laughed merrily at me as though I was a small child. "I will see your body in due time," she smiled. Then she walked over to where I lay and sat down next to me on the feather-filled bed.

"You have a very handsome body, Heb," she told me. "I look forward to the time when I can explore it."

Oh my Goddess! I must be in a dream. May I never wake! My body responded with passionate excitement. I quaked and burned and shivered, all the while clutching the bed linen, trying to hide the evidence of my feelings, yet reaching for her at the same time.

She gently took my exploring hand, kissing my fingers tenderly, her lips lingering on each one. "Be at peace, Heb. The intimate time spent together between a man and a woman is holy and sacred. We have no need to rush."

"I am sorry, your Majesty," I murmured, chastened by her words and actions. In my life I had known nothing except haste and overwhelming need to relieve my body.

"There are ways that I wish to teach you, so that we may honor The Golden One—that is Het-Heru—in our being together and thus honor our Pharaoh and the coming generations."

"I am ready to learn, Majesty" I muttered under my breath. "I am a good student."

"Not just yet, Heb," and she laughed softly again. "Anticipation and proper timing are part of love."

I watched her as she got up and strolled casually around the room, inspecting each piece of furniture. Then she smoothed the clothes stacked on the table, stroking the fabric with her fingertips. She was dressed in a simple flowing pale-blue gown, which was cut low in front. Her arms and wrists were bare of decoration, but she had a sash laced with gold thread fringe on the ends, which she had tied around her narrow waist. On her ankles she had golden chains with tiny bells that tinkled with each step. The whole picture of her was of extreme ecstasy and beauty.

In the light from the torches and candles, I could see the curves of her body under the gown. The mound that I would penetrate in time. I could feel the lump of my excitement throb violently under the coverlet. I wanted to push the bed linen aside so she could know how much I wanted her, but didn't dare. She was my Pharaoh's Queen and a Noble Priestess as well, and I was intimidated by her.

"Are you hungry?" she asked, without looking at me.

"Yes, very much," realizing too late the double meaning of her question and my reply.

She turned and gazed at me, seeing my aroused body under the cover. Without displaying any surprise, she smiled, her eyes looking deeply into mine, teasing me gently. Then she continued, "I meant, have you eaten yet? I could have something brought in for you," she added graciously.

"Um, well I haven't eaten much all day. I'm not too hungry. Perhaps just some fruit." My body desired impatiently while my mind raced with a single idea, around and around. To hold my beloved. To kiss her. To caress her. To make love with her. To enter her Holy Sanctuary of bliss.

She interrupted my daydream. "I will get something for you to eat. Wait here." She left and returned with a small bowl of dried fruit and a goblet of thick barley beer, which she placed on the table. She sat in one of the reed chairs and pointed silently to the empty one, while she nibbled delicately on a date.

I got up, wound the bed cover around my nakedness, and sat next to her. While I tried to eat, she watched me, seeming to scrutinize every detail of my actions, all the while examining my bare chest, shoulders, arms, face. I could feel my pulse beat strongly in my neck. "You are making me nervous," I laughed hollowly.

"Oh, I'm sorry, Heb. Would you like for me to talk while you eat?"

"Yes, please. I love the sound of your voice."

"Thank you for saying that." She smiled slowly in feminine delight. "Very well." She looked away as she collected her thoughts. "I know much about you, Heb, but you know nothing of me."

"Mm, hm," was my only reply, my mouth full. A slight breeze blew into the room and I could smell her fruity, sweet kapet perfume drifting towards me. How much longer would we have to wait? I both anticipated and feared what would inevitably transpire.

"I was born the youngest child into a noble family north of here. My mother had a dream when she was pregnant with me, of the name Atalana. It isn't a Ta-Meir Res Resu name, you know."

"I had often wondered about that," I replied.

"She dreamed of a far-away place. There was a woman in the dream, a lady of noble stature, who lived in a large house surrounded by much water."

"Like irrigation ditches?" I asked, teasingly.

She giggled at my joke. "No silly. Like the northern sea at the end of the Nile, only bigger." "Oh," I replied.

"My noble family has lived in Nekken for generations. I was the youngest child, with several older sisters and brothers. I was spoiled and pampered, especially by my father. We adored each other. Then when I was four, my father was killed in a hunting accident."

Her gown revealed the tops of her breasts gleaming in the firelight. I stared, distracted, at the cleft between them, not quite listening to her story.

"Are you paying attention?"

"Oh, yes," I breathed deeply.

"Hmm," and she shook her head in mock anger.

But her eyes twinkled and I saw through her ruse. I noticed that there were flecks of gold in those dark brown eyes. Some of the hair on her long wig had fallen over one shoulder, curling around one of her breasts. She moved the tresses behind her shoulder. Was it for my benefit, so that I may have an uninterrupted view of her loveliness?

"After his funeral," she said, picking up the thread of her story, "I began to have visions of Het-Heru. In vision She told me that I would marry Pharaoh. When I spoke of this to my family they only laughed at me. They thought I was having childish fantasies, due to the death of my beloved father."

I had finished all the fruit and was sipping the thick beer, vastly interested now at the mention of the Neter of love, beauty, and pleasure.

"The visions continued until I was nine, at which point I announced to my family that I was going to serve Het-Heru at her holy Temple at Enet-ta-Neter."

The wind blew more strongly at that moment and the torches flickered wildly, but didn't go out. I got up and pulled the curtains shut to block out the wind. I could hear the palm trees rustling outside.

"I think She's listening to me and sent the wind to let me know she hears," Atalana said.

"Who?"

"Het-Heru, of course."

I stared at the seated woman, becoming more aware in every passing minute of her uniqueness…and something more. A sense of being chosen, selected by the Neter. I pulled at my lip. My brow furrowed as I studied her, trying to understand her and my part in Het-Heru's unknown plan.

"Now you're making me nervous," she giggled.

I shrugged in apology.

She continued her story. "I coaxed my eldest brother to take me to Enet-ta-Neter. When I arrived, I discovered that I had been expected by Mukalia."

"Who's that?"

"The High Priestess at Enet-ta-Neter." "Oh," I said without comprehension.

"The Priestesses took me in, taught me. I never left in all those years. Not until later when Ankhamun went to Het-Heru's Temple to present offerings and obtain the Neter's blessings for children - and discovered me there."

"That is an amazing story, Atalana." It was the first time I had called her by name. I was getting bolder and less intimidated.

The young woman gazed at me. "I'm glad you can say my name. I was beginning to think you had forgotten it."

"Oh, no," I exclaimed. "You have a beautiful name." She didn't know how many times I had repeated her name to myself in the silence of my chamber.

"Thank you, Heb." She paused. "Do you want to hear the rest of my story?"

"As you wish, your Majesty," I said politely. After all she was a Queen and I was her servant, but my body kept jogging me into physical awareness. Periodically I would think of Pharaoh in the adjoining apartment and shudder. How could I make love to her with the King in the next chamber?

As though she could read my mind, she continued. "When Ankhamun saw me, he fell in love with me instantly."

"So did I," I murmured thoughtlessly. I hadn't intended for her to hear my words.

"I know, Heb," she replied with great tenderness. She reached over and placed her soft hand on my arm, sending hot chills throughout my body.

Anticipation was proving to be a far more difficult task than unfulfilled desire.

"And do you love him?" I asked impulsively. The words popped out of my mouth before I could stop the question. I was half-afraid to hear the answer but needed to hear her say it.

"Yes, I love him very much. I think I have been in love with him since I was a little girl," she replied emotionally.

Frustration, physical yearning and guilt, coupled with the intensity and meaning of her words were painful. I pulled away from her touch, folded my arms over my chest to protect myself, and pushed against the chair's back, withdrawn, moody and hurt.

"I didn't mean to upset you, Heb. But you asked. You would have to know, sooner or later. Please don't be angry with me," she cajoled.

I felt contrary and stubborn, not really meaning to pull away, yet deeply wounded and confused. "I used to wish that he would die, so I could have you all to myself. It was terribly wicked of me, but I couldn't help it," I blurted out, hoping to shock and hurt her.

"Yes, I understand you couldn't help it. I'm not upset with you. But jealousy is a vicious enemy, hurting everyone around us and ourselves as well."

Her lecture only made me feel angrier and I drummed my fingers of one hand upon the table. How could she love both the Pharaoh and me?

"Do you still wish for his death?"

"No," I confessed. "Not anymore," I added meaningfully.

"I see," she replied, thoughtfully. "I'm glad. Because he loves you, too. He trusts you with his life. And with me." I wished she wouldn't remind me of what I knew only too well.

She caressed my cheek as though she owned me, raising gooseflesh where her fingers lingered. I loved the feel of her fingers on my face. I felt myself yielding to her gentle touch and I uncrossed my arms.

"I have been wicked, too," she said so softly I had to lean forward to hear her words.

"You?" I asked with astonishment. "How?"

Her narrow lovely face twisted into a grimace in the torchlight, tormented by some inner pain. I wanted to reach for her, to comfort her, but refrained due to a lifetime of training as a servant.

"I have never spoken of it to anyone." She reached for my hand and I eagerly held it, giving her as much comfort as I could muster.

Suddenly I realized we had become co-conspirators, telling each other our darkest secrets. Eagerly, I waited to hear more, knowing as I did, that a special knot was being tied between us. "I promise I won't say anything to anyone."

"Especially not to Ankhamun?" she asked fearfully.

"Especially not to him."

She swallowed hard, searching for the right words. I could tell that none of them were easy.

"Shortly before we were to be married, Het-Heru appeared and told me Pharaoh would never have children. Not with me. Not with anyone." Tears sparkled on her cheeks and she brushed them away. "I couldn't bring myself to tell him. He was so happy. And I loved him so much. He believed our love would bring many children, many sons. I was afraid to tell him, afraid that he might change his mind about marrying me. I kept hoping what I heard wasn't true. That one day I would discover I was pregnant. But the Neter was right after all."

She removed her hand and sniffled. I handed her a corner of my bed-cover to wipe her nose. "Atalana, I...."

She held up her hand to stop me. "I don't want your pity. This terrible lie has festered inside me for too long. I...I...just needed to tell someone." She sat up straighter in her chair, unburdened at last.

"I'm glad you trust me."

"I do, Heb. I trust you completely." She looked at me wistfully. "Do you hate me? Now that you know I deceived your beloved Pharaoh?"

"Not at all. I think I love you more than ever, if that's possible."

"There's something else." She lowered her eyes to the empty alabaster fruit bowl on the table and began to play with the edge of it. "It wasn't Ankhamun's idea for you and me to become lovers, to make a child for Pharaoh." Mustering up courage, she looked shyly into my eyes. "It was mine."

My bruised feelings were mollified at hearing those few words. I wanted to stand at the open portal, to shout to the world "The Queen wants me!" I could have raced down the long hill to the Holy River and swam across its wide expanse without effort. I could have jumped so high that I would have flown into Nut's body and beyond. I could have swept up Atalana's body in my arms and laid her gently in my new bed, to caress and love her until the imperishables fell from the sky.

Then I remembered my Master. Even though Pharaoh himself had given me permission to be intimate with his Queen, I was fully aware of my divided loyalty. So instead I forced myself to sit very still, though throbbing violently inside. The veins in my groin ached with an agonizing pressure, my heart beat as though I had been running, but I remained motionless.

Atalana watched the intense effort I was exerting over my body, struggling to prevail over my khat.

She stood up, walked around behind me and leaned against me. I could feel her soft breasts against my back. The overpowering, spicy scent of her perfume made my head spin and I gripped my thighs.

She stroked my damp hair, wet with the sweat of my desire. Then she kissed the top of my head, running her fingers gently over my forehead and down my face. I laid my head back against her, the sweetness of her touch like a healing balm, and closed my eyes. She came around in front, kissed my eyelids, my cheek.

"Heb," she whispered in my ear.

"Yes, your Majesty," I murmured, my eyes still closed, ecstatic from her perfume and her touch.

"Please call me Atalana."

I summoned up all my strength to do as she asked. "Atalana," I rasped.

"Tell me how much you love me," she prompted.

"I love you more than life itself."

"Atalana," she inserted.

"I love you more than life itself…Atalana." I heard her sharp intake of breath.

"And you love the Pharaoh, also?"

"Yes, I love the Pharaoh." I opened my eyes and started to pull away from her touch.

"No, Heb, you must love both of us. Please don't make this more difficult than it needs to be."

"I'll try," but I was uncertain, wary of an unknown future, not understanding her words nor her motives.

She held out her hand. I took her small delicate one in my large, callused hand. She helped me to stand. The cloth was still wrapped around me and I moved awkwardly.

"Heb," she said quietly. Then she stood on tiptoe and gently kissed me on my lips, placing her hands on my bare chest. I was surprised at how short she was, but then I was a tall man, taller than most. Her head came barely to my shoulders. In my mind, she had loomed tall, like a statue, like a Neter.

I returned the kiss hesitantly. My body throbbed violently, desiring her, knowing that she desired me, too. It took all my strength to resist.

"Relax," she coaxed me.

"I'm afraid," I confessed.

"I am, too," she replied. "Come, let us lie down together," and she led me by the hand to the bed.

I lay down, moving to the middle to make room for her.

My body was shaking violently, but this time out of nervousness. My earlier erection had softened and I felt shame once again, this time at the loss of my masculinity.

Atalana slid onto the bed next to me, lying on her side, stroking my head again, talking to me quietly. "It's all right, Heb. Don't be embarrassed. What you're experiencing is natural, under the circumstances. This must be very difficult for you. Just close your eyes and relax." I did as she instructed.

"Take a deep breath," she said, running her fingers gently over my face and hair, then around my neck and shoulders.

I did so.

"Another."

I could feel my body calming for the first time in many seasons. Her hands felt like the softest linen on my skin and I breathed in the delicious sensation. I could sense the pervasive weariness of my body, from holding myself stiffly, not allowing myself full physical freedom for a long time. I sighed in relief and my body's tension eased.

"That's good, Heb," she murmured. She stroked my forehead in long, slow caresses.

I reveled in the relaxed, floating feeling that washed through my physical body. "Do you do this with Pharaoh?" I asked innocently.

"Of course. This was part of my training at the Temple."

"I like it a lot."

"I'm glad." She giggled like a young girl. "Now be quiet and let your thoughts relax."

For many minutes only silence filled the room, while she rhythmically stroked me. Our breathing patterns changed, and we began to breathe in unison.

"Imagine that you are floating in Nut's sky."

In my mind's eye I saw thousands of stars in a black velvet sky, twinkling, beckoning. I began to float towards them, then travel past them, still buoyant on airy serenity. I felt as though the whole universe of stars was made up of love and contentment. Het-Heru's golden face drifted past me in the darkness of the universe. I sighed again with inexpressible happiness, even forgetting for a moment the young Queen lying next to me, the woman I had desired so much for so long.

I don't know how long we lay together. When an oil lamp began to sputter and go out, I opened my eyes, having returned from the star kingdom, surprised to find myself resting on the soft bed with the Pharaoh's queen still next to me.

"How do you feel?" she asked gently.

"Peaceful."

"What did you experience?"

I described the stars and my impressions. The harmony of our breathing. My sense of absolute freedom and inner harmony. She listened intently.

"You have accomplished what many initiates have to struggle towards for years to attain." She sounded amazed. "Have you ever undergone training in a temple?"

"No, never," I responded in some confusion. "I've never even left Abtu Palace."

"I don't understand," she mused to herself. "You surprise me, Heb. Although, taking everything into consideration, maybe I shouldn't be."

I was puzzled.

She changed the subject, or so I thought. "How did you happen to save Pharaoh from the camel accident? How did you know about the scorpions in our bed?" she interrogated me.

"I had dreams," I replied simply.

"What kind of dreams?" She pressed me for details.

"Het-Heru came to me. I would see something happening. At first I thought I was making it up. But later the pictures proved to be true. With the camel incident it didn't come for many months after the dream. With the scorpions," I shuddered at the remembrance, "it was immediate."

I felt her shudder too. "And Het-Heru?" she questioned.

"Um, yes, Het-Heru. When my Mother died she gave me a carved amulet of Het-Heru. I guess I looked at it so often, it affected my dreams."

"Do you still have this amulet?"

"Yes. Do you want to see it?"

"I'd like to see it very much." She sounded excited.

I rolled to the opposite side of the bed. I got up, making sure the cloth was still draped modestly around me. I found the worn and stained pouch and extracted the amulet. "Here it is."

She took it cautiously in her small hands and examined it quickly. "This is like my medallion!" she exclaimed.

"I know. When I saw you that first day, I was struck by the similarity."

"I'm beginning to think none of this is coincidental."

"What do you mean?"

"That somehow you and I, and Pharaoh, too, have been brought together for some important reason. Do you know what I mean?"

"Yes," I replied slowly. "I have had that idea several times in the last few days."

"I will have to think about this some more." She stretched her willowy body, yawning as she did so. "I need to go now."

"Please stay a little longer," I implored. "We haven't…" I didn't finish my sentence.

"I know. But it's late and Pharaoh needs me."

I didn't question her further but felt a deepening disappointment.

"We have had a good beginning," she yawned again.

"We have?" To me we had done little more than talk and I was dejected.

"More than you know." She stood on tiptoe again to kiss me on the cheek. "Good night, my dearest friend."

"Good night, Atalana."

She quietly opened the door to the Royal Chamber, closing it softly behind her. Then she was gone, with only the scent of kapet on the pillow and the returned throbbing of my body to remind me that she had ever been there at all.

CHAPTER FIVE

ENET-TA-NETER, TEMPLE OF HET-HERU

Many days passed without another visit from my beloved Atalana, while Pharaoh kept me busy with his personal business. By night I replayed our brief time together incessantly, remembering her touch, her scent, and her silky hands. Once I glimpsed her in the main corridor, but she kept her eyes averted and walked by me wordlessly and unsmiling. I felt a sharp pang. "Had I done something to anger her?" My body grew increasingly restless and I wondered if I should send for Bashta.

One evening, with light still present in the western sky, I heard a light tapping on the door separating my room from the royal chamber. Then the door eased open.

"Heb?" Atalana whispered. "Are you there?"

I jumped to my feet, my heart beating wildly. Fortunately, I had not invited Bashta to my room. "Yes, your Majesty, I am here."

"I want to talk to you."

I pulled out one of the reed chairs for her and she rested in it, all the while holding out a piece of papyrus for me to see.

"I've sent a message to Mukalia and she has answered me." She waved it at me, breathless and happy.

"Who is Mukalia?"

"She is High Priestesses of Het-Heru. I studied with her at Enet-ta-Neter. Don't you remember I told you?"

"Oh," I replied, noncommittally.

"Please sit down, Heb."

I perched on the edge of the sturdy chair, at the moment uncomfortable seated in her regal presence. I looked at her questioningly.

"She is the Hem Neter, High Priestess, a very special woman."

"Uh, huh," I replied, still not understanding.

"She has asked me to bring you to the temple for the full moon ceremony but to come a few days earlier." She leaned in closer. "I told her about you and your dreams, and she is very interested in meeting you."

I wrinkled up my head. "Why would she want to meet me?"

"Don't you understand? This is a great honor. I've never known her to speak to anyone except the other priestesses."

I tried with great difficulty to comprehend what the Queen was telling me, but I had nothing with which to compare this to. I remained silent.

"I also asked the Sentyt to cast a chart, to see what the stars could tell me."

"About what?"

"About a child, of course." Her laughter tinkled like the silver bells on her anklets in the small chamber. "Don't tell me you've forgotten about that." She teased me mercilessly.

I blushed so violently that the Queen became concerned.

"Are you all right?" she questioned me.

"Yes," I replied slowly, my embarrassment beginning to fade. "And I haven't forgotten. I thought perhaps you had changed your mind."

"Oh, no, never!" she cried passionately.

"I don't understand. When I saw you, you acted as if you were upset with me."

"No, my dearest," she touched my hand and the thrill of the contact coursed through my body, bringing with it the old familiar sweet pain. "I thought it was best not to arouse suspicions in the palace. You never know who might be watching."

I let out a noisy sigh and nodded. "Of course, you're right. I didn't think…"

"You agree with me?" she interrupted.

"Absolutely. No one must know about…"

"That's correct." She smiled a slow delicious smile at me, the corners of her mouth crinkling with delight.

Instantly I wanted to kiss that mouth, but restrained myself, as usual.

"Mukalia is the wisest person I have ever known. I trust her to tell me, us," she corrected herself, "about the child. What the Star-Beings have to say."

Mukalia didn't sound like a local name. Who could this woman be? A foreigner? How could a foreigner become a Hem Neter? And who or what were star-beings? I didn't ask these questions out loud, but Atalana seemed to intuit my thoughts. Something she did often enough to make me uneasy.

"Mukalia is an Ancient One" she murmured respectfully.

"I've never heard of ancient ones."

"I know. Very few have. But she is the last. And she wants to meet you!"

I tried to muster up an appropriate expression of honor but failed miserably. "I'm sorry, your Majesty…"

"Atalana, please," she countered.

"I'm sorry, Atalana. I do not understand. Who is she? Why would she want to see a servant?"

She patted my shoulder gently. Blood flooded into my upper torso and my Min member began to become erect.

"You will understand when you meet her. I really don't know any more than you do." She stood up. "The moon will be full soon. Prepare to leave tomorrow. Before Nut swallows Ra-as-Atum in the west, we will travel to the Temple of Enet-ta-Neter." She kissed me quickly on the cheek and left, while the sensation lingered a long time.

On the following day, sometime before noonday, a young female servant appeared at my door. The young woman was dressed in a long skirt that was tightly wrapped from waist to ankles. The only other clothing she wore was several beaded necklaces and beaded anklets. "The Queen requests you to accompany her to the Temple of Het-Heru." She handed me several items. A handled basket made out of the exterior of sturdy papyrus reeds. In it was a white cloak with a bone clasp. A starched linen collar embroidered with stars and images of Het-Heru. A pleated linen kilt. A heavy leather belt with an attached golden scarab to secure the kilt. And a white nemes to protect my head from Ra's heat.

"Prepare yourself and meet Her Majesty in the Great Hall."

"I will be ready presently." The girl left wordlessly.

I hurriedly dressed myself in the elegant attire, kohled my eyes, tied on my stiff, new leather sandals, packed a change of clothing, and rushed to the Great Hall through the long main corridor. The Hall was filled with other people, Grand Vizier Ptah-un-Atum, Custodian of the Crown Shu-un-Atum, other officials, nobles and the priests. Shu-un-Atum's face looked drawn and creased with anger, and he crossed and uncrossed his arms impatiently. Waiting on his throne was Pharaoh dressed in his robes of office, Hedjet crown firmly on his head, holding his heqa and nekhekha in front of him in a position of authority. Atalana stood next to him on the dais. She maintained a solemn expression but her eyes danced with excitement.

Grand Vizier Ptah-un-Atum thumped the floor with his ceremonial Vulture staff.

"Ankhamun-Heru, Son of Ra, Speaker of Truth, Defender of Ma'at, Lord of the Diadem of Nekhebet, Protector of Life, Beloved of Amun, King of Hedje and Lord of Upper Ta-Meir Res. Ankh. Uja. Senb." All in attendance bowed including myself. "Ankh. Uja. Senb," we repeated.

He thumped the staff again.

"The servant Heb."

The Royal Couple nodded at me solemnly. I bowed very low before the throne, my hand to my ab in ceremonial greeting of loyalty. "Your Majesties. Ankh. Uja. Senb."

Ankhamun spoke in a formal voice. "We thank you for accompanying the Queen to the Temple of Het-Heru at Enet-ta-Neter for Her Majesty's Sacred Pilgrimage."

"Your request is my pleasure, your Majesty," I replied. I glanced questioningly at Atalana.

As always, she seemed to intuit my thoughts. "To accompany me to the Temple of Het-Heru is a great honor and privilege. You, Heb, have shown yourself to be a loyal and trustworthy subject, worthy of such honor." She grinned for a moment, then quickly regained her solemn composure.

Now I understood Shu-un-Atum's anger. He had wanted the honor for himself. Not only that, I'm sure he had never forgiven me for the incident with the camel long ago.

The Queen's dark eyes were outlined in dark green; the lids colored green powdered with silver. She wore a pale green gown with a green and silver striped collar over it. She wore the beautiful alabaster medallion of Het-Heru over the collar, the same I had seen on the day of her crowning. She wore an elaborate wig, the many corkscrews, braided with turquoise and malachite beads, cascading over her back and shoulders. Her hands, arms and ankles were covered with many silver bracelets and anklets. A tiara plated with electrum, the head of a vulture perched over her forehead, completed her outfit.

I took a deep breath as I took in her appearance. Atalana only seemed to grow lovelier with every circuit of the moon.

Pharaoh clapped his hands and a soldier appeared, the muscles on his arms and legs gleaming with the warmth of the late morning. "Please escort the Queen to the boat."

"With pleasure, your Majesty." The athletic young man bowed low, his hand on his ab in fealty.

I followed them through the wide corridor and out into the courtyard. Atalana climbed aboard the same golden chaise that had carried her to her husband and King. She was transported down to the quay from whence she had arrived several inundations ago. I walked behind her silently, holding my reed bag packed with my belongings. I had thought to pack my camel hide pouch as well. The large felluca waited for us at the dock. We boarded without the muscular soldier while the sailors set sail to the Temple of Het-Heru. The trip was long, sailing against the strong current with the wind at our face. We had to zigzag, tacking against the current. Thus we didn't arrive at Enet-ta-Neter until almost atmu.

The sailors helped Atalana to disembark. Then the boat left, to return for us after the moon began to wane. Our bags were picked up by young temple Initiates, who disappeared into the complex with our belongings.

A number of Priestesses gathered around to welcome Atalana. An older woman with a long wig stood waiting. I recognized her. She had traveled to Abtu Palace with Atalana for the coronation.

Atalana immediately went over to the older priestess and bowed her head slightly, the beads in her wig tinkling against each other as she did so. "Shara-Het," she said softly, hugging the matronly woman.

"It is good to see you again, my daughter." She examined Atalana's elegant appearance with pleasure and a little awe. "Time and the Neterw have made you a Queen."

Atalana blushed and lowered her eyes. "Thank you, Shara-Het."

"Mukalia has been asking for you all day. I will take you there immediately." She glanced at me.

"This is Heb. Mukalia wants to see him, too."

"That is what I've been told," replied the Sentyt Priestess good-naturedly. "Heb," she acknowledged him, "welcome to the Companions of Heru." Her eyes were full of questions for me but she refrained from voicing them.

The Holy Temple complex at Enet-ta-Neter was expansive, although certainly not as large as the Palace at Abtu. The complex, one large building and a number of smaller ones, stood alone on a sandy plain, on a rise overlooking the Mother River Nile. A small village was close by, around the bend of the river, out of sight. The complex was enclosed by a low mud brick tenemos, which could afford no protection to its isolated female inhabitants. Why was it there?

Atalana intuited my thoughts again. "The wall is not for defense but to delineate the boundaries of sacred energy contained here."

Shara-Het linked her arm affectionately through the Queen's, at ease with the young woman she had known for so many inundations, and led us through the tall mud-brick entryway, about ten cubits high, into the temple complex.

As I walked through the simple gate, I was greeted by the six massive columns of Het-Heru standing before the main Temple. Instinctively, I fell to my face in the dust, prostrating myself before Her Holy Image. A soothing warmth, not just from the sand, pervaded me and my eyes smarted with tears.

I felt rather than saw as the Queen walked over to a piece of cloth spread out before the main building for her, took off her tiara, and gracefully laid face down on it, arms outstretched towards the Temple Building, honoring the Holy Place of Het-Heru, Mistress of Heaven.

Her action took me by surprise. I had never seen noble persons prostrate themselves before now, except to Pharaoh. I felt a little disconcerted yet somehow pleased.

After a few moments we both got to our feet as if on cue.

Atalana straightened her clothing, placing the metallic tiara back on her lovely head. I noticed that her eyes were moist, too.

I felt an overwhelming flood of sensations. First I felt harmony and peace, the magnitude of which I had never felt before. It was as though I had come home, to a home more accepting and loving than any I could ever have imagined. The second was a sense of being safe and secure, as if I had returned to the womb of the Universe, protected against all invasions. The third was joy and happiness totally unbounded by palatial injunctions, social interchange and fear of looking foolish. I wanted to dance around the courtyard like a child at play. I felt bigger than myself, expanded with life, accepted, nurtured and loved for who I was. I began to hum to myself with a happy little tune that I made up on the spot.

"It is wonderful, is it not?" the young Queen asked me, fully comprehending my feelings.

I breathed a happy sigh. "Wonderful, yes!" I exclaimed. "I wish that I had words to describe it all."

"I've always felt that here. I had almost forgot what Enet-ta-Neter is like. I'm so glad to be back!" she replied breathlessly.

The older woman stood smiling at us. Without another word Shara-Het escorted us across the complex to Mukalia.

"Why does it feel like this?" I asked in awe, walking next to my beautiful Queen.

"Everything here is created in Divine Order, as it has been done for ages. The buildings, walls, columns, all are constructed in an harmonious design and in a particular size and shape, so that all we have to do is be here in our physical bodies in order to learn and grow."

"Really?"

"Yes," she replied eagerly, warming up to her subject. "Our ancient ancestors were brilliant. All the stone used here is sacred as well. It not only holds and echoes vibrations and sound, but also can contain ideas, thought, prayers, even energy from Het-Heru."

I looked around in appreciation of the Per Neter, Home of the Neter Het-Heru. "Amazing."

We passed to the right of the large main building towards a large body of water, a man-made lake at the edge of the compound, surrounded by swaying palm trees. Near the lake was a small, mud-brick building. Atalana walked inside without hesitation. I had to duck beneath the low doorjamb to enter. It was dim inside and cool. Several oil lamps were on the floor, illuminating the occupant. On a small pallet in the corner lay the oldest person I had ever seen. Her face was crisscrossed with so many wrinkles, I could hardly tell that the old one in front of me was human.

"Atalana, my dear girl," the old woman rasped. Her voice replicated the sound of frogs in the lake beyond. She held out skinny arms shaking with palsy.

The Queen knelt down beside the old woman, took hold of the hands, veins purple and swollen with age, and tenderly kissed the backs of them. "Holy Mother," she said.

"Pah! There is nothing holy about me that is not also holy within you," replied Mukalia with amusement. "Have you forgotten everything I've taught you since going to Pharaoh's court? Call me Mukalia or simply call me Mother."

"Mukalia," replied Atalana with a wide smile. "No, I haven't forgotten. I'm so glad to see you again," and she gently hugged the old woman, being cautious of the brittle old bones.

"I have been watching you." Then Mukalia pointed at me, trying to sit up on one gnarled elbow. "Is this your young man?"

"Yes, this is Heb. Heb, this is Mukalia."

I stepped forward and knelt beside the old woman, who took my hand in her thin one. As she did so a cool breeze blew through me, a soft gentle wind that seemed to emanate from the elder reclining on the pallet. I thought I could hear bells tinkling and a soft internal glow filled me with tranquility. I instantly felt at ease with her. "Reverend Mother," I said. Indeed I felt reverence for her.

"I'm very glad to meet you at last, Heb," the old woman sighed and lay back on the pallet, groaning.

Mukalia seemed familiar, as if I knew her. But how could I? I would certainly have remembered her if I had met her before. She was unforgettable.

"Your Holiness," I replied. A faint memory flickered through my thoughts. Was she the old woman in my scorpion dream, standing behind Het-Heru?

She investigated my face with her rheumy eyes. The heavy droopy lids almost covered her irises. Her eyes were like none I had ever seen before, black and deep as a well. I stared at them, unable to look away. I could see the stars of Nut's body shining clearly through them. I blinked and shook my head, trying to clear the vision.

Mukalia chuckled, a low throaty sound. "Yes, you are the one." She patted my hand affectionately.

"I beg your pardon?" I asked politely.

"I told you," replied Atalana, with the musical laugh I loved so much.

"Sit down, both of you. There is so much I have to tell you, Heb, and I don't have much time."

We sat down on a worn carpet, close to the old woman, and made ourselves comfortable. I took off the new sandals, which had rubbed my ankles raw. I preferred going barefoot. Atalana slipped hers off too and removed her heavy tiara, placing it on the ground. The oil lamps flickered with the evening breeze.

Mukalia passed a hand over her eyes, a sigh making the bony chest rise and fall. The dark brown skin stretched across her thin face and arms looked as dry as papyrus and almost transparent with age. "I don't know where to start. There's much for you to know." She closed her amazing eyes.

All I could hear was the steady thump, thump of my ab. Atalana reached over and gently took my hand and together we waited silently, expectantly. But for what?

So much time elapsed that I thought the old woman had fallen asleep. Then she suddenly opened her eyes and looked at Atalana, then me, then back to Atalana.

"You want to know about a child, your child," she began.

"Yes," replied the Queen.

"It will not be as easy as you have thought. There is an older man."

"The Pharaoh?"

"No, one with a lean, drawn face and the eyes of a hyena. He waits like a spider, spinning his webs." The face of Shu-un-Atum popped into my mind.

"Yes, that one," Mukalia prompted me.

"What about him?" I asked. I was getting used to others reading my thoughts as easily as I could read hieroglyphics.

"Be….very…careful."

"We will." Atalana looked at me questioningly, fearful.

"But that is not what I want to talk about." The old woman abruptly changed the flow of the conversation.

"What do you want to say, Mother?" asked Atalana, gently.

"You know, I am the last of what you call the Ancient Ones. All that is left alive in Ta-Meir Res of my Muan people. The rest are gone now. The ones who asked for a small bit of land for themselves. We worshipped Creator Source and all its manifestations." She turned to me momentarily. "What you call Atum." She was interrupted as she hacked a deep phlegmy cough, momentarily unable to breathe, and pointed to an earthware cup.

I silently handed it to her.

She drank some of its soothing liquid and handed it back to me. "Where was I? Oh, yes, I remember. That was in the days of Auset and Ausar."

I must have looked puzzled because Mukalia hastened to explain.

"They were nobles from the realm of Titania."

"Ausar and Auset? The Neterw?"

"Heavens, no, boy. They weren't deities. They were real people like you and me. They were Titanians," Mukalia said, as if that explained it all. "They only became star-beings after they died, when their ka migrated to the stars. Not everyone who lives becomes a star-being. You have to lead an extraordinary life. As they did. But, no, they weren't Neterw."

My head swam, trying to comprehend. What she was saying was in conflict with everything I had ever been taught.

She talked slower now, apparently hoping that I would be able to follow her story better. "Ausar was a prince of Titania, a high noble lord, and Auset was his wife. He had traveled far to find my people, the Muans. He knew that a time of trouble was coming and that we could help. But there had been a calamity in our homeland long times before. Many had died while others had been scattered like chaff in the wind on many small islands in the vast sea. Thus Prince Ausar had difficulty in finding us. However, his distant ancestors and mine had a common heritage. He still retained a drop of Muan blood and was able to intuit where we were living.

"Not only that, but the Titanians were excellent sailors," she added. "He discovered remnants of our people and came to the island where I was living. I was a young woman then. Prince Ausar explained to us that he believed a massive catastrophe would soon befall his homeland. Titania would be completely destroyed, similar to the way the land of Mu had eons before. He asked us for our help, to travel with him to the land of the Hwr, where Titanians had established a colony some ages before. We would help them build a new life, where survivors of the coming catastrophe could begin anew, safe from a watery grave." She paused and cleared her throat.

I looked at Atalana and she was completely enthralled in the tale. She looked at me, her eyes glowing. "Mukalia has told me these stories before, but I never get tired of them. Go on," she encouraged the wizened old woman lying before her.

"Most of my people were reluctant to leave. They knew that it might mean a quick death of their bodies to leave our home. And they would never feel the vibration of our Motherland ever again. It was very pleasant on our island and we had been left in peace for a hundred generations. But Prince Ausar was persuasive. I was young, just coming into my first moon time, and decided I would leave with him. In my youthful exuberance I looked forward to the adventure. Others made that choice as well, mostly Elders, healers, gardeners and masons. Our group's number totaled sixty times six, a sacred number indeed." She bent over and drew a design on the dusty ground. Two pyramids intersecting each other in a six-pointed star. "This was one of our sacred symbols," she explained.

So many questions were forming in my mind but I decided to let the old woman talk. She might answer my questions in the telling of her story.

"We then sailed to Titania. Many of my people aged quickly and died on the trip across the great sea. I miss them but fortunately I can still talk with them."

"How do you do that?" I interrupted her, puzzled.

"They are there, in the great collective home in the stars. They no longer have bodies but their hearts are still alive. They have become Star Beings."

For many moments Mukalia was quiet to allow me time to digest her words. After a time she continued again. "A fleet of boats awaited us when we arrived at the busy dock. I had never seen such buildings and temples as I saw there at the capital ringed by canals. The Titanians were masters at architecture. The energies there in the port city were far too overwhelming for us, however. The dizzying vibrations of so many people scurrying about, talking incessantly, interfered with our quiet connection to the stars and Creator Source. So we decided to stay on the boat, with the sacred water to nurture us."

"Prince Ausar tried to convince his people to leave but they laughed at him and his fearful predictions. Only a small number of Titanians chose to journey with us. Ausar organized them to gather provisions, as they would leave Titania forever, bound for a different land." She gestured with her arms. "What you call Ta-Meir. Ausar took some animals I had never seen before, along with plants, seeds, and food for the long trip. I met Lady Auset when she came aboard, shortly before we sailed. She was a fine woman, loving and kind, able to intuit like my own people, and we became friends. His brother Setekh and sister-in-law Nebt Het joined us, as did his cousin Ptah, a master builder. Ausar's best friend Djehuti joined us as well. I was amazed at the Titanians' ability to carve symbols to represent ideas and words; they were fascinated with language in all forms. On the long voyage Djehuti taught me some of the symbols, but those were very intricate. Being a library myself, I thought that my way was far easier—to store information in my body rather than have to record so many symbols on numerous disks of gold or stone."

"Is that like hieroglyphics?" I asked.

"Yes, Heb, you are quite right." Her thin voice was beginning to fade. She touched Atalana's arm with a shaky hand. "I need to rest now, my daughter. We will talk more in the morning."

"Of course, Mother," replied the young Queen. "I'm sorry if we have tired you."

"No, no, my dearest one," Mukalia hastened to explain. "I'm not used to so much talking." She looked at me. "You will return, too, young Heb?" It was more of a command than a request.

"Yes, Mother Mukalia. I will return." I kissed the old brow and the elderly woman smiled in appreciation. Then she closed her eyes and immediately began to snore.

Atalana put out the oil lamps. We tiptoed out of the mud-brick building. Ra-as-Atum had left to travel the night through Nut's body while multitudes of stars glittered in Her black sky.

Atalana found her way easily back to a building near the main temple in the light of the waxing moon. "I will find something for us to eat," she told me. "You must be very hungry."

My stomach growled. I hadn't noticed that I was hungry while we were talking with Mukalia, but now I was ravenous.

She found her way to the kitchen where priestesses and initiates prepared and ate their food. An oil lamp had been left burning. Food had been prepared for us before they had retired. A jug of beer stood ready for us along with a cold pot of lamb chunks cooked with grains and herbs. Some dried figs and dates were waiting in an earth ware bowl and the table had been set with two clay platters. We found ourselves too hungry to start a fire and heat up the lamb stew, so we ladled the cold food onto the platters and began to eat and drink, finishing with a desert of the dried fruit. The food tasted wonderful after our long fast.

Afterwards we wiped the platters clean and put them away on a shelf. "You can't sleep with the rest of us in the dormitory," Atalana giggled. She seemed more like an ordinary young woman than a Queen in these surroundings. "I will take you to the guest quarters," which turned out to be a mud-brick hut just outside the compound's mud-brick walls

In the hut, straw pallets were placed on the ground for visitors. An oil lamp had been lit for me. "I will see you in the morning," she said and then she was gone. I took off my elegant new clothes and carefully folded them and placed them in my bag that one of the initiates had brought here. I washed myself thoroughly in the basin provided and laid down naked on the pallet, pulling a coarse linen sheet over me. I noticed that the energies I had felt within Enet-ta-Neter were not as strong outside in the visitors' quarters. I wanted to think about what Mukalia had told us, but a peaceful lethargy darkened my mind and I slept soundly.

CHAPTER SIX

MUKALIA, THE LAST OF THE MUANS

I was awakened by the sounds of cattle lowing in the compound and bells jingling around the necks of goats and sheep. I thought I heard a goose honking in my hut. I opened my eyes to see a female with several fluffy babies in tow snuffling under my mattress with her bill, looking for insects. When I sat up, the babies ran off, alarmed at my unexpected movement, with their mother honking after them.

I chuckled to myself and put on an ordinary kilt, tying it at the waist. I decided to leave the sandals off. Blisters had already formed on my toes and heels from the new leather rubbing my skin and anyway I was used to being barefoot.

I walked to the low wall and stepped over it easily, walking in the direction I hoped was the kitchen. As I entered the area, I again felt the surge of sensations, but not as intensely as the day before. Perhaps I was getting used to them.

I heard the sound of female laughter and followed it to its source. Atalana was there, surrounded by girls and women of the temple, all of them seated on reed-covered stools or on the ground, giggling, chatting, and eating together. The Queen sat on a stool, dressed in a simple undecorated white dress, identical to the others. The heavier fabric covered her womanly body just to the knees. I had never seen her legs before. They were delicately curved, ending in slim ankles. She wore no jewelry except an ankh pendant, the key of life, on a chain made of small blue faience beads. Her feet were bare like mine and she wore no wig. Her short hair gleamed. "Good morning, Heb," she said and returned to telling a story, which were making the others laugh.

"Good morning, your Majesty." I felt rather uncomfortable as the only male around, as though I was defiling the sanctity of the place. Shara-Het was nowhere to be seen. I sat on the floor near the entrance, hoping to be inconspicuous. A young girl dressed only in a short flaxen kilt approached me. Judging by her short hair with three braids down her back and her flat chest, she couldn't have been more than ten inundations. The girl shyly offered me a large bowl, filled with raisins mixed with dried cooked grain and a pitcher of still-warm, fresh milk. I poured the milk over the mixture and ate heartily, watching Atalana out of the corner of my eye.

Restless, I handed the empty bowl back and strolled outside. Ra-as-Khepera was still low in the east. I saw some girls milking cows, while others were bent over, tending the large garden within the border of Enet-ta-Neter. I could see stalks of grain blowing in the wind and many green vegetable plants.

Shortly Atalana joined me outside and I bowed automatically.

"Did you sleep well?" she asked.

"Yes, your Majesty, did you?"

"It's the best sleep I've had since I left here." She stretched her body. "I've been waiting for you. I thought I'd take you on a quick tour before we go see Mukalia."

I nodded in agreement, eager to see the rest of Enet-ta-Neter. "How long have you been awake?" I asked her.

"Since before dawn. I was participating in the morning rituals." She started walking, pointing to various buildings. "You've already seen the kitchen, the visitors quarters, and Mukalia's home near the sacred lake."

"Sacred lake?" I questioned.

"Oh, yes, Mukalia tells me that it was here when the Ancient Ones came to Enet-ta-Neter long ago. Originally it was a natural lake but as it dried up, they had to devise a way for water to it fill it from time to time, except during the annual Nile flood, raising the level from the water below."

"Mm, hm," was my only reply. Many things didn't make sense to me.

Atalana headed for the lake. "We must wash in the sacred water before we go into the Per Neter." When we arrived, she peeled off her short shift and lowered herself into the clear water.

I politely looked away, yet my eyes kept drifting to her nude body. Her aristocratic long neck and full breasts with their pinkish-brown nipples glistened with water. I found my organ growing uncontrollably.

"Come on in, Heb," she called, splashing water at me and giggling, not offended at my body's excitement.

I quickly untied my skirt and climbed in after her. The chilly water felt wonderful in the morning heat and my ardor cooled, too.

She ducked her head under the water and then scrubbed her thick hair vigorously. I followed suit, feeling naked, as indeed I was, in her royal presence.

She stepped out of the lake, dripping and smiling. "Ah," she exclaimed. "That felt good." She shook her head like a dog, droplets sprinkling around her on the hot sand, mindful but pretending that she didn't notice that I watched her. She slowly pulled her white shift over her head, the material clinging to her wet body, watching me with amusement and something else I couldn't identify.

I got out quickly, picked up my kilt from the ground and shook off the sandy particles that had attached to it. I could feel her eyes on me, watching intently, her jovial mood suddenly subdued. I hastily wrapped the cloth around me and tied it, not wanting to make eye contact at that moment.

My mind and body were at odds with each other and I longed for Bashta's familiar comfort and release.

"You have a magnificent body, Heb," she said softly.

"Thank you, your Majesty," I replied shakily. I kept my eyes downcast on the ground. Red tendrils crept up my neck to my face.

"Heb," she complained. I looked up in time to see her roll her eyes in mock offense.

"Atalana," I corrected myself.

"That's better." Then she took my hand and led me to the Holy Temple of Enet-ta-Neter. I was comfortable with her small hand in mine and could have walked anywhere with her. When we arrived at the large building I saw pairs of lioness heads high on the walls overhead, used as water spouts. The heads had been fashioned out of clay and then dried in a hot oven before they were placed on the walls. "These are the other face of Het-Heru and symbolize Sekhmet," she explained.

"I know who Het-Heru is, but what is Sekhmet?"

"You'll see." She giggled with a secret joke of her own.

The desert air had quickly dried our bodies. Seven stairs led up to the Temple Building, the stone steps burning our feet. I saw many torches and oil lamps burning to illuminate the darkness inside. I could hear chanting and singing within, a solitary female voice. We walked through a short corridor then turned left into the immense sanctuary. When we arrived at the portal to the sanctuary, I gasped in amazement. One entire wall and the ceiling had been plastered white over hewn stone, which gleamed in the torchlight. Both then had been subsequently painted. The ceiling had been dyed a deep amethyst blue-purple; hundreds of five-pointed stars were painted on it, as though we were standing beneath the Duat of Nut's body.

The scent of myrrh was heavy in the air. Many lamps were lit, illuminating the temple. Empty offering bowls were situated on low flat rocks near the altar.

At the entrance to the chamber, Atalana picked up a smoldering incense bowl, added a chunk of incense. She purified me, letting the myrrh smoke waft around my body and head. Then she did the same to herself and set the bowl down again.

Next, she led me to the center of the Holy Chamber.

Before us stood a wide stone altar with a tall wooden Naos box placed on top of it. The doors to the elaborately painted box were open. Within the box stood an impressive golden, life-sized statue of Het-Heru, Neter of love, music and beauty. Het-Heru held an ankh in one raised hand, while clasping Her holy Waas Sceptre in the other. The cow horns with the sun disk of Ra in between graced her head. Atalana explained that the Neter's head, body, and carved ceremonial tools were made of the finest sycamore wood, sacred to Het-Heru, then completely overlaid with gold leaf. A beautiful cloth was draped around her golden body. Her eyes were fashioned of two cut and shaped crystals, making her look so alive that she seemed to stare unblinking at us. Her lips were curved in a welcoming smile and I felt a sudden impulse to hug the statue, so similar to my mother's amulet was She.

Behind the statue of Het-Heru and the naos box she resided in was an impressive carving covering the entire wall. Almost reaching to the ceiling, two extremely tall images of Het-Heru, one on the left side, one of the right, stood facing the inside edges of the wall. Rays of light connected each of the Het-Heru's foreheads in a direct line to two stars at the top of the wall. Between the Het-Heru's were two Heru's pictured as falcon birds, standing back to back, each looking towards his female consort, Het-Heru. Each of the two Heru's was perched on a column of four straight lines, their bird-eyes resolutely staring at the abs of the twin Het-Herus.

A thick gold disk, larger than a serving platter, lay on the floor, propped up against the stone altar that supported Het-Heru's statue. On its interior a circle was carved, around which eight Het-Heru's held the circle in their upstretched hands, and four images of Heru, two at the top, two at the bottom of the circle. Inside the circle were many images of animals, kings, gods and Neterw. I had no idea what the designs meant but I could feel vibrations coming from the disk. I bent over to pick up the disk, in order to examine it more closely. A spark discharged itself into my hand most painfully as I reached for it. "Ow!" I stepped back, nursing my singed fingers.

"That is a holy relic," Atalana explained quickly. "A zodiac of Zep Tepi. No one but Mukalia, Shara-Het, and the Sentyt initiate-in-training are ever allowed to touch it."

"Why didn't you tell me sooner?"

"I never thought you would try to pick it up," and she suppressed a giggle.

"What do the symbols mean?" I asked, peeved at her.

"I'm not completely sure. I was never initiated into its mysteries," she continued. "I think it is a record of our land and the stars of the Duat."

"What is it for?"

"It is used in ceremonies, to usher in Star Beings and sacred energies."

This wasn't the first time Atalana had mentioned the Star Beings. I was going to ask her about them, but I felt gooseflesh rising on the back of my neck. I whirled around to see an immense black statue fashioned out of volcanic basalt standing in a darkened niche on the wall behind me, her sleek, lioness face and woman's body powerful and foreboding. Her powerful leonine face was covered with an ornate headdress, topped with a disk of Ra, while a cobra coiled through her hair. Her statuesque body was very feminine, alluring. However, Her black eyes seared into me like fiery stone.

"Who is this?" I had never seen the likeness before.

"Sekhmet, the feminine principle of creation, desire, and passion. Remember the lion heads on the wall outside?" I had an irresistible urge to touch the statue but I refrained, remembering my last encounter with a sacred object.

"Go ahead," urged Atalana. "She won't hurt you."

"Are you certain?" I queried. I hoped she wasn't teasing me.

"Absolutely. Touch her."

I walked over to the black statue, towering over me, and tentatively reached out my hand. I felt warmth emanating from Sekhmet and the coolness of the basalt stone simultaneously. I felt encouraged, so I moved around to Her side to see Her in profile, stroking Her smooth arm. As I did so, Sekhmet's arm moved beneath mine and the statue turned to look at me.

I jumped back and yelled to Atalana. "She moved! Did you see that? She moved!"

Atalana had been watching, her mouth gaping open. "I did. I saw her move." She blinked her eyes in disbelief. Then she broke into peals of nervous laughter. "It looks like you have another Neter who wants to communicate with you," she joked with me, her voice muffled, hand over her mouth, trying to stifle her amusement. "You are very popular with Neterw!"

"It's not funny, Atalana."

"I know, but I can't help laughing," and she laughed out loud at my consternation and fearful response, her laughter echoing in the large sanctuary.

I walked over to where she stood, glowering at her. "Did you know this would happen, too?"

"No, Heb. Honestly. I've heard tales about Sekhmet from others but I never believed them…nor experienced it myself…before now. We should talk to Mukalia about this," she added, trying to ameliorate my hurt feelings.

"That is a very good idea," I replied curtly from my wounded male pride. "Let's go now," I said, forgetting my interrupted tour, hoping for answers to my growing list of questions.

"All right, Heb," but she still sounded like she was ready to laugh again any moment. "Follow me," and she led me out of the temple to Mukalia's small house.

The old woman was sitting up on her pallet, obviously waiting for us. She smiled in anticipation, the deep wrinkles around her mouth and eyes like aged furrows in an ancient earth. "So, the Neter Sekhmet has claimed you for her own."

I looked into her bottomless eyes, but her face was unreadable. "How do you know?" I questioned the Ancient One.

"The seed energy of my people, the Ancient Ones, is strong in you, as it is in Atalana. We have the gift of sight."

"How could that be?" I questioned.

She cleared her throat and began to explain, her voice raspy with age. "For more time than you can imagine, the land of Ta-Meir Res has been populated with Muans and Titanians." I must have looked confused because she quickly explained. "The Muans were my people, Heb. From the Motherland Mu." I nodded.

"Long before Ausar and Auset arrived here, the Titanians had colonized this territory and brought some of my people here to help with building. Only we Muans knew the sacred incantations of sound and words of power that would make building their large structures so easy."

Atalana interrupted briefly. "Hekau," she explained.

"Yes, exactly, my daughter," the old woman nodded in agreement. "Hekau, words of power." Then she continued. "Some of my people had intermarried with the Titanians and also with the natives who lived here before we arrived. Therefore, the blood of the Motherland flows through many peoples' bodies and hearts in Ta-Meir Res."

"But my mother is from a foreign land."

"Hm. And what of your father?"

"I don't know anything about him."

"Well, it must be your father who had Muan blood."

"But what does that have to do with me? And the Queen?"

"Often the spiritual force of Mu lies dormant. With every passing generation, the seed power of Mu generally diminishes. However, with some people, the power emerges fully again and those individuals are different from their contemporaries.

Those blessed with Muan energy can see, feel, hear, and do things that others cannot. Often they are visited by star-beings, like Het-Heru and

Sekhmet. Many of them like Atalana find their way here to Enet-ta-Neter and to me. When Atalana told me about you, I knew you were one of us. All of the Priestesses and Initiates here have strong Muan blood-energy, thus called by the Neter of Love, the cosmic force which bound the people of Mu together long ago. Het-Heru has called you, too. She has great plans for you."

"I? A humble servant?"

"You are not a servant here, except for the Neterw. And serve them you will…and have."

"I don't understand, Reverend Mother."

"Soon, in less than one inundation, comes the Sopdit New Year in conjunction with the Great New Year. This is highly auspicious and very rare. Do you know of this?"

"No, I've never heard of these New Years."

"Atalana has. Haven't you my daughter?"

"Yes, Mukalia. The Sopdit comes only comes once every one thousand, four hundred and sixty one inundations and the Great New Year every two thousand…" She hesitated, trying to recall the numbers. "Two thousand, one hundred and sixty inundations."

"Very good, Atalana. I see you were paying attention to your studies." The old crone smiled. Only a few back teeth remained, and those were blackened by advanced age. "And can you tell this young man what that means?"

"It means," Atalana searched her memory, "a coming of a new time. An important beginning and ending. This conjunction has never happened in living history."

"Nor mine either. I've seen both but never at the same time," replied the ancient woman.

How could that be, I wondered. That means that Mukalia is…I mentally calculated her age, but dismissed it as impossible.

"I look forward to it." Mukalia paused for breath. "You see, the star

Sopdit is the Great Provider and the Great New Year ushers in a new age with many wonderful changes. We are in the age of the Twins right now but very soon will cycle into Apis, the Bull joined with the Cow Mother Het-Heru. Important changes are coming." She grew more excited. "I have known for many inundations that this time was drawing near. I, too, play my part in the great cosmic drama."

"What is that, Mother?" asked the youthful Queen.

"I will tell you, in due time."

I listened to their interplay, bewildered and feeling like an ignorant child who has walked into a tutoring session with elders speaking a foreign language.

"I'm sorry, Heb. I didn't mean to leave you out," the empathic old woman said kindly.

"Mukalia, you said that you have seen a great new year and a sopdit new year. That means you are five thousand, nine hundred and twenty seven inundations." I was proud that I was able to perform the difficult mathematical computations.

"I'm actually a little older than that, but it is a close approximation." She grinned toothlessly at my bafflement.

"But that's impossible!"

"No, my dear boy," Mukalia said in a quavering voice, patting my arm. "Here I am, to prove it is possible."

I kept shaking my head, "No, I don't believe it. It cannot be. No one lives that long."

"My people are, were, capable of living for aeons. The Titanians thought we were immortal, because we resided in physical bodies for so long."

"There's no way to prove what you say," I argued stubbornly.

"I have seen many changes in Ta-Meir Res and in the lands surrounding her," she reasoned with me. "I came here as a young girl with Auset and Ausar. The land was green then, with many lakes and trees. The rains came and went for hundreds of inundations, then stopped completely. The trees were cut down and the land dried up. The desert mother, with her scorpions and snakes, began to claim Ta-Meir for her own. Only the sacred water of the Nile flows now and a few oases exist to the east and west. I have watched many generations emerge as babies, grow old and die. All this I have seen with my own eyes." I wanted to run out of the door. I couldn't believe her fantastic story. The old woman was completely mad!

Atalana stopped me with her words. "I told you she is an Ancient One. The Ancient Ones could live for many, many inundations. Mukalia, as you see her now, looks exactly the same as when I came to Het-Heru's temple when I was only nine. In that time, she has not changed at all."

"That cannot be, Atalana."

"But it is, Heb. You must trust me."

I pulled away, upset at their joke, angry and confused, yet curious, too.

"Heb, I want you and Atalana to travel north to Rostau. See the ancient Hwr and the Great Pyramid that Ptah and Djehuti built, with our help. You must stand between the paws of the Hwr. Then you will believe me."

"I have heard of these places. But I thought they were only stories, to entertain children when they were bored."

"Pah!" cried the old woman. "The Pyramid and the Hwr are as real as you and I, and this mud-brick house." She began to cough violently and spat up foul brown mucus into a cloth. "I'm all right now," she said eventually, reassuring us. "Time is getting short." She turned to the Queen. "Could you bring me some broth?"

"Yes, Mother," and she left the house in a hurry.

I fumed in a corner of the tiny house, knowing Mukalia's seeming sincerity yet doubtful of the clarity of her mind.

The old woman lay down, still coughing periodically. After a while concern for her well-being diminished my temper and I sat down beside her. "Can I do anything for you, Old Mother?"

She shook her head no and coughed some more. Gasping for breath, she gripped my hand tightly and squeaked in a thin voice, "Take very good care of Atalana. You are all she has."

"But the Pharaoh…"

"She is beyond his help. You will hold the future of Ta-Meir Res in your hands."

I gulped. "Het-Heru has said the same words to me… twice."

"I know. Het-Heru is a Star Being and has communicated Her wishes to me."

"You have mentioned that word before. What is a Star Being?"

She swallowed and struggled for air. Finally she continued. "A Star Being is an emanation of star energy that was alive during the creation of the worlds of life. Each human being contains a little of that star energy, and can gain more by working with a Star Being. The star-being Het-Heru is quite ancient, existing before the beginning of time, creating with the Passion of Mother Sekhmet, the Mighty One. In fact, Het-Heru holds time in her hands, and shapes it like a potter molds clay. She was a guide and teacher for my people of Mu long ago, as she is for you and the people of Ta-Meir Res now. Listen to her carefully…" She laid back, eyes closed, exhausted with her efforts to talk.

Atalana returned with a steaming bowl of vile-smelling broth and knelt at the old woman's side. I was glad for her return as my mind was spinning out of control, awash in the new ideas that the old woman presented to me.

"Can you eat a little of this?" she asked Mukalia.

I helped Mukalia sit up. The ancient woman opened her mouth obediently and Atalana spooned some of the black broth through her lips. The woman swallowed and opened her mouth again. Soon she had finished the soup and lay down, closing her eyes.

"Rest now," Atalana murmured. There was no response from the old woman. The Queen felt the withered wrist and sighed with relief. "She is only sleeping," she whispered to me. "She will feel better soon."

We left the small enclosure and I breathed deeply of the fresh air outside, wild improbable thoughts whirling around inside my head. "What was in the bowl? It smelled terrible."

"You won't believe me if I tell you."

"At this moment I might believe anything."

"It is beetle broth."

"What?!"

"I told you wouldn't believe me!"

"You mean, a soup made out of beetles?"

She laughed merrily. "Well, the green scarab beetles are boiled in water all day, then their bodies are removed and only the liquid is consumed. Mukalia claims the beetle broth keeps her young, a recipe for longevity." She chuckled at the disgusted look on my face. "Come, let's find something to eat," she encouraged me.

"As long as it isn't beetle broth," I replied adamantly.

"I promise you I will find something else," she laughed.

I followed her to the kitchen, which was already crowded. The smells of roasted goose made me salivate. I hoped it wasn't the mother goose I had encountered earlier with her chicks. I hadn't eaten anything since my simple breakfast. Atalana placed some pieces of goose on a plate along with freshly-baked flatbread and some dates. "Let's eat by the sacred lake."

When we had found a shady place under some palm trees, we began to eat hungrily, hanging our feet in the cool water. "You've had quite a morning!" she teased me.

"Mukalia has old age madness," I responded seriously.

"No, Heb," she replied. "No more so than you or me."

"You don't believe her fantastic stories!?" I countered with doubt.

"Yes, I do. Her stories are always the same. If she were lying, they would change, don't you think?"

"Maybe," I hesitated. "Although she does seem to know about other things. How did she know about Sekhmet's statue and me?"

"She knows things that I can only begin to guess at. One thing is for certain. She's not like anyone else I've ever met."

"That is surely the truth," I agreed and decided I could not fathom the mystery. "I would like to go see the Hwr and Pyramid as she suggested."

"I, too. Let us make a trip there sometime in the future."

I had finished the goose and bread and washed my greasy hands and face in the sacred water. Atalana was delicately picking off pieces from the cooked goose leg from the dried clay platter and putting them in her mouth. "This tastes better sitting outside. I miss the open air and the casual atmosphere. So different from the formality of the Palace."

"Yes." My eyes began to rove her body and I felt the familiar tingling sensations arise. I found it difficult to be in the Queen's presence without that happening. For the second time that day I wished for Bashta's skillful ministrations to relieve me of the overwhelmingly painful yet pleasurable passion that was rising in my body.

"Soon, Heb," she read my thoughts, "we can be together, but not just yet. I'm sorry if being with me is so difficult for you."

"I don't wish to offend you, your Grace," I muttered, yet my hands longed to touch her soft skin.

"I'm not offended, Heb. I'm flattered. I, too, wish to join with you. But we must wait until the full moon."

I looked up in anticipation. "The full moon?"

"That is when Het-Heru's power is at its strongest." She got up, came over to me and sat down, putting her head in the hollow of my shoulder. The conflict of desire over restraint was splitting me in half, and I sat very still, trying to regain my composure. "I don't want you to fight your feelings for me," she murmured in my ear. "Your feelings are sacred, holy." She kissed me gently on my cheek, which blazed with the touch of her lips. "Dearest Heb," she breathed. "I love you."

"I love you, too, Atalana."

"I know, my darling. I have known since the day we met."

I turned my face towards hers. Her eyes burned with an intensity I had never seen before. I saw the images of Het-Heru and Sekhmet merge into her countenance. She kissed me passionately on my lips, her eyes open, staring into mine. Her power over me was complete and I responded in kind.

She pulled back from my eagerness. "Now gently, like this," and she demonstrated, lightly pressing her warm lips to mine, in a whisper of a kiss.

It took all my self-control to kiss her softly in return while my whole body ached and throbbed with longing and desire. I wanted to lay her down upon the hot sand and make love to her. I wanted to kiss every part of her, to listen to her moan, as Bashta moaned when we were together. But I didn't love Bashta. I loved Atalana. And Atalana was Queen. Instantly Pharaoh's face swam into my awareness and I pulled away, guilty and remorseful.

"Soon, Heb," she responded in hushed tones, although her body trembled as violently as mine. "We will be able to fulfill your desires very soon." She stood up, towering over me.

How could she possess such self-restraint?

"Let us go to the guest quarters and I will soothe you."

"Yes," I replied, not knowing what she had in mind, but filled with yearning for more of her touch. I picked up our dishes and carried them with me and left them in the kitchen. Then we continued on to my guest quarters.

The windowless room in the guest building beyond the temple wall was dim. No oil lamps had been lit since it was too early. I lay down upon the pallet, still quivering and breathing heavily. Atalana seated herself next to me, and I closed my eyes expectantly.

She sat close to me, leaning her back against the plastered wall. She began to rhythmically stroke my hot forehead, humming to me with the sweet voice I loved so well. Her hand shook with unfulfilled desire, but soon we both relaxed and began to breathe in unison. I soaked up her touch through my skin, the fever of my unrelenting hunger melting into serenity.

After a while she placed her hand on my chest, over my ab, and spoke. "Beloved Het-Heru, fill Heb with your healing energy. Grant him peace. Gift him with the knowledge that he and I are but one body, one mind, one heart."

I floated beyond Geb's earthly body, out into Nut's stars, buoyant and finally at ease. I saw the gold-encased wooden statue of Het-Heru in my mind's eye. The shimmering Neter drifted near me in the darkness of space, her crystalline eyes smiling at me, comforting me, and I felt weightless. I felt Het-Heru's great love wash over and through me, strengthening me. Het-Heru's love was a tangible thing, something I could touch, smell, taste, and embrace. She cradled me within Her infinite love. Atalana floated near me, and as I watched, Atalana and I merged together and became a glowing star in Nut's dark body. I fell deeply asleep within the softness of the Neter's love and Atalana's touch.

CHAPTER SEVEN

ANCIENT HISTORY OF MU, TITANIA, AND ZEP TEPI

It was almost atmu when I awoke. Atalana sat motionless next to me, her eyes far away, and her slender hand still resting on my chest.

"Mukalia wants to see us," she whispered.

"How do you know? Did she call for you?"

She shrugged. "I just know. I hear her in my mind."

I sat up and stretched. "I have slept away the whole afternoon."

"How do you feel now?" she asked.

"Better," I reported. My body didn't shiver and burn with love-fever as earlier, and I felt somewhat detached from my physical being. A new and comforting sensation.

"Good," she smiled at me.

I washed my face and hands in the basin in the corner, splashing water over my head. I ran my fingers over my damp hair, which was getting too long. Time to shave it again. I knew the way to Mukalia's house and I led the way this time, Atalana following dreamily. I recalled our picnic at the sacred lake and my overwhelming passion for her, but it seemed much had passed since that moment. An endless aeon of time.

When we entered the little mud-brick hut, Mukalia cried out with delight. "Heb. Atalana. I'm so glad to see you again." She sounded much stronger than before.

I bent over and affectionately kissed the wrinkled cheek. She hugged me in return, with a strength I couldn't believe in one so old.

Atalana embraced the ancient woman with tenderness and devotion.

We both sat at her side. The love that poured out of the old woman's eyes was like that of Het-Heru in my dream/vision and I reciprocated that love as best I could. Atalana seemed very far away. Although her body reclined next to me, she drifted in another world, distant and serene.

Mukalia began again. "My dear ones, there's so little you've seen of life out there." She pointed beyond the temple grounds. There's much for you to learn and you must learn it quickly."

"Like what?" I prompted.

"People don't always show you their true face, as I do. You must learn to listen beyond their words, to feel with your body's wisdom, to intuit the truth in every situation. You must trust your ab. The ab is the seat of wisdom and you can take action based on that knowingness. Yet you must always remember to love them all, friends and enemies alike. That is the key to life and happiness. That is what we taught them." "Taught who, Mother?" I asked.

"Prince Ausar, Auset, Djehuti. All of them. They were good students and they learned quickly, especially from the Elders. They enjoyed hearing my stories, too." She paused, a fleeting look of sadness passed over her visage. "I miss the Elders terribly. I miss all of them, but most especially the Elders. Soon I will join them and leave this worn out shell behind." "You mustn't say that, Mother. You will be with us a long time." I beamed at the old one.

"Never fear. I will always be with you, Heb," she replied solemnly, and squeezed my hand. She sighed. "It has been difficult for me. Learning to be an Elder, a Healer, a Storyteller, after everyone had gone, even though I was born a Library." She paused, looking contrite. "I'm sorry. I don't mean to complain. It has been my perfect lesson in life."

I was confused again so she explained. "Here, in Ta-Meir Res, when the Ancient Ones began to leave their bodies, I had to take up their work along with mine. It wasn't easy but I did the best I could. I needed my people to give me strength, but after a while there was only me. So I drew upon their wisdom and that of Star Beings, too." She looked at me pointedly. "You know how difficult it is to live in a body."

I nodded. "Yes, I know," as the day's events and fluctuations and recent emotions surged through my mind.

"You will have to learn many new things, too, Heb. New strengths. New wisdom. You will have your library of memories to sustain you." She nodded. "You are strong, Heb. Stronger than you realize. I know who you are. And so does Atalana."

The young Queen looked up at the mention of her name. "Yes," she murmured confidently. "Heb is quite strong. He has been learning quickly. I have been teaching him, Reverend Mother," she added.

"I know, my daughter. You both are learning well."

"Teaching me?" I didn't recall any lessons.

"Everything that Atalana does is for a purpose, my son," replied Mukalia. "She is a good teacher, a powerful priestess. I know how difficult it has been for both of you. But that will be eased somewhat at full moon."

"What happens at full moon?"

"You will see."

I quivered with anticipation and apprehension.

"There is nothing to worry about, Heb. You still have a few things left to learn though, before they arrive."

"Who arrives?"

"The people. Throngs of them will come in time for the full moon. It will become very noisy then." She laughed a reedy laugh.

Atalana spoke up. "Is it time to show him the crypt, Mother?"

"I think that is a good idea, dearest one. Then bring him back here." Atalana got to her feet.

What was the crypt? I cringed, thinking of all the unusual experiences I'd already had and wondering what else waited for me.

"This way, Heb," and she stepped outside. We quickly washed our hands and faces in the Sacred Lake.

Then I followed her to the Main Temple building and we entered again, past the Holy Sanctuary where Het-Heru and Sekhmet stood. We went to a darkened chamber near the back. There was a hole in the floor. I looked down and saw a rickety ladder descending deep into the ground. Atalana climbed down the ladder and I clambered after her. Torches burned in the still air. She picked her way carefully through the narrow corridor. The ceiling was low and my head narrowly missed hitting the top of the corridor. The air was dusty in the underground passage.

Atalana paused at a small doorway. She got down on her hands and knees and crawled through the tiny opening. On the other side, she stood and continued down a set of carved stairs. I followed behind her, squeezing my large body through the narrow doorway and walked down the few stairs to the bottom of the crypt.

At the bottom the chamber opened into a long passage. The gleaming white limestone walls were beautifully carved with mysterious symbols. Baskets of woven papyrus reed stood to one side. "That's where we keep the sacred implements," she told me and showed me the jewelry and tools used for ceremonies.

Rectangular wooden boxes stood in narrow niches to the sides of the chamber. Each box had symbols painted on the top and sides. Atalana went to one with a spiral painted on its lid and slid open the cover. Inside was the shriveled-up remains of a human form curled up like a baby. I sprung back, suddenly fearful and sickened at the sight.

"This is an Ancient One, Heb," she explained. "She was buried on her side in the dry sand outside until she mummified as you see here. Then she was brought inside and buried with the others under the original altar, before the temple as you see it was built over them. That way they could offer the wisdom stored in their bones to the living. I and the other Priestesses come here often to consult with them."

I shuddered at the idea of talking to dead, withered bodies.

"Bones and Stones," Atalana murmured.

"What did you say?"

"Sacred energy is stored in bones of wise people. And also in certain sacred stone. That is what our Temple is constructed of. Sacred Stone. Under which are housed the sacred bones of the Wise Ones.

"Yes, I remember you told me."

"You don't forget anything."

I grinned in appreciation of her words. I was used to learning things quickly and efficiently, to perform my task as Custodian of the Palace.

She closed the lid and proceeded down the corridor. She showed me other niches, each one filled with a box. One had a spider web painted on it. It must have been very old because the paint was almost completely flaked off, even in the dry, still air of the crypt. "This is one reason why Enet-ta-Neter is so holy and powerful," Atalana continued. "Because it is built on the remains of the Ancient Ones, containing their wisdom and holy energy. We can heal sick people using this energy."

A special niche, encased in white limestone, held a very small box. This one had a five-pointed star painted on it, the symbol of the Duat. Atalana paused before it, stroking the wood reverently. "This is another sacred relic. The box contains a bone of Ausar," she told me.

"Could that be true?" I wondered to myself. The Temple inhabitants presided over Mysteries too vast to contemplate. I touched the box and could feel Ausar's life-giving energy pulse into my hand, up my arm, and flood into my body.

"Ausar was the wisest of the wise, spending years traveling and teaching." She continued to the end of the narrow passageway, where the last niche stood waiting. It contained a single box, with the lid left open. The box was empty. The cover had a carefully drawn image of a star on it, this time a six-pointed star. "This is the sacred symbol for Mukalia's homeland," she murmured respectfully, tracing the lines of the star with her slender fingers. "We will inter Mother here after her body dies. She has become the greatest Elder of them all, although she is too modest to admit it. Thus she will remain in this sacred room, close to the others, so that we may honor her greatness and partake of her continuing wisdom."

I felt sad, thinking of the wise old woman's eventual departure from the land of the living. And realized with a pang that I would miss her.

When we returned to Mukalia, Shara-Het was sitting with her, holding the old woman's hand. They were deep in conversation and stopped abruptly when we crossed the threshold. "Excuse me," Shara-Het said and quickly departed. She didn't look happy to see us.

Atalana scrutinized the old woman's face. "What did she have to tell you, Mother?" she asked pointedly.

"She has cast a horoscrope for you, Heb and the baby and wanted to talk over the results with me."

"And?" Atalana wanted to know more.

"It will be a healthy boy, intelligent, quick, and courageous."

The crone's face was impassive, but guarded. I felt an unpleasant twinge in my stomach. Was there something she wasn't telling us?

The young Queen's expression lit up, delighted with the knowledge that had been shared with her. "Ankhamun will be pleased."

"Do not tell him anything," Mukalia warned. "He will find out in due time."

"All right, Mother," she replied but her brow wrinkled. "But I do not like to keep secrets from my husband."

"It will only be a secret for less than one inundation. Promise me you will do this."

"I promise," she agreed, but tears sparkled in her slanted eyes.

"Come and lay down next to me, girl," Mukalia asked. Atalana did as requested, curling up in the old woman's arms. She began to stroke Atalana's wet face, as the Queen had done for me. She began singing a song to the young woman, completely oblivious to my presence. The words were obviously foreign.

> *Ee ah co la no*
> *Ee ah co la no*
> *So me ee go ee ah wah*
> *My ah ke'e oh.*

Then she repeated it, over and over until Atalana's eyes closed and her breathing became regular. The tears stopped.

I left the house noiselessly and found my way to the kitchen, delicious smells permeating the air. As I entered the aromatic kitchen, all the female voices were stilled with my arrival.

"Don't let me interrupt you," I begged.

Several of them giggled and they began to talk again, but now self-consciously.

I helped myself to the cooked food, went outside, and sat down, leaning against the building. I ate and watched the evening star of Eosphoros rise in Nut's body. I had seen, heard and experienced much in the last several days. Most of it was beyond my ability to understand, so I filed it away in my memory. Some of it was lovely. But seeing the mummified bodies of Ancient Ones was frightening. I couldn't imagine talking to the dead remains of anyone.

A mature young Priestess came outside to where I was sitting. "May I join you?" she asked pleasantly.

"I would be honored," I replied.

Her face was plain but somehow pleasing. The elegant features of the Queen I loved were missing in this ordinary face, but I felt completely at ease with her, something I rarely felt in Atalana's company.

She sat down on the still warm sand next to me. "I am called Tietra-Het."

"Tietra-Het. Pleased to meet you. I am Heb."

"Yes, I know." She hesitated for a moment then spoke. "You love her very much, don't you?" she asked bluntly.

Did Priestesses always speak their mind so honestly? "Who?" I temporized.

"The Queen, of course," she answered.

"Yes, I do," I replied. I was sure she knew in any case and was simply making conversation.

"That is good," replied the young woman. "She deserves happiness."

"I will do my best to please her."

"I am sure you will." She modestly looked down at her bare feet, running her hand through the sand, picking up some, letting the grains slide through her fingers, then again, over and over.

Was it my imagination or was she flirting with me?

"I am glad you are here visiting us," she continued.

"I am pleased to be here," I responded.

"We hardly ever have men stay here. Except priests during sacred rituals. And those who are sick, of course," she added quickly.

"Tietra-Het." Someone was calling her. Shara-Het appeared around the corner. "It is time to go to the Temple."

"I'm sorry. I must leave you now," she said and stood up abruptly.

I stood, too. "I welcome the chance to talk with you again," I said formally, out of earshot of the Elder Priestess.

Tietra-Het left without speaking, joining the others trooping off to the temple.

I wandered over to the garden, inspecting the maturing plants in the moonlight. They were well cared for by the Priestess gardeners.

Then I heard Mukalia speak my name.

"Heb."

I turned around in surprise, surprised to see her frail body behind me.

But there was nothing. I saw only the darkness around me with the moon waxing to full in the sky, so I ignored the message.

I heard it again, more urgently.

"Heb!"

"I'm coming, Mukalia," I replied out loud and hurried to her hut.

Atalana was gone and the old woman was sitting up, smoothing back her thin white strands of hair with trembling hands. The oil lamps had already been lit for her so I could see her better than during the day.

"Ah, good, Heb. You heard me."

"Yes. I thought I was imagining your voice."

"No." She chuckled. "You heard me well." I kissed her and sat down.

"I haven't finished telling you my story." I looked around for my companion.

"Atalana has heard the rest. But you need to know." She cleared her throat noisily. "You remember what I told you about Prince Ausar?"

"You and your people came here in a boat with him along with some Titanians."

"That is correct. When we got here, the land was lush and fertile. It wasn't dry as it is now. We prepared the soil, with the assistance of the people already living here. They were quite friendly and helpful. Many were descendants of Titanians who had formed a colony here ages before, the great-great-great-grandchildren of Geb and Nut. Some carried the seed of Mu, my people whom the Titanians had kidnapped and brought here."

"But I thought you came to Ta-Meir Res willingly?"

"Oh, yes, those of us who came with Ausar and Auset were volunteers. The others before us were not as fortunate and were practically slaves to their Titanian masters."

"How terrible," I replied.

"Yes, it was terrible then." She sighed. "When I came here with the Titanians, it was far different. Ptah and his masons, along with some of my people began building a city in the north. They called the city Ineb Hedj . They also carved the statue of the Hwr from a gigantic stone on sacred land, partly to commemorate their flight from Titania, partly as a marker for a star-gate. In the third winter, it rained almost non-stop. Periodically the earth shook and we were afraid. Then a great flood covered the plain, up to the Hwr's chin. Fortunately, we Muans had intuited what was coming and advised the Titanians to move to high country while we waited for the floodwaters to abate. We told them to save food and seeds from the previous harvest, so no one would go hungry.

"During that dreadful time, the sky was dark in the daytime and terrible lightning storms made everyone edgy and irritable. Prince Ausar was tremendously unhappy. He believed that the earth shaking, along with the flood and storms, indicated that his beloved land had been destroyed, as he had predicted.

"Auset tried to comfort Ausar but he was inconsolable. The water dissipated slowly but we had to begin building all over again. Everything had been destroyed except the Hwr. Djehuti and Ptah decided to create a temple around the Hwr, to protect it from further floods. Only we Muans knew how to move the massive blocks of stone that formed the building and the walls around it.

"In the next year, after would later be called an inundation, Ausar could not restrain himself any further. He made provisions to travel to the great ocean, to see for himself if he was correct. He was gone a long time and Auset was afraid he would never return. When Ausar did return, he told us he had found a muddy expanse of ocean, all that was left of their glorious civilization. The sea had become dangerous, with maelstroms, powerful cross-currents and waves many times taller than the Hwr. The sea boiled and churned and lightning flashed constantly across the sky. The sky was dark even during the day as angry clouds covered Ra's face. The sea grave covering where Titania had once been had become unnavigable. Although he sailed completely around the circumference of the area, being careful to avoid being pulled into the churning whirlpools and currents, he returned without finding a single survivor or any trace of Titania."

"How was it destroyed?"

"No one knows for sure. Some say that the great crystal the Titanians used for power had somehow exploded. Others thought Titania was obliterated as punishment for their fall into evil ways. Perhaps the earth mother simply stretched her body as she is prone to do, and they got drowned in the process." She shrugged.

I stretched my own cramped body and changed positions.

Then Mukalia continued. "Life continued for a generation while we planted and harvested, and the city of Ineb Hedj grew. The rain that watered our crops was indecisive. Sometimes it would rain well, then become more infrequent, then we would have rain again. With every passing season the weather grew warmer, always warmer."

"When the building of Ineb Hedj and the Hwr temple was complete, we asked Ausar for some land to call our own. We intuited Enet-ta-Neter was holy ground. Ausar granted us permission to settle here. There was a lake, which in the intervening time mostly dried up, except for our refilling it through irrigation.

"Ausar was a restless man, in some ways a typical Titanian, not content to sit on the land and watch others build and farm. So he made plans for another longer trip. He wanted to determine for himself if other Titanians had survived, as we had. Auset cried and begged him not to leave again, but he was unwavering in his decision.

"He was gone for so long that Auset began to despair that he would ever return. Ausar' brother Setekh, a greedy, impatient, cowardly man, plotted. He waited for a while after Ausar' departure, then married Auset against her will, although he was already married to Nebt Het."

She drank a little from the earthenware mug next to her and continued. "There was a short, but bloody civil war, and when it was over, Setekh was the victor and had himself crowned King. The next few generations were bad and crops failed in the dwindling rainfall. Hunger reigned supreme."

"Generations? How long did Titanians live?"

"Not nearly as long as Muans. But they lived to great ages."

"Why don't we live that long now? If we are descendants of Titanians and Muans?"

"That's a good question, Heb. I will consult with the Star Beings and let you know."

"Thank you, Mukalia."

"Let's see. What was I talking about? Oh, yes. Eventually the rains stopped altogether and the land dried up. When Prince Ausar did finally return, the land was parched and arid. Only the blessed sacred river saved us from starvation. We used the water to irrigate and later could predict the seasonal flood. Ausar had brought news that other Titanians had survived the great catastrophe and were living in other parts of the world. However, when he found out about Setekh, the Prince forgot about the survivors in his fury. And the two of them did battle. When the war was over, Ausar lay dead and Setekh was victorious once again.

"Auset, Djehuti, Nebt Het and Ptah brought Ausar's broken body up the river to us, praying that we could do something, to bring Auset's beloved husband back to life. They knew we could live practically into eternity and believed we were capable of great healing magic.

"In those days there was no temple as you see it today. We lived simply in huts made from the leaves of the palm trees. We had created a large altar, fashioned from crystals, in the shape of a six-pointed star. Stars were sacred to us, especially Sopdit and those in Orion's belt, from whence we had originally traveled to earth and where we will return."

"You came from the stars?"

"Yes, my dear boy. We all come from the stars. We Muans came from the stars, then to Eosphoros, and eventually to this place." She pointed a long bony finger through the open doorway at the evening star, following

Ra in his aging path across the sky. "The Titanians came here first through Her Descher, the red planet. That's why the Titanians are different from us as people. They like to explore, while we are content in our homes."

My head reeled from the web of wild and puzzling stories, details, ideas and conceptions the old woman spun. "How did you travel? Did you have wings? How long did it take?"

"Slow down, Heb. First of all, we traveled in our light bodies, not physical ones. So we didn't need a vehicle. And we could travel anywhere in the space of a thought." She cleared her throat and drank again. Her weariness was becoming evident. "Over the altar we had formed a Gold Light Temple in the shape of a pyramid, a sacred design."

"A pyramid?" I asked excitedly. "Is that the one you want me to see?"

"Heavens, no, Heb. Our pyramid wasn't solid but made out of gold light, as I said."

"Oh," was all I could think of to say. I tried to imagine a structure constructed out of light.

"You've gotten me off track," she grumbled. "Let me see. Where was I?"

"I'm sorry."

"Oh yes. When they brought us Ausar's body, it was already beginning to decay in the heat, turning green with putrefaction. We quickly brought his dead body to the altar and began to chant and sing."

"Is that the same song you were singing today?"

"Partly. Now don't interrupt me anymore or I will completely forget my story." I grimaced in apology.

"Our Elders and Healers worked on him, invoking the Gold Light from Creator Source which might resurrect his Titanian body, as it used to do with ours. Many animals came to join us in the sacred circle, a common occurrence when we did our holy work. Among them were vultures, crocodiles, an ibis, jackals, a lioness, several cows, falcons, a black dog, an ostrich and a hyena. They didn't hurt anyone and seemed to want to add their energy to ours. Unfortunately, Ausar wasn't a Muan, so we could only bring him back to life for a short while. Just long enough for he and Auset to merge in a final loving embrace and to say good-bye to each other."

I couldn't discern whether or not Mukalia was making up all these details. But one thing was for certain. She was a fabulous story-teller.

"After Ausar died, we left his body on the altar overnight. In the morning only a few bones and the skull were left and some feathers from a falcon. We took one of the bones and buried it beneath our altar."

"Atalana showed it to me today," I piped up.

"Ah, that is good." She patted my cheek affectionately. "Then Djehuti and Ptah took the rest of the bones and departed. We heard later that they had built a beautiful Temple to Prince Ausar at Abtu and buried his skull there. They also buried bones at other sacred places in Ta-Meir Res."

At the mention of Abtu, I sat up, more interested now. "I have heard that," I added.

"Auset, his widow, kept the bird feathers and remained with us for a while, learning our ways. After three seasons she gave birth to Heru and they both lived here with us in Enet-ta-Neter, while the boy grew into a man. We often worked our healing on him, as he was a sickly boy. I'm sure you know the rest of the story. After he had grown to manhood, Heru declared war on the aging Setekh and deposed the greedy king. The people were joyful, since Setekh had been a corrupt and depraved leader. They crowned Heru as King in his place. Heru worshipped the sacred falcon as a symbol of his kingship and in remembrance of his father. Auset meanwhile moved to an island far south of here, Per Auset, where she mourned in solitude for her beloved husband the rest of her days.

"Ptah and Djehuti were greatly impressed with our gold light pyramids. They decided they wanted to create a pyramid on the sacred land where the Hwr was situated. We tried to teach them and their helpers our old ways, how to manifest light and substance from Creator Source, but they were unable to do that. Their vibrations were too dense to work with the subtle energies. So they formulated a plan to build a pyramid out of stone instead.

As I've said before, we of the Motherland knew how to reproduce sacred sound and light energies to work with heavy objects. With some practice, the Titanians were able to do so on their own and found that even the heaviest objects could be cut, transported and placed on the plateau near the already-old statue of Hwr. You know her as Sekhmet. Once they learned, it became child's play."

"Sekhmet?" I had promised not to interrupt, but I couldn't help myself.

"Yes, my dear boy, Hwr is a statue of Sekhmet, the Lioness. The Titanians worshipped the sacred animal of the lioness as a vital creative force in the universe, powerful, strong, proud, a natural leader as they were themselves. So it was only natural they would want to create a statue in that image. The Hwr was also a symbol of the age of the lion, the star age of their escape from the great catastrophe. And besides which, Sekhmet the lioness, is a guardian of the doors of creation, which is holy. Between Her paws, the Hwr, lies the doorway to cosmic knowledge. That is why I want you to go there, to stand between Her Paws, and be blessed with the sacred information."

My head was swimming in confusion at the bewildering array of details.

"Before building began on the sacred plateau, however, Djehuti drew up plans for three pyramids to commemorate the destruction of his homeland, as well as to honor us Ancient Ones and our common ancestors, the Star Beings. He did so by aligning the pyramids to the stars in Orion's Belt as it was during the sinking of Titania. Ptah was given the job of building the actual structures. Ptah also constructed chambers beneath the ancient Hwr leading to the pyramids. Regeneration chambers, he called them. They thought they could become immortal, like us Ancient Ones." "Unfortunately," she smiled sadly, "the chambers never worked.

"They finished the first pyramid. But Ptah and Djehuti grew old, ready to die, long before they completed the pyramid project with all three pyramids but promised they would return to finish it. Djehuti even recorded the date they would return, which pointed to the two stars from whence each would arrive. I trust they will keep their word. Only time will tell.

"Before his death, Djehuti carefully recorded the stories of Auset and Ausar, Setekh and Heru, and other notable Titanians, an epic saga. He also wrote down everything he remembered of their homeland, their knowledge, and all the things that he had learned from us Ancient Ones. With the great passing of time the stories and the people in them became legends, then elevated to Neterw. I don't know if that's such a bad thing. We Muans know unseen forces, like creativity, justice, destructiveness, passion and love exist in the universe. The Titanians' descendants just created stories to explain them. Stories are always easier to remember than facts anyway."

The old woman's body relaxed, having completed her tale.

I was speechless at her brilliant reweaving of myths into history, if indeed that was what she had done.

Just then Mukalia reached out to me in terror, her body went into spasm, while her eyes rolled back in her head, only the whites showing.

"Mukalia." I shook her gently, but she remained stiff in seizure. Then I cried out, "Atalana. Come help me!" I leaned over the old woman and listened to her breath. It came in ragged patches. "Atalana!" I called again.

I had just gotten to my feet and was about to run through the darkened complex to find the Priestess-Healer-Queen when Atalana, out of breath, showed up at the opening. "Did you call me, Heb?"

I don't know how she had heard me in the large temple complex, but at the moment I was more concerned about the old woman. "Mukalia," was all I said, but in an instant Atalana understood. She knelt beside the old woman, vigorously rubbing her wrists and then her feet. Then she put her hand on the thin chest and began to keen in a voice I didn't recognize. Four other priestesses arrived at that moment, Shara-Het and others whose names I did not know. They formed a line next to the pallet and also made strange sounds, sounding like a harmonious concert of voices. Their hands hovered in the air over the ancient body of the High Priestess from Mu like frantic birds.

Shortly thereafter, Mukalia's body relaxed, her eyes returned to normal and she coughed.

"Are you all right, Mother?" Atalana inquired anxiously.

The old woman sighed. "Am I still here?" she asked.

"Yes, Mother, you are still with us."

"Ummmm," replied the old one, sighing in disappointment. "I thought as much."

"You frightened us," I said.

"There's nothing to be frightened of, boy," she replied in a tiny voice. "The next world is far more pleasant than this one." Several of the Priestesses volunteered to remain with the old woman through the night and the rest of us left the small hut.

As Atalana walked with me back to the guest quarters, she held my hand tightly. "I don't know what I'll do when she is gone."

I squeezed her hand in response.

When we had arrived at my temporary home in the visitors' quarters, Atalana impulsively buried her head in my shoulder, her slender arms around my neck, and began to weep. "Oh, Heb, she is so wise, so helpful. She can't die and leave me. Whatever will I do without her?"

I stroked her small head and held her tightly to me, her tears wetting my chest.

I lifted her tear-stained face, bent over and kissed her on the lips, softly at first. When she didn't resist, I kissed her deeply. I could feel her instantly respond to me. I held her body very close, my erect manhood pressing urgently against her slender body as I kissed her again and again. I could feel her heart beating rapidly.

With great effort she pulled herself away from me. "Not yet, Heb. Not here. Not now. I'm sorry. Please forgive me," and weeping harder, she ran away from me into the dark night.

I got out my mother's amulet, extinguished the oil lamp and lay on my pallet, holding the wooden carving to my chest, exploding with desire and burning with longing for my beloved Atalana. "Oh, Het-Heru. Help me," I implored. "Help me." I remembered the lioness Neter and began to pray to Sekhmet, too. I would not sleep much that night, but tossed and turned until the sky began to lighten with Ra-as-Khepera, the golden orb of dawn —and new beginnings.

CHAPTER EIGHT

Full moon ceremonies
and the Star Child

I awoke to bright sunshine, groggy and stiff from too little sleep. I must have dozed off after the fiery disk, Ra-as-Khepera, rose in the east. My head ached from the heat. It promised to be a very hot day.

I washed myself in the basin, and still dripping, climbed the small wall and headed for the kitchen. When I arrived there, it was empty. Everyone was gone. Where could they be? I helped myself to a bowl of dry cooked grain and goat's milk, sprinkling a few dried grapes in it, took it outside and ate it quickly. None of the priestesses were in the garden either. Then I heard feminine voices, raised in homage, emanating from the Temple.

Then I saw them, the ones Mukalia had talked about. Crowds of people were arriving for the Full Moon ceremony, mostly by boat, others riding donkeys or camels or on foot. Was the full moon tonight? I had lost track of time.

Nobles mixed with the rekkit, common people, old and young, male and female, adults and children, sick and healthy alike were gathering at the Holy Sanctuary. Some of the wealthier had brought large tents, which their servants were setting up beyond the perimeter of the Temple complex, as though they were here for a festival instead of a solemn occasion. Poor people made themselves comfortable on papyrus reed mats. Children played and shrieked in merriment, throwing sand at one another or chasing geese that had wandered outside the tenemos boundary.

I spied the women and girls emerging from the Temple. They had finished their rituals as they heard the crowd gathering. What I was to discover later was the pilgrims were an essential component in the Full-Moon ceremonies. I saw Shara-Het walk among the poorer folk, bending over, talking to one here, another there. She came towards me but disappeared into the kitchen. When she emerged, she was carrying baskets of food to distribute. I replaced my bowl in the kitchen and strode over to help her. Some of the young initiates took baskets, too, and they were quickly mobbed, unfamiliar hands open in supplication, hungry from their long journey to the Temple of Het-Heru, the Golden Neter of Love and Healing.

Some people were too ill to walk and had been brought to Enet-ta-Neter by their families. I saw Atalana gesture to them and walked to the Temple, while family members followed her, carrying their sick relatives into the sacred chambers. Others, able to ambulate on their own two feet, followed her as well.

Hours later, the Temple complex was swarming with people. Except during Pharaoh's coronation, I had never seen so many people gathered in one place before. The quiet purity of the temple had been transformed into a noisy carnival. Perspiring heavily in the hot, still air, I walked into the Temple building. The Holy Chamber of Het-Heru and Sekhmet was filled to capacity with sick people, while many others waited outside, perspiring in the fierce sunlight, flies buzzing around, annoying those already too sick and exhausted to brush them away. I noticed the golden disk I had tried in vain to pick up had been removed from the sanctuary, probably put away for safe keeping. All the Priestesses including Atalana, dressed in white robes now, were busy administering to the people. I was surprised that no one recognized

Pharaoh's Queen humbly offering assistance. Wounds were cleaned and dressed. Herbal potions were handed out. Some were receiving the sound therapy I had myself experienced. All in attendance were given sacred water from the lake to drink. Younger Initiates followed the priestesses around, too inexperienced to practice healing, but observing and learning from the actions of their elders. Meanwhile, Het-Heru, the Neter of love, Her crystal eyes gleaming, blessed them all while Sekhmet watched from Her darkened niche, Her cat-woman features both fiercely protective and nurturing.

It was late in the day when all sick people had been tended to and had left the Temple complex perimeter. Most visitors were returning home, but some had started cooking fires, preparing to spend the moonlit night outside the compound. Several would be spending the night on the roof-top of the Temple, hoping for divine dreams.

Atalana and all the other priestesses and initiates had retired to the sacred lake, to purify themselves again in the holy water. Out of respect and to allow them privacy, I stayed far away. I could hear girlish giggling from many of them, as they washed and splashed each other. I went to the kitchen to see if I could find anything to eat, but the pantries were bare. All the food had been given away earlier in the day. I wandered around the people gathered outside and I was given some roasted meat and bread to eat. At a large tent, I was offered barley beer, but I politely declined. I wanted to have my wits about me for the coming ceremony.

When the women had finished bathing, they returned to dress for the ceremony later tonight. I waited until all had left, then went into the sacred lake, removed my kilt, and bathed myself thoroughly. I wanted to be well scrubbed for whatever lay in store for me. When I was sparkling clean, I got out and allowed myself to dry in the still hot air, then dressed myself.

I decided to see Mukalia, to check on the old woman. On my way, I must have stepped on a bee or some other venomous creature. "Ouch," and I hopped on one foot, the other radiating with a burning pain. I quickly hobbled over to her house, favoring the bee-stung foot.

She was resting quietly on her back, eyes gazing at the ceiling until she spotted me standing in the doorway.

"Heb, my son," and she opened her arms.

I hugged her hesitantly, both afraid I would hurt her as well as in pain myself. "Mother Mukalia. How do you feel today?"

"Wonderful, now that you are here."

I grinned at the compliment, then grimaced.

She examined me with her sharp eyes. "Let me see your foot."

"It is nothing."

"Pah! Don't be such a baby. Come here," and she moved over for me to sit on the pallet next to her, which I did gladly.

She examined the calloused bottom. A red welt was forming there.

"I see. A small creature has taken out its anger on you for stepping on it. You must be more careful where you walk." I smiled at the notion of angry insects.

She sat up straighter, cradling my foot in her lap, while she wrapped her two hands around my injured extremity. She closed her black eyes and hummed to herself.

I felt intense heat, then soothing coolness, then nothing at all.

"There, that's better," and she lay back down, satisfied with her work.

I held up my foot and found that all trace of the insect bite was gone and so was the pain.

"Thank you, Mother."

"It is nothing," she echoed my earlier words.

"How did you do that?"

"I imagined Gold Light surrounding your foot. Gold Light is very powerful, as you must know by now." Abruptly she changed the subject. "What is the most important thing you can learn from me?"

"Eating beetle broth?" I asked jokingly, now that the pain was gone.

"No, my dear," she patted me on the arm affectionately. "It is to be able to feel wisdom—to know the right thing to do—within your body."

"That is why you keep telling me to listen to my heart. To feel with my heart."

"You are correct," she grinned at me, the gaps between teeth making her look silly, although her words were solemn. "Wisdom is the ability to feel, to know inside your body, that harmony feels good. Disharmony feels bad. It is just that simple."

"Hmmmp," I replied. "I didn't know that."

"Creator Source, the one you know as Atum, has given us the ability to determine what is good and wise, versus what is wrong and ignorant. The rule of Ma'at says that harmony is best, feels the best. People prosper within harmony. Without harmony, there is chaos both within oneself as well as within the whole world. One's harmony, then, affects everything." I was eager to reply, but she interrupted me. "Are you ready for tonight?" she teased, changing the subject once again.

"I don't know. Am I?" I questioned her in the same manner.

She pretended to examine me from head to foot. "Hmmmpp. As ready as you will ever be, I suspect." She smiled broadly, the gaps in her mouth where teeth were missing gave her a comical air.

"Can you tell me anything about tonight?"

"No, I'm afraid I cannot. Or will not. As you prefer. But I believe you will find it interesting—at the very least," she added mysteriously. She placed her shriveled palm over my ab. "No matter what happens, you must always listen to the wisdom in here. You can never go wrong if you do that one simple thing."

"I will try, Mother," I replied affectionately.

"You will do more than try, young man," she said with mock sternness. "You will do it or I will come to haunt you, like a khabit."

I knew she was teasing me again and I felt my love for her, warm and tender as though she was my own mother.

She held my chin in her hand, staring at me with her impenetrable eyes, yet I could see affection and trust shining back at me. "I love you, too, Heb," she rasped softly. "Now go," she croaked commandingly. "Your Beloved waits for you." I imagine my face was a mixture of contradictory emotions, because she added, "Pharaoh and the Neterw give you their blessing. And so do I."

"Will you be all right?" I inquired.

"I will be perfectly all right. I will see you in the morning," and she grinned mischievously.

I returned to my guest quarters, which were now full of strangers, lying about on the many pallets provided. I pulled out the clothes I had worn to Enet-ta-Neter and changed, ignoring the strangers' curious looks. I kohled my eyes, while looking into a polished piece of copper on the wall. I put on my new sandals and walked to the Temple, nervous yet excited. The full moon was just rising over the eastern horizon and it glowed over Het-Heru's Temple with an eerie orange luminescence.

When I walked into the Sanctuary, I was astonished to find that all the women, young and old alike, were dressed in elaborate Temple clothing of the finest white linen and sacred jewelry.

Shara-Het wore a Menat, similar to those shown in carvings of Het-Heru around the Temple Complex. It consisted of a necklace with small beads of numerous strands, the ends of which are caught into two strings of heavier beads, each ending in a counterweight in the back. Later I realized that the menat was infused with Het-Heru's Divine Spirit during invocation rites and could thus transfer life-giving force to the wearer.

The Priestess's eyes were outlined in green. Every one of them wore black wigs. They were clustered in front of the golden statue of Het-Heru, obviously waiting for me in order to begin. The sanctuary was quite full. I hadn't realized how many females were associated with the Temple.

Atalana looked magnificently regal. She seemed more beautiful than ever seen by the light from those torches. Incense burned in nearby braziers, myrrh, the favorite scent of Het-Heru. The chamber was smoky with its delightful yet heavy aroma. Atalana's eyes were glazed as if in a trance and had a far-away look. I began to feel the other-worldly effects of the chamber myself. The room took on a misty quality. I saw Atalana through a dim haze of smoky golden light, which permeated the large sanctuary.

They chanted in unison, shaking their sistrums in time to the words, while I listened. "Ra Ma....Ra Ma....Ra Ma" Father. Mother. Then they formed one line and walked in a westerly direction around in a circle, still chanting. "Ra Ma." "Ra Ma." "Ra Ma." I joined the circle. "Ra Ma." Around and around we circled four times, chanting continuously, finally stopping, facing east, the direction of the rising Moon.

The Priestess of Purification, Uab, sprinkled holy water from the sacred lake, first on the statue and altar of Het-Heru, then on Sekhmet, then on each of us celebrants. Next she took a smoking bowl of myrrh and did the same thing, purifying and cleansing us with its smoke.

Shera-Het stepped forward, holding up her arms. "Awaken Mighty Quebsnuf, Son of Heru, Lord of Air. We welcome you in peace. Guide us and protect us during our sacred vigil."

Everyone rattled her sistrums and menats, then turned, facing south.

Tetra-Het stepped forward this time. "Awaken Mighty Duametef, Son of Heru, Lord of Fire. We welcome you in peace. Guide us and protect us during our sacred vigil." Rattling of sistrum again.

Then we all turned as one, facing west.

Another priestess, whom I didn't know, stepped forward. "Awaken Mighty Imset, Son of Heru, Lord of Water. We welcome you in peace. Guide us and protect us during our sacred vigil." She bowed.

In unison, we faced north, as yet a fourth priestess stepped forward. "Awaken Mighty Haapi, son of Heru, Lord of Earth. We welcome you in peace. Guide us and protect us during our sacred vigil."

A fifth priestess held up her arms in supplication, while we all faced center. "Awaken Mighty Khepera, lord of beginnings. We welcome you in peace. Guide us and protect us during our sacred vigil."

A mighty rattling of sistrums and menats was heard as we again faced the fabulous gleaming statue of Het-Heru.

Then Atalana, Priestess-Queen, took my hand and we stood directly in front of Het-Heru. The Neter's crystalline eyes gazed benevolently down upon us. I noticed that the gold disk of the heavens had been placed at Het-Heru's feet once again, and it was glowing. I didn't know if it was the reflected strange light of the moon or if the object itself had started to glow of its own accord.

The rest of the holy women grouped around and behind the two of us, also facing the statue. They chanted as if with one voice. "Oh, Divine Lady, Beautiful Being, Protectress of women, Beloved of Heru, Mistress of the House of Heru, Bringer of Love and Joy, Mother of the Light, Neter of Singers and Dancers, Healer of Illness, Het-Heru of the Seven Faces, The Golden One, Mistress of Heaven, We bow to thee Mighty Het-Heru."

Then Atalana spoke. "I beseech you Lady Het-Heru, Divine Mother, bless this man and me. Bring joy and love to our bodies and hearts. Make us perfect vessels for the spirit who will join us. Protect and bless our child, who will be seeded under your Divine Love."

With astonishment I saw the statue of Het-Heru raise her golden ankh and point it at Atalana and me, curved end forward. I looked around but no one else seemed surprised. Then I heard the statue speak. "You have done well. I am proud of both of you. You have surpassed all the challenges in your paths so far." I saw stars shining in her crystalline eyes and felt the floating sensations I had experienced twice before. My body took on an unreal quality as though I was no longer exclusively physical but had become suffused with gold light, merging with Het-Heru's own.

Then Atalana and the other Priestesses turned and faced the statue of Sekhmet, who was standing in Her darkened niche. They began to chant again. "Mighty Sekhmet, Eye of Ra, Great Mother of the World, Divine Feminine Creator of the Cosmos, Lady of Fire, Neter of Passion and Desire, Destroyer of Evil, Defender of Righteousness, the One who Existed before all the other Neterw, we bow to thee Lady Sekhmet."

Then I heard Atalana's clear and musical voice as she invoked Sekhmet. "Hear me Oh Mighty Sekhmet. Bless this man and me in holy passion and sacred union. Let us honor the universe with our love for each other. Help us in the creation of new life. Defend and protect our child. And be with us in all the coming days, to safeguard us from Evil." She bowed to the statue and I followed suit.

The statue raised her arm to us in benediction and the temple vibrated with her immense power, as though we were experiencing a mild earthquake. Thunder boomed through the Temple and the ground shivered and rolled. Fiery sparks flew from the statue's eyes.

My skin raised in goose flesh and my hair stood on end.

"I am with you and I bless you!!" a deep feminine voice reverberated throughout the Temple. Then a loud roar followed, echoing throughout the great hall.

Atalana and I turned to face each other.

She and the others began to sing, not words as such, but sounds of power. The harmonic tones echoed in my brain and I unself-consciously joined my baritone voice to their higher pitched ones. Atalana and I melded into one and we flew on the sacred sounds through the air over the temple grounds. We became as a giant bird, soaring past the moon through the starry night. "I" didn't exist in that moment, only "we." We flew over the Nile, sparkling in the moonlight. Thirstily I drank in the watery essence emanating from the holy river below. Then gracefully, delicately, we returned to the Temple and landed, separating once again into our individual human selves.

I felt the center of my forehead being anointed with a fragrant oil and my head exploded with images. Het-Heru and Sekhmet stepped down from their stone pedestals and began to dance around me. Het-Heru transformed into Mukalia and the old woman held out Het-Heru's ankh for me to hold. Pharaoh's face drifted before me, fatherly concern etched in his features.

"You will hold the future of Ta-Meir Res in your hands," he promised. I saw myself being carried in a golden chaise to the holy river Nile by the Neterw—Ausar and Auset, Djehuti and Ptah, Setekh and Nebt Het—and I sailed with them in a large barque to Titania. A giant light exploded around us and they were gone. I floated in the churning muddy water, strewn with dead bodies. Volcanoes began erupting all around me and Sekhmet emerged from a lava cone, glowing red. I became a baby, cradled in the Neter's leonine arms, who then placed me on an empty Pharaonic throne in the Great Hall of Abtu. The palace's once-majestic walls were crumbling into ruin and I felt a great overwhelming sadness.

I felt Atalana's soft, warm hand squeeze mine and my vision began to fade. She led me out of the Sanctuary, away from the other Priestesses, down the main corridor and up a curving stairway. By the light of burning torches, I could see the Neters of the Hours carved into the wall. Each one protected one hour of the night, when Ra was far away and darkness filled the land. We arrived at the temple's second story, and Atalana led me by the hand into a large chamber.

She shut the massive wooden door behind us and locked the wooden latch. Torches burned high above us in brackets, illuminating the walls, which were overlaid with white, shining alabaster. Scenes of the story of Auset and Ausar had been carved into the marble, then tinted with natural colors. On the northern wall was the royal/divine courtship and marriage. The second facing east depicted Ausar's long journey while Setekh claimed Auset and the throne. The third southerly wall was the doomed battle between the two brothers. On the westerly fourth wall showed Ausar's dead body, penis erect, making love to his long-suffering wife, who had transformed herself into a kite, a small hawk. Heru arose from their union as a falcon to ultimately win victory over Setekh. The carvings on this last wall were explicitly sexual and I found myself becoming aroused as I looked at them.

In the middle of the enormous chamber was a thick pallet filled with goose feathers, covered with soft linen. Next to it stood Atalana. My beloved Atalana. As I watched, she slowly and gracefully removed her wig, then her jewelry and finally loosened her gown, which fell to the floor at her feet. I examined her naked body gleaming in the torches' glow. I could clearly see every curve of her body. The nipples on her breasts stood erect. Her narrow waist flared out into desirable hips and thighs. Her slender curved legs ended in slim ankles.

My body throbbed intensely.

I walked over to where she stood to kiss her, but she held me at arm's length. She began removing my clothing, all the while keeping her eyes on mine. She undid the leather belt and unfastened the collar and casually dropped them. Slowly she unwrapped my linen kilt and let it slide down my legs to the ground.

I drew in a sharp breath at the sensation, my heart racing with excitement.

"You have a wonderful body, my love," she murmured, lightly stroking my chest and shoulders in rhythmic circles. "I've always thought so, from the first moment I met you." She lightly traced my lips with her index finger. She brushed my cheek with her mouth, then kissed my shoulder, my arm, my lips, letting her fingers graze my inner thighs with a feathery touch. She stood on tiptoe and gently bit my earlobe, swirling her tongue around and inside my ear. She had been well trained as a Priestess of Het-Heru, Neter of Love.

She was breathing as heavily as I was and I took courage from that. I gathered her impulsively into my arms and kissed her. My tongue explored the sensuous lips, the strong teeth, and dove deep inside her mouth. I broke away and looked deeply into her gold-flecked brown eyes. Her pupils were dilated with excitement. She stared back at me, unafraid, welcoming, jubilant. Firelight flickered in those brown pools and I could see passion reflected in them and something more. A ferocity, as if she had also become Sekhmet, a feral creature of the night. The light from the torches shimmered over her body, making her appear golden. A smooth, golden lioness. She held my face in her hands and kissed me with wild abandon, undulating her breasts against my chest, her pelvis against my leg.

I began to kiss her all over, her full breasts with their upright nipples, her taut belly, her long neck, her lovely face, her mouth. Now, finally, she was mine, to love as I wished. All those endless days and nights of desiring her flooded through me and my love was in my mouth and my hands, caressing her wetly with my lips, hungrily touching her silken skin. I cupped her breasts and sucked her swollen nipples while she groaned with ecstasy. The sound of her pleasure inflamed me and I licked her breasts, her slender throat, her earlobes. I knelt down and placed my mouth over her swelling labia and she swayed with the contact. She grabbed my head fiercely while I breathed in her natural perfume and explored her with my tongue. Then I stood again, kissing her passionately, feeling her teeth against my lips.

She fiercely pushed me back and I fell gently onto the soft bed. I reached up to touch her, but she took my arms and laid them at my side. She knelt next to me and began caressing my skin with her fingers. Sliding over the muscles of my shoulders, down my smooth chest to my belly and up again to my neck in one long, continuous motion. Then she repeated it, over and over, lingering and teasing, gentle but insistent, her fingers burning fiery hot. She brought her hand down to my knee, then caressingly up my leg, past my thigh to my belly, just barely touching my erect manhood, with its attached balls of flesh, with the edge of her fingers. My body shuddered with ecstasy. She flicked my nipples with her tongue, then moved lower and licked my taut belly, then bit at the wiry hair around my pelvis. Periodically she would nip me in playful love bites. I moaned involuntarily. Every sensation, every touch pushed me further over a sensual abyss into oblivion.

I made little attempt to struggle but allowed Atalana to capture my body as she had captured my heart. I glanced at the wall depicting the union of the Neterw. I don't know if it was the flickering torchlight playing tricks with my eyes or my engorged imagination, but Ausar's penis seemed to grow larger, while his wife's wings spread over him and engulfed him completely.

My swollen phallus ached to enter Atalana and I arched up to meet her, but she avoided me. Then she kissed me, deeply and without reservation, until we were both breathless.

She fell onto the pallet next to me, panting.

I started to speak. "Atalana, my dearest…"

"Shhh," she commanded and put her finger to her lips.

Beyond the closed door I could hear the sound of the women chanting, echoing from the sanctuary. "Oh, Divine Lady, Beautiful being, Protectress of women, Beloved of Ra, Mistress of the House, Bringer of Love and Joy, Mother of the Light, Neter of Singers and Dancers, Healer of illness, Het-Heru of the Seven Faces, The Golden One, We bow to thee Mighty Het-Heru." Then they repeated the chant. "Oh Divine Lady…"

"Don't pay any attention to them. Close your eyes and remain still," Atalana whispered. "Allow yourself to sink into your feelings, Heb." She rolled over to face me and touched me once again with a light flick of her fingertips, teasingly and intimately. I was her captive.

I groaned in response. "Don't stop," I pleaded.

"Let your feelings grow as your body does," she murmured next to me, lying back down and held my hand tightly in hers.

"I will explode if we can't touch," I replied.

"No, you won't. Trust me. Allow the sensations to travel from your loins up your body and out through the top of your head.

With great difficulty I tried to imagine doing as she said, but couldn't.

"Breathe, Heb. Breathe the feelings through your body and out through your head into the temple."

She lay next to me, eyes closed, her body quivering like mine. "Like this," and she demonstrated deep intakes of air with sharp sighs of exhale.

I began to breathe as she instructed and found that I could channel my passion through my body and out through my head. My body grew more aggressively sexual with every breath yet I continued to send its sensations out from the top of my head and into the temple chamber as she instructed.

"I'm getting dizzy, Atalana," I gasped after a while.

"That's good, Heb. You're doing it right," and she continued with her rhythmic breathing as well.

My body began to shake and vibrate with ungovernable tremors, as though it would break apart.

"Let your body do what it wishes," she murmured, feeling me tremble next to her, "and keep breathing. The shaking will eventually stop of its own accord."

In and out I breathed deep gasps of air, then expelling it explosively through my mouth and body, while my body shook with unimaginable energy and force.

"More, Heb. Deeper. Breathe deeper. Send your passion for me into the Temple, out into all of Ta-Meir Res, into the sky of Nut, to share with all the stars in the sky."

I breathed and sent my ardor as she directed. I had never felt such intense energy in my body as I did now. Every part of my body was on fire, vital, and filled with fervent desire.

I could hear her next to me, moaning and breathing. Her body shook as mine did.

"Now open up your head, my darling. Let the energy of our child fill you."

As she spoke I was suddenly flying within Nut's body of stars again, careening and spiraling through the heavens, dispensing desire and passion behind me in a path of golden light. Het-Heru and Sekhmet were with me, encouraging me forward. A silvery light loomed ahead, outlining faintly the shape of a human being.

"There he is," Atalana cried. "Can you see him? Our baby. Our boy."

I reached out to touch the figure but he eluded me, laughing and floating around me in a scintillating trail of silvery sparkles.

"Now, Heb," she shrieked. "Sit up and face me."

When I had done so, she sat on my lap, trembling uncontrollably, entwining her naked legs around my waist, holding onto my quaking shoulder for support with one of her hands. With the other she eased herself onto me.

I felt her wetness and pushed my member deeply into her. My body shuddered as I felt her inner muscles clench tightly around me, grasping me in their fervent grip.

"Don't move, Heb. Just breathe. Breathe your passion up through your body, out through your head, and merge it with our child. Send your seed to our love child."

But I found it impossible not to move. My body had a stubborn will of its own. I began to rock back and forth inside of her, while I breathed deeply, directing the profound energy upwards.

Atalana clutched me, her fingernails digging deep into my back, moving her body in response to mine. Then she kissed me ardently. "I love you, Heb" she proclaimed. "I love you!"

"I love you, too, Atalana." I could feel powerful sensations start at my feet and speed upwards through the whole of my body. The top of my head seemed to burst open, as I violently filled her with my hot seed. Golden light-energy erupted like a volcano from the top of my head out into the temple and beyond. At that same moment she screamed loudly and moved in her own delight. When she had finished, her body slumped in my lap, her head falling on my shoulder, arms wrapped slackly around me.

I held her tightly. We didn't move. Except for the rise and fall of our chests, we were motionless, wordless. The skin of my body seemed to pulse with a new energy. Slowly our heavy breathing returned to normal while our bodies relaxed in the glow of our lovemaking. Tenderly I extricated her from our tangled position and helped her to lie down on our bed. I lay next to her, holding her in my arms like the lovely flower she was.

She closed her eyes, sighing deeply. She snuggled closer, her head resting on my chest. We were together. Finally, completely together. Forever. I gazed at her loveliness. And I was filled with serenity and fulfillment, in a way I had never felt with Bashta. I noticed the chanting from the Priestesses had stopped.

"I hope I didn't disturb them too much with my scream," she giggled in response to my thought.

I laughed in reply. "What does it matter?" I asked.

"Nothing matters now, my dearest love," she answered, opening her eyes. She gazed at me tenderly and joyfully. "Except that I feel all sticky," she added with loving humor and moved away a bit.

"Me, too." I glanced down and noticed my belly, groin and thighs were covered with blood, her blood. Blood was smeared on her, too. Startled, I sat up. "I didn't know…"

She saw where I was staring and nodded. "…that Ankhamun is incapable," she murmured, gazing at me tenderly.

"Yes. Why didn't you tell me?"

"It wasn't necessary. You would know soon enough" Atalana sat up to explain. "He thought that I could heal him. But I couldn't." She started to weep with both a wife's grief and a priestess' frustration.

I held her close to me, comforting her, kissing her hair, her eyes, her tear-drenched cheeks. Her naked body gleamed in the torchlight.

She cried until she had emptied the cauldron of sadness from within her. Then she pulled herself away and wiped her eyes. She glanced at the bed linen, soiled with blood and semen. "We need to burn these." I nodded in agreement and started to get up.

"Not now, my love. Let's just be together for a while longer." She snuggled into my arms, laying her head on my chest again. For a long time neither of us spoke but reveled in the sensation of our togetherness.

"Heb?" she murmured after a time.

"Um, hm," I replied.

"When you first were brought in to meet me after the wedding… remember that morning?"

"As though it was yesterday."

"I could see your excitement, even though you tried to hide it. I felt a response in my own body and knew that we were connected. I didn't understand at the time. Now I know." I hugged her, my hands embracing her naked back.

"I love you very much, Heb. But differently from how I love the Pharaoh," she murmured in my ear. "I don't know how to explain it. But… " she paused for emphasis, a trace of her earlier ferocity returned. "Nothing and no one will ever get in the way of our marriage. I am his life, Heb. Do you understand?"

"I think so," I replied with irritation, disappointment and jealousy coloring our recent lovemaking with a bitter shade of black. "But I don't like hearing it."

"I know, my dearest. I know. Can you be content with what we do have?"

I breathed and exhaled loudly, trying to overcome my rising anger. "Being with you is more than I could have ever dreamed, could have ever hoped. Every night I prayed to Het-Heru to help me when…"

"You prayed to Het-Heru?" she interrupted me.

"Yes. I was in so much pain from loving you, wanting you so much, so I asked for Her help."

"Oh, I think I understand even more now," she said and turned over on her side. She pushed a lock of hair away from her forehead where it had matted. She lay silently musing, distant, remote as a queen on her throne.

"I should go now," I said, hoping to be as cruel with her as she had just been with me.

She turned to face me. "No, my darling. Stay with me awhile longer. There's no need to rush off."

My obstinate pride erupted. "How could you say these things to me?

How could you have made love to me when you feel as you do about…
Pharaoh?"

"I hope someday you'll understand, Heb. I'm not a woman who can live
her life the way she chooses. I am an instrument of the Neter. And part of
Her plan is that I will be a mother, the mother of the next Pharaoh." She
rubbed her belly, crimson with the blood from her maidenhead.

"I don't understand you," I said, realizing the accuracy of my statement
as I said it. "I thought you love me."

"I do love you, Heb. I love you more than you can ever know. We are
one body, one heart, one mind. And we always shall be. But I cannot, will
not, let my love for you interfere with what I must do." I felt sick to my stomach, yet the truth of her words resonated in my mind.

"And you, too, Heb. You have an important part to play."

"I don't want to play any part!" I spat at her stubbornly.

"I've wounded you with my words," she murmured and tears welled up
in her eyes. "Please forgive me, my darling." She embraced me tenderly.

I relented immediately, feeling her luxuriant soft skin under my hands
and next to my chest as she hugged me. "I can never stay angry at you."

There was a soft knock on the door.

"It is Shara-Het," Atalana whispered. "We must go now."

I held her tightly, afraid to let go, afraid that everything that had passed
between us was a dream. Or worse yet, that I would never be with her again.

She kissed me passionately yet again, then pulled away from my embrace and got to her feet.

I stood also, suddenly shy and awkward at our parting.

"Remember, Heb. You and I are one soul, one body. Wherever you go,
I am with you." She slipped on her Temple Gown, then rolled the soiled
bedlinen into a ball and picked it up along with her belongings, and crept
out into the darkened quiet temple.

I stood motionless for a long time in Ausar and Auset's chamber, gazing
around at the alabaster carvings, pulling at my lip with mixed emotions of

elation and confusion. My head ached where the ointment had been applied. I hungered for Atalana, but I was alone, vastly, utterly alone in that chamber with the elegant carvings. Unlike earlier, the loving couple carved into the stone looked distant and aloof, even diminished in the flickering torchlight.

I addressed myself to Ausar as if he could hear me. "Is your bone actually buried beneath this Temple? Are you a real survivor from a distant land, as Mukalia says? Are you a Neter? Or are you just a made-up story to tell cranky children at bedtime?" The carvings on the walls remained stubbornly mute.

I wrapped my skirt around myself, picked up the rest of my clothing and walked back to the guest quarters. Sounds of snoring greeted me when I arrived. I washed myself thoroughly, cleansing away the tell-tale signs of lovemaking, and went to sleep on my pallet, awakening often with uneasy dreams until morning.

CHAPTER NINE

MUKALIA AND HER
GOING-HOME CEREMONY

"Heb." I was awakened by a soft voice at my ear.

"Atalana?" I sat up and looked around. She wasn't there. Most of the guests had departed. The remaining few were washing and dressing, preparing to leave. Otherwise, I was alone. I decided to trust my new ability and responded to the voice. I wrapped my old kilt around me, tucked it in at the waist, quickly washed and proceeded to the kitchen.

Atalana was there with the other women, looking lovely as ever, but quiet and contemplative. She smiled sadly at me. "Mukalia has asked to see us as soon as possible."

We immediately set off for the small mud-brick house. As we walked across the compound, Atalana reached out and held my hand tightly.

"Everything is about to change, Heb," she said with a catch in her voice. "And I'm afraid."

"Don't be afraid, dearest," I replied. "I'm here with you."

"Promise me," she began.

"What is it?" I replied.

"Look after our child…if anything…happens."

I examined her face but it was unreadable. "I promise." I felt a sudden pain in my solar plexus. "But nothing will happen," I added.

She brought my hand to her mouth and kissed it. "You are a good man, Heb. I'm honored to be carrying your child."

"How can you know…" but I didn't have time to finish. We had arrived at Mukalia's small hut and entered the mud-brick building.

Shara-Het and others were there. They had finished bathing and dressing the old woman in a golden gown that was far too big for her withered body. Tietra-Het was combing out the tangles in the sparse white hair.

Mukalia smiled broadly when she saw us. "My children!" she exclaimed and we took turns hugging and kissing the Ancient One. "Today is the day," she announced happily. "I am going home."

I looked quizzically at Atalana, who turned her face from me and wiped her teary eyes.

"Heb, my boy, would you do me the honor of carrying me to the Sacred Lake?"

"It would be my privilege," I replied to the old woman. "And my pleasure." I picked up her frail body in my arms. She didn't weigh as much as a handful of straw. I walked to the lake with my precious bundle, with the rest of the women following. When we arrived, I set her down on the long stone bench next to the water.

"Ah," she cried in her funny, croaking voice. "It is a beautiful day." She looked around and I followed her gaze. Great flocks of many types of birds were flying overhead, then landing to perch in nearby palm trees.

"Yes, it is, Mother," replied Atalana, her voice cracking.

"You must be happy for me, my dear," replied the old woman. "You, too, Heb."

"I am happy for you," replied the Queen. "I'm just sad for myself."

"No need for that, my child. I'll be as close or closer as I am right now."

I recognized with a tug in my chest that the old woman, Mukalia, the last of the Ancient Ones, was going to depart the earth this morning. I didn't know what to say or do. So I stood quietly, allowing myself to be filled with the magic and mystery of the woman who had come to Ta-Meir Res as a girl from her Motherland, later becoming a Companion of Heru, High Priestess of Het-Heru, finally attaining the status of a Great and Wise Elder.

In the short while that we had gathered, I was amazed to see animals of every kind beginning to gather near the Sacred Lake. Not only all the domesticated animals from the Temple compound, but wild animals as well were arriving to say farewell to the wise woman who would be leaving soon. Several lionesses with cubs in tow arrived, followed by a magnificent he-lion, his ancient mane a dusty golden brown. He roared and they lay down lazily near the water on the far side of the lake. Jackals and hyenas appeared from the desert beyond the compound. They were joined by the Temple's goats, cows, and geese. The lions seemed to pay no attention to the prey so close to them, nor did the domesticated animals act afraid of the predators in such proximity.

Mukalia had noticed them as well and smiled broadly. "You see, Heb," as she gestured at them. "This is what happens at a sacred Muan ceremony."

The other priestesses and initiates were arriving also, bringing lotus flowers with them. They arranged the flowers around her and adorned her with them. Several of them placed glistening stones around the ancient body. Mukalia's eyes shone brightly with love and pleasure, as she looked from one to the other in the group. A small group of the full moon participants followed the temple's inhabitants, rich and poor alike, and stood on the outskirts of our group. Unlike the carnival atmosphere from the day before, they were all quiet and respectful, even the children, as if they somehow understood.

"Heb, my boy," Mukalia spoke softly.

"Yes, Mother."

"You have the sacred seed in you. The Seed of the Motherland. You must nurture it. It is your heritage, your gift. A precious gift." Her eyes misted over. "Feel, Heb."

"Feel?"

"Your feelings in your Ab are your wisdom. That is why we return the Ab to the body once the body has mummified. We always have need of our wisdom. Look to your wisdom. Listen and feel." She breathed a deep sigh and laid her head down wearily. "It is time now."

Each of the priestesses took turns kissing Mukalia goodbye. Many of them sniffled as they did so. When the old woman kissed me on the cheek, she whispered in my ear, "Your son is destined to be a great man, Heb. Take good care of him and teach him what you have learned here."

"I will," I whispered in return. "Thank you for everything, my dearest Mukalia."

When Atalana's turn came, the Queen burst into tears. "I can't say good-bye to you, Mother. Please don't leave me."

The old woman patted her cheek, trying to comfort the young woman. "Do not cry, dearest daughter. My time here is done. And now I must continue on my journey to the stars, to rejoin my people." She held the quivering chin and kissed Atalana on the mouth. "Be brave, my darling. You have a small one to think of now."

She turned to face our group. "I bless you all!" and she waved her hand in a benediction. Then, "My family—will you sing my song to me? I want to die like a Muan." Without waiting for a response, she closed her eyes and folded her hands on her chest. With the flowers arranged around her scrawny neck, she looked as if she was already dead.

I don't know if it was a strange trick from Ra, but Mukalia's body began to glow with a bright gold light. The light was so intense, it hurt my eyes and I had to shield them with my hands. The animals moved closer. I was especially concerned about the carnivores attacking, but they appeared oddly placid and benign.

Atalana began to sing, followed quickly by the rest of the women. I didn't know the unfamiliar words so I hummed the tune along with them.

Ee ah co la no

Ee ah co la no

So me ee go ee ah wah My ah ke'e oh.

A magnificent falcon suddenly appeared overhead, wheeling and soaring above us. It flew so close that I could see the details of its feathers on its outstretched wings. Then with a cry it dove down to the body of Mukalia, sailed along the length of her and flew off into the western horizon, screeching its farewell.

Atalana bent over, listened at the ancient chest and shook her head. Mukalia had gone into the day, quietly and peacefully, in the Muan way. Her mouth was set in a radiant smile.

CHAPTER TEN

ABTU PALACE, POISON, SNAKES, AND THE KING'S CHILD

Atalana and I arrived back at Abtu Palace, accompanied by ceremony, as when we left. We were participants in a ritual greeting by the Pharaoh with a short speech by Shu-un-Atum, who seemed as angry as before. His gaunt beetle face was generally unreadable, but his brows were deeply furrowed. Shu-un-Atum and Ptah-un-Atum hovered close by the dais on which Pharaoh sat on the huge wooden throne. I noticed that Ankhamun's face looked unnaturally gray and had visibly aged in the short time we were away. When the formalities had ended, he stumbled and almost fell, then had to be helped down from the dais by several servants. I rushed to his side to assist him down the long corridor to the inner sanctum.

The Queen and I exchanged furtive glances as we helped the old King down the hall. Mine was a question. Hers full of guilt.

When we laid him down in the massive sleeping rack, Atalana's face was drawn with worry. She scolded him tenderly. "My darling, why didn't you send word that you were ill?"

"I'm all right, my dear," the King replied. "Just a little tired. Nothing to worry about." But as if to deny his own words, he doubled up, clutching his abdomen and grimaced in pain.

"Call for the Court Senu, Physician-Priest," she said tersely to a serving girl, who rushed off on her mission.

"What can I do?" I asked helplessly. I had never before seen the Pharaoh so frail and helpless, and I trembled with anxiety.

"Nothing, Heb," she replied with tight lips. Then she turned to me and smiled wanly. "Why don't you rest after your long trip?" She took off her cloak and turned to her husband.

Thus dismissed, I went to my chamber next door. Over the next several weeks, many people came and went from the King's bedroom, but I was never summoned. I fumed in silent frustration. I took my meals in my room, afraid I might miss my Beloved if she came to me. I paced my room like a caged animal or lay in my bed for hours on end, gazing at the ceiling, thinking of the magnificent one at Enet-ta-Neter, painted with stars from the Duat in Nut's body. I thought of the dramatic death of the Ancient One, Mukalia and of the birds and animals who had come to her final rites. I remembered the Sentyt Priestess Shara-Het, who was Atalana's friend. She would already have been initiated as High Priestess – Hem Neter – now.

Thinking of the few precious days Atalana and I had spent at the Temple, culminating in our ecstatic union, made my body turn to fiery flesh. I ached for her. I longed for a single word, a look, even to just stand in her presence. I touched my own skin, remembering both her gentleness and her ferocity. I closed my eyes and pretended it was she. Every moment carried with it the exquisite torture of remembrance and unsated hunger for her. In my mind I replayed every scene of the time we spent together, every loving look, every touch during our time at Het-Heru's Temple.

Was Mukalia correct? Was Atalana now carrying our child? I remembered my sacred oath to Pharaoh and would never allow those words to leave my lips, not even in the quiet confines of my room. Each endless day merged into wearisome night and then back into day again. I lost track of time, even forgetting to eat until Bashta brought food to me. I couldn't look at her, but turned my head and murmured my thanks.

The whole Palace was hushed, as if we might disturb the King's rest. Often I got out my mother's amulet of the Golden Neter Het-Heru and prayed. "Lady Het-Heru, please heal my Master. Help him to return to his vigorous self." But the Neter, who had always answered my pleas before, was silent. I felt lost and abandoned, not only by the Neterw but by the woman I loved as well. Never once did I see Atalana, nor did she come to my chamber.

Very early one morning I heard a disturbance in the corridor. I opened my door and peered out. A crowd had gathered, among them Shu-un-Atum and Ptah-un-Atum. A few women were weeping and I became instantly alarmed.

Then I noticed Atalana was standing at the door to their chamber. "Pharaoh has recovered," she reported wearily to those within earshot, who passed the good news on to others. From my close vantage point, she looked pallid and thin; her clothes hung on her formerly voluptuous body as if they had been made for someone else.

Pharaoh's two half-brothers exchanged a quick glance between them, then walked past her and entered Pharaoh's room.

Atalana seemed to suddenly wilt like a lotus at sundown, catching herself on the wall before she could fall. I impulsively moved over to her and took her arm, then braced her to walk into the room she shared with the old King.

"Thank you, Heb," she breathed quietly and pulled her arm away quickly. Then she closed the heavy door behind her, closing me out.

The group in the hallway muttered, but it was a happy sound. "The Pharaoh is well!" they rejoiced. "The Pharaoh lives!"

I suddenly realized that I was very hungry and walked outside to the noisy cooking area. The place smelled of delicious soups and herbal concoctions. Since everyone there seemed to be talking at once, paying no attention to me, I helped myself to some bread and a little soup. As I stood eating, I noticed that Bashta was sitting in a corner, quietly nursing our young daughter. I nodded my head at her and she broke into a beatific smile at my silent acknowledgement. She took the child from her breast, set her down and covered her breast modestly. The little girl immediately put her thumb in her mouth. Then Bashta got up from her stool and came over to me.

"Good news," she said shyly.

"Very good news," I replied.

"You must have been very busy with the King," she said, but it came out more as a question.

I nodded in reply, not wanting to tell Bashta I had been avoiding her, while waiting for some word from the Queen.

"I've missed you," she whispered close to my ear, so that no one else could hear. She need not have bothered. No one could have heard her in the uproar.

"Mmm, hmm," I said noncommittally and patted her on the cheek, as one would pat a faithful dog.

Apparently that pleased her, for Bashta's face glowed like a newly-lit torch. "Our daughter has grown much," she reported.

"I can see that," although I really hadn't much noticed.

"Every day she looks more like you." It was obvious that she wanted to talk further with me but I felt uneasy, guilty and a little bored in her presence. "She is already walking, did you notice?" When I didn't answer, she continued. "I've named her Sebat. Is that alright with you?"

"Certainly. That's fine. Good name," I added inanely. "I must get back now," I told her quickly.

"Of course," and she timidly touched my arm. "When will I see you again?"

"I'm not sure." That was one of the few things I had said to her that was true, since I had no idea what Pharaoh might need of me, or Atalana either. How ironic that both Bashta and I both hoped for love from one who could not or would not give it.

As if someone had read my mind, the conversation turned to the Queen. One of the serving girls said to the kitchen staff, "Did you know? The Queen nursed Pharaoh night and day. She wouldn't let anyone else touch him. Hardly ever ate or slept. Thank the Neterw that she was so well trained in healing. Otherwise we might be praying to Ausar today."

I shuddered at the words. Yet it helped me to understand why Atalana looked and acted so weak. I felt ashamed that I had been thinking my own selfish thoughts those long days and nights, while Atalana herself had become sick while caring for her ailing husband. I wished fervently that Atalana would call for me, or come see me in my chamber. Something. Anything. So that I could lend her my strength. And perhaps also so I could study her eyes for signs of renewed love for me.

Days passed and I busied myself in affairs of the running of the Palace again, since the Pharaoh had no further need of me at present. It was good to be active, to keep my mind occupied with trivial details. It kept me from thinking of her. Yet back in the silence of my room I lay awake long into the night, unable to remove the images that haunted me. Once or twice I even allowed Bashta to briefly come to my chamber, to attempt to soothe me with her hands and body. Then I sent her away again, unable to slake my unfulfilled longing and desire.

One night, late as usual, I was musing to myself. Remembering scenes, replaying them over and over in my head. Touching myself as though it was my Atalana touching me. When I heard a scratching at the inner door. I got up quickly, trying to hide the evidence of my pleasurable thoughts, as I hurried to open it. It was Atalana, standing there in the darkness of the doorway.

"Heb," she whispered. "I must speak to you."

She pushed herself past me, while I closed the door hurriedly. She paced up and down in the small chamber, then finally came to perch in the reed chair by the small table. I sat across from her, waiting, holding my breath, watching for a sign, listening intently. The intense throbbing in my body accelerated until it was almost unbearable. Then she spoke again quietly. "I am sure that I am pregnant. We will announce the news tomorrow." I started to speak, but she hushed me with a glance.

"I am afraid that rumors will start in the Palace, that this child is not the Pharaoh's." She bit her lip and looked down at her hands clenched before her. "He has been so ill. So how could he have…?" She looked at me with clear meaning in her face and tone of voice.

"I know, Atalana," I replied.

But she interrupted me before I could finish. "They were trying to poison him while we were gone!" she whispered with an angry flash in her eyes. "If I had returned a day or two later, it might have been too late."

"Who?"

"Shhhh," she cautioned me.

I inhaled deeply, taking in the news as silently as I could.

"I'm not sure if he will fully recover. There has been much damage to his body from it. I did everything I know how. Herbs, potions, incantations, rituals. But even now he can hardly get up from his bed."

"Oh, no!" I whispered in return. "The Pharaoh." I hung my head.

"We must be very careful," she said to me, staring deeply into my eyes. "Now more than ever. No one must even get a hint of what has passed between us."

"I understand," I said. But did I really? "Will I ever get to be with you again?" I asked mournfully.

"I don't know, my dearest." She touched my hand tenderly then and the thrill of our contact ran through my body. "There is much danger, and I don't know from what corner it may come next."

"I love you," I replied simply. "Let me protect you."

"I don't know how you can. Keep vigilant and mindful. I will need someone to test all the food before it is served to us."

"Of course," I agreed, thinking to myself that it would be an honor to die for the two people I loved most.

"No, not you!" she hissed. "Anyone but you."

"But…"

"Not you! Find some other person who is willing to take this terrible job." She clutched my hand with her slender fingers so hard that I almost yelled. "You must stay strong and well. In case…"

"Yes, all right." I didn't want to acknowledge what case she was referring to.

"Promise me."

"I promise."

"Good," and she exhaled loudly in relief, releasing my hand. "If anything happens…"

"I will let nothing happen…"

"…if anything happens," she continued stubbornly, "You must take the child and find refuge, somewhere safe, and raise him for us. He must survive to rule this Kingdom. The King and I have discussed this and you are the only one we trust." I nodded in assent and she smiled grimly.

"Very well, then. I must return before anyone notices I'm gone. Good-bye, my dearest love." She reached up to give me a quick kiss, then hurried to the door. I heard it close behind her, leaving only emptiness and silence.

"Goodbye, my love," I replied sadly. I lay down and put my arm over my eyes, weary to the bone.

There was much stirring in the Palace the next morning, as the Pharaoh was prepared to seat his throne for the announcement of the coming child. I stayed far away from both of them, tending to menial kitchen duties for the celebration feast, honoring my word. I would not let the remotest part of my being reveal the truth to anyone.

The sacred smell of myrrh permeated the Palace, while the sounds of chanting, singing, and sistrums filled the air. When I happened to see the entourage pass by on its way to the Throne Room, I was shocked at how small and shrunken the King looked, carried on a sedan chair, draped with gold cloth. Atalana walked behind him, head high, dressed all in white, beautiful. She had recovered some of her strength and I rejoiced. Sometime later I heard cheering emanate from the Great Hall. I imagined it was in response to the joyful news that the King and Queen had announced. I felt a pang, both that I wasn't there to be part of the celebrating, but also because of my secret, that wasn't mine to share. I turned instead to making sure all was in readiness for the banquet to be held in the King and Queen's honor. I was relieved there were so many tasks to oversee, so that my mind would be distracted.

It was the last time Pharaoh Ankhamun would be presented in public. His health, as Atalana had feared, was deteriorating daily and he kept to his bed, hardly able to stand. Atalana tended to him constantly and was very seldom seen as well. Once I saw her pass by in a corridor. The thinness following her nursing her husband after we returned from Enet-ta-Neter had passed and she looked plump and rosy, the pregnancy making her glow from within. I bowed my head as she passed, so I don't know if she looked at me, if she was smiling, or not. I could smell the scent of kapet about her, wafting to me in an invisible embrace, the only embrace we could share. It wasn't enough but it was all I had. I turned afterwards to see her soft curves disappearing down the hall. The pregnancy didn't show from the back. Apparently it was superstition that if a coming child is a boy, the pregnancy only shows from the front. It seemed so with Atalana.

Atalana Meruti, my beloved Atalana. The very thought of her name aroused passion in me and a longing that never ceased, only disappearing from awareness when I was busy, and returning full force when I was not. I made sure to stay busy from dawn until late at night, only collapsing into bed when I simply could not stand up any longer. Then I slept fitfully, dreaming, always dreaming of her, only to stagger from my sleeping mat while Ra-as-Khepera rose in the east.

I resumed my relationship, if you could call it that, with Bashta. Although I'm sure she wanted more from me, she never spoke a word of it. She was like the devoted cow that followed the farmer around, begging to be milked. As I think of this now, I am ashamed of myself. But there wasn't any more of me that I could give. My heart was promised elsewhere. And Bashta was only too happy to do whatever I asked of her. When Bashta and I were physical, I closed my eyes and pretended it was Atalana, so my spirit wouldn't rebel as the pretense.

Shu-un-Atum and Ptah-un-Atum took to caring for the Southern Kingdom of Ta-Meir Res during the King's long illness. They seemed more cheerful than I had seen but I avoided them whenever possible. Ptah-un-Atum's oily obesity increased while his brother's skinny weasel-like qualities grew in the same measure. Although the Palace was glum during the King's long illness, the brothers made no attempt to hide their joviality. Regent Ptah-un-Atum held many state banquets and endless festivals, which continued on sometimes for days. Notorious courtesans from nearby areas were often in attendance and I was ashamed at the conduct of the new court.

Sometime after the annual harvest, I found out that Pharaoh's child had been born. A boy-child. Atalana, standing in for the invalid King, while holding the child, attended a Royal Ceremony where Catfish was officially honored as the next Pharaoh. The baby's squalls made everyone in attendance nod in approval. "A strong, healthy child," they commented knowingly. Sentyt Astronomer-Priests had erected a birth chart for the baby and announced that he would grow to be a good and wise king, strong and fearless, yet kind and compassionate towards his people, a favorable servant of the Neterw. His public child-name was Catfish. A good choice and I silently gave my approval. Although I had assisted in fathering Catfish, I continued to remind myself that this was Pharaoh's child, not mine. After a while I almost came to believe it.

Celebrations were held, I was told, all over Ta-Meir Res to celebrate the birth of the next Pharaoh. The land was at peace and the people were happy with the continuation of the Royal Line. I held my tongue and kept my worries about the Kingdom to myself.

I was concerned when Bashta was called in to wet nurse the baby. Atalana may have had no milk although it was standard practice for a Royal Queen to forego nursing her own child if she chose. In any event, Bashta weaned our daughter and took to feeding Catfish from her own non-royal, but ample breasts. When I held Bashta in my arms at night, I imagined that there was a direct link from her breasts to the young baby and thence to his mother, the Queen. In that way I was still connected to Atalana Meruti. Therefore, I kissed, fondled, sucked, and caressed Bashta's breasts more than ever, to her moaning delight—and mine as well. However, after I was sated, I sent Bashta back to the servant's quarters, in the hoped-for but unlikely event that Atalana would come to me in the chamber adjoining hers. She never did.

Only weeks after the birth of Catfish, I was summoned to see the Grand Vizier, Pharaoh's half-brother Ptah-un-Atum. His brother Shu-un-Atum lurked in the shadows, an appropriate place for a man who was half scorpion. I was appalled to see Ptah-un-Atum's massive figure sitting on a small chair, which threatened to collapse beneath him. The stink of him was everywhere in the room, as if his body was putrefying while still alive. I wrinkled my nose in disgust, hoping he wouldn't know why I made such a face. He didn't; he was as oblivious to me as a grain of sand in the desert. He was stuffing sweet honey cakes into his mouth with noisy relish, as he addressed me.

"Heb," he said, between munching and swallowing.

"Yes, Grand Vizier," I replied ceremonially. There was no sense in offending him; he was gaining in power every day.

"From this day forth you will attend me as you did the Pharaoh Ankhamun. Before his illness took him to bed," he added.

"Yes, Sire."

"I am to be the child's Regent when the King is dead, until he is old enough to ascend the Throne."

I thought Ptah-un-Atum to be very presumptuous, considering the King was still alive, but said nothing. I nodded and hoped that my face was appropriately respectful.

"Therefore, I am to be accorded all rights and privileges as if I were your Monarch," he continued, belching noisily. "When the time comes, that is," he added hastily, wiping his mouth with the back of his hand.

"Yes, I will do so." But my stomach turned squeamishly in anticipation.

"When the child is fully grown, I will pass the kingdom on to him."

If there's anything left of it when you're done, I thought.

"My brother, Shu-un-Atum, will become my Grand Vizier when I attain the Status of Royal Regent."

I nodded in Shu-un-Atum's direction but he only glowered at me in response. He obviously had never forgiven me for my impudence and royal favoritism.

"You used to do a magnificent job of running the Palace, so you will resume that as well," he mentioned casually, doubling my work as if I was two men instead of one. "That's all." And he waved me away as one would brush aside a pesky fly.

I bowed and was leaving the putrid-smelling chamber behind, when I heard a voice in my head. "Go quickly to the Queen!" The Golden essence of Het-Heru appeared above me and I felt a great urgency.

No sooner did I leave the Great Hall when a sudden sound of screaming echoed from the other side of the Palace. The King's private chamber. I ran down the winding corridors as fast as I could.

I heard more screaming, then the rushing of many feet. "The Queen!! Look to the Queen!"

The great door to their chamber was open wide and people were filling in fast. I pushed my way through them, to see a figure lying on the floor. Atalana. She held the small boy-child Catfish clasped tightly to her breast, who was squalling at the top of his tiny lungs. I looked into her eyes and with great effort she motioned with them towards the open window. I saw several black, shiny vipers slithering out through the columns and understood in a moment what had transpired. She had protected the baby, our baby, from the poisonous snakes. How had they gotten into the King's bedchamber? Had someone deposited them there? Bashta was suddenly beside me, taking the wailing baby from the Queen's arms, rocking him, soothing his cries.

I knelt down beside Atalana, quickly examining her bare feet and legs. There were many puncture wounds from the murderous snakes on her ankles and calves. Her breathing was rapid and ragged. Gasping for air, her chest heaved from the effort. I gathered her into my arms, willing my strength into her body. It might be only moments before the serpent's poison consumed her. Even now it was defiling her blood with its fiery venom.

She attempted to speak, but had difficulty getting her words out, her throat constricted with the poison. Her eyes were filled with terror. It was with extreme effort that she communicated with me. "Wait for me, Heb," she whispered through clenched teeth. The pain must have been unbearable.

"I will."

Then her body went limp. A long moan escaped from her lungs, rattling in her throat. Then her eyes glazed over. She was dead. In a heartbeat she had gone, leaving me alone without her! Tears ran down my face splashing on my bare chest.

I wanted to hug the lifeless woman in my arms and hold her tightly. I wanted to kiss her still lips and cry out for her to return to life. I must not. I had an important secret to keep. I sat trembling in agony as I held her now lifeless body, amid the din of the jostling crowd. My emotions almost tore me in two.

All around us soldiers and priests and servants stood silently and still. They were in shock at what had transpired. Unbelieving what their eyes and ears told them. Unable to move or even think.

Bashta came over to me, still holding the Royal Child, and tapped me on the shoulder. "The King," she murmured.

Then I heard it, a small, quavering voice behind the growing wall of people. "Heb. Heb." My King was calling to me. Resolute, unwavering duty told me to go to Pharaoh at once. I turned to a serving woman, who knelt down and took Atalana's lifeless body from me. I rose and went to his bedside.

He grabbed my arm. "Heb, is she…" He couldn't speak the unspeakable, unthinkable words.

I simply nodded, my wet face tight and drawn.

"Quickly, Heb. Get the heqa and nekheka."

I looked around the room for the leather trunk with the royal implements of power in it, engraved with gold hieroglyphics. They were wrapped in their sacred cloth inside. I removed both of them from the trunk and brought them to Pharaoh Ankhamun. His hands shook violently as he refused them.

"Take these," he whispered. "They will verify that my son is King." I nodded, though not fully understanding what the Pharaoh was telling me. I was still in shock, like the rest of those in the room.

"You will need to know this" and he whispered the child's secret King-name into my ear, the name that would be his when the baby became Pharaoh. "Remember it well," Ankhamun groaned, in his own grief and pain.

"I will," I promised him.

"Heb," he whispered again, his thin lips next to my ear. "Take the child now. Run away. Hide him until he is old enough to be King. If he stays, he dies. Do you understand?" He tried to sit up but fell back.

I nodded dumbly.

"Do this one last thing for me."

"I will, Your Majesty."

"And remember your sacred oath to me. Now go quickly," and he pushed me away with what remained of his failing strength.

I turned from him and would have kissed my darling Atalana goodbye, but could not. I must keep the secret. Women were already keening their mourning cries. I moved to the Queen's lifeless side and quickly unfastened the beautiful necklace of Het-Heru from around Atalana's pale neck. Somehow I knew Pharaoh's son would have need of it also in the coming days.

I stood up and saw Bashta's face near the open doorway. I strode over to her quickly. She was pale, but strangely calm. "Come," she urgently pulled at my arm. "We must leave."

Had she heard the Pharaoh's words to me? I didn't know, didn't care. We rushed out of the Royal Chamber. I stopped for a moment in my adjoining chamber to pick up the old leather bag with my mother's two amulets. Then we hurried through the hall to the now-empty servant's quarters. Everyone had been roused to the King's Chamber. There was much rushing to and fro, cries, loud voices, so no one noticed us.

Our daughter Sebat lay sleeping and Bashta shook her gently to rouse her. The child complained with a sniffle. Bashta laid Catfish down, removed all his royal garments, grabbed an old swaddling cloth, and wrapped him in it and then in another heavier cloth to keep him warm. We could hear the noisy chaos and confusion all around us, the only thing reigning in the Palace at that moment. Dear, practical Bashta handed me several woven blankets to carry, while she wrapped another one over one shoulder, tying it at her breast with the baby inside. I wrapped the other one around Sebat then put one around my shoulders as well. I picked up the daughter of our bodies, slinging the small child over my shoulders, letting her hold onto my neck. She clung to me for dear life, shivering and shaking, whimpering sleepily.

Then Bashta led the way to the quiet kitchen, wrapped some bread and dates in a clean cloth, and turned to me. "What is the fastest way for us to get to Waset?" she whispered.

"I don't know. What do you mean? Why Waset?"

"My family lives in Waset. We will be safe there. He…" she looked down at the tiny lump cradled against her bosom inside the blanket, "will be safe there."

I nodded. I didn't know that Bashta had a family somewhere. We had never spoken of such mundane things.

Then we hurried out of Abtu Palace, looking like an ordinary man and his wife traveling with their two small children. The Neterw shrouded us with their magickal bodies and no one seemed to take notice of us. The small crescent moon shone dimly in Nut's body. Mother Nile looked silvery and dark, a road for our escape. We carefully picked our footing down the steep slope and found our way to the quay. A number of small boats were moored there. We took the most battered one, got in and I raised the sail, while Bashta threw off the woven papyrus ropes. Fortunately I had learned some sailing when I was a young man or we would have been lost.

The wind blew fiercely on the sails but the currents were easy to navigate. With desperate speed, tacking against the current, we sailed strong and true, south to Waset. Catfish slept against Bashta's body while Sebat slept on the floor of the small boat. Bashta and I turned often to anxiously scan the river behind us, watchful of other boats that might be coming our way. But all night we didn't see any. I sailed with great care, the baby as precious cargo.

Later, in the pinkish light that precedes the golden orb of Ra-as-Khepera rising in his scarab body, I pulled over to the bank and lowered the sail. The baby was awake, nursing at Bashta's breast, while our girl-child slept.

Bashta silently handed me a piece of bread, but I shook my head, unable to eat from anxiety. "We better travel on foot now. I'm sure they are looking for us in a boat. How far are we from Waset, do you suppose?" I asked her.

"I'm not sure, but I think we may be very close. We should be there by midday. There's the trail," and she pointed to an old, well-worn path along the river, strewn with rocks but clearly recognizable.

"We should get out and walk the rest of the way to Waset. In case anyone saw us take this felucca. I wouldn't want to be recognized."

"You're right," she agreed.

"Are you up to it?" I questioned.

"Of course." She shrugged her sturdy peasant shoulders in affirmative response.

She turned and awakened our daughter, who stretched her little body. Bashta gave the child some bread and dates to eat, before we would start our trek, and Sebat hungrily gobbled down her hurried breakfast. Then we got out of the boat and I pushed it as hard as it could into the river, letting the currents take it back north.

"Let me hold Catfish for a while," I said and Bashta agreed. She held our little daughter's hand while we walked for a while, picking our way around the rocks and stones on the path. The pink light had changed to gold, while the intense blue of the sky unveiled itself above us. Nut's body stretched as she gave birth to the shining disk.

I held the sleeping babe. His little body and head seemed dwarfed against my large arms and hands. It was the first time I had seen him so closely. He looked helpless and fragile.

The path along Mother Nile widened ahead, with room for maybe four people to walk abreast, with large rocks to sit upon, to provide rest for weary pilgrims. The stones on the path had dissolved into gravel, which made our walking easier. I looked behind me and saw Bashta and our daughter walking hand in hand. The little girl took small faltering steps on her chubby legs and her mother slowed her pace to match.

As I waited for them to catch up, I looked down again at the infant. Catfish was sleeping soundly after having drunk his fill earlier from Bashta's breast. He made little sucking motions with his toothless mouth, and milky bubbles formed as he did so. I touched his rosebud lips with my finger and, in his sleep, he grabbed hold of it with his miniature hand. I felt a swelling of emotion in me unlike that I had ever known before. Protective. Ferocious. And softly loving all at the same time. Atalana's baby. Atalana's and my baby. Our son. No, I quickly corrected myself. Pharaoh's son.

All at once, I remembered Het-Heru's words, "You will hold the future of Ta-Meir Res in your hands."

Oh no! Het-Heru, what have you done? I turned and handed Pharaoh's child back to Bashta, overcome now with a deluge of feeling. It was the first time I had allowed myself to think of the terrible consequences of last night.

I fell on the path as one who has broken his legs, unable to stand any longer. I clawed frantically at the grit beneath me, hoping to hear answers in the grains of crushed earth. "Why?" I cried ferociously, while tears poured down my face. "Why?" I clawed at the sand with my hands, as though it could tell me the answers. But there were no answers. The rocks were silent, while the intense sun beat down upon my back. On my knees, I pounded the ground, then picked up some of the sand and threw it as far as I could, did the same with stones and rocks. I heard them splash in the river beyond the path. My fingers were bloodied from the effort, but I didn't care.

I implored wordlessly. *Please, I beg you, any Neter who can hear me. Make me wake from this terrible dream. It cannot be real. I will not let it be true.* Her face was in my memory. How can she be gone? I sat up, listening intently, hoping.

The wind blew past my ears, but wordlessly. No consoling answer could be heard.

I examined my bloody fingers as though they belonged to someone else. It felt good to bleed. It took my mind off the greater pain. I looked up as though Atalana might be hovering above me. My darling one. How can I go on without you? Never being able to see your smile again. Smell your perfume. Watch the breeze blow your hair like fine threads of silk. Feel your velvety hands on my skin. Wrapped in my arms. Our skin, sliding along together. You are my blood. My cells. My skin. How can I breathe without you?

You brought life to my body. You brought light to my heart. It cannot beat without you. My blood is sluggish without you. My heart pumps but with a different beat. The pain is a wound that will never heal. What can I ever look forward to? What can I ever have that will make me feel alive again? Who could ever replace you? No one. No one can ever replace you.

Like a drunken man who cares not who can see or hear my piteous prayers, I entreated the endless sky. "Het-Heru, hear my pleas. Bring my love back to me. Make her alive once again!" Then I said to myself: *I cannot tolerate this. I want to tear my aching ab from my chest. Come to me, Ammit, the Devourer, take it now. I am lost without her. I am nothing without her. I am dead without her. Let me die now.* I beat my fists against my chest, as though it would stop my life.

I waited in hopeful anticipation. But all I heard was the steady thump, thump inside my chest. I die not. I live…but without joy. My joy died. My heart does not know I died with her. My Khu has departed my body. She has gone without me. I am lost, I cannot find my way without her. The world is cold and dark. I am tired of living. I am tired of life. There is nothing else I want now. Nothing to live for. But yet I live. Does not my Khu know it is time to take me home to Ausar?

Then I called out in as loud a voice as I could muster. "Auset, wrap your loving wings around me and warm my cold, tired bones. Take me. Let me fly with you to the next world, where my beloved waits for me as yours does for you. Ra, let your old weary rays disappear into darkness. Do not shine upon me as Khepera, the beginning. It is the end of day. Hide the moon in Nut's body above me. Help me rest in peace. Let me think about anything else but Atalana. Heh, let me sleep for a million inundations and awake in her arms. Let us be joined together in the next life, with Ausar. Anpu, shower of the way, lead me. I am ready to go. Take me now."

Still my heart beat and my lungs filled with air and expelled again, while blood continued to flow through my veins.

Other people around me may smile and go on with their lives, not knowing that they live with a dead man. Khat—dead meat.

I am dead.

Yet my heart beats. I can hear it. I can feel it. Why must I live when she is dead? Dead. Dead. Dead. Suddenly the faces of Ptah-un-Atum and his wily brother Shu-un-Atum appeared and I shuddered. Will they mummify her properly for the next life? Will they let her rest in her tomb in peace, while her Ba flies far in its daily life? Will they glorify her name? Or will they obliterate her cartouches from the palace and temple walls and columns? Will they pretend that she never existed? Will those a hundred years, a thousand years from now not know the exquisite glory that was Atalana?

"Oh tears, wash away my pain. Wash me clean. Let me forget her. Let me live whatever I have left of my life in peace. Let many days go by without thinking of her. Let me never speak her name again. Let me forget. Het-Heru, help me. Help me…." And I fell exhausted in the sand in the piercing sun, my spirit torn into pieces, my body overwhelmed with uncontrollable shaking, tears mingling with sweat, burning my eyes.

"Heb!"

I raised my head momentarily. Bashta had been watching me, listening to my confession, while she wept bitter tears over the head of the sleeping babe in her arms. Catfish, my son. Our son, Atalana's and mine. No! I sternly reminded myself of my vow. The son of Pharaoh.

The plump mother wiped her face with the back of her hand, her visage tight and pale, angrily staring at me.

I don't care if she is angry. She loves me without its return. The emptiness of unrequited love. But I don't care. Can't care. Those in love are selfish. All I know is my own grief, my bottomless, self-centered grief. "Atalana," I whispered to the hot air around me, as though the Queen might magically materialize in that remote setting. When she didn't, I lay my head down again, breathing in the dust from the road, beaten and hopeless.

"Heb!" Bashta again interrupted my despairing monologue. Her voice rasped with irritable weariness and emotion. Her countenance was severe and drawn. Her features looked tense, her attitude remote. I had never seen this look before.

"We must continue quickly," she told me between gritted teeth. "We need to get to my father's house soon, before soldiers are summoned to look for us. For him," she added with a conspiratorial look towards the babe she was holding.

"You are right," I agreed, and with the greatest effort pulled myself up to stand upon my leaden feet. "Show me the way," I mumbled. I picked up my other child, my daughter Sebat, slung her over my shoulders, holding her by her legs, while she clung to my neck with her small arms. And we continued our urgent trek towards Waset in mutual silence. I walked now as an old man, my steps uncertain and stumbling, my once-straight back bowed with unnamable, unmeasurable grief, my mind numbed by pain and despair. Dust rose from my shuffling feet as I followed the woman—the mother of my daughter—leading the way toward Waset and safety.

CHAPTER ELEVEN

FLEEING TO WASET INTO
THE PROTECTIVE BOSOM OF MUTTUY

The mud-brick house was identical to the hundreds of other mud-brick houses in the poorer section of Waset. A ragged cloth hung over the doorway, flapping in the breeze. The smell of onions and garlic and spices emanated from deep within. Several girl-children played outside, drawing pictures in the dust with sticks, and giggling. Except for a scrap of material around their waists, they were naked. The grime of the dust mixed with their sweat, rivulets of dirty perspiration lining their young faces. One looked somewhere around eight and nine inundations old, that awkward age when girls look like young camels, with long, skinny legs and arms; the other one or two inundations younger. Bashta stood at the entrance and called out "Muttuy!"

An older woman, thick in the hips and breasts, moved the cloth aside and peered out. Then she saw us and her face lit up. "Bashta, my little dove!" She reached for her daughter and Bashta allowed herself to be swallowed up in the mammoth folds of flesh that was her mother. "Come in, don't stand outside in this heat," and she stepped aside to let us in.

Bashta entered first and I held Sebat's hand as we stepped over the threshold. Sandy gravel covered the floor. The gloom of the windowless room smelled of many bodies. The main room of the house was bare and undecorated except for a few straw mats on the ground. With much noise, the two young girls swooped in after us, then hid behind the large woman. They peered around the wide hips, their large brown eyes shy but curious.

The woman Muttuy, Bashta's mother, motioned for us to sit. I almost fell onto a mat, exhausted with fatigue and sorrow. Bashta continued to stand, aloof and apart from me.

"Come here child," the woman commanded Sebat. The girl looked at her mother Bashta, with a questioning look.

"It's all right, Sebat," Bashta answered her. "This is your grandmother."

"Yes?" the older woman replied. Her face broke into a huge grin, showing several of her camel-like teeth missing. She had a cheerful, welcoming countenance and I felt instantly at home. But Sebat stood her ground, her back pressed against Bashta's thighs.

"Hello, Sebat," Muttuy chuckled, while the two young girls peeked out at their cousin.

"Mama, this is Heb," Bashta pointed to me. "Heb, this is my mother, Muttuy."

Muttuy wiped her hands, greasy from preparing a noonday meal, on her garment, then held them out to me, while I continued to sit cross-legged on the floor.

I reached up and squeezed the leathery hands gently. "I'm glad to meet you," I said as cordially as I could, then leaned back against the hard wall.

"Heb," she nodded in response. "What have you done to your hands?" She motioned to my knuckles, bloodied on the gravel path coming here.

"It is of no concern."

She seemed unconvinced.

Bashta began to undo the blanket holding the young prince-child.

"And who is this young one?" The Mother moved closer, and tenderly stroked the tiny hand of the young infant that Bashta had revealed.

"This is Catfish," Bashta replied very quietly, but said nothing more.

Muttuy looked from the sleeping child, to Bashta, to me, and back to the child again. Her face wrinkled a bit in concentration. Then she made the pronouncement: "He looks a lot like you, Heb," she smiled. "Not much like you, though, daughter."

Bashta turned red, bit her lower lip, and remained silent.

"Well," Muttuy broke the quiet tension, "I'm so happy to see you. Can you stay?" Without waiting for reply, she continued,

"Sit. I'll make you all something to eat."

"I was hoping, that is, we were hoping, that we could…stay here…for a while." Bashta fumbled with her words. She put her hands on Sebat's shoulders, standing in front of her, for emphasis.

The older woman scrutinized her daughter's face, examined eyes reddened by lack of sleep and excess emotion, suddenly solemn. "What has happened? Did they turn you out of the Palace?"

Bashta didn't reply. She was starting to sway from exhaustion and her eyes were rimmed red and bloodshot. A few tears trickled down her cheeks and she angrily wiped them away.

Muttuy took hold of Bashta's chin in her palm. "What is it that you are not telling me?" she demanded.

Bashta turned her head, pulling away from the maternal grasp and examining eyes. "Atalana, the Primary Wife of Pharaoh, is dead," she murmured.

A sudden jolt in my chest accompanied her words. I felt it best to say nothing and lowered my eyes.

'Dead? The young Queen?"

"Yes, mother."

"How? What happened?"

"Vipers," was all that Bashta replied, always a woman of few words.

"Vipers? How? Did they get into her chamber?"

"Yes." Questioning Bashta could be like pulling ticks from the hide of an uncooperative dog. The mother looked exasperated and turned to me for help.

I stood up on shaky legs, weariness and emotion taking their toll, and put my hand on Muttuy's fat forearm for emphasis. "We came here because we are in danger," I said simply. Truth would be the best course of action for this very direct but compassionate woman.

She gasped but waited to hear more.

"Atalana…the Queen…has been murdered," I said with great difficulty. My voice was quavering and hoarse. I struggled to speak. "The whole Palace is in an uproar. There are enemies everywhere. Pharaoh was worried that …his…child…would be next." I looked at the baby in Bashta's arms. Catfish was stretching and making little mewling noises, starting to wake up.

"Great Neterw, do you mean…?" Muttuy was speechless, her eyes wide, the whites showing above the irises in alarm.

I nodded my head yes, about to say more.

"Shhhh…" She silenced me. The girls clinging to her made Muttuy suddenly irritable. "Go outside and play now!" She pushed them towards the doorway and they reluctantly left. She looked out through the rag at the doorway to make sure they had gone an appropriate distance and turned back to me. "The King's child?"

I continued in a subdued voice. "The King asked me to take the child to safety, to hide him. Bashta said the child would be safe here with you."

Muttuy looked around at her meager surroundings, embarrassed at her poverty. "The King, yes, the King." She put her hand to her mouth, stunned, trying to understand the entire situation but obviously overwhelmed.

"No one must know who this child is," I continued, staring at her intently, forcing upon her a wordless promise. "Or he may be the next to die. There are enemies…"

"We must tell no one," Muttuy whispered, now a co-conspirator, taking charge. "Say nothing to your father or anyone else," she directed Bashta and then looked to me. "You must tell no one what you have said here today." She glared at me aggressively. "Too many mouths, too many wagging tongues. We could all be put in danger." Bashta and I both nodded in agreement.

"Soldiers will be coming," she predicted. "We must make plans." She moved the cloth away from the doorway and looked out, as if she could see them already.

Catfish started crying at this point, and Muttuy was her practical, maternal self at once. "What are you doing for milk?" But then two wet spots appeared on the front of Bashta's short-sleeved robe and she instantly knew. "You have been his nurse?" "Yes," Bashta replied.

"You must feed him then. I will go and prepare food for the rest of you. She turned to see Sebat lying on one of the mats, sound asleep. "Poor child. Did you travel long?"

"We have traveled all night and part of today." I realized just how hungry and tired I was and yawned involuntarily.

"There is water out back. Wash yourselves, then rest, while I cook."

We did as we were told. Soon we had washed the dust of the trip off our bodies. Muttuy gave us some clean clothes to put on. We ate delicious fish, fried in oil with lots of onions and garlic. Some freshly baked coarsely ground flatbread completed our simple meal. I had rarely eaten fish. Fish were considered creatures of Setekh, and thus never served to nobles. Only poor people, rekkit, ate fish. Because of that restriction, fish was rarely brought to the palace. I enjoyed every succulent morsel, crisp on the outside, tender on the inside, smacking my lips in pleasure.

The infant Catfish was soon sleeping soundly in a small basket in the main room. I was directed to a mat in one of the smaller rooms in the back of the house. When she had finished nursing, Bashta laid down on the mat, then turned her back to me. I was soon snoring, in the oblivion of fatigue. The respite wouldn't last long.

It was dark when I woke up. I glanced next to me. The mat was empty. Bashta had already gotten up. I heard the sound of an infant crying, Catfish, and stretched myself. The sound stopped and I knew Bashta was nursing him. My eyes still felt heavy and swollen.

My body ached everywhere, but the worst was the deep ache in my chest. It was like a tight band around my ribs, heavy and constraining. I put my arm over my eyes, trying to block out the memories of the last several days. I could see Atalana's face clearly in my mind, the golden glow I loved in her face and eyes. Her smile. I will never see her again. The words had a finality about them. Never. How could I live with never? I felt hollow inside, as though the life-force had been torn from me and died with my beloved. I was used to taking charge, issuing orders, making plans. I had no plans now. No reason to issue orders. No reason to live.

Then I thought of my small son in the next room. Pharaoh's son, I corrected myself. I would have to live for him. I would have to make plans for him. I would have to protect him, hide him, until he was old enough to assume his birthright. To take the throne of Ta-Meir Res. And I would have to care for him—for Atalana's sake. She would want the best for her son. And I would have to teach him what Pharaoh Ankhamun would want him to know and learn. To be strong and wise, gentle and compassionate, like the old King himself.

At this moment, though, I didn't want to do anything. I wanted to take myself to the river and fling myself in, and let the fierce current drown me. I wanted to bury myself in the hot sand and become like one of those mummies I saw at Enet-ta-Neter. I wanted the terrible sensations that threatened to overwhelm me be removed magickly. I wanted respite from what seemed an intolerable burden. To live while my beloved no longer existed was unimaginable. But I knew that there would never be rest from that burden. I would carry it with me all the days of my life.

I heard talking in the next room, adult voices mingled with children's high pitched laughter. I decided I had better get up and join them. I eased myself off the mat, feeling very old, very tired and shuffled wearily into the main room.

"Heb," Muttuy greeted me cordially, cradling Catfish in her arms. He had a milky smile on his tiny lips. His eyes were drowsy. "Did you sleep well?"

"Tolerably," I replied. I looked over at Bashta, but she averted her eyes. I drew a deep breath. Our relationship was irrevocably altered now.

Muttuy watched us, her eyes keen as a hawk. "This is my husband, Udimu."

I clasped hands with the stooped, unassuming man, thin but wiry. He looked as though he could easily be overpowered by his large wife, which wasn't far from the truth.

"I am glad to know you, Heb. Welcome to our home."

I found that these two short sentences would be the most Udimu would say at any time. He was a quiet man, like his daughter Bashta. Quite unlike his voluble wife. Or perhaps, because they never had a chance to talk much around her, as she filled up any void with words.

"Thank you, sir. I am glad to be here. Thank you for your hospitality." I tried to summon up a whisper of a grateful smile.

He shrugged in reply and clapped me hospitably on the shoulder.

"You have already met our daughters." Muttuy was the ever-present hostess.

I nodded and smiled at them. They sheepishly grinned back at me.

"We also have two sons. They are in the local militia. You will meet them soon," the woman continued. Then her brows furrowed, as she thought about the full extent of what soldiers in Waset would now mean.

"Um hmmm," was my reply.

She continued, unabated. "Udimu has killed two ducks for dinner," she announced proudly. "Are you hungry?" My stomach growled, much to my surprise.

"Yes, I am, thank you," I added politely.

"Have some figs, then. It will be some time before the food is ready."

She left to go outside to the cooking area, the baby slung in one arm. She was used to doing chores with a baby in tow. Udimu left with her, presumably to add wood to the oven, but in reality he was too reticent to continue conversing without his wife present.

The two girls, also taciturn, left to go outside. They called to Sebat to join them and the little girl hurried outside, glad to be in the company of youngsters again. I could hear them greet the neighborhood children with squeals of laughter.

Which left Bashta and I alone in the main room. The tension between us was palpable. "Would you like to show me around Waset?" I suggested cautiously. I needed a break from the confinement of the small hut.

"All right," she agreed, reluctantly. She led me on a hike through the narrow winding streets of Waset, past the deserted marketplace, down to the river bank. I stumbled and shuffled like an old man. It was as though I couldn't control my body. I was getting numb, yet my heart throbbed in agony.

We sat down on the bank, quietly contemplating the swiftly moving River, neither speaking for a long time. A few fellucas were returning home from the daily fishing. Their sails rippled in the wind. Ra-as-Atum was low in the west. I could smell many cooking fires and my stomach rumbled in anticipation.

"Bashta," I began hesitantly, not sure where to begin or how to breach the new distance between us.

She turned to look at me, the first time in over a day. Her eyes were hard like the pebbles on the beach. The only expression in them was anger.

"I am sorry," I said lamely.

"Sorry for what?" she snapped, a harsh tone to her voice, one I had never heard before.

"Sorry I never told you…about…Atalana. My feelings." This was more difficult than I thought it would be.

"All the time you were with me. You were wishing you were with her." It was more of a question than a statement.

"Yes, it's true. I didn't know what to do. I couldn't help my feelings."

"Hmmmp," was her curt reply. "Did you ever love me? Care about ME?"

I searched my feelings. "Yes, I care about you."

"But you don't love me?"

I sighed. "No, I didn't. Don't." I reached over to touch her, to comfort her, but she pushed my hand away.

"I thought you were preoccupied with your duties. That you were a cautious person who needed time to care more deeply for me. That eventually you would come to love me as I love...loved...you." The change from present to past tense didn't escape me.

A few tears trickled down her chubby cheeks and she quickly wiped them away. "I am glad to know the truth at last."

"I don't know what else to say. Except I'm terribly sorry."

"Yes, you're sorry that she is gone." Her words cut me deeply.

I hung my head, ashamed of my past behavior. I had used her, taken advantage of her affection for my own selfish needs. Pretending that I felt something for her so I could find an outlet for my lust. "I am the worst of men," I muttered. My guilt added to the already onerous burden of emotions. Even though I was suffering, Bashta seemed to ignore that fact.

"I will never forgive you," she pronounced.

"I don't blame you," I replied sadly. And I realized that I didn't hold a grudge, indeed I had no feelings for her at all. How could I have laid with her, made a child with her? The past was a blur. My former life seemed like a dream except for the sharp pain in my chest when I thought of Atalana, which was every waking moment.

Bashta got up, brushed the sand off her robe and wordlessly left me seated on the riverbank. I could find my way back to her home, but I didn't feel like joining in the family dinner just yet. I wanted some time to be alone and think.

Images of all the women in my life who had left me passed through my mind. First my mother had died and left me alone when I was a young boy.

Then Mukalia, just as I was getting to know her. Now loyal Bashta had ripped me out of her heart. And…worst of all, Atalana. My dearest Atalana.

How I missed being able to touch her soft skin, feel her caresses. Never to kiss her again, hear her gentle voice, see her beautiful face. I wallowed in my grief, glad that no one was there to see me blubber like a baby. Heavy racking sobs shook my body for the second time today.

When I had begun to regain my composure, I got up and washed my tear-stained face in the cool water of the Nile. I could feel a shell beginning to envelop my heart. I would never again cry or allow my feelings out. Then I felt a presence behind me and turned to look, suddenly fearful and anxious. Soldiers? There was no one there.

"Heb," I heard my name being called.

"Who's there?" I looked around but couldn't see where the sound came from. Had Bashta repented and came back to join me? To forgive me?

"Heb, I won't ever leave you."

The voice was soothing and calm. All around me on the riverbank was a golden glow. From the sunset? No, I knew at once it was the Neter Het-Heru. In the yellow glow I recognized the face similar to my beloved—Het-Heru. The Neter and Atalana had merged into one. Did that mean that Atalana had become a Star Being? I wished that Mukalia was here to answer my question.

"You have done well and I am proud of you," Atalana-as-Het-Heru continued. "If you have need of comfort, I am here. I will always be here."

I felt a light touch on my shoulder and my body relaxed. The pain eased somewhat and blessed peace washed through me. The relaxation was sharply defined as my torment eased. "Thank you, Golden Mistress. I am so glad to hear your voice and feel your presence."

"Fear not for the little one. We have plans for him. Keep him near you and teach him well. For the time being, do not tell him who he is and where he has come from. Let him enjoy his childhood. There will be plenty of time later on for his responsibilities."

"I will do as you ask, Lady Het-Heru."

"Trust your feelings, Heb." The words reminded me of the old one, Mukalia. "They will guide you truly."

I thought of the ancient woman who had such fabulous stories to tell. Such wisdom to impart. Although I had only known her for a short time, I loved her as if she were my mother. She was a magnificent woman and I was grateful to have been on intimate terms with her. Het-Heru was a wonderful influence on me as well, and my heart was lighter than before. "Thank you, Great Golden Lady," I began, then realized Het-Heru was gone.

Twilight was lengthening. Dinner would be ready. I must return before it got too dark to see my way back to Muttuy's house. I felt amazingly better on my return walk and began to hum.

CHAPTER TWELVE

HIDING IN PLAIN SIGHT

Each passing day of my new life was much like every other. Bashta, Sebat, the baby and I were given the small back room in the family home. I think it was the room formerly occupied by the two, now-grown sons. Bashta continued to be distant with me, although polite in front of her family. I'm sure her family noticed the strain, but refrained from speaking of it —at least in front of me.

Extra clothing for us appeared as if by magick. We received several kilts for me, an ankle-length robe for Bashta, and some swaddling clothes for the baby. Perhaps the neighbors donated items. I asked no questions, but merely went along with anything that Muttuy suggested. I became taciturn and withdrawn, a shadowy figure, like a khabit, in the household. I noticed that most of the family members were also quiet, deferring to the powerful woman who was head of the household.

Bashta continued to nurse Catfish, although his primary care began to be taken up more and more by Muttuy. Catfish was usually to be found perched on the older woman's hip or strapped to her broad back. The matriarch was formidable and intractable. "I will guard this child with my life!" she declared to me on more than one occasion, when we were alone. I was relieved, as I knew nothing about caring for children.

I wore clothes like the rest of the poorer townspeople. I fished with Udimu and quickly began to smell of fish as he did. I found it impossible to remove the scent of fish from my fingers, no matter what I did. I was accepted without question as one of the family and performed daily chores with the others.

Het-Heru helped in the healing of my grief. Every night I walked to the banks of the Great Mother Nile river bank near sunset. Every night I had nightly visitations from the Golden Neter. Every time She appeared, I felt more and more at peace. It was as if the flowing currents of the Holy River took me further and further from the life I had known at Abtu Palace. It was as though Mother Nile swept through me, cleansing me on every level, making me into a new man.

Muttuy had been right. Soldiers arrived very shortly in Waset following our hasty departure from Abtu Palace. They came looking for Pharaoh's child along with a man and woman servant who had disappeared at the same time as the baby.

Fortunately, I had already buried the heqa and nekhekha that Ankhamun had given me, along with Atalana's necklace, in Muttuy's house. I had dug a deep hole beneath the floor in the main room, and covered over the precious items with the sandy soil and straw mats.

Shu-un-Atum also came to Waset, his skinny beetle body carried on a royal pallet through the streets, hoping to find a glimpse of us in the crowds or in the homes. But he and the Royal Guard had underestimated the power and unity of the rekkit of Waset. When Muttuy made it known that we were not to be found, without question a remarkable wall was thrown up between us and the spies that descended from Abtu Palace. It was as though we had simply become invisible or didn't exist at all. Her two soldier sons were no doubt responsible for our protection, at their mother's bidding I'm sure. After a period of frustration, the army left with the newly appointed Grand Vizier.

After perhaps three passes of the moon, we in Waset heard very sad news. The Pharaoh Ankhamun, beloved King and Protector of our land, had passed on to the next world. Ptah-un-Atum, half-brother to Ankhamun, would be coronated as the next Pharaoh, continuing the Dynasty. I shuddered at the thought of that vile man sitting on the same throne as my beloved King used to do. We were told he would take as his wives the three elderly widows of Ankhamun. He was apparently intent on inheriting everything he could get his greedy hands on. His brother, Shu-un-Atum, was installed permanently as Grand Vizier. It seemed that vipers still flourished in the Palace!

When I first heard about Ankhamun, I felt great pain in my khat and in my thoughts. My whole life had revolved around the King. I hardly knew myself without him. It was because of him that I had been educated and given a position of some importance. It was because of him that I had a good life. It was because of him that I had a relationship, although too fleeting, with Atalana. He had trusted me and loved me, and I loved him more than if he were my own father. And he had trusted me to raise his child, to teach Catfish and help bring him to power at some point in the future. I was bereft of my Father King and felt even more alone than I had since coming to Waset. On my evening meditations, I got out my old amulet of Het-Heru and prayed for Pharaoh. I also asked Ausar and Anpu to watch over the old man, to assist him in the dangerous journey through the Duat to the afterlife.

A few days later my pain and sadness turned to anger. I was angry our good king had been poisoned. Angry that someone had also killed the Queen, my darling Atalana, and forced her child into hiding. Angry that someone had so disrupted our peaceful life, that no one in Ta-Meir Res could feel safe. Who was responsible for such heinous acts? I could only guess, but suspected Shu-un-Atum and his brother. Would the new Pharaoh be strong enough to protect us? Would neighboring countries see our weakened country as prone to invasion? Catfish was a helpless baby, unable to do anything for the country, nor did he have any powerful protectors. I dare not bring him to Abtu Palace. He was in danger of assassination like his parents.

Other people also questioned the chain of events, speaking in whispers among themselves. How did the Queen die? Why had the death of Pharaoh followed so soon after hers? Pharaoh's child and heir to the throne had disappeared or died, a mystery no one could solve. What would happen to our country? Would our society collapse into civil war or be invaded by outside countries?

Townspeople gathered in Muttuy's small house, to discuss what they should do in case war came to the area. There were a number of soldiers in Pharaoh's army who were loyal to Waset, who could protect us, but otherwise we were on our own. The community began to build a mud brick wall around the perimeter of the town. Everyone became involved, even the children, stamping straw into the mud to make stronger bricks. A few farmers on the outlying area taught their sons to become sentinels, to alert the town if any invasion was spotted on their way to us. Perhaps we were being unduly suspicious, since Waset was a small town without much importance in the Southern Kingdom. A few noble families lived here in Waset, but otherwise we had no powerful allies and no important trade or wealth to pay for a war. We did have ancient sacred Temples nearby, but that wouldn't be of much use to defend ourselves against an invader.

Nevertheless, the town prepared for a possible siege. Caches of food were stored in the central part of Waset, as well as in several other strategic locations. We had some local wells within the town, so we were assured of having enough water. Weapons were in short supply as well as any material to make weapons. We hoped…and prayed…it would not come to war. But anything was possible.

For seventy days, during the sacred period of mummification, our country was in mourning. Men, as well as women, wept openly in the streets. Our Ruler was much beloved and would be greatly missed.

After the period of mourning, we heard that Pharaoh Ankhamun's mummified body had been taken to Abtu Temple, to be presented to Ausar, god of the underworld. Ankhamun's spirit was now joined with the Neterw in the Barque of the Dead. His remains were buried in a mastaba near the sacred temple. His body, along with his Ba and Ka, contained the wisdom he had gleaned throughout his life and priests would be able to consult him for advice. For three days after his entombment, an official period of feasting and celebration was proclaimed. No one worked in Waset during the festival, except doing what was absolutely necessary. Bonfires were lit along the banks of Mother Nile, to bring Light to the Neterw as they journeyed with Ankhamun.

I avoided the festivities, feeling glum and hopeless. My appetite had greatly diminished in the time since Bashta and I had fled from Abtu Palace, and I was thinner than I had ever been in my adult life. I ate only beer and bread, refraining from fruit, fish and meat, during the three-day celebration, hoping that my fasting would bring strength to my beloved Pharaoh in the next world. I shaved my head and cut off my beard. Indeed I removed all hair from my body. From then on, I would continue to remove my hair on a daily basis.

I had no incense to burn and no sacred oils to anoint myself with, being poor. Incense and oil were costly, having been brought from distant lands. Usually only nobility and the priesthood could obtain these. However, I did my best to perform rituals at the banks of Mother Nile, praying to Het-Heru and the other Neterw, to speed Ankhamun's journey through the Duat to reach the Barque of the Dead.

After the Festival of the Dead, life resumed its normal pace in Waset. The war that we all feared had been averted, however, by the apparently smooth succession of Ptah-un-Atum. All the people in Waset breathed a sigh of relief. They decided, however, to save the caches of food. One never knew when the food stores might come in handy.

It had become my evening habit since arriving in Waset to go to the banks of Great Mother Nile, to offer up prayers to Het-Heru. This nightly ceremony brought me great comfort. Every evening, just before Ra-as-Atum retired in the night sky, I would wash myself, put on a clean kilt and perform my nightly ritual in the dying day along the banks of the Nile. Sometimes the evening star Eosphoros would be present. I associated Het-Heru with that gentle planet.

I remembered a little of the ritual verse and actions that had been performed at Enet-ta-Neter, when the Golden Neter had sanctified my union with Atalana, and incorporated those verses into my prayers. Every night as I performed my ritual, Het-Heru would appear in a golden vision. I talked to her as easily as I might talk to another human being. Had I had gone mad? Perhaps I had. Yet Het-Heru blessed me with Her presence and because of it, I was at peace.

One evening as the sun was dying in the west, I was once again at the banks of the river, performing my simple ritual. When I was done, I was inexplicably filled with the most happiness I had experienced since the time I spent with Atalana at Enet-ta-Neter. Once I was done with the formalities, I luxuriated on the bank, staying to watch the full moon of Djehuti rise in the east. It was huge and brightly orange colored. My body trembled with excitement. Strange, I thought to myself. What is this? What is happening to me? I would have sworn on Ma'at's feather that I heard the voice of my Dearest call my name. Atalana?

"Heb," the Khabit-of-Atalana murmured. "I have missed you, my love."

I looked around, thinking perhaps someone was playing a joke on me. I was all alone except for some boys playing with sticks, knocking stones into the river and jostling each other in the moonlight. They were too far away to see me well. It couldn't be them.

"Heb," she repeated again. "Hold out your hand."

I did as I was told, holding out my hand with my palm up. I felt a presence, a pressure on my hand. Then soft stroking, tickling my palm. I smiled involuntarily. "Is it really you?"

"Don't you know my touch?" she replied.

My ab filled with delirious joy. "How do you come to be here?" I asked.

"I have never left you, my dear one. But this is the first time I've been able to make such direct contact."

"Why can't I see you?"

"Perhaps if you closed your eyes, you could."

I did so, and in my mind's eye I could see Atalana in all her loveliness. Her glowing smile lit up my heart. She held out her hand and I imagined that I held it. Still with closed eyes, I brought her soft hand to my mouth and kissed it. Ah, yes, you may think that I am well and truly mad, first conversing with a Neter and now a dead woman. But who knows what mysteries exist within the universe? Who may know what is possible and what is not? I didn't care. My beloved Atalana was here with me in this moment and that was all that mattered.

I lay back on the warm ground and held the invisible spirit in my arms, her head resting on my shoulder. I had so many questions to ask her, but I was afraid that the moment would end too soon. So I simply "felt" her, and cherished the sensations that I thought I had lost forever.

"You look different, my dearest. You are so thin. You have shaved your head, too."

"Yes," I answered simply.

"You have turned yourself into a priest." She sighed a little.

"I have?" Her words astonished me. "Why do you think that?"

"You come here every night, to make homage to Het-Heru. To consult with He. To fill yourself up with Her Golden Light. You have forsaken the world of ordinary people. You have become celibate and enter into the spiritual plane nightly. You desire to make yourself a better person. Is that all true?"

"Yes, but mostly I have sought…"

She interrupted me, which was so like her. "What else does a priest do?"

"I don't know. Enter a group at a temple, go through initiations."

"Haven't you been initiated through your experiences in life?"

"Oh, yes," I agreed. "Many…. difficult initiations."

"Well, then." I could almost feel her shrug.

"And are you not selected by Het-Heru, who comes to teach you?"

"Yes." The idea of being a priest had never occurred to me until now.

"It is through your ritualistic behavior that you opened the door for me to come through tonight."

"I have? If that's what I accomplished, I'm grateful." I laughed then, startling myself with the sound. It had been a long time since I had laughed.

"I am grateful, too," and she snuggled closer.

"But I'm just making all this up, aren't I? Seeing Het-Heru. Feeling you here with me?"

"Are you?" she challenged me.

"I don't know."

"That's a good answer," she replied. "The path requires you to be open to whatever happens, without trying to make sense of it."

"Ah, I see," but I didn't really. What I was experiencing was very mysterious.

"And how is little Catfish?"

"He is growing so fast, my love. Every day he looks more and more like you." I could feel her smile in the darkness.

"Ahhhh." She sounded pleased. "And Bashta?"

"That is over and done." I didn't want to tell Atalana about my foolish behavior on the day of our long trek or Bashta's subsequent anger with me. I still carried the shame of that day with her.

"Too bad. She is a good woman."

"Yes," I agreed. "But she isn't you."

"Don't you think you should look to the future now? To find a real flesh-and-blood woman to make a life with? Not a Khabit."

"No!" I exploded. "I will never find another. All I want, all I have ever wanted, is you. That, and raising your son to become Pharaoh one day."

"How do you propose to go about doing that?"

"I'm not sure yet." Then I told her about Muttuy and the robust woman's pledge to the young child. I finished with, "Muttuy is a wonderful woman. Between us I think we will teach him well."

"Then perhaps that is why you became involved with Bashta. So she would lead you to Muttuy, who will help in Catfish's education and care for him. Since you won't be with any other woman."

"I never thought of it that way before."

"The Neterw lead us down paths that are full of challenge and mystery, yet there is purpose behind all of it."

"I suppose so."

I felt Atalana move away from me. "Darling, my time is about done. I must leave. There are only small slits in the curtain of time that I can slip through to be with you."

"No, please don't leave!"

"My dearest, even though you may not feel me and hear me, I assure you I'm always with you. Know me in your heart and feel me in your body. We are connected through the vast reaches of Nut's heavenly body and Geb's earthly one."

"Will I get to see you again?"

"I don't know. Perhaps. But wait for me, just in case." Her image and her voice drifted away like fog in the chilly night air, and once again I was all alone on the banks of the holy river. I was disoriented and light-headed and it was with difficulty I made my way back to the family home.

CHAPTER THIRTEEN

The Baby Catfish;
Heb returns to Enet-ta-Neter

My simple life in the house of Muttuy and Udimu was pleasant and the days passed peacefully. My food was cooked and my clothes were washed by Muttuy and the girls. The family seemed to adopt me as one of their own and they even began to introduce me as their cousin. After a while it seemed I had never lived anywhere else. I helped to care for my new family with delight and a growing sense of loving reverence for them and for nature all around us.

Every day I went out to fish with Udimu, sailing out in his tiny felluca, catching fish for the family table with fishhooks, harpoons, traps, and nets. Although the nobles of Waset avoided eating fish, a creature of Setekh, we poor families needed flesh to nourish our bodies. The river provided for us abundantly.

I helped sow seeds in a plot in their tiny backyard, a first for me. I never ceased to be amazed at the miracle of the seed's emergence. A tiny seed, containing the life energy of that particular food, astonishingly grew into a vegetable or grain, feeding and nurturing us. Muttuy's two daughters were amazingly adept at coaxing food to grow. We had delicious vegetables, onions, garlic and sometimes melons for our table. Gardening was not an easy task in our dry land. We had to carry the precious water from Mother Nile through the town in heavy goat-stomach pouches to irrigate our always-thirsty plants. The townspeople only used the wells in emergencies. The rest of the time every one of us dipped our containers into the life-giving river.

I also continued my "studies" with Het-Heru on the banks of that river every evening.

Once, Muttuy took me to the marketplace, to shop for things we couldn't grow, raise, or catch ourselves. She had Catfish firmly strapped to her back. "I won't let this child out of my sight!" she declared.

I had never gone to a town market before arriving in Waset, but she went often, sometimes every day. As we approached the bazaar, I could hear the cacophony of many voices, mingled with the sounds of animals, birds and children. I looked around, unable to take in the whole setting in a single glance. Everywhere was talking, mingled with shouts and laughter. Naked children ran rowdily through the marketplace, knocking over merchandise, bumping into people, to the chagrin of their mothers. Vendors haggled with customers, hoping to get the best prices. Frenzied trading and heated arguments could be heard from time to time.

Although Waset wasn't a large town, the items for sale were varied and numerous, some brought from far away. Everything one could want or need, provided one had to means to purchase it. Customers wandered among the colorful booths, pausing to bargain or trade, sometimes hoping to sample the wares. Vendors waved flies away with small palm fronds. The rekkit, common people, mixed with nobility, all shopping in the hot dusty day. Soldiers from the militia mingled with mothers, babes wrapped in slings.

I was fascinated by the various smells and textures of herbs, spices and oils. Dried herbs like mint, oregano, and lemon balm. Spices like turmeric and mustard, cinnamon and cardamom. Salt, a necessary condiment for our desert country. Without it, one could dehydrate quickly in the heat. Frankincense. Myrrh. Kapet. Incense and oils for sacred anointing.

I wrinkled up my nose at the pungent odor of various animals closely grouped together. Honking geese, quacking ducks, donkeys and goats, along with the occasional screech of young camels each exuded their own smells. All of these animals were for sale, the smaller ones contained in hemp cages. Camel tenders stood holding the reins of their animals, just weaned from their mothers. The young camels knelt on the hard ground, placidly chewing their cuds. Camels, I found, were a precious commodity, and most people could not afford to buy one. Placed on blankets next to the camels were an array of leather whips and saddles for sale. Periodically one would screech loudly, the sound ear-splitting if one happened to be close by. Water buffalo and long-horned cattle were tied up, waiting to be sold. Cages held live pigeons ready to kill and eat, a real delicacy. They were too precious for Muttuy's family. Each pigeon provided less than one meal to an individual.

Goats, along with goat's milk and creamy white goat's milk cheese, were available. "I love this," Muttey whispered to me as she purchased an extra-large packet of cheese, wrapped in oiled flax, paid for by some fish Udimu and I had caught and she had preserved in salt brine. She broke off a large piece of the soft, fragrant cheese and popped it into her mouth, then wrapped the remainder, placing it lovingly in her large reed basket. "Sometimes if we have extra food, we bring it to the marketplace to sell," she explained. The same vendor asked if we were interested in a goat stomach pouch for water and other liquids. "No, thank you," Muttey replied. "We still have several good ones." She turned to me and sighed. "I would like to get a she-goat someday, so I could make my own cheese."

"The little one is growing fast, Muttuy," the vendor casually mentioned, wiping her hands on her stained gown.

"Yes, my nephew's son," the large woman lied.

"He is so darling. What a handsome boy." The woman touched one of Catfish's little hands. I was amazed to see the baby was unafraid of the attention, grabbing hold of her finger, and smiling to her. As we continued to shop, others came up to us, entranced by the child. Catfish seemed to enjoy the interest and was his tiny, charming self to everyone. The child would smile at each of them, glowing in their praise, reaching out his chubby hands to touch them, to make contact. I had known Catfish was agreeable at home, but had not seen that he was so well-behaved in public.

"Catfish is a very special child," Muttuy murmured to me.

"Yes, indeed," I agreed.

As we walked around, I was particularly entranced with the sights of hundreds of items for sale – the colors and shapes of produce; metallic items glinting in the hot sun; sparkling gemstones, and other wares—all laid out on cloths on the ground, in harmonious arrangements. Produce sat warming in the hot sun. Dates of many varieties, both fresh and dried, and figs too. Watermelons and other melons. Hot peppers of many shapes and sizes. Green and purple grapes. Peacock feathers. Hand-made flax and hemp cloth from family looms. Cracked corn and wheat for animal feed. Rendered animal fat for cooking and lamps. Fresh fish from the River and chunks of meat, dripping bloodily. Necklaces, armlets, anklets, rings, and earrings made of many materials—faience glass, polished lapis lazuli, malachite, azurite, turquoise from Bakhet, amber, and gold—for those wealthy enough to afford it. Carved and polished alabaster vases. Earthenware pottery designed for many uses—from cooking and baking, to water jugs, eating bowls, pitchers, mugs, oil burners, and flower vases. Sturdy hemp ropes of all lengths and thicknesses were to be found. Carved camel bone and goat bone hair fasteners and other personal items for decoration. Emollient face and body oils made from a mixture of precious oils, honey, goats milk, spices, and myrrh to protect one's skin from the arid climate. Cactus plants, whose yearly flowers were delicious. Golden honey fresh from local hives. Bowls of dried black, yellow and red lentils, fava beans and chickpeas. Dried grapes. Freshly-made bread. Grains for cooking. Copper knives and cutting tools. Imported carved and polished wooden items from Kush, very rare and expensive, meant for the wealthier citizens of Waset. The rekkit would have to content themselves with wooden items made from common acacia, tamarisk, or sycamore trees. Stone plows. A couple of dark-skinned slaves and a few indentured servants, willing to work hard on your land. Palm fronds for fans and fencing. Dried meat and salted fish in oil. Bows and arrows for hunting. Reed baskets and fishing nets. And finally Sacred amulets of Neterw, ankhs, and djed pillars made from wood, stone, or precious gemstones—blessed at Enet-ta-Neter, Abtu, Nubt, and Per Auset Temples.

Some vendors were hawking pieces of beef, goat, lamb, goose, and fish cooking on small braziers. Delightful aromas arose from the smoking and spitting food roasting over the hot coals. "I'm hungry," I mentioned to Muttuy as we wandered from booth to booth, my mouth watering in anticipation.

"We are almost finished," she replied. She stopped and fingered a lapis lazuli armlet lovingly, then put it back. They were a poor family, so luxuries were out of the question.

After we had traded for items we needed, Muttuy and I returned home, passing the Nile as we did so. Women and girls were washing clothes on rocks lining the river. They were bent over, beating each piece of clothing on rocks, then wringing out the water with reddened hands. A few children were being bathed too, while others played and splashed in the cool water. Today the Holy River was calm and deep blue, sparkling gently in the sunlight. Other times it was ominously dark purple, with waves washing the banks. Often at atmu, as the sun disk was falling into Nut's black, star-filled sky, the river glowed redly from Ra's reflection.

During inundation, filled with soil washed down from rainfall in the southern mountains, the black swirling water was sometimes impossible to navigate. Udimu and I stayed home then, repairing nets. The town was set far back from the banks of Mother Nile, to avoid being flooded during those times. However, farmers looked forward to that special time, where the land would become fertilized by all that rich, black silt overflowing the land. The rest of the year they would have to labor from dawn to dark, sweating by the fiery light of Ra. If they were lucky or wealthy, they would have water buffalo to help them till the furrows. If not they would spend many back-breaking hours bending over the damp soil, hoeing, then placing each precious seed in the furrows. That way, water would evaporate less in the lower level of ground, conserving the precious, life sustaining liquid.

Wealthier farmers had constructed a system of wooden dikes and gates leading from the Nile to irrigate their land. Donkeys and other animals plodded around and around, moving the waterwheels which then pumped the water from the river onto the land. Otherwise a farmer and his entire family would have to laboriously hand-carry pouches of water to the plants each and every day. Once in a while it would rain, but never enough to irrigate properly.

When Muttuy and I arrived home, the family gathered around us, eager to see what we had bought. Muttuy had purchased a number of items. Precious sea salt from the Northern Oasis, traded many times until it arrived at our home. The goat cheese. A large packet of lentils and another of fava beans. Tiny parcels of cumin, coriander, and mustard. Some cabbage and horseradish. A few dates and date sugar. Some flax material and a length of rope. Two sharp fishhooks to replace older ones that had broken. "These are made out of a special new metal called bronze," Muttuy explained proudly. "They are supposed to stay sharp longer than the copper ones we use." She had traded well today. She unloaded a packet of grapes dried into raisins.

Her two daughters grabbed the raisins, running outside before we could stop them, stuffing the plump raisins into their mouths.

Muttuy shook her head in mock anger. "Udimu," she turned to her husband. "Why don't you go catch a duck? I noticed some down by the river. I'll roast it for a special feast tonight."

The man nodded, collected his bow and arrows, and went out to capture our succulent main dish.

The large woman squatted on the ground in front of the food mat and began chopping onions and some garlic in preparation. Then she got out a sunbaked oven pot, added the onions, garlic, the raw beans and lentils, sprinkling mint, dill, and thyme on top, then pouring enough water over the mixture to stew it. She paused, wiped her brow, checked on the bread dough she had left in an earthenware bowl earlier in the day, ready for baking.

My stomach made gurgling noises as I watched her preparations. Hoping to speed up the cooking process, I put several more sticks of wood into the clay oven, which caught fire right away.

Muttuy deftly sliced some ripe cucumbers she had picked from a nearby vine into a bowl, adding a little vinegar and salt. Finally she took out the bread dough, patted it, shaping it into a round flat loaf, pressed some sesame seeds into the top, and put it into the now-hot oven. When Udimu returned with the fat duck he had caught, she then plucked and gutted it, cut it into pieces, basted the pieces with oil and sesame seeds, and added it to the onion, garlic and bean mixture. Then she put the stewing bowl with its fragrant ingredients on top of the oven to cook. Our dinner would be a feast, worthy of a noble house tonight. I then thought of Catfish's royal mother and father and sighed, remembering the Palace meals, each one a banquet compared to our meager supper.

When Muttuy was satisfied that dinner was progressing nicely, she cut off a tiny piece of goat cheese and handed it to Catfish, who stood watching the preparations. He immediately popped it into his mouth, sucking the soft, salty cheese. The baby, as I had told Atalana that magical night on the River bank, was growing fast. He was learning to walk. He had a number of teeth—and he talked. That boy talked. Perhaps it was the time he spent with the voluble Muttuy, or maybe it was a natural inheritance from his intelligent mother.

He was asking questions all the time. He was inquisitive about everything and everyone. I think the first word he uttered was "why?" He was coddled and cuddled and fussed over by everyone in the house. Muttuy called him "the prince." Although others took the name as a joke, I knew what she meant. Catfish called her "nana." And he called me "Heb."

I was worried he would become spoiled with all the attention, but Muttuy was firm. "This child will need all the love that we can give him and more. He must have a strong foundation that is based on love and caring. He must know that he has a family that stands behind him, supporting him. He will have enough burdens to think about later on." Her words made sense to me and I didn't question her.

Although Bashta still nursed Atalana's child, she did so less and less often, as he learned to eat solid food. She spent much of her time away from the house, to avoid me I surmised. Catfish had the usual mother-child relationship with Muttuy instead. When the boy once asked me where his father was, I quietly answered "Your father has gone to live with Ausar." My answer seemed to satisfy Catfish and he didn't ask again.

One late afternoon Bashta came into the main room from outside, bringing a man with her. I recognized him as one of our near neighbors. Although I recognized him by sight and had often greeted him, I didn't really know him at all. He was accompanied by Sebat. Bashta was blushing and went outside to the cooking area to find her mother and father and bring them back inside with her. The neighbor and I eyed each other up and down, like two dogs sniffing out unfamiliar territory. The atmosphere wasn't unfriendly, just awkward. I was the first to speak. I smiled. "Please sit and be at peace," I welcomed him.

Yet when Bashta returned with Muttuy and Udimu, the man was still standing bashfully, shuffling from one foot to the other, folding his arms across his chest, then unfolding them. Bashta went over to his side and took his hand. "This is Tenti," she announced. "He has asked me to marry him," she concluded with her usual and direct simplicity.

Muttuy cast a quick look at me, but I was smiling broadly. "Congratulations," I said. "To both of you."

The matronly woman crossed the room and clapped the man on the back. "So you are the one who has occupied my daughter all this time?" She laughed good-naturedly. "Welcome to the family," and she hugged him so tightly he gasped for air. Udimu clasped hands with Tenti. And in this uncomplicated manner, the betrothal was finalized.

Muttuy got out some beer and bread and together we celebrated the coming event. Sebat climbed up on the man's lap, already familiar and comfortable with him. As I observed Bashta and Sebat with him, his gentleness and good humor impressed me. On Muttuy too, who was beaming the whole time. Tenti had the temerity to debate the town's affairs with the matriarch, so he was strong minded as well. And most importantly, he clearly adored Bashta. I was glad for her, surprised and pleased at my reaction. Even though I didn't love her, I could have been jealous. But I found no such emotion. Suddenly I felt very old, as if I was not a young man any more but an Elder. Where and how had I come to be this way? Het-Heru and my evening prayers came to mind.

Catfish was weaned very soon after that afternoon. A simple ceremony was held shortly thereafter in the family home and Bashta and Tenti were pronounced married. She and Sebat left with their few simple belongings the same day. Since they were only moving down the dusty street a short distance away, there were no long farewells. We would be able to see them often. Catfish was to remain with Muttuy and Udimu.

A strange emptiness pervaded our home for some time. I missed Sebat's constant running through the house, laughing and playing with her cousins. She had been part of my life. And yet, at the same time, I also felt detached. She was not really my daughter, only by accident of blood. Sebat belonged to Bashta and her new husband Tenti far more than she ever did to me. And Catfish was bonded with Muttuy. Detachment was not a word I had entertained before, but I thought about it a lot after Bashta's wedding. I was detached from everyone it seemed. Did I truly love anyone? Was I close to a single soul? The answer rose from deep within me. Het-Heru and Atalana. They were my family.

When I realized the depth, the truth of this, an idea came to me. Or perhaps Atalana's words had inspired me. Suddenly I knew that I must return to Enet-ta-Neter.

I broached the subject with Muttuy and to my surprise, she was encouraging. "I think that is a wonderful idea. You must go," she advised me. "This will always be your home, but perhaps there is something calling you to the Temple. Catfish will be just fine with us. What would you do with a small child, anyhow?"

"I don't know what to say. I'm not even sure what I'm looking for."

"You will find out. I know," and she put her finger to my heart. "The answer is within you and in time you will know. But please remember what I say. This is your home and you will always be welcome here, to stay or go as you please."

"The moon will be full in a few days. I'd like to go right away."

The kind woman smiled. "I will ask Udimu if he will take you there tomorrow."

Words caught in my throat, so I hugged her instead. I was blessed with having known some very wise and powerful women. Muttuy not least among them.

Udimu took me in his felucca early the next morning. We had with us some provisions from Muttuy, bread, a pouch of beer, some dried fish, a few dates. It was a long trip up the Nile and she knew we'd be hungry long before we arrived at the Holy Temple. I felt excited and more alive than I'd felt in ages. I was anxious to get there, but it was hours before we arrived at the pier at the outskirts of Enet-ta-Neter. I practically leaped out of the boat, helped Udimu tie it up, and together we quickly walked through the portal to the entrance of Het-Heru's Sacred Home.

Crops were growing in the field. Cows and goats wandered around. It looked similar to when I left it. Was it even in this lifetime? It seemed so long ago when I had been there with Atalana. As I entered, I felt the surge of energy and power enter me as I did the first time. My heart quickened a beat or two. I led the shy Udimu to the kitchen. Shara-Het was seated on a stool, sewing a torn garment with a tiny bone needle. When she saw me cross the threshold, she stood up and came right over to me.

"Heb, how wonderful to see you again!" She gave me a quick hug and turned to see Udimu.

"Shara-Het, this is Udimu. My…um…father."

"I'm pleased to meet you."

Udimu grunted in his common taciturn way in reply.

She turned back to me. "Are you hungry?"

"Famished," I told her.

"Sit here. I will prepare something for both of you."

Soon we were eating delicious hot and spicy soup made with green vegetables, chickpeas, and hot peppers, with flat bread to sop it up with. We had fresh Nile water to drink. As we ate, Shara-Het chatted about the Temple. New initiates had arrived, but not as many as formerly. "I think the younger people are not as interested as once we were."

"Hmmp," I replied, my mouth partially full.

"Would you like to visit Mukalia when you're done?"

"What?" I exclaimed, turning pale, almost choking on my food. "But…"

"No, my dear. I mean her bones."

"For a moment, I thought you meant…"

Shara-Het laughed merrily at my consternation. "I'm sorry. I forget that you are not entirely accustomed to our ways." The older woman continued to shake with laughter. Her thinning hair billowed around her head like a white veil.

I joined in, both of us laughing at my confusion. Soon both of us were roaring with laughter. It felt good to laugh again. "It is wonderful to be here," I said, when I could finally muster some words.

She gently touched my hand affectionately. "It is good for you to be here."

"I don't think I'm ready, though. To visit Mukalia." I remembered my trepidation on my last visit to the crypt.

"That's all right, Heb. Whenever you are ready." She grinned a little. "Mukalia isn't going anywhere."

Shara-Het made arrangements for Udimu and me to sleep in the guest quarters. I slept soundly and dreamlessly that night. The older man left early the next morning. He would sail back to Waset, to Muttuy, to Catfish and the girls. As he left, I thanked him and then went to go find Shara-Het. I found her down by the Sacred Lake, basking in the warm sunshine.

"Good morning, Heb. Has your father left already?"

"Yes, he did. He asked me to thank you for your hospitality."

She smiled. "He's not your father, is he?"

I wondered how she knew. "No, but it is a long story."

"I could use a long story right now," and she grinned at me.

Thus encouraged, I told the Elder Priestess everything. About Bashta and me. The death of Atalana. Pharaoh giving the baby Catfish to me to protect. The flight from Abtu Palace. Being taken in by Bashta's family. Everything. Except for one important detail I had sworn to withhold.

"We had heard about Atalana," said Shara-Het softly. "I felt very sad."

"Yes, it was a terrible tragedy and…"

"I mean I'm very sorry for your loss. I know what she meant to you."

Startled by her compassionate words, I felt the old familiar pain again. "I thought I was over it."

"I know," and she patted my hand. "You are twin souls who found each other, but weren't destined to make a life together this time."

My rebellious eyes welled up and I cleared my throat, wiping my eyes. In a voice husky with emotion, I asked, "How do you know all this?"

"It is my job as Hem Neter to know more than most people." She looked at me with tremendous kindness. "I miss her, too. She was like my daughter."

The two of us sat for a long time in silence, feeling the sun at our backs. I was infinitely comforted by someone knowing the truth at last. I didn't have to pretend or make excuses or feel guilty. The breeze blew around me. I could hear the scream of a falcon overhead. Insects buzzed in the air. I sighed in the simple pleasure of the day.

Shara-Het was the first to break the delicious silence. "So, Heb. Why have you come here?"

Her direct question surprised me into a quick answer. "Het-Heru has called me home," I replied without thinking.

"Hmmm," was her answer, then continued. "You know this is a Temple for Priestesses."

"Yes, I know. But perhaps an exception could be made?"

"Perhaps. I have never known a man whom Het-Heru has called to Her Service before now. Yet…you do have a strong connection to Her." I could tell she was thinking out loud, trying to make a decision. She stood up. "I will go and invoke Her right now and ask what She wants us to do." With that, she left quickly and walked to the Temple.

I knew the answer before Shara-Het returned. I would become the first Priest at Enet-ta-Neter. Yet my training had begun long before.

CHAPTER FOURTEEN

SHARA-HET AND ACCEPTANCE

I was still sitting by the sacred Lake when Shara-Het returned. As she walked up to me, I was grinning broadly. I knew what she would say.

"So, it is arranged," she smiled back. "I have been at Enet-ta-Neter most of my life and have never seen a Priest in residence here before. You must be very beloved by the Neter, considering the changes that we must make in your behalf."

"I don't know about that," I replied humbly. "I only know She has always been with me, now more than ever."

"All right, then," Shara-Het continued. "You will stay in the guest quarters permanently. We will build for a special house for you there, so that you are undisturbed by our full moon visitors. Het-Heru will not allow you to sleep in the Priestess' quarters. At least, not yet."

"Uh huh," I murmured drowsily. I didn't care if I had to sleep on the rocky ground, under the stars of Nut's belly.

"We will arrange for you to get white robes, for rituals. A lady in a village near here makes them for us. You will need to visit her today, so she can fit you properly. You may eat with us and share ceremonies with us, and be here on the temple grounds all day long. There are many who will delight in your training. Except for special rituals and meals, you must return to your house outside the perimeter when darkness falls."

"That is fine with me," I agreed.

"You will rise before dawn, bathe in the Sacred Lake, dress in your white robe, once you have it, then join us in the Sanctuary for morning ceremonies." The Hem Neter looked very serious, giving me instructions, and I refrained from chuckling. "Then you will change into your ordinary robe and join the other initiates in their daily training. This could also involve cooking meals, cleaning the premises, and tending to the garden and our animals. During the full moon, you will work with different Priestesses, to learn the various forms of healing with our patients." I nodded.

"As with the other initiates, if you are found lacking in the necessary spirit, you will be asked to leave." Now she smiled broadly. "I somehow don't think that will happen, however."

"Thank you, Shara-Het. I will do my very best."

"I know you will, Heb." She wrinkled up her forehead. "I have a feeling that your initiation process will be greatly speeded up. You may be ordained much sooner than most." She motioned for me to follow her and we walked to the kitchen/dining area. When we arrived, I was cordially greeted by all who had met me during my last visit. In all, there were 122 women and girls at Enet-ta-Neter, of varying ages. There were a few initiated Priestesses; some who were still in training. Most however, were women and girls from the local villages, spending the inundation time in service to Het-Heru. Their ages varied from about eight or nine inundations, to Shara-Het, the oldest woman in residence, now that Mukalia had passed on to the next world.

One Priestess walked up to me. "Hello, Heb. Do you remember me?"

I instantly recognized her face, but couldn't remember her name. "Yes, you are...ah..."

"Tietra-Het," she helped me.

"I'm sorry," I apologized. "I remember our conversation, but couldn't recall your name."

"That's all right." She smiled benignly.

Shara-Het broke in. "Tietra-Het, would you take Heb to the village seamstress? He will need to be fitted for some temple garments right away."

"Of course," the younger woman replied. "I would be honored."

"Why don't you have something to eat first?"

The whole company of Priestesses, Initiates and others, gathered around and we helped ourselves to the cold luncheon. Once Tietra-Het and I had eaten our fill, we bade farewell to the others and began our short trek to the village.

"You look very different from when I last saw you," she began conversationally. "You are much thinner now."

"Hum, yes, I believe I am."

"I heard about the terrible events at the Palace. It was a great tragedy. You were very close to the King and Queen, I believe." She was being deliberately vague and I appreciated it.

"I was, yes." I changed the subject to something far less painful. "How long will it take to get there?"

"Not too long. We will be able to go and return before night falls."

"That's good," I replied. "Is it safe around here?"

"None of us has ever had any trouble."

"I just don't want to be recognized by anyone outside of the Temple."

We walked for a while in silence, picking our way along the sandy gravel on the narrow path along the river bank to the nearby village. I glanced sidelong at the young woman. She seemed younger than Atalana, certainly far less distinguished and self-confident. But of course, she wasn't a Queen. "How did you happen to be chosen for Enet-ta-Neter?"

"We are traveling to my home village. Young girls are often asked to serve at the Temple during inundation, since we cannot farm during flood time. I went to the Temple for a few inundations. I felt more at home there than at the home of my family. One day I was called to see Shara-Het at Mukalia's hut."

"You knew Mukalia?"

"Oh, yes, she was a wonderful woman. We all loved her very much."

"I'm sorry to interrupt you. Please go on."

"Mukalia had wanted to see me. She asked me if I would like to stay and begin training to become a Priestess. I told her that I would like that very much. And from that day on, I lived at Enet-ta-Neter. I am pleased that I had the Calling."

I enjoyed Tietra-Het's simple way of speaking. As we walked on, I became more and more at ease in her presence. "How long have you been there?"

"Let me see." She counted on her fingers. "I think it has been about fifteen or so inundations since I was called."

She wasn't much older than me. We were practically contemporaries, except that we were generations apart in experience. I could tell that Tietra-Het wanted to say more. I allowed her to talk without encouragement.

Finally, and with some hesitation, she asked, "Do you miss her?"

"Who?" I asked blandly, deliberately elusive, although I blushed uncontrollably. I was glad to be walking behind her on the narrow trail. For some reason I also enjoyed teasing her.

"The Queen. Atalana."

I stopped my teasing immediately. "Yes. I miss her very much," I said simply.

"Oh…" was her only response and she looked ahead, quiet, withdrawn into herself.

We continued the rest of our walk in awkward silence. Awkward, I think on her part. I was enjoying the sunny day and seeing the new country around me. I felt good to have a purpose, again. To know what each day would bring and to learn new things. I strode along, humming to myself.

Once we arrived in the village, Tietra-Het was greeted by some of the villagers. She greeted them in return, but took me directly to the home of the seamstress, a tiny woman who bustled around, taking my measurements, sometimes having to stand on a chair to reach my shoulders and chest. Very quickly she was done.

"Come back day after tomorrow and I'll have these ready for you," she told me. "Would you like something to eat or drink?"

"No thank you," Tietra-Het replied. "We must return right away." I thanked the woman, and we headed back to Enet-ta-Neter.

"You're a very tall man," she giggled, out of earshot of the village seamstress.

I smiled in return. "She's a funny little lady," I replied.

"But an excellent tailor."

Having nothing more to say, I walked on steadily in the late afternoon. The sun was still hot, but not unbearable. We nibbled on some dried fruit, not stopping. Tietra-Het seemed to be in a hurry to get back to the Temple and I followed her lead. Once we returned, she turned to me. "I must go now," she murmured and walked off in the direction of the dormitory.

"Thank you," I called after her.

She waved in response.

Not knowing what to do with myself now, I wandered around the Temple enclosure. I found myself heading towards Mukalia's hut and changed course. I wasn't ready to see her empty habitation. The sun was getting low and soon I would have to go to the guests' quarters. I wondered if it had been made ready for me yet. I don't know if I was getting good at mentally calling others, or whether I had picked up the signal myself. But Shara-Het appeared, as if she had magickly emerged from the sand below my feet.

"Would you like to see where you will stay?"

"Yes," I replied. "I was just wondering about that."

She smiled and led me past the wall, to a small room apart from the other guest quarters. My small bag of belongings was already there. It seemed comfortable enough.

"We will see you at our evening ritual, followed by our meal. In time you will participate in it." And Shara-Het left quietly.

My little room was in a hut made of mud brick, as all houses were. However, unlike palaces, these walls were bare of decoration or whitewash. A wash basin with water in it stood on a low table near the door. I washed briskly, changed into a clean kilt, and walked to the Temple for the evening ritual with Het-Heru. I hummed a little tune of my own making as I walked, happy for the first time in years. Truly happy—and at peace.

CHAPTER FIFTEEN

A PRIEST OF HET-HERU

My time spent in the Temple was exciting and rewarding. The other Initiates felt as I did, having been called by Het-Heru to some Divine Purpose. We shared that in common.

The first lesson I received was simple. Everyone in the Temple had an assignment. Each one was as essential to the running of the Temple as any other; there wasn't a hierarchy of importance at Enet-ta-Neter. No occupation and no individual was more or less important than any other. We were all part of the divine organism known as the Temple, "Per Neter", home of the Neter.

There were ordinary tasks such as sweeping the floor of the Sanctuary or pulling weeds, tending animals or cleaning up after meals. These were usually performed by the Initiates and others in temporary service to the Temple. However, only the Initiates would learn and practice the details of the Twelve Holy Tasks, while ordained Priestesses normally didn't share the more mundane concerns of the Temple.

Sacred Tasks included purification, communicating with the Neter, chanting the appropriate words of the litanies, or organizing and ordering supplies.

Shara-Het had one Sacred Task for many years, that of Sentyt, Sacred Oracle and Astrologer, the Priestess overseeing Divine Timing. She was currently undergoing training as an Initiate, to eventually become ordained as Hem Neter, the vastly important job of Senior Priestess, running the entire Temple as both servant and physical incarnation of the Neter Het-Heru. Before her, Mukalia had embodied that role, at least nominally after she became physically ill. But, because of the great love and respect for the old Muan, no one had been willing to take over that service until Mukalia's body had departed the living world. Even in her depleted physical state, the amazing Muan Elder could hold the energy of the Temple together almost more than anyone else at Enet-ta-Neter.

During the learning of the duties and responsibilities of each Sacred Task, I discovered that one must also learn personal accomplishments: learning how to quiet one's mind and body, how to encourage visions, and how to intuit the presence of the Neter. Also one must learn how to comfortably operate in both the mundane and divine worlds equally well. An initiate was instructed in how to purify oneself prior to rituals in the Sacred Lake and how to paint holy symbols on one's body. Since Enet-ta-Neter was also a Dream Temple, one had to learn how to interpret one's own dreams as well as that of others. Het-Heru's Temple was a place of healing and midwifery (like the Great Golden Lady Herself) so we had to study healing herbs, potions and magical chants, as well as to develop a compassionate manner in dealing with sick or troubled people, along with pregnant women ready to give birth.

Once all these skills and tasks had been acquired at a reasonable level of competence, one was ordained as Priest or Priestess.

Then a second training and initiation period was conducted for the complete absorption into, and the study of, one specific Sacred Task. Each Sacred Temple task was rotated periodically; one would not hold a Sacred

Task for life. However, a Priestess, or in my case a Priest, could expect to hold a position for a length of time inundations long. Training for a Sacred Task was too intense to change frequently. One must acquire ever deeper understanding of the current Task before one moved on to another. If a Priestess died in service, another would begin the Initiation process to fill that position. A Priestess could be initiated into several Divine Tasks in her lifetime, but certainly not all Twelve.

At the beginning of the yearly inundation, Priests and Initiates from Nubt would make the trek to Enet-ta-Neter. Then Nubt Priests and Het-Heru Priestesses would come together to reenact the marriage of Heru and Het-Heru. Outside of the ritual, however, they were discouraged from becoming too friendly.

Tietra-Het stayed a distance away from me following our afternoon together. We didn't have any further personal conversations. She was a Mer Priestess, overseeing the specific physical needs of the Temple. Our conversations were therefore limited to mundane matters or participating in rituals. I didn't question her decision, but was relieved not to be involved on any deeper level with her. I intuited that she was attracted to me. I didn't want to repeat the difficult lessons I had learned from my time with Bashta. I was ready to learn selflessness, not requiring a woman to care for my needs.

I learned my priestly duties well and enjoyed working on behalf of those who journeyed to our Temple for our assistance. My inner life with Het-Heru was full, and I was rarely lonely.

As I trained to become a Priest of Het-Heru, I noticed that my personality, character, even my physical body and sensations began to change. I was becoming more like Het-Heru in every way—a healer, visionary, oracle, compassionate, kind and loving, while appreciating and experiencing the joyous, healthy, sensual side of physical life as a divine heritage. I had always enjoyed food and drink, touch and sensation, beautiful scenes and agreeable aromas, but these became elevated, sacred experiences. I felt blissful when I partook of simple physical pleasures. Just as my ghostly visit from Atalana helped me understand I was training myself to become a Priest, so my program within the Celestial Energy of the Temple was training me to become an earthly version of Het-Heru.

This all-important detail was never divulged or even recognized until one was actually in training. The power of wanting to become a Neter might draw those people only interested in misusing power for their own personal gain. Rather, as I developed more heavenly instincts, humility and a desire to serve our community became foremost in my awareness.

I began to understand that Pharaoh, as High Priest of the Kingdom, had a tremendous responsibility to lead appropriately, to be a humble servant of the people he served. His position was not one of absolute authority over his people. Rather it was his task to merge the mundane world of Ta-Meir Res with the magickal and divine world of the Neterw—in the spirit of Ma'at—to create balance, justice, peace, and harmony for all.

I was delighted that my ability to scribe and understand hieroglyphics could be put to good use in the position of Kher Heb.

Not only that, but I learned to keep records when I was Custodian and Overseer in Pharaoh's Palace, another function of Kher Heb.

The Sacred Task of Kher Heb entailed not only keeping all the written records of the Temple, but also Reciter of the Holy Words during a ritual service. My former training in the Royal Palace helped me learn the new tasks faster than usual. I didn't have to learn hieroglyphics from the beginning and I already was skilled in keeping records. Once I had completed my first initiatory process and was ordained as Priest of Het-Heru, I began my training for Kher Heb, Keeper of the Sacred Papyrus.

One day after our morning ritual, I began practicing the Sacred Litany in the Sanctuary for the upcoming Festival of Het-Heru. Het-Heru's Special Day would be celebrated soon, within the span of a moon's cycle. I wanted to make sure I pronounced each divine word perfectly. This would be my first time, as Initiate for Kher Heb, to perform the long litany in public and I confess I was a little nervous.

My hope was to be a good initiator; to evoke, through the words of the Sacred Text, the essence of Het-Heru. My baritone voice reverberated off the Temple walls as I practiced out loud. Surprisingly, my voice sounded pleasing; I had never been a singer, so I had no way to know my natural ability. I remembered that my Mother was supposed to have a beautiful singing voice. Holding the ancient Rite papyrus in my hands, I found a certain rhythm of chanting came naturally to me. I remembered Atalana and Mukalia singing to me and how that helped to heal my pain. Suddenly I understood my role in the Temple. Words of Power, Hekau, spoken correctly, melodiously, and with the correct tempo and pitch, had the power to heal!

Thus, the process of becoming Kher Heb entailed more than I could have ever guessed. As I realized this, my skin was covered with gooseflesh. If I had any hair left, it would have stood on end. This was a realization of major proportions. I wanted to jump up and down and laugh out loud at my discovery. Oh, how I wanted to share my new-found knowledge with Atalana! No one else was with me in the Sanctuary. So instead I grinned to myself.

I had extra papyrus at hand and wrote down what I had just intuited about sound. Although other Kher Hebs must have realized what I did, I wanted to preserve it for future generations of Priests and Priestesses. I thought about all the miracles that had transpired in my life up to this moment. Perhaps I should write them all down. Thus, I made a momentous decision to record my life history. I temporarily forgot Het-Heru's Celebration in my excitement.

I decided this was to be my own personal journal, one that would record my journey and help me to become a better Priest. As I wrote, I made connections between what I had learned in the Temple and what I had experienced in life.

I paused as I thought of Atalana again, this time in a whole new light. She was a Priestess of Het-Heru. She had been trained as I had been trained. When she had become a Queen, she was still a Priestess. When she and I were together here in Enet-ta-Neter, she was a fully-ordained Priestess. So she must have held one of those Twelve Sacred Tasks. What was it?

I began to think in reverse, to try to remember everything she had said and done while I knew her. She couldn't be a Sentyt, since that was the task of Shara-Het at the time. Mukalia was the only officiating Hem Neter. I doubted Atalana was a Kher Heb, since she didn't seem to know the intricate hieroglyphics as I did. What was she then? I thought about all the Sacred Tasks available:

> Khener—holy chanter and singer
>
> Ur Hekau—professor of magickal words
>
> Sau—protector of the sacred space
>
> Senu—physician
>
> Mer—overseer of goods and supplies
>
> Uab—purifier
>
> Hem—hostess
>
> Maa—seer and communicator with Het-Heru
>
> Setem—keeper of offerings.

Although I would never know for sure, I decided that Atalana must have held the Sacred Position of Maa. Her abilities of divine seeing and working with Het-Heru appeared to be the greatest of her many assets. I remembered the Ceremony before and during our sacred lovemaking, how Atalana appeared to embody Het-Heru. Memories of that precious time filled me with joy and I smiled. Atalana had taken charge of all that transpired that momentous night. Her combined passion and sensuality sent me out of my body into the stars. I remembered the star-child that we connected with in the realm of Nut. I had sent my seed to him through Atalana. Her connection to Het-Heru was therefore strong, as we created that child within her womb. The child of Pharaoh. The next Pharaoh, if luck had anything to do with it.

Atalana was very close to Mukalia who, as Hem Neter, was the incarnation of Het-Heru on the physical plane. Did Mukalia train Atalana for a new and highly important duty, one not usually taught at the Temple? How odd that Mukalia could have lived for thousands of years, yet died the day after my momentous lovemaking with Atalana.

Since Het-Heru is the Divine Mother of Pharaoh, I must have participated in the deliberate creation of a Pharaoh, through Atalana, one of Her most beloved Priestesses.

Atalana told me that Ankhamun had been unable to fulfill his duties as husband. Thus Atalana was still a virgin when we had joined in the unbearably ecstatic merging to make the child, Catfish. The blood on her legs and mine was testimony to her virginal status. Yet, Atalana seemed to know all of the joys, positions, and techniques of physical love. How had that occurred? Was she trained to do so? Did Atalana learn about human love making as part of her duties as a Priestess of Het-Heru? Did the Sacred Ceremonial Ritual of the Marriage of Heru and Het-Heru include physical lovemaking techniques? Was Atalana the one who participated in that Marriage Ritual?

Thinking back further still, I remembered that Pharaoh Ankhamun had gone to Enet-ta-Neter to encourage fertility, so that he could have an heir. We servants had heard that he participated in mysterious fertility rites and rituals. Was Atalana part of those rituals as well? He then had fallen in love with Atalana and made her his Queen. I remembered also that the first time I had seen Atalana she had reminded me of Het-Heru. Was that part of her duty as Priestess? Was she supposed to bring the incarnation of Het-Heru into her physical being, into the Palace, in order to make a child, a royal child? If Ankhamun was a Royal Servant of the Neterw, maybe Atalana was also!

She told me that she had a vision before her Wedding, that Pharaoh would remain childless. She had married the King anyway. Did she know that there would be another man, a man who was close to Pharaoh, loyal in every way, who could help bring a child into being?

I was breathless. Was everything planned with Het-Heru, Pharaoh, and the Priesthood acting together as one for the greatest good of Ta-Meir Res? Was I part of the plan as well?

If so, no wonder that Het-Heru came to visit me.

No wonder I had dreams of protecting Pharaoh.

No wonder the King had gone to Enet-ta-Neter and had fallen in love with Atalana.

No wonder Atalana decided to marry Ankhamun anyway, even knowing that she could not have a child with him.

No wonder I had fallen in love with her and that Atalana had chosen me to have a child with.

No wonder I practiced being in touch with Het-Heru every evening on the banks of the Nile.

No wonder I had come to this moment of discovery.

"She must have known that we would come together, that she would have a child with me!!" I shouted those words out loud and looked around quickly. No one had heard or seen me. I would have to protect my writing and still my enthusiastic tongue. I could not divulge my discoveries. Catfish must not be put at risk. Too much planning had gone into bringing him to life to endanger him now.

I wanted to see Shara-Het, to ask her questions. I forced myself to practice the Sacred Litany first, knowing that I might not have any more time today. Once I had finished, I rushed out of the Sanctuary to find the older Priestess.

Shara-Het was in the kitchen by herself, eating dried fruit. "Heb," she greeted me warmly. "How is the practice going?"

"Very well," I replied, my excitement showing through.

"What is it, Heb?" I'm sure she could intuit my excitement, although it wouldn't take an oracle to do so at this moment.

"I, um, well, that is, I need to know about Atalana." I was apprehensive. What if she didn't know the answers?

"Come with me," she replied, smiling. I followed her to the peace and sunshine at the Sacred Lake. We were alone; no one else was around. She sat down on a stone bench near the water. I sat on the warm ground at her feet. I had always liked Shara-Het. Now that she was becoming Hem Neter, I felt a growing spirituality in her.

"What has gotten you so excited?" she asked me gently.

"I don't know where to start."

"At the beginning is always a good idea."

"Yes, you're right." I told her of my chanting and my subsequent reve-lation about it. "Chanting the sacred words promotes healing," I added breathlessly.

"That's correct, Heb," she replied.

"It is?" I was astonished at the veracity of my discovery.

"Of course."

"But no one ever told me."

"Being an Initiate and then a Priest mean that you learn wisdom your-self. We can teach you the ceremonies and prayers, but you must go further, discovering the wisdom for yourself. Once you are able to do that, you will never forget the wisdom, unlike prayers you simply memorize. We allow and encourage people to arrive at their own understanding in their own way and time."

"I see," I replied.

She motioned at the Per Neter complex of Het-Heru all around us. "All of these buildings, columns, walls, carvings, statues, and altars contain the stimulus for you to glean the hidden wisdom. They are like doorways into sacred realms. Wisdom is embodied in the physical Temple, through many generations of sacred practice, as well as brought here by Het-Heru herself. When you study and live in the Temple, wisdom enters through your eyes, permeates your skin and bones, and becomes a part of you."

"Oh...." I said, as more realizations beginning to surface within me. "I can learn only so much from you; then I must learn the rest by myself."

"Yes. We have no magickal formula for wisdom. And wisdom is the goal of all of us here at the Temple, even when we don't yet know it. Wisdom cannot be taught. It can only be learned through the body and senses. Without wisdom, one cannot truly become a Priest or Priestess." I nodded.

The older woman continued. "That is why it takes a few people longer than others to be ordained. You were accepted into the temple because you had already learned much of the wisdom. We knew you could readily access divine information, so you would be a wonderful applicant to our Temple.

"I have questions that came up after I understood about sacred sound."

"What is that, my boy?"

"Was my relationship with Atalana and all the things that happened to me ordained by Het-Heru?"

"You must ask Het-Heru herself for the answer to that. I couldn't tell you."

"Do you know?" I was not to be put off by her vague answer.

"Even if I did know, it wouldn't be appropriate to tell you. So you must ask the Golden One."

I wrinkled up my face at being put off by the Initiate of Hem Neter. "All right then. I have another question." She smiled benignly.

"Was Atalana taught by Mukalia—to perform sacred rituals of the flesh?" I gulped with embarrassment as I asked the question.

"Do you mean did she act as Het-Heru in matters of lovemaking?"

"Yes," I replied. "That is what I mean."

"Atalana was one of the most gifted Priestesses I have ever known. She was chosen by Het-Heru at a very young age. She left a wealthy, comfortable noble home to live and study with us. Early on she showed a great ability to manifest the Mistress of Heaven through her own body. Although this was the task of Mukalia as Hem Neter, the wise old Muan elder decided to teach all of what she knew to Atalana. Not just the knowledge of Enet-ta-Neter and Ta-Meir Res but also of Mu. The Muans believed that the physical body was a holy temple. Thus everything that the body experienced was holy and sacred, including all manifestations of lovemaking. Although Atalana was never allowed to experience the ultimate fulfillment of love that might bring a child into the world, she was taught everything else that might pass between a man and a woman.

"But she was a virgin."

"Yes, she was a virgin. Atalana practiced these methods once a year, with various Priests of Heru from Nubt, at the Festival of Het-Heru."

"The one I am studying the litany for?"

"Yes, the very same one. Interesting that you are getting messages about Atalana at this time, isn't it?" She sighed. "Of course, this training only began once she had reached her moon time and was becoming a grown woman."

"Of course," I agreed, taking a deep breath, thinking of the possibility of Atalana being intimate with other men.

"Atalana became so proficient in these abilities that she began to perform healing for men who came to the Temple, those who were unable to experience lovemaking. Remember that in no way did she take the place of the wives of these men. Rather she became the embodiment of Het-Heru, evoking and manifesting the divine loving and spiritual sensuality of the Neter to heal these men."

I felt pangs of jealousy as Shara-Het continued her narrative and struggled to get past it.

Shara-Het must have intuited my discomfiture. "I'm so sorry, Heb. I got carried away with my story. I know how much my precious daughter Atalana meant to you. Please understand that her training was not profane in any way." She extended her hand and I squeezed it gently in appreciation.

"Thank you for telling me that." I breathed in response.

"I believe that you are similar to Atalana. You, also, are very connected to Het-Heru and can evoke Her Presence. Perhaps that is why you are, were, so attached to Atalana, and she to you."

"Did she love me, Shara-Het?" I needed to know that at this moment.

"I think she loved you more than either of you could ever appreciate. I think the roots of your connection go very deep, maybe to the beginning of Time."

I wrinkled my forehead again. "I'm not sure what you mean."

Shara-Het smiled again and stood up. "You will understand eventually. Of this I am certain. Please excuse me. I must spend quiet time before the evening ritual. See you later, Heb."

"See you at the ritual, Shara-Het."

The older Priestess began walking towards the Sanctuary, then turned. "The wisdom is all around you, Heb. Just allow yourself to feel it." She left me alone by the sparkling water of the Sacred Lake. I got up and moved to the edge, letting my fingers trail in the cool water, thinking about what we had discussed. With her mysterious manner and smiles, Shara-Het had encouraged more questions than she answered.

By the time of the event at the Festival of Het-Heru, I had memorized the extensive litany. My voice took on a rich tone during its recitation, surprising me and all those in attendance with the pleasing quality. The crowds seemed to bring out a deeper quality in me and my voice. My Mother Nyla had been a singer, too, so I came by it naturally.

After that celebration, we found more and more people were coming for medical attention, needing assistance with childbirth, as well as those who wanted to sleep overnight for dream incubation. This occurred not just at the Full Moon but all during the month. No longer did we have idle days to sit in the sun and dream. Now we were busy with those seeking our help—along with their relatives—from morning until atmu.

When I asked Shara-Het about it, she replied, "It's because of you, Heb."

"What have I done?"

"Nothing that you know of," and she gave me one of her enigmatic smiles.

What did she mean? I wasn't doing anything different. I hoped that I could discover the answer before long.

We at the Per Neter of Het-Heru found that we needed to finish our morning ritual, then change and attend to the sick and ailing now arriving in droves to Enet-ta-Neter. We would eat hurried meals and finish our day with our evening ritual. All the rest of the time belonged to our patients.

I worked with the Senu Priestesses who tended the sick, ailing, unhappy, or pregnant. I learned fast although I preferred to chant the liturgy that accompanied the healing or childbirth rather than personally apply poultices, offer herbal concoctions, set bones, wash wounds, or deliver children.

Thus I continued in becoming the sacred Kher Heb, the Keeper of Words. I practiced the chants while performing healing duties. I found that women particularly would undergo great healings of mind and body if I held their hands while I chanted.

Several of them mentioned that as I did so, I was surrounded by a Golden Light. I didn't take them seriously, though. I knew that Het-Heru had come to participate in their healing, and I was pleased at the results. I didn't take it personally, however.

Atalana never again appeared to me as she had on the moonlit night in Waset along the river. But I felt as though she was always with me, through Het-Heru. Sometimes I thought I could hear Mukalia's voice, too. These abilities to see and hear the unseen Divine World greatly enhanced my studies, my chanting, and my healing work.

CHAPTER SIXTEEN

CATFISH BECOMES A WARRIOR

I could hardly believe so much time had passed when Udimu arrived at Enet-ta-Neter with a request from Muttuy. She requested that I come to Waset. Catfish was now twelve years old and wanting to join the army. She planned to discuss this with me and perhaps other issues as well.

I talked with Shara-Het after the evening ritual. I had already been ordained as Kher Heb inundations ago, so my presence would be missed. However, she encouraged me to go to Waset with Udimu. An Initiate for Kher Heb could fill in for me while I was gone.

After a night's rest, Udimu took me by boat back to Waset. Our trip was uneventful, the River peaceful and calm. He was quiet as usual, his face covered with deep wrinkles now. I could tell by looking at his face just how much time had elapsed.

Udimu left me at the boat dock, while I made my way to their home through the dusty streets of Waset. When I arrived at the mud-brick house, I could see some of the building was crumbling away. It needs to be repaired, I thought. The little girls no longer played outside. I supposed that they had homes of their own now.

Muttuy was outside, cooking. She was stirring an earth ware pot that was steaming. The smell of fresh bread cooking in the round mud-brick oven was delightful and my mouth began watering in anticipation. I went over to Muttuy and received a warm welcoming hug. Was it my imagination or had she put on even more weight than before? Surely Tauret's influence (the hippopotamus Neter of pregnant women, mother of Sobek) was strong in Muttuy, both mothers of vital men, and powerful in their own right as well.

"Heb," she cried in delight. "I am so glad to see you again." She eyed me up and down and nodded in appreciation, taking in my bald head, hairless arms and legs, and Priestly garb. "Your new life agrees with you."

"Yes, it does," I agreed quietly.

"Well, then. Sit down. Are you hungry? Do you want something to eat?" Before I had a chance to answer, she was spooning out some of the fish soup that was cooking into a wooden bowl. She slapped a small still-steaming loaf of flatbread down on the table next to it. "Go ahead. Eat," she commanded.

I grinned in response and did as I was told, tearing off a large section of bread, stuffing it in my mouth. Then I tasted the soup. "Delicious," I announced. "You are still a great cook."

The hefty woman smiled, gaps between her teeth more apparent than ever.

All the time I was eating Muttuy told me about the events of Waset. The marriage of both her daughters to men that she, Muttuy, approved of—naturally. One of them, the younger woman, was currently pregnant and I got to hear the details of the advancing stages of pregnancy. She told me of news that reached them about the politics of Ta-Meir Res. "The Pharaoh is an outrage," she whispered to me. "What can Maat be thinking of? There is no balance or harmony in the Palace or anywhere anymore."

"Why are you whispering?"

"They have spies everywhere."

I looked around at the tiny home. "Everywhere? Who?"

"You have been secluded in the Temple, so you probably haven't heard any of the gossip that has gone on."

"No, tell me," I encouraged her.

"They have orgies, they say, sometimes right in the throne room." She looked disgusted.

I thought of Ptah-un-Atum and his proclivity to excess and didn't doubt the gossip.

"But not just with women. Boys too. And sometimes animals as well." Her eyes were wide with indignation. "What is the matter with him? How dare he insult the Neterw like that?"

I was about to reply when she continued her narrative. "His brother is no better, they say. He sends troops to every corner of Ta-Meir Res, to listen to the street gossip, to find out if anyone speaks badly of Pharaoh. The soldiers break into people's homes. Arrest innocent men or murder them in their beds. Seize any possessions or land if they want to. Many people have died."

"Oh, no."

"Yes." She put her hands on her hips for emphasis. "And he has with him a select number of troops who guard him against assassination. It's really awful." She paused for a quick breath. "But that's not why I've asked you to travel here."

I had finished eating. She removed my bowl, wiped it clean, and put it aside, without once losing her train of thought.

"Catfish will be twelve inundations old very soon," she said. "Or at least twelve inundations from when you brought him here to me."

"Yes?"

"I haven't told him anything about himself. For all he knows, his rekkit parents are both dead and he was an orphan when you brought him here. He is such a smart boy," she smiled then. Her beatific face lit up. "I think I love him more than any of my own children, but don't tell them," she added in a conspiratorial tone.

I shook my head no.

"And you'll see. He's quite handsome, too. But he has a temper. I've tried to help him deal with that because I've told him it will hurt him. He must treat people with compassion." She shrugged her shoulder. "Perhaps he will outgrow it. He's still just a boy." Then her eyes widened. "But what a boy. He is already as tall as you and very strong. His voice has changed already as well. Two of my sons are here in Waset, in the local militia. They left Pharaoh's army, as it was getting violent against the people. They have played with Catfish for years and taught him how to ride, how to shoot, how to throw a spear better than some adults much older than he. He is really amazing. You should see him. But of course you will."

"Where is he now?"

"Oh, he's with Wahankh and Wosret. I told them you were coming but he wanted to go hunting first. I wouldn't be surprised if he brought home a lion." She grinned at the thought.

"He sounds a lot like his grandfather, Menamen-Ra. He was quite a hunter and warrior too."

"Hmmm, well that could be. Catfish gets it from somewhere. Blood will always tell in the end." We heard a noise from outside.

"Ah that must be them now."

All of a sudden the three men burst into the house, talking all at once, their manly presence filling the entire building. While still in the main living area, they threw down their spears, bows, arrow quivers, and unbuckled their daggers and belts, dropping their adorned mace heads along with their leather headpieces, making a terrible clanking racket along with the clamor of their deep, excited masculine voices.

"Nana," Catfish came out to Muttuy. "Look, Nana!!" He held up several geese and four rabbits they had caught on their hunting expedition. He threw them down on the wooden table.

"Not there!' Muttuy exclaimed. "Catfish!! They're all dirty and bloody!" She moved them quickly to a pail next to the cooking area.

Then she wiped her grimy hands on her apron and held out her hands. "Come here my darling boy. I'm so glad you're home."

She hugged the tall boy close to her, then hugged her other two sons as well. They held back a little shyly seeing the stranger Heb.

"Do you remember Heb?" Muttuy asked the young boy.

"How are you, Heb?" Catfish asked politely although without much feeling.

Of course the last time I had seen Catfish he was still a baby. He probably even didn't remember me. He held out his hands and I squeezed them in greeting. "Greetings Catfish."

"Have you ever met my sons?" The huge woman inquired of Heb.

"No, I haven't." I examined them closely. They were strapping young men, sturdy and muscular. They looked to be much younger than I was when I knew Atalana.

"Wahankh and Wosret meet Heb." She turned to me in explanation. "They are twins."

"Ah," I replied. "I am glad to meet you at last."

They nodded at me. Appropriate names for such warriors. Wahankh means strong in life, while Wosret signifies powerful one.

"They don't look like identical twins," I mentioned.

"No, they aren't," Muttuy agreed.

Wosret had a wide scar across his cheek, making him look fiercer than the other, and was a little taller than his birth brother. Wahankh had let his hair grow too long and it was touching his ears, which stuck straight out from his head. They both were exceptionally tanned from the sun and wind; their skin had the consistency of old leather. There were permanent lines at their eyes and mouth from squinting in the glaring sun. When they smiled, their teeth were dazzling brightly white, I imagine in contrast to their dark skin. Wosret's teeth were crooked.

Then Catfish asked, "What are we having for supper?"

I stared at the young man, amazed to see how big he had grown and how deep his voice had become. He certainly looked older than twelve. Muttuy's report was very accurate.

"It's all ready. Wash your hands. Then sit down and I'll serve you."

They sat down on the eating mat inside. All the remaining space seemed to be taken up with the three warriors' masculinity, as if their bodies were enormous. The warrior qualities of Heru made them look as if they had sprouted wings, filling up the entire room.

As they ate noisily, Muttuy chatted, the same as she had done earlier with me.

Then Catfish interrupted. "Nana, have you decided if I can join Wahankh and Wosret in the militia yet?"

"I was just talking to Heb about that when you arrived."

"I'm big enough even if I'm not old enough."

Wosret spoke up. "Ma, remember we were fourteen inundations when we joined up, but we weren't nearly as big as Catfish here." He jabbed him playfully in the ribs with his elbow. Catfish made a fist and punched Wosret in the arm in return.

"Yes, yes, I know that's what you want. There are some considerations though, we must speak of. She looked at her two grown warrior sons. We need to speak in private with Catfish's guardian."

"We'll go wash off in the river," Wosret replied. "Come on, brother." They left with as much noise as they had arrived, daggers, belts, and other appurtenances clanging around them.

Muttuy just shook her head in mock exasperation at the din.

Catfish turned expectantly to me. "I didn't know you are my guardian. Nana never told me."

"Yes, before Pharaoh died he put you into my custody," I replied.

"Pharaoh? Why did he do that?" The boy's face wrinkled in confusion.

"I have accidentally gotten ahead of my story. There are some items I must show you first." I looked at Muttuy, who nodded in agreement. She handed me a small spade and I removed the straw mats, then dug into the soil in the living space. Catfish watched me with interest.

I took the dirty bag out of the ground and returned to the mat. I wiped off the dirt and shook the items out of the cloth bag which had deteriorated into strips of rags. I laid the heqa, nekhaka, and the Het-Heru necklace on the table between us.

Muttuy took a deep breath of anticipation, studying the boy's face intently.

Catfish touched the items gingerly.

"Do you know what these are?" I asked him.

"This is a heqa and nekhaka, like those the Pharaoh has."

"Yes."

"Where did you get them?"

"I got them from the old Pharaoh Ankhamun."

"What? Why did he give them to you?"

"He wanted me to be able to prove that his son was the real Pharaoh when the time came for him to assume the throne."

"His son?" Now Catfish had a mistrustful look on his face.

"His son, who was just a tiny baby at the time. The Queen had died at the hands of a traitor, who planted poisonous snakes in her chamber. The Pharaoh was suffering from being poisoned. Their son was in danger as well. Just before I took the child to safety, King Ankhamun gave these to me for safe keeping. We had to hide them all this time. I wanted you to see them, to let you know who you really are."

Catfish blinked several times. "I? Who am I?" He asked slowly.

"You are Pharaoh's son and the son of the King's Royal First Wife, Queen Atalana." Saying her name was more difficult than I thought it would be. In fact, this whole conversation was difficult in the extreme.

"I? I, a king's son? A prince? The next Pharaoh? Living in this house?" He laughed loudly. "Surely you are playing with me." His temper was starting to rise up like a cobra's hood.

"This is no joke, Catfish," interjected Muttuy.

"Bashta was your wet-nurse and she brought us here to Muttuy and

Udimu, where she thought you would be safe until the time was right to announce your birthright."

"So my mother and father were the King and Queen?" He sounded as though he needed to keep asking, the story was so preposterous.

"Yes, that is right, Catfish," I replied.

"That would explain…" Catfish began.

"Explain what?" Muttuy asked.

He turned to her, but yet talking to himself. "Why you treat me as you do. Why I must learn things that the others never had to learn. Why sometimes you look at me so strangely."

I could tell that this young boy, almost a man, had inherited both his father's acute understanding of people as well as his mother's quick mind. I had kept my secret pledge so well that in my mind Catfish WAS the son of Pharaoh and Atalana.

"Do I look like him?" Catfish asked almost shyly.

I studied him for a moment. "You are taller and your features are more like your mother's. Narrow face, high cheekbones, slender build. But you are as strong as your Grandfather Menamen-Ra, who was an excellent warrior as well. I understand he had a temper too. Perhaps you can channel that into compassion."

The boy blushed hotly and glanced at Muttuy. She shrugged and smiled at him. "What he says is true. You must learn how to deal with your anger, for when you are a King."

The boy looked thoughtful. "Did you know all about this, Nana?"

"Yes, my darling boy. I have known it from the beginning."

"And what is this?" Catfish asked again, stroking the necklace of Het-Heru. He seemed to be accepting the truth at last. "It is beautiful."

"This belonged to your mother Atalana. She wore it on her wedding day and other times as well. I took it off her body the day she died. I thought you would want to have it as a keepsake."

The young man picked up the necklace and held it to his chest, in a gesture I would never have expected. "Atalana," he said softly, tenderly. "My Mother. I will treasure it always," Catfish almost looked as if he would cry, but instead he seemed to shake himself as a dog might, summoning up the strength that was his heritage. "What were they like?"

Your mother was the most beautiful woman…Queen…I have ever seen. Sometimes she looked like the Neter Het-Heru. She was very smart and helped your father run the country. Your father, King Ankhamun, was a very kind man. He treated everyone with courtesy, as though they were worthy of his respect. He believed that peace was more important than war, although if war came, I suppose he would have fought, like his father before him. But he made treaties and bargains to keep peace. The happiness of his people was always more important than his own. No one went hungry, even if he had to take the food out of his own mouth. During his reign Ta-Meir Res was prosperous, peaceful and happy."

"Not like those hyenas now inhabiting the palace," Catfish spoke in anger. "Have you heard?"

"Yes, Muttuy was telling me today."

"They must be brought to justice. How dare they defile the throne of Ta-Meir Res? Now that I am King, I will go remove them," he finished hotly.

"No, Catfish! We must wait for the right time," Muttuy spoke up quickly. This was the longest I had seen her quiet. "You cannot just march into the palace and demand that they relinquish the throne to you. What do you think would happen? Do you believe that they would allow you to live?"

"Hmmm, I see that you are right as usual, Nana," spoke the young prince. He turned to me. "Then it is even of more importance that I join the army, learn how to become a warrior, so that I can take my country back when the time is right."

"There is merit in what you say," I agreed. "But do not be too rash. You are still young. There are things for you to learn yet."

"Nana," he pleaded. "Let me go with my brothers and learn to fight. Those offal in the palace will destroy Ta-Meir Res otherwise."

She patted his hand fondly and looked to me. Obviously he had been listening to his "nana" about a lot of things.

What would the Pharaoh have said if he were still alive? And Atalana? What would she say to her son? I must be father and mother, King and Queen, for this boy before me. It was a huge responsibility, one I wasn't sure if I was up to. Then I felt a light pressure on my shoulder while a golden glow emanated all around Catfish, bathing him in the light of Het-Heru.

"What does your heart tell you?" the Neter asked me.

I am afraid, I thought.

"The boy has a destiny to fulfill. How best can he do that?"

To become a warrior, I replied. I knew it was the right answer as soon as the words left me.

Catfish was waiting.

"Yes, you can join the militia," I agreed with a worried heart.

His beaming smile erupted at the good news.

"But your foster brothers must know who you are so they can look after you properly. There is no sense in being kicked by a camel or having some other accident until the time comes for you to assume your crown." I remembered Pharaoh Ankhamun and his experiences with the camel and the scorpions.

"I will tell them everything," Muttuy agreed. "I know they will be delighted. They have always loved Catfish like their little brother."

After having seen the three of them together, I couldn't help but agree. Then an idea suddenly occurred to me. In thinking about it later, I knew it was a vision from Het-Heru. Her divine plan was so simple. "There's just one more thing," I added. They both turned to me expectantly. "You must have training to be a good and wise King as well as a strong warrior."

"What do you mean?" asked Muttuy.

"I would like him to learn from the best scholars so that he can be educated in reading and writing hieroglyphics, understanding people, agriculture, diplomacy, bargaining, compassion, city planning, and whatever else a King will need to know."

Catfish scowled.

"I know you are impatient to become a warrior, Catfish. But remember you are also going to have to learn to be a King. A good King," I added, "like your Father." He sighed impatiently.

Always practical, Muttuy spoke up. "But how will we do that? We don't have any money?"

"We will need to tell a few more people about Catfish, then," I replied. "People with money and influence."

"But how…" she began.

I held up the heqa and nekhaka. "Here is proof. Everyone knew the Queen had a boy child. Don't you suppose they want to know what became of him? Don't you think they will be overjoyed to know that he survives?"

A wide grin broke over Muttuy's massive face. "Of course," she said softly. "After years of Ptah-un-Atum and his brother, the people are ready for Catfish, aren't they?"

Het-Heru's plan for Catfish was straightforward yet wonderfully intricate, while the timing was perfect, I still smile about it after all this time. Leave it to a Neter to think of every important detail!

After twelve years of rule, Ptah-un-Atum and his brother Shu-un-Atum were profoundly hated and deeply feared by all the people in Ta-Meir Res. Where once the rekkit openly loved and worshipped their Pharaoh, they now spoke in angry whispers whenever they came together, to complain about the repulsive current ruler and his treacherous and dangerous Grand Vizier.

I was further surprised to discover the extent of Muttuy's influence in Waset. She not only knew most of the poorer townsfolk by name, but she also recognized the more powerful and affluent members as well. Because of her ability to instinctively discern who would not be appropriate to know the secret, she avoided those people who may have been loyal to the current

Pharaoh or at least disloyal to Catfish. Working surreptitiously through one or two people at a time, so as not to arouse suspicion in the Pharaoh's loyal soldiers and citizens, Muttuy organized dozens of influential and trustworthy people, letting them know about Catfish and the eventual plan of his enthronement. Catfish shouldn't be put in any danger. Fortunately, Waset was a small town, in the backwaters of the Nile, isolated from the more important cities of Nekken or Abtu. The town began to buzz with excitement and anticipation, where formerly only hopelessness and impotent anger had reigned.

I decided to linger in Muttey and Udimu's home for a while, to oversee plans, interview tutors, as well as to acquaint myself with the people who would ultimately be responsible to help Catfish become Pharaoh. I sent a message to Shara-Het of my intentions and she was a devout supporter of them. In fact, she asked to be allowed to teach the boy the spiritual side of life. When I talked to Catfish about it, he was reluctant, especially to be around so many women. We decided that at the proper time, Shara-Het would instead come to Waset and teach Catfish in his own home. In the meantime, the family strove to help the young man overcome his natural proclivity to react with anger when frustrated or thwarted.

All the years of my own education in the Palace and at Enet-ta-Neter turned out to be extremely valuable. There was no one better suited than myself to teach the 2,000 complex hieroglyphics, so Catfish and I spent hours each day on his lessons. The boy turned out to be an excellent scholar and very quickly picked up the difficult characters, the bilaterals, the determinatives, the standards, the mathematics as well as the everyday hieratic. I was proud that he could comprehend the writing of Djehuti so well.

The other subjects he needed to learn, however, were beyond my ken. I was able to ascertain the appropriate teacher for each subject, following Muttuy's advice. She was a woman naturally wise as well as smart in the ways of the world.

The best teacher of agriculture turned out to be a local farmer, whose crops and methods of farming were the best in the area. He was proud to show Catfish everything he had ever known or learned from his relatives. We had to keep the farmer on his feet, however; he prostrated himself every time Catfish showed up at his farm. It became our private joke that the farmer walked around with perpetual "dirt on his nose." However, it wouldn't be a good idea to arouse suspicion in others by the farmer's behavior.

The unofficial, unelected leader of the community was none other than Muttuy. Had she not been a poor woman, she may have been an appointed leader. As it was, Muttuy, along with the local nomarches and nobles were able to put together a curriculum of political knowledge, diplomacy and expertise that would serve Catfish and the country well for years.

Catfish was determined to study warfare with his foster brothers and the local militia without delay, so we allowed him to do so every morning from Khepera until Ra. After that the sun was usually too hot to be outside anyway and he concentrated on the more intellectual components of his studies.

Muttuy asked General Herusmatauy to teach Catfish about military strategy and handling of troops. The General, who lived just outside Waset on his family's farm, had gotten too old to lead troops anymore. But his still-alert mind and detailed memory were a welcome adjunct to the physical training Catfish received each day. Catfish was lucky to glean knowledge from the old General's years of battle and excellent strategies. Not only that, the General had served as a young cadet under Catfish's grandfather, Pharaoh Menamen-Ra, so loyalty to the Royal family ran deep.

Watching the diverse elements of Catfish's education come together, I was exceedingly grateful to Muttuy for being the person she was. I couldn't think of another individual who might have woven together the tapestry of experienced teachers as she did. When I expressed my gratitude, the woman just beamed with happiness.

"I love that boy," was Muttuy's happy reply.

She was not the only one who loved him. I was astonished to find how many people were honored to participate, even slightly, in the growth and education of Prince Catfish. I hoped they wouldn't be disappointed in the young man. I also hoped that Catfish wouldn't get too arrogant from the exalted treatment he was receiving. However, what I discovered is that the years of being in a poor but loving family, being treated as an equal, and expected to show respect and kindness, had taught him better than any school or teacher could have ever done. Especially because he had never known who he was and what destiny had in mind for him, he had remained – mostly—humble.

There were several noble families who were especially instrumental. They paid for his teachers, although I suspect many of them would have taught the future Pharaoh without charge anyway. These wealthy dynasties also made sure Catfish had the finest weapons, as well as good food to nurture his body, while others fed his mind. Several times they sent their servants to Muttuy's house with an elaborate meal for the entire family. I had to discourage them from doing so, as I was worried what townspeople would think of it. I certainly didn't want Catfish to be put in danger from wagging tongues. When I explained the situation to them, they agreed. Instead they made arrangements with different merchants at the local market to save the best meat, grain and produce for Muttuy when she came to shop, and to charge her nothing in return. Meanwhile, Udimu continued to fish for the family.

I went on Muttey's reconnoiters and recognized the son of a noble family. Aapehty had been a patient at Enet-ta-Neter Temple. I was glad to see that he had recovered from his illness. The family was happy to see me again too, and proudly invited me to teach hieroglyphics to their son. Sometimes Aapehty and Catfish would compete to see who could learn the difficulties of that system better. Catfish was better at translating the letters, words and concepts, while Aapehty could draw the complicated figures better. I encouraged them to send Aapehty to Nubt to become a Priest-Scribe initiate, to become a Kher Heb like me. But their son's delicate health would outwit our plans. The boy died suddenly of a lung ailment before he could apply to Nubt. Catfish grieved for his friend Aapehty, the first time death had affected him, his parents notwithstanding. I saw a sudden maturation as a result. Catfish went with the family when Aapehty was entombed in the family mastaba seventy days after his death, once the boy had been properly mummified in the ways of their religion.

After the long ceremony, Catfish came to me that evening to discuss his thoughts with me.

"Why did Aapehty have to die?" he asked me the question that has haunted mankind since the beginning of time.

"I don't know," I replied honestly. "What do you think?"

"But I thought you are a priest. Aren't you supposed to know these things?"

"The Ba travels outside the body every day and must be fed. The Ka continues to grow and learn. But I have never been taught why a person dies."

"He was too young," Catfish sniffed. "And I miss him."

"I understand. I miss certain people too." I felt a twinge of pain as I said so, thinking of Atalana and my love for her. "But there are ways we can stay in touch with those we love after they are gone."

"How?" Suddenly Catfish was listening intently.

"It takes practice. The kind of practice that Shara-Het would like to teach you."

"Oh that. I meant to really be in touch."

"That is what I mean also."

He wrinkled his forehead. "Are you certain?"

"Yes, I have done so for many years now." I refrained from telling him about Atalana, though.

"All right then. I'm willing to learn. You may send for her."

I smiled at his imperious tone. Catfish was getting a lot of practice in commanding others.

The following day I sent a message for Shara-Het to come teach Catfish. Within a week she was living at the family home, sleeping in my room, while I slept on a mat in the main living area. I was happy to give up my space, since I felt that what she had to teach Catfish would be invaluable in his growth and progress. Without a spiritual grounding, the boy-man would be less like his father and more like his grandfather. That wouldn't be good for Catfish or for Ta-Meir Res either. There had been enough violence and enmity already. I was also glad that Catfish had come up with the idea himself. I secretly blessed Aapehty for having died, in order to give Catfish the impetus he needed for this part of his education. Was his death another piece of Het-Heru's overall plan for the young prince?

Shara-Het was more of a mentor and friend to Catfish than a teacher. She demonstrated and lived the ideals she wanted Catfish to learn, rather than taught him. She was gentle, kind, respectful, truthful, compassionate, and loving. They had no formal classes per se, nor did he want to study and practice the rigorous rituals and ceremonies. Catfish had no patience for healing either, unlike his Priestess Mother. But he proved an apt enough student for the ethics of a virtuous life as well as a basis for a sound, compassionate rulership.

One day I happened upon a conversation the two of them were having in the back near the cooking area.

"Oh, pardon me," I said to both of them, planning to leave again.

Catfish stood up in acknowledgement. "Heb, please join us."

I was impressed to hear his newly-attained polite tone and words. I looked to Shara-Het who nodded.

"Thank you for inviting me, Catfish." I determined to sit quietly and not disturb them, but to merely listen.

"You know, Catfish," continued Shara-Het, "This country is based on Ma'at's Law of Truth, Balance, and Harmony. The Pharaoh is a representative of that Neter, dispensing justice rather than disharmony. Not only that but the whole country can suffer from injustice or thrive under harmony. It is up to Pharaoh."

"I know that, but what about Pharaoh Ptah-un-Amun and his brother…" he replied suddenly angry.

She interrupted him quietly. "They have not been taught properly or they would not behave in such an unseemly and unkingly manner."

"Can't we stop them?"

"I'm afraid it is too late for someone to teach them the understanding of the Laws of Ma'at. But it is not too late for you."

"What happens when a King does not respect Ma'at?" Catfish inquired, not yet mollified.

"The Neterw have a way of removing that individual and replacing him with someone who is better for Ta-Meir Res."

"Like me," he replied, grinning, pleased at last.

"Yes, like you, when the appropriate time comes."

"When is that?"

"I cannot say," the Elder Priestess replied. She was getting old. I could see strands of white hair peeking out from her wig. "It is up to the Stars and the Neterw to determine when the time is correct."

"Can you give me a hint?" the prince blazed back.

Her eyes twinkling, Shara-Het replied, "When you are older."

I smothered a laugh and tried to look serious. But then the other two broke out in peals of laughter, and so did I.

Shara-Het was aging. She would be better cared for in the quiet of Enet-ta-Neter by the younger priestesses than here at Muttuy's house with the many comings and goings of local residents. Soon after that, Shara-Het returned to Enet-ta-Neter, while I stayed to oversee the education of Catfish.

She and I had talked before she left.

"You may never return to Enet-ta-Neter as a Priest," she said to me, smiling, although her eyes were sad.

"Yes, I have thought of that," I replied. Neither of us was surprised at the other. "Perhaps I am supposed to be a different kind of Priest."

"May Het-Heru bless you and all you have done and will do for Her," the elderly Hem Neter Priestess said to me.

"Em Hotep," I replied. "Thank you for everything."

We hugged briefly and then Udimu sailed with her to Het-Heru's home at Enet-ta-Neter.

CHAPTER SEVENTEEN

SHU-UN-ATUM AND DROUGHT

Several peaceful years went by. Our lives flowed as easily as the Nile, beside which our town of Waset stood. Catfish's training was progressing well. We were all extremely proud of him.

In the meantime, his foster father Udimu was pitifully aging—his hands, fingers, shoulders and back had grown swollen and feverish to the touch, which then began to twist in on themselves in a painful, crippling condition. Even though I practiced the healing arts on him, he continued in his illness.

Thus he was unable to fish anymore. It was fortunate for us that we were fully supported by several noble families, or we would have had to call a halt to Catfish's education while he fished for the family.

The young Prince amazed everyone with his capacity for knowledge. He quickly learned whatever he studied. He continued to grow until he was taller than anyone in the village. Due to the demanding, physical training he received with the local militia, his muscles filled out and he appeared to be older than his less-than-fifteen inundations. Fortunately, his other training helped to keep him from becoming a hardened soldier. He had a generous heart and was loyal in the extreme, although he could be willful if the situation demanded it. He worried us with the recent development of a streak of wildness, perhaps due to the influence of his soldier "brothers" Wahankh and Wosret, or maybe he was simply showing off for them.

Catfish took unnecessary risks, putting himself in needless danger from time to time. He went hunting for lions by himself, even though he was still inexperienced. He demanded that members of the militia practice fighting with him using various weapons, without protective padding or holding back their lunges and parries.

"I'm having fun!" he explained to us.

He ignored our pleas to be more cautious, so we hoped that aspect of him would diminish as he matured. In time I would come to see this quality as life-enhancing, but at the time I was quite concerned for his safety.

I missed the routine of Temple life. But it was important to be in close proximity to the Prince. Yet I doubted he even knew I was present most of the time. I performed my own private ritual at the banks of the Nile each morning and evening, calling on Het-Heru, asking Her to remove my turmoil and loneliness. Her comforting presence, combined with the soothing sound of the Holy River, helped maintain my inner peace. Without these spiritual practices, I'm sure I would have experienced immeasurable grief and pain. Rituals were my salvation against the yearning and heartache for my long-lost love. Time never diminished that ache.

Then our peace was abruptly shattered.

Our Pharaoh, Ptah-un-Atum was dead. Although none of us had liked the former King, nevertheless there had been a semblance of normalcy during his reign. The pudgy Pharaoh Ptah-un-Atum had minded his own business, ignoring the rest of the country, allowing us some freedom. Our seeming autonomy actually reflected a total lack of concern for his subjects and overwhelming selfishness, as we would soon discover. His skinny brother, on the other hand, was vicious, cruel, and manipulative in the office of Vizier. What would he be like as King, with absolute power at his command?

When we heard how the Pharaoh had died, we trembled in fear. Shu-un-Atum had arranged for the assassination of his brother, and then had himself coronated immediately. Grand Vizier Shu-un-Atum ordered several of his own loyal guard to murder his obese, older brother, to kill him as he lay with his concubines. Once the former King was dead, Shu had himself crowned Pharaoh in his stead, not waiting the traditional seventy days of mourning and mummification before assuming the throne.

They say that often one disaster follows on the heels of another.

Not long after the coup d'etat, that same year, the annual Nile flood came late, but the floodwaters were marginal. The Nile Meters showed the river level as dangerously low. Without the thick layer of nutrient-rich black silt left by the overflowing river, our fields lacked the necessary vigor to bring our crops to harvest. Farmers planted anyway, in the blistering sun, the heat more intense than normal. The level of Mother Nile's life-giving water sunk to the lowest that anyone had known since before Ankhamun's time, and irrigation ditches dried up quickly.

Drought! That word brought terror to millions of our citizens. We all had heard stories of people starving in their homes.

People prayed to and made offerings to Hapi, Neter of the Nile, to encourage Him to bring the life-giving flood waters to their fields, but to no avail. Farmers entreated Ausar, Neter of green plants, to bring them a high quality harvest, in spite of the lack of flood-water nutrients. But the sun disk Ra beat down mercilessly, scorching plants the farmers had coaxed into life from seed. Day by day they searched the sky, hoping for rain clouds that would save them from the forces of Setekh, Neter of chaos and the life-draining desert. But the sky remained blue and no rain fell. Even wild ducks and geese seemed fewer in number and more difficult to catch, as though they, too, shunned our hungry land.

Insects decimated the remainder of the straggling crops, weakened by drought and heat. Farm animals began to die. So did our most vulnerable —young children and the elderly—their bodies piled on the West Bank of the Nile, as whole families lined up to bring their departed to holy ground on the other side of the river. Often a newly-dead infant would be brought to the West Bank, lying in the arms of a grieving parent. Mothers and Fathers wept inconsolably at the loss of their young ones, the vanished future of Ta-Meir Res, as giant communal burial ditches were hastily dug to accommodate all the dead as well as to protect against disease. Everyone had more than their share of flies that year, from maggots growing in the vast multitude of bodies decomposing in the blistering sun. The insects' fat, glistening, iridescent bodies alighting everywhere and incessant buzzing made everyone ill-tempered, while water buffalo and cattle bellowed madly, swishing their tails in vain at the pesky insects swarming around them.

Had the Neterw turned their backs on us?

The new King Shu-un-Atum had sent soldiers to guard the precious newly-planted farms along the Nile, until those turned to dust as crops withered in the fields. We had more than the normal numbers of khamsim, and our precious top soil was blown away in those blistering winds. Famine spread throughout the country. The royal coffers were empty, the result of the former king's excess spending. Ptah-un-Atum had not planned for the future, so there was little food stored in the granaries.

Without a surplus of food or money to buy food, people throughout Ta-Meir Res began to starve. Food riots broke out in towns and villages, as fathers fought with one other to find enough food to feed their families. Those outbreaks were brutally quashed by the new Pharaoh's troops while fields and marketplaces literally ran with blood.

We in Waset were the least affected by these events as we had incredible good fortune—the surplus of food stored from many years before. Some of it had spoiled or rotted, or had been eaten by insects and rodents in the intervening years. However, there was enough food for the entire town and nearby farms so long as the inundation became normal the following year. If not, we would be in as much trouble as the rest of Ta-Meir Res.

Because we were so isolated from other, larger towns, no one outside of Waset knew of our secret cache. Our little town was fairly unimportant in the larger scheme of Ta-Meir Res, unlike the major cities of Nekken and Abtu.

Was this largesse due to divine intervention again? Another of Het-Heru's plans? Although we were grieved to hear about the losses everywhere else, we knew that our salvation was no accident. It was to provide for the Prince and the rest of his village. We performed rituals of celebration and brought offerings, thanking Amun, the protector Neterw of Waset, for our precious gift.

Civilian and trooper spies alike were willing and ready to report any complaints to Pharaoh, especially if it meant that they might be paid with food. The merciless heart of King Shu-un-Atum was primarily obsessed with his own security and wellbeing, believing many people were plotting against him. In that regard, his suspicions were probably well-founded. Men who plotted against others generally believed others were doing the same to them. Under his leadership, many citizens were consequently arrested and simply disappeared. We never found out what happened to them. Perhaps they starved in prison. Maybe they were cruelly murdered and their bodies thrown to the jackals. No one knew. Had the Pharaoh tried even a little to assist with our current calamity, such as trading with neighboring countries for food, we might have forgiven him. Instead he surrounded himself with ever-growing numbers of soldiers, guarding himself against his own worst fears. Thus enmity against him grew daily, even in the gentlest of hearts.

Rumors began to circulate that the Neterw were angry at Pharaoh Ankhamun's demise, as well as his Queen's, along with the disappearance of the infant prince, and were now extracting retribution on the country. Were we all co-conspirators in those tragedies because of our own non-action? Some of the Priests claimed that we were responsible for the terrible tragedies, that we had somehow violated Ma'at and had invited the disaster upon ourselves. Some of us accused our fellows of bringing the punishment of the Neterw upon our shoulders. Others felt guilty and tried to repent their evil ways.

Soon even the greenest of Ta-Meir Res along the Nile flood plain was becoming arid desert, or bone dry, black mud flats now turned to hard clay, fit only for scorpions, not human beings. When the people of Ta-Meir Res nicknamed the new Pharaoh "King Serqet" (King Scorpion) behind his back, the name stuck. Anyway, it seemed to me a fitting name for the man who reminded me of a repulsive, yet highly dangerous insect, an insect who could sting himself to death in order to get even with others.

As soon as he found out about the King's assassination, Catfish was ready to take up arms and attack Abtu Palace. We had to argue him out of that disastrous plan. He, and the slowly-growing army following him, were unprepared to undertake such a campaign. We lacked the necessary manpower, resources, weaponry, as well as money to feed and house the thousands of troops needed in order to reinstate the prince as rightful ruler. We were years away from being successful. As I said, Catfish was a risk-taker, so to him the bold idea was a good one. In desperation, we called upon General Herusmatauy, who spent many hours talking to the Prince, helping him to understand the error of reckless planning and poor timing. In the end Catfish relented and we all drew a collective breath. But I could clearly see the course he was on and it was only a matter of time before he would confront the Power of the Throne, wresting away that position to claim it for himself.

One afternoon Muttuy returned from getting water at the river. She huffed and puffed as she came in through the doorway, beads of perspiration all over her face and neck. I took the heavy water jug away from her immediately, concerned at the alarming rust color of her face. She tried to motion me away with a wave of her fat hand, but she was clearly exhausted.

"Too hot," she panted, trying to catch her breath.

"Sit down, Muttuy, you are not well."

"I'm fine. Just a little overheated is all. Give me a moment and I'll start supper."

"No, please sit down." I led her to a gnarled wooden bench, one of the few pieces of furniture we owned.

She sat down with great effort. "Perhaps I am a little unwell at the moment," she relented. "Where is Catfish?" she inquired.

"I'm not sure."

"He should be home for supper soon."

"Yes, that is so." Catfish was never one to miss a meal and Muttuy was a good cook. "You have time, so rest now." She leaned her cheek upon her hand and closed her eyes.

I was alarmed as I had never seen the woman look this sick. I gave her a few salted nuts to chew and cut open a pomegranate for her to suck on. Then I got a cloth from the brick counter near the oven, dipped it into the water jug, dabbed the moist rag on her forehead, then along the back of her neck, moving aside her graying hair as I did so.

"Ah that feels good."

I left the wet cloth on her neck, while I felt the artery on her neck with my finger. The blood vessel throbbed madly. "You are overheated. You need to stay out of the sun. Let me go to the River to fetch water for a few days while you rest," I pleaded with her. I thought she was in danger of having a brain seizure, too, because of her color, but was unwilling to tell her so at present. If it was that, I could give her some herbs to help remove the excess blood in her head.

"That is woman's work," she retorted.

"I know, but you need to stay cooler for a while and rest."

"Hmp," was her stubborn answer.

I could see who Catfish emulated with his willful manner.

"And furthermore, you must lose a little weight, as I have been telling you."

"Yes, yes. You tell me all the time. Why can't you let an old woman eat in peace?" she answered.

"Muttuy! Muttuy!" Udimu hobbled into the house, using a stick as a cane, then through the living area to where she sat outside. He was becoming more and more crippled all the time, but at this moment he moved with astonishing speed.

"I'm here," she replied tiredly.

"Have you heard?" The aging man, usually so taciturn, was speaking quickly. "I heard it in from some boys down at the quay."

"What? Heard what?" she answered irritably.

"The Pharaoh Shu-un-Atum. He sent troops to Khemenu to bring order to the food riots. But the mob turned on them. They began to fight, digging sticks and hoes against daggers and spears. Many soldiers were killed, along with some townspeople. But there were so many they overwhelmed the soldiers, who ran away!! Can you believe it?"

Muttuy sat up straight, the rag fell off her neck onto the dusty ground. "When was this?"

"Just days ago. A couple of fishermen sailed from Khemenu and ended up here. Do you suppose the soldiers will follow them? Will they find our food stores? What will happen to us?"

"Hush, old man, let me think," and Muttuy stood up, wavering a bit, still dizzy from the heat.

"But Wife, this is serious. What about Catfish?"

"Not now. He'll be home any time. Let's talk to a few people first. Maybe the General will know what to do."

As the elderly couple continued to wrangle, the late afternoon sunshine dissolved into an eerie orange-gold light while my body became heavy. In my vision I floated far away from their home, leaving Waset. Before I knew it I was passing through the mud brick tenemos of Enet-ta-Neter. There stood the holy Temple and with it the sacred energy enfolded me like a swaddling cloth. I entered the Sanctuary containing the golden statue of Het-Heru, Mistress of Heaven. Behind me stood the protective lioness, Sekhmet, her black basalt body quivering, ready for action. I stood between the two Divine Females, safe from the violent world, free from decisions, but alone in my fear.

"Tell me what to do," I whispered to them. If I spoke any louder, the magick spell would be broken and I'd be back in Waset again without knowing Their wisdom. "What is happening?" I asked them.

"You hold the future of Ta-Meir Res in your hands." The now-familiar words of the Golden Neter echoed off the walls like the silvery sound of sistrums. "Everything is as it should be. The Prince has a destiny to fulfill and you will help. You have always helped."

"But how?"

"You will know. The time is approaching when all will be made clear."

The Neter's words made no sense to me. I suppose they would become significant in retrospect.

"Trust your heart, Heb. It is the seat of your wisdom." Mukalia's words resonated. The withered old woman's face merged with the golden Neter. Their eyes were the same. Deep. Ageless. Unfathomable.

Behind me I heard a growl. I turned to see Sekhmet glowing with a reddish light. "I am the avenging Eye of Ra. I will protect the boy-King," Her menacing voice reverberated in the Sanctuary.

I shivered and became a small, helpless boy again, trying to pull a shadowy Pharaoh off a dying camel, skeleton hands tearing at my fingers. Scorpions crawled out of beds. Snakes slithered through columns. I heard the sound of wood splintering. A spider wove a web all around me. I heard a scream of passion and panic. Faded wooden statues danced to the beat of sistrums. Blood drummed in my ears. A baby sobbed. Silver sparkles raced through stars of Nut's body, the constellation now made up of fiery spears and arrows. A lion sat on a collapsing throne, the Pharaonic Hedjet crown on his head, which then became the face of Catfish. I saw Abtu Palace in ruins around him.

"Het-Heru," I cried in terror. "Help me!"

"I am here," Her Golden Voice breathed inside and around me. "I will always be here, waiting for you." I reached out to touch Her, but Muttuy's voice broke the spell.

"Heb!"

"What?" The vision was gone as quickly as it had come.

Muttuy was pulling at my arm. "Come with me, Heb. We need to meet with others, to discuss what must be done. I fear there is little time to waste."

I knew that no matter what was decided tonight, everything would work out perfectly, as it always had. Catfish would become the Warrior King he dreamed of being, taking each step on the long road to the Throne. My task was to tell them my vision, so all the participants would know that the Neter Het-Heru, Celestial Mother of Pharaohs, was still orchestrating the events. Because there was nothing to fear. Then why was my body trembling?

CHAPTER EIGHTEEN

PLANNING FOR CIVIL WAR

We stood grouped in a huge gathering room in the largest house in our town. Muttuy had sent runners to every loyal family and they had gathered here. It was home to a large, extended family of great political and financial means, their power going back generations. The house was a lavishly built and extensively decorated mud-brick mansion, plastered and painted with the skill of dozens of artisans. Expensive floors of variegated marble were laid in six rooms and the main hallway. Ra-as-Atum had already disappeared in the West, so beautiful lotus lamps, filled with precious oils so pure they hardly smoked at all, illuminated the gathering of rich and poor alike. I hadn't seen a structure this lovely since I left Abtu Palace fifteen inundations before. Behind the residence were a number of smaller houses, including rooms for servants, storerooms, a chapel, and a second kitchen.

A dozen or so people had gathered to listen to what I had to say. These consisted of only those townspeople involved in our scheme of restoring the Prince to his throne.

The Nomarche of Waset introduced me. "Here before you is an ordained priest of Het-Heru, trained at Enet-ta-Neter. He has had many visions of the Golden Neter, and only today had another one. She has an important message for us." A couple of men talked loudly in the back of the chamber.

"Shhhh," someone hissed.

I cleared my throat. "The Neter Het-Heru, Celestial Mother of Pharaohs, assures me that She is in charge of events unfolding in our country. Because of Her, there is nothing for us to fear. She knows that the Pharaoh currently sitting on the throne is an abomination and will be removed. She will put Catfish on the throne at the appropriate time. She is guiding us through our troubling times. In the meantime, you must trust the messages I receive."

My vision was well-received by everyone at our hastily-created meeting. An ordained priest with a message from a Neter was a potent force.

Muttuy was the first to speak after I did. She had difficulty standing because of her great weight, and rocked to and fro on her bare feet. "We have the blessing of Het-Heru. There is no better time to fight than now," she said. "King Serqet is despised. The people are afraid and hungry. The mobs attacking soldiers in Khemenu are just a symptom of the general unrest in Ta-Meir Res, which will not end until justice prevails and the people are fed. Let us not stop the natural current of the river's flow toward the sea; indeed, let us hasten it along."

"We should be circumspect," said the General. His hands were shaky with palsy, but his voice was clear. "If we reveal Catfish's real identity precipitously, it could put him at unnecessary risk. Let us continue to keep the secret. We will know when the right time is at hand. I can feel in my Khu that we must be even more careful than before or we could ignite the whole situation."

Catfish spoke vehemently. "But we cannot sit and do nothing! We must help our fellows to fight against the Pharaoh's evil. People are starving. I'm sure there are other countries that could help us. Can we not bargain for food on our own, without our government needing to interfere?" He had become a tall man, taller than any in the room. Atalana's high cheekbones were etched on her son's oval face and I thought to myself how handsome Catfish had become. His slanted eyes were fierce with emotion. "Do we have to stand aside while the rest of Khemenu is slaughtered? They are blameless. All they want is enough food to eat. Is that so terrible? We must take action!"

The Prince's passion caught everyone by surprise, including my own. It was perhaps the first time I had heard him argue for the common good instead of his own interests—and it certainly would not be the last.

Several members of the local militia were present, along with Wahankh and Wosret, nodding in agreement with the case set out by Catfish.

Wild arguments broke out on all sides of the problem and a number of voices spoke up. Here are what some of them had to say.

The Nomarche's son, standing near the entry way, spoke first. He reasoned, "We don't owe anything to Khemenu."

Muttuy turned to him and interjected. "Women and children of Khemenu are likely to be killed. The Neterw would want us to protect the innocent."

"Fighting would put Waset in jeopardy. We must refrain from action."

"Everyone will be slaughtered like spring lambs if we don't do something soon!" Wosret shouted.

A short, thin man spoke up with hesitation. "I'm certain these events will pass and will be soon forgotten. I say we take no further steps."

"Would you care to see Pharaoh's men come for you?" Wahankh, Muttuy's other son questioned him hotly.

Tenti, Bashta's husband spoke. "This is just the beginning of a long conflict. Perhaps we should wait and see which way the wind blows."

"Khemenu is only the first of many towns to rise up and fight for their lives," said a camel-tender I recognized from the market.

"We are not ready. We lack supplies and men," General Herusmatauy said with authority. Several others nodded at his reply.

A farmer, whose farm was situated near Waset, spoke up. "We would have to share our food supplies. Once we start to fight, the whole country will find out we have extra food and come to take it away from us. Then we would starve, too."

"If we fight, we will all be killed or imprisoned."

"No, the Pharaoh is too afraid to take on the whole country. He would have to back down. He wouldn't have enough soldiers to fight us all." Muttuy's voice was hoarse with feeling.

"There's nothing to fear. All this will blow over quickly like a spring sandstorm," replied Tenti.

"You're wrong, Tenti," Catfish interjected. "This is the beginning of civil war. We cannot escape it," he continued with quiet authority. The light from the lotus lamps shone on his youthful countenance, making his face look rather golden. "I know this as surely as my hand is connected to my arm. Therefore, it isn't a question of whether or not we take action, but how and when to do it. It is folly to go seeking war, but a greater folly to ignore war when it comes seeking us." He looked around at the assortment of stunned, fearful, angry and excited faces all around him. "So who is with me?"

"I am, little brother!" yelled Wosret.

A chorus of voices chimed in. Pandemonium and cheering broke out in that sumptuous room.

In the end, we were all convinced by the dynamic line of reasoning that Catfish put forward. The country was aching from years of neglect by and violence from the two brothers. People were without food and punished when they demanded to be fed. When people are hungry, they will do almost anything. Fear of starvation is more pressing than fear of a Pharaoh, even a violent one. Within a short time the Prince would prove to be correct; civil war was in the making. We had no time to waste.

Catfish had studied hard and long, absorbing all the important lessons that could turn a boy into a King—most importantly compassion for his suffering people. It was obvious to all of us in the splendid and regal room that night that Catfish was becoming that King. The mantle of leadership had been offered and he wore it magnificently on his broad young shoulders. That night Catfish became both a man and a leader. If all our plans went well, we could offer him the Crown soon. Het-Heru had chosen well.

Muttuy organized the attendees into working groups. One group would locate artisans to fashion bows, arrows, slings, and maces, as well as blacksmiths to forge daggers and spears. Another group would recruit volunteer soldiers from among the young men of the town. Yet a third group would be responsible for the sewing of cloth into simple tents, to protect those soldiers from the elements, as well as to create spare clothing and leather makers for sandals. Then another group would be in charge of putting together food for the troops and to recruit cooks as well.

Still yet another group would travel to foreign countries, to trade and bargain for food—or steal if they had to. This meant that a collection would need to be taken up, as money and valuable items were necessary for trading. We couldn't simply go to other countries as beggars with empty hands, expecting them to help us for nothing. I remembered the conflict Menamen-Ra had with the Assyrians long ago, and thought to advise accordingly.

We had to find those willing to volunteer their valuable household camels, in order to carry heavy packs on humped backs, so that our troops wouldn't have to do so and would be free to march and fight.

Emissaries were sent to various other towns and villages, to discreetly uncover what, if any, similar war plans were being concocted there, or what tactics King Serqet might be planning against us. These envoys were instructed to encourage and organize similar resistance wherever they went, without alarming the authorities loyal to the Pharaoh's government. Consequently, the rebel forces grew in numbers with speed and secrecy.

Especially at the capital of Ta-Meir Res at Nekken. Queen Atalana's family had come from that bustling city. I'm sure those Noble families would want to be involved in the restoration of the King.

During the next few weeks townspeople were involved in the planning process. One could see them pass here and there, whisper to each other, and go about their business with an air of urgency. Otherwise, the rest of the town believed only that we were preparing for possible civil war and nothing else. We all agreed with General Herusmatauy. As long as our troops were few in numbers, inexperienced and untrained, as well as ill-equipped, we should keep the identity of the Prince confidential within our own ranks.

Meanwhile, the Prince hardly came home to sleep or eat. He was enmeshed in the process of preparation. He personally oversaw the preparations and talked with the organizers of various groups. He gave inspiring talks wherever he went and to whomever he spoke with. He was tireless, encouraging, and praising the work of every individual, further honing his leadership skills to a fine edge. Even those who had no idea he was our candidate for future king were impressed by his behavior and gladly joined our ranks. His leadership abilities grew, shining through the young man. Atalana and Ankhamun could be proud of their son.

During all this time King Serqet was busy, too. Although he had no idea of the forces beginning to array against him, his natural paranoia was instinctively mounting. Since he was reluctant or unable to trust even those closest to him, no one was able to properly advise him as to the wisest course of action in the wake of the tragedy in Khemenu. He continued to send spies and soldiers to all the major towns in Ta-Meir Res, to report as well as to intimidate, imprison, and murder. The soldiers involved in these heinous acts were often drunkards, cowards, bullies, and otherwise brutal, violent men. The Pharaoh preferred to hire them over men of real valor and integrity. He didn't seem to mind that the scum of human society was responsible for carrying out his orders. Thus he further alienated his subjects.

The Viziers were too afraid of the new Pharaoh to arouse his murderous, cold anger, so instead they were condescending and toadying, mollifying the King's concerns. King Serqet slept with a dagger, stationed the strongest soldiers at all his doors and openings, and had tasters sample all his food in case it was poisoned. Sometimes he barricaded himself in his quarters for days on end, refusing to see diplomats, princes, envoys, or messengers alike.

He openly reviled the wives and concubines he had inherited from his fat brother and avoided them at all times. They were older than him anyway. The truth was King Serqet felt ill at ease with any woman once he removed his kilt and exposed his private parts. The scars from his childhood had become deep crevasses of suspicion and wariness.

Although he was too close to his situation to understand, the King had created a prison out of his own behavior, fears, and mistrust. Like the scorpion he was named for, Serqet lived in the dark with his stinger poised over his head, ready to strike at a moment's notice. Thus the King was virtually alone and a prisoner in his own Palace, effectively shutting out the truth of the situation, and scheming in a void, helping to create the very thing he was most afraid of—rebellion.

Just as we had overseen the Prince's education, now Muttuy and I were in charge of the growing rebel army in Waset.

"Do you think we're doing the right thing, Muttuy?" I asked.

"Do you mean raising an army and fighting? Yes, I do. Why do you ask?"

"I get a little afraid sometimes."

"But you were the one who received the vision from Het-Heru."

"Yes, but a vision fades in time and I begin to doubt my own memory."

"Well, even if you didn't receive a vision or even if the vision wasn't from Het-Heru, we still have a good plan. And it is progressing well."

"That is for certain. I can't believe how much people have come together to cooperate with each other, in this large enterprise."

"When people are united in a common goal, it is easy to do."

"I suppose you're right."

"It's almost atmu." Muttuy went outside, to begin preparing the evening meal. Nowadays she cooked so much food, it appeared as though an army was coming to eat. Perhaps it was. I smiled momentarily at the thought. Several women walked into our house, to help Muttuy prepare supper.

Udimu hadn't arrived home yet; probably he was still at a neighbor's house drinking barley beer and gambling. Unable to fish anymore, the old crippled man had taken up the new activity.

I left the house and walked through the dusty streets to the bank of the Nile, to perform my evening ritual. That and the Mother River always soothed me.

Along the way I met people that I knew quite well by now. Several men smiled as they walked by on the way back from fishing all day. They had fish hung from a line and each held one end of the rope.

"Em Hotep," I said.

"Em Hotep to you," one of them replied.

"Fishing was good," I commented politely.

"Yes, thank you, it was," the other replied and they continued their trek home.

I passed the market place but it was quiet at this time of evening. All the merchants had folded up their mats and gone home long ago, to eat and rest. There were torn cabbage leaves, squashed tomatoes, and a broken watermelon in the dust. Some splattered pigeon blood. A broken earth ware container of wheat had overturned, a few grains spilling out onto the street. Wild birds were gobbling up what was left behind.

I continued to walk until I felt the soft breeze from the river gently touch my face.

I was still concerned about Catfish. His life hung in a delicate balance. He was untried on the field of battle. Furthermore, he was young and reckless. How did I know that the outcome would be positive? How did I know that the King's forces wouldn't just trample our plan and us with it into the dust? The Prince didn't understand the depth of the King's malice. King Serqet was a dangerous foe, one who would stop at nothing to destroy anyone and anything that opposed him. I remembered the story Ankhamun had told me about Shu-un-Atum's boyhood. Once beaten and humiliated at the hands of a father who was supposed to love him, he wouldn't be concerned about unbridled, reckless, and murderous retaliation towards those he didn't care about. How could I tell Catfish that the King was like a scorpion, perhaps even stinging himself, until his goal was accomplished – death of our Prince and all those who supported him.

I thought of my Meruti, dear Atalana. What would she advise if she were here? Would she think we had a chance to defeat the terrible ruler who showed a pitiless heart as once he had been given no mercy. What would Ankhamun counsel? He might have argued for peace at any cost. Were we beyond that now, with no turning back?

I longed for the quiet solitude of Enet-ta-Neter, to regain my bearings and composure. If only I could spend a little time there, to participate in the group rituals. To talk to Het-Heru in Her own Per Neter Temple, where Her energy was strongest. To discuss my misgivings and fears with Shara-Het. To feel once again the strength of the Temple, which would also provide peace.

I thought of the beautiful columns with the face of Het-Heru, which looked so much like my own dearest love. Atalana could have been the model for those columns. Her slanted eyes and beautiful features were similar to the Neter's.

With a rush, I took a deep breath. It had been a long time since I had felt my loss so keenly. It was an old ache in my chest. A catch in my throat. A stinging in my eyes, as though I was downwind of cooking fires. A knowledge that as much as I wanted it, my own dear Atalana would not be coming back to me in her lovely physical body. All I had were memories and feelings, sometimes a fleeting vision—and her son. I would need to protect him with every bit of strength in my body, even though I wasn't a warrior.

I sat on the sand, pulling my shenti around my legs for warmth. The night was cooling off fast as it did this time of year.

I hadn't given myself the luxury of thinking about Atalana in quite a few inundations. I had always been too busy working, to give full attention to my memory. Or maybe I was afraid to feel what was still so strong and unhealed inside me. I remembered the day I first saw her, golden and lovely as a Neter, taking on the task of Royal First Wife. I remembered the time we spent at Enet-ta-Neter. The day we swam and the drops of water sparkled on her golden skin, enticing me. The pleasure of her eyes and lips smiling at me. The way her body felt in my arms. Oh Neter, no, I couldn't go down that road again. That road led to madness, and to unfulfilled longing. I had spent enough time there. I couldn't, wouldn't go back. In earlier times I had Bashta, but now I had no one. It had been fifteen inundations since Atalana had gone to join Ausar in the Duat—and I had no one. How could so much time pass so quickly? I had once asked Heh, the Neter of Millions of Years, to make time move faster. He had listened to my plea. Time indeed was progressing rapidly.

Did I want anyone with whom to share my life? No. No one could replace Meruti Atalana. I must focus on Catfish instead. He is my life. He is my dearest love's child, grown into a man. No, not a man yet, but very soon.

Now I remembered where I had started, my concern about the welfare of Catfish and our group's ability to bring the young man to the throne of Ta-Meir Res.

The stars were already twinkling in the darkening sky. So much time had elapsed while I had sat along the Nile, thinking and remembering. My stomach growled with hunger. I got up, arranged my shenti, and collar, and walked back to the small house of Udimu and Muttuy.

CHAPTER NINETEEN

Catfish and Heb
to Enet-ta-Neter

As I ambled home along the now-familiar streets of Waset, I felt a sudden tightening in my abdomen. My head began to swim and I felt dizzy. My ab began to pound harder than a dunbek. Hurry, it told me, so I walked faster. The deep shadows of buildings around me seemed to reach out ominously and my anxiety grew with every step.

Then in my mind's eye I saw them—an army of man-size scorpions pouring through the town like floodwater, unstoppable, daggers raised menacingly. I could hear cries, as the occupants of the houses tried to protect themselves against the merciless scorpion army. A wave of blood poured out from each doorway, staining the dusty ground red. It seemed as though even the buildings were screaming in pain and fear. As quickly as the vision appeared, it faded from my mind.

They were looking for Catfish! I began to run as though a khaibit was after me. My bare feet pounded on the dirt, raising a cloud of dust behind me. I passed many homes with lamps burning. The occupants would be sitting down to eat their evening meals, unaware of the danger I knew we were all in.

When I breathlessly entered the simple home of Udimu and Muttey, my skin was cold with dread. "Muttey!" I called out anxiously.

"I'm in the cooking area," she yelled back.

With a few strides of my long legs, I was outside. The two women who were helping her prepare food looked up at me.

"Catfish and I must leave right away," I told her. We must not delay. Something bad is getting ready to happen. I saw it."

Muttey studied my eyes. She trusted me implicitly, even without knowing the details of my concern. She turned to her friends. "I will finish with the cooking tonight," she dismissed them with a motion of her hands.

Wiping their hands on their clothing, the women left, muttering to each other. Muttuy turned to me when they had gone. "I will pack some clothes for him."

"No. He needs a disguise to hide from Pharaoh's wrath. I'll take him to Enet-ta-Neter tonight. I'll shave his head and make him look like an Initiate, so he won't need regular clothing. He can wear an extra robe of mine." I turned to see Udimu, his crooked body an apology of flesh.

"I'm sorry, son. I cannot take you there. But I will get several of my friends to help. They can use my felluca." He hobbled out into the night.

"Thank you, Udimu," I called after him.

"What can I do?" Muttey asked, her face drawn and tight with worry.

"Pack some food. We will need to leave immediately."

"Right away," and she began to wrap bread, dried fruit and some meat in cloths for us. "What has happened?" she asked as she prepared.

"I'm not sure. Perhaps someone has divulged our secret. All I can see is an army of scorpions with daggers, coming here to find Catfish." I glanced around the area for the young Prince, but he wasn't at home. Icy claws of fear tore at my stomach.

"Muttey, where is Catfish?" I asked her anxiously.

"He was just here," she looked around. "I don't know where he went!" she cried in terror. I put my hand on her shaking arm to calm her.

"Does he visit friends with Wahankh and Wosret?"

"Sometimes." She wrinkled up her eyebrows. "Let me think. Which house would it be?"

"Nana?" Catfish entered the house then and we both sighed with relief. Muttey and I raced to his side, talking to him in unison.

"You must get away tonight."

"I'll take you to Enet-ta-Neter. I think you will be safe there."

"Don't bring anything with you."

"Udimu is going to find a friend to take us there."

"Wait a minute," the young man stopped us both. "What are you talking about?"

"The King's troops are coming to find you," I said, summing up my concerns.

"Coming to Waset? Now?" he asked.

"Yes," I replied.

"How do they know where to find me?"

"I'm not sure. Someone must have talked," Muttey told him.

"We need to leave now. Tomorrow morning will be too late," I urged him.

"All right, Heb," he agreed. "But must I go to Enet-ta-Neter?"

"They won't find you there. I will disguise you as an Initiate."

Udimu entered with several of his friends. "Here we are. They can take you to Het-Heru's Temple right now."

He quickly introduced us. "Heb, this is Baenre and Iawy."

"Thank you so much for helping us." I clasped hands with both of the men. Iawy and Baenre were younger than Udimu. They were both wearing kilts, well-worn, stained, and thread-bare but otherwise wore no other clothing or adornments. Their tough, lean bodies were browned and leathery from their time in the sun. From the smell of them, they had been drinking quite a lot of barley beer. "Are you capable of making a long journey?" I asked them anxiously.

"Yes, we are fine," Iawy replied. He hadn't shaved for days and the stubble on his face made him look older than he actually was. The other one smelled of stale sweat mixed with barley beer. Udimu's gambling associates? Could we trust them? Udimu surely wouldn't recruit undependable people.

Muttey got out a small spade and hurriedly dug up the middle of the living area, retrieving the heqa, nekhekha, and Atalana's necklace from their hiding place under the dirt. "I'm sure you will need these at some point," she commented, as she wiped her sweaty face. Gooseflesh rose on the back of my neck and my stomach clenched. She wiped the items off, wrapped each in a clean cloth and arranged them carefully in my pack, which also contained the Het-Heru talisman, the carved carnelian signet, and papyrus of my writings.

Meanwhile, Catfish sat down on one of the outside stools while I proceeded to scrape all the hair off his head, upper torso, neck, and arms with a copper razor. The razor wasn't as sharp as I would have liked, and he had areas where blood oozed out. I got out my second temple robe and he donned it. It was a little tight for him, but I would get a new one for him later. This one would have to do for now. The Prince now seemed somewhat believable as an Initiate. I picked up my heavy pack.

"Here is food for the journey." Muttey handed Catfish the parcels she had packed, along with a goat-stomach container of water. She and Udimu hurriedly hugged both Catfish and me. "Go with the blessings of Het-Heru and Amun. Make haste," she added, pushing us out of the house into the dark street beyond.

"Be very careful," I warned Catfish' foster parents, thinking of my vision.

"I promise we will not let them know where he has gone," Muttey replied. Udimu nodded in agreement.

The four of us ran to the dock where the felluca was tied. Catfish was the youngest and got there before the rest of us. The older men were not able to run very fast, but we all finally made it to the dock. Fortunately the streets were dark and empty. It was quite late. We were all panting, out of breath by the time we arrived. There was no activity at the quay, while the boats floated quietly on the dark water. I took it as a good sign. Iawy, the man with the stubbly face, untied Udimu's small felluca, while Baenre raised the sail. Catfish pushed the boat out further in the water and we all clambered in. It reminded me of the urgency with which Bashta and I left Abtu Palace fifteen inundations ago, at night, also escaping from the danger of Shu-un-Atum.

The men quietly sailed the boat downstream to Enet-ta-Neter, lost in their own thoughts. The silvery orb of Djehuti was just a sliver of light in Nut's body. Baenre adjusted the two triangular sails, letting them billow out to allow more speed, while Iawy adjusted the rudder.

"You must not tell anyone you took us to Het-Heru's Temple," I hastened to explain to the two friends of Udimu. The four of us took up almost all the available room in the little boat. I didn't have to talk very loud to be heard.

"I understand," replied Iawy. "Udimu explained it all to us. We would rather have our innards torn out than let King Serqet ever get his hands on this young man here," and he nodded at Catfish.

The Prince grimly nodded at them in appreciation. "I hope it won't come to that," he replied tersely.

I scanned Mother Nile both upstream and downstream, anxiously looking for other boats. So far, there weren't any. Did we leave in time? Were Pharaoh's troops even now leaving Abtu Palace to journey to Waset in order to find Catfish? If so, we would come upon them around dawn. That would not be good for us. The soldiers would surely question anyone they encountered as they sailed south. Pharaoh would be looking for a young man. Catfish stood out, not only because he was the right age of the boy in question, but also because he was so tall!! He would be difficult to hide anywhere.

"I wish I had brought my weapons," Catfish grumbled. "All Muttey let me bring was this old hunting knife." He held up the dull, copper-bladed knife attached to a poorly carved stone handle.

"Your weapons would have been most unwise," I replied. "You are supposed to be a Priest Initiate, not a warrior. How could we explain those if we were spotted?"

"But without them, I am helpless and unable to defend us."

"Hmmm, perhaps Het-Heru will protect us in a different way." I certainly hoped that was true.

"I trust my dagger and mace more than I trust any Neter," the Prince quipped. In time he would repent those haughty words.

Baenre cleared his throat and spat into the river beyond our small boat. "Your Majesty," he addressed Catfish as if he were already crowned, "if Heb is correct, then no weapon will protect you against Pharaoh's solders. They are vicious men. Not only that, but you would surely be outnumbered if Heb's vision of their numbers is correct."

Catfish gazed at the dark water, holding his temper. I could feel rather than see him set his jaw angrily, yet he did refrain from speaking. "Heb?" he began after a few moments of silence.

"Yes, Catfish."

"What if we do encounter Pharaoh's troops?"

"Greet them in a normal way. We are priests returning to Enet-ta-Neter after a short holiday, to continue our Temple work."

"But what if they don't believe me? I don't think I have the right attitude for a Priest."

"Hmmmm," was my reply. Maybe he was right. Perhaps the soldiers wouldn't be taken in by his disguise after all.

"I have an idea," the prince continued. "When we see their boat..." he began.

"If we see their boat. We don't know if we will actually meet them," I temporized.

"If—or when—we see their boat," the prince continued stubbornly, "I would have time to climb over the side of the felluca and hide in the water, holding on to this rope." He pointed to a papyrus rope that was tied to the mast. "I'm a very strong swimmer and can hold my breath longer than most." He crossed his arms defiantly across his chest, the white temple garb gathering tightly across his chest and upper arms as he did so.

Perhaps he wouldn't convince the soldiers in his too-tight robe. I hadn't realized how big Catfish had grown until now. "But what about crocodiles? Or a hippopotamus?" I asked fearfully. "They are more numerous the further downstream we go."

"Crocodiles," he repeated, as though he had forgotten about them, thought for a moment, then shook his head. "I will slip into the water anyway. Better to take my chances with the possibility of a crocodile than the probability of a regiment facing us." He turned to peer aggressively at the river as though he could already see crocodiles and soldiers challenging his existence. Catfish reminded me of stories I had heard about the deceased pharaoh Menamen-Ra, and the Warrior King's dogged determination to fight whoever or whenever needed. The young man was so like his grandfather. I had taken on the task of guardian so well that I forgot that Menamen-Ra's blood did not flow through the young man's veins.

All of us in the little boat were anxious and fearful as we continued our trek down Etures, the southern section of the river. Baenre and Iawy took turns sailing and handling the rudder of the small craft, but none of us would sleep that long, exhausting, anxious night. We jumped at every floating log and whirlpool we ran into, imagining that each one might be the prow of a boat from Pharaoh's army. We periodically nibbled on the food that Muttey had packed, more from nervousness than hunger. As the dawn of a new day, Ra-as-Khepera, approached, my stomach knotted with even greater apprehension. We would be most vulnerable during daylight, and we still had a distance to travel before we arrived at the dock of Enet-ta-Neter.

"How many hentis do we have left to go?" I asked the stubble-faced man. His eyes were red from sleeplessness and barley beer.

"We'll get there before Ra is high in the heavens," was his answer.

I scanned the banks anxiously, looking for familiar landmarks that would signal our approach to the safety of the Temple. Although it wasn't hot, my Temple Robe was drenched with sweat.

Catfish tied the papyrus rope securely around his wrist, ready at a moment's notice to slip into the cold river.

Quietly we glided along the water, riding on the shallow keel of the boat. It was the first time that I had been on the river since the low flood waters had taken its toll on Ta-Meir Res. I was appalled to see how shallow the level of Mother Nile had become. The water had receded at least the height of two men standing on one another's shoulders, much less than usual at this time of year.

Tall sedge plants hugged the shore, their roots buried along the edge of the river. Many had turned brown and had fallen over, their roots drying out in the parched riverbank. Ibis and heron birds were wading in the shallow water, pecking in the mud, looking for insects, worms and small fish to eat. Blooming lotus plants were dotted here and there in the backwaters, giving a colorful relief to the greenery. Far from the banks fan palms stood like friendly sentries, their spiny leaves motionless in the still morning air. Drought-hardy acacia and tamarisk trees were flourishing further inland from the water's edge.

In the distance loomed harsh, dry hills and inhospitable mountains, glistening in the glare of day. They seemed to float above the landscape, a mirage in the shimmering heat.

Ordinarily during this season, farms would be lushly green with crops of grain and vegetables on either side of the river. However, as we passed numerous uncultivated fields, I could see how the drought had claimed the usually-fertile land, as it stood dry, parched, and dusty brown. Once we passed a farmer standing in his barren field, the family water buffalo drinking at the water's edge, while a young child sat on the back of the farmer's donkey, watching us sail by. The buffalo, donkey, and their owners looked equally scrawny. If the drought continued, the precious buffalo would be butchered to assuage the family's starvation. However, the farmer may not be able to afford another buffalo to help with the plowing next growing season, and his family could eventually starve anyway or else have to leave their farm to find food.

Several vultures circled overhead while more perched in a passing acacia tree. I wondered what creature was dying in the arid morning. Long decans passed, each agonizing moment filled with dread of the possibility of King Serqet's soldiers, a form of human vulture.

To take my mind off my nervousness, I began to quietly chant the familiar litany of the morning ritual. Catfish quizzically looked at me; I smiled in return and continued. I recited the familiar prayers to Het-Heru, summoning Her protective and loving energy as the Vengeful Eye of Ra. To surround our felluca and keep us safe from harm. I relaxed a little as I did so. My eyes were heavy with sleep, but I forced myself to stay alert and awake.

As we rounded a familiar bend, I could see the tall two-story building of the Temple of Het-Heru looming in the distance. I awkwardly stood up, dangerously rocking the small boat. "There it is," I yelled. I saw several women going about their daily tasks, watering vegetable plants by hand in the communal garden and I waved furiously at them. Either they didn't see me, or else they thought I was a pilgrim, seeking medical help from the Senu Priestesses.

The prince quickly untied the rope from his wrist, unnecessary now that we had arrived at the Per Neter, the Temple of Het-Heru.

As Iawy tied up at the quay of Enet-ta-Neter, Catfish and I leaped out of the boat. Once they handed us our few belongings, Baenre turned the boat around to immediately return to Waset. I knew they were protecting the young prince. Their delay here at the Temple might make a difference in his survival. If noticed, they might be forcefully questioned and tortured, and admit to being from Catfish's home town, or worse, that they had just come from delivering him to Enet-ta-Neter. It was best they return to Waset right away. They waved to us in farewell and were soon tacking back and forth through the strong currents, traveling north to Waset.

I stumbled from fatigue and relief, leading Catfish to the main entrance through the tenemos wall. I saw several Priestesses, in their white robes, heading towards us. One of them broke into a run when she recognized me.

"Heb," cried Tietre-Het, spontaneously throwing her arms around me in greeting. "I am so glad to see you," she continued, then quickly released me, feeling my body stiffen.

"I am glad to be here," I replied solemnly. I put down my small bag. "Tietra-Het, I'd like you to meet Catfish."

"Em Hotep, Catfish," the Priestess smiled in welcome.

"Hello," the tired adolescent mumbled. He looked as if he would fall down on the ground and be instantly asleep.

"Shara-Het will be so surprised to see you. Why didn't you let us know you were returning?"

We had already entered through the mud-brick entryway on our way towards the Sanctuary. I prostrated myself momentarily before the lovely columns of Het-Heru, then stood up, picked up my precious belongings, resuming our walk. Once again the Divine Energy of the Sacred Temple walls swirled through my exhausted body. Nervousness drained from me in those sacred surroundings, while Celestial Vibrations of Het-Heru, the nurturing Mother Cow, began to fill me with blessed peace.

Catfish had been watching everything I did and said with interest, his intelligent eyes alert, even though his reddened lids were swollen from lack of sleep. He carried his small bundle with him.

"I had no time to send a message," I replied, as we walked together. "I need to see the Hem Neter right away," I continued, adding an urgent formality to our conversation that we normally didn't use together.

"Here she is now," Tietra-Het replied. Then she abruptly walked away, a little upset perhaps by my lack of affection. "Shara-Het," I called to the elderly Hem Neter Priestess. I noticed that she walked with a limp. The folds of skin on her arms and below her chin were flabby and sagging. She was aging fast.

"Heb, my dear boy, how are you?" She held out her hands to me. I handed my bag to Catfish, then lovingly squeezed her gnarled hands with mine. The veins were beginning to show purple through her thin skin. "Not so tightly," she pulled her aching hands away.

"Oh, I'm sorry," I apologized.

"I am having difficulty with them lately," and she rubbed them gently together, hoping to assuage the swollen, aching joints. "The healing herbs don't seem to be helping anymore."

Then she turned and gently patted Catfish on the shoulder, looking up at the lanky young man. "Catfish," she said quietly. "You've grown even taller, I think. And you've shaved your head."

"Em hotep, Shara-Het," he smiled with affection at his mentor, running his hand ruefully over his bald pate.

"Where can we talk in private?" I whispered into her ear, remembering the urgency of the situation.

"Let us go to the Sacred Lake." Still limping, she slowly led the two of us over to the stone bench by the water, under a large palm tree for shade; that was her favorite place to relax and meditate. She sat down and I sat next to her. Catfish stood nearby, looking at the Lake which was bone dry. The river had not risen high enough to fill it. Reeds and sedges around its edges were slowly dying, although the date palms at its edges were still intact.

When the two of us had relaxed on the bench, I turned to the aging Priestess. As usual, I was my straightforward self. "Shara-Het, we need your help. I may have put you all in danger. But I didn't know where else to go."

"What is it, Heb?" she questioned me.

"Last night I had a vision. Pharaoh's troops have been sent to Waset to find Catfish. Perhaps someone was trying to win favors with King Serqet, and decided to notify the authorities that the Prince was still alive and se-cluded in Waset. I'm not sure," I finished with a shrug. Visions weren't al-ways lucidly detailed, but the urgency of my vision had been clear enough. "The only place I could think of to hide him was here at Enet-ta-Neter. Now that we're here, perhaps we have put your lives at risk as well."

"Now, now," said Shara-Het, patting my hand. "There is no reason to think that."

"My plan," I continued, "is to make Catfish look like one of the Initiates. To portray him as having been here for a long time. That we fool anyone who comes here looking for the prince, to find only the devoted servants of Het-Heru." I looked to Catfish. He nodded his head and yawned widely. I must find him a bed soon. "He'll need bigger Temple robes, too; this one is too small for him."

She smiled gently. "Yes, I can see that. He has become a big man."

"Maybe too big to hide?" I asked anxiously.

"No, I think he will be all right. I believe we can accomplish this plan, with Het-Heru's help of course. She is his Divine Mother after all. But we cannot tell anyone else of his identity. I am the only Priestess here who knows that he is…" She broke off her sentence. "You know."

I nodded conspiratorially.

"I will tell everyone that Catfish is one of your students from Waset. That he has come here to begin his Initiation."

"That is perfect," I breathed.

"He will have to follow the Temple regimen, of course," and her grey eyes twinkled at the thought.

"What?" Catfish spun around hearing that last sentence.

"It wouldn't hurt you and will help to make the masquerade complete. I doubt anyone would question you if you are able to repeat the chants and litany, and perform parts of the Sacred Tasks."

The young Prince looked at me, beseeching me with his eyes. "Do I have to?" he asked.

"Just until the danger is past," I agreed with Shara-Het.

"How long will that be?"

"I'm not sure. It might be a lengthy time."

"Very well," the prince agreed reluctantly.

So began the sacred instruction of the future leader of Ta-Meir Res.

Following our conversation with Shara-Het, Catfish and I took a long nap. We rested from our stressful trip, then had some supper, followed by washing ourselves in a stone basin, to purify ourselves for the evening ritual.

I glanced at Catfish who looked ridiculous in the undersized robe, his hairy ankles showing fully. I had no idea that he was so much bigger than me. Not only that, he was remarkably tall, taller than me, taller than anyone I had ever seen. "I'm afraid my robe wasn't a very good idea, dear boy."

Catfish rubbed his eyes ruefully, then stretched his shoulders backwards with a yawn, straining the fabric of the garment across his chest. If he moved any further, he would have ripped his robe. "That is all right, Heb," he acknowledged with a grin. "We were both in a hurry from urgency. I understand."

I didn't find out until sometime later that soldiers of King Serqet had been dispatched from the capital of Nekken, not Abtu as I had feared. They had traveled on the southern section of the Holy River, while we sailed along a more northerly part. Thus they had never known of our hasty flight to Enet-ta-Neter. The troops arrived before the light of Khepera emerged over the eastern horizon in Waset. I counted ourselves lucky that we had left as early as we did.

However, although Catfish and I had been very fortunate, and my vision timely, there were terrible events brewing in Ta-Meir Res and elsewhere.

I was to see the terrible tragedies for myself during the evening ritual.

I assumed my old task as Kher Heb, while Catfish and the other initiates watched, or partially participated, depending on the length of their training.

I was embarrassed at the ridiculous appearance of Catfish's ill-fitting robe and determined that Tietra-Het would take him to the local village, to be measured for new robes the following day.

I was surprised at the young man. Rather than his stubborn, yet jocular self, the Prince seemed respectful, even genuinely interested in the ceremony, chanting the repetitious words that he picked up. He began to blend in with the others, and so I ceased paying attention to him and focused instead on the litany.

"Nefer Nebet Hetepet Het-Heru.

Nefer Nebet Hetepet Het-Heru.

Nefer Nebet Hetepet Het-Heru." I continued to chant.

As I did so, I found myself falling into another vision, or was it the second part of the original one? In any event, I again saw Pharaoh's soldiers arriving in many boats at Waset. These were bloodthirsty, cruel individuals, showing no mercy. They questioned every man, woman, and child they could find, often breaking into homes to do so. "Where is the prince, son of Ankhamun?" was the standard query. Most Waset residents had no idea about Catfish, having never been taken into confidence about him. Angry soldiers took out their frustration on the residents and many citizens were killed that morning. However, one nosy old lady in Muttey and Udimu's neighborhood had observed the unusual comings and goings in that family home over the last several years. She volunteered information about the elderly couple and their family, in particular the tall young man who had arrived as a baby in Waset so many inundations ago.

Fueled with this information, the soldiers stormed Muttey's home as she was preparing supper. In my mind's eye I saw them attempt to interrogate the boisterous woman, who hotly refused them.

"Don't you have anything better to do than to bother an old lady?" she said rudely. She had been standing near the oven, kneading bread. She wiped her floury hands on the front of her frock. "Why don't you find food for your countrymen instead?"

"We know about the Prince," the captain of the guard interrupted her aggressively. "Tell us where he has gone."

"Prince?" she looked around at the hovel she had lived in all her adult life. "Does this look like a Palace to you?" I'm sure she had meant the comment to be humorous, but it came out sarcastically instead.

In response, the soldier hit Muttey on the side of the head with the handle of his dagger, knocking her to the ground. Udimu happened to enter their home at that moment, and hobbled over to her defense. Before he could reach his wife, he was stabbed through the back and chest by an impatient soldier, coughing up spurts of blood as he collapsed, then died on the spot.

The Captain yelled at the troops responsible for the murder. "What are you doing? He might have given us important information!" He turned to Muttey, but she just glared at him from the dusty ground. "Tell us where the Prince has gone, old woman!" he shouted.

"I don't have any idea what you mean," she replied angrily, looking up at him, maintaining control of herself with great difficulty. Tears flowed down her cheeks.

The man pricked the sharp end of his blade against her fleshy throat. "Tell us or you die. We know all about your plans for an uprising against Pharaoh."

"I know nothing about a Prince or an uprising," she continued tremulously, now visibly shaking with fear.

The Captain of the Guard pulled back his arm and with a swift stroke, decapitated the helpless woman. Muttey's dismembered head rolled around the bloody cooking area, coming to rest near the body of her dead husband, her dead eyes staring, wide with horror.

At that moment I shrieked and so did the Prince. The evening ritual came to an abrupt end.

Catfish fell to his knees on the floor of the sanctuary as he began wailing. "Nana!!" he called to her in a voice full of horror and grief. The only mother the young man had ever known had been brutally murdered. "Nana!" he howled like an injured animal.

CHAPTER TWENTY

MURDER, RUIA, AND OSORKON

With my arm around his shoulder for support, I helped Catfish back to the guest quarters where we had rested earlier. The young man walked woodenly, as we made our way through the Temple complex to our little hut. At least he had stopped crying. How had he been able to see what I had seen? His Mother, Atalana, had been endowed with special gifts by the Neter. Perhaps Catfish had the gift, too. Or maybe it was because the traumatic event prompted a sudden intuitive vision. That had been known to happen with even ordinary people. At any rate, the Prince and I had simultaneously seen the bloody murders of Udimu and Muttey.

When we arrived at our little hut, Catfish sat down limply on the mat, staring in front of him, his face a blank mask. I sat next to him, waiting for a sign that could help him through his misery. I wasn't sure if anything I said or did right now could be of much use to recover from such a ghastly experience. He had lost the only mother and father he had ever known in the most brutal deaths imaginable.

A young Temple Initiate named Ruia arrived at our doorway, holding a hot carved stone cup of an aromatic herbal concoction. "This will help him to sleep," she said shyly. I could tell by her mannerisms during the evening Ritual that she was not a new initiate, but she was unfamiliar to me. Many inundations had passed since I had left Enet-ta-Neter. I glanced twice at her when we assembled in the Sanctuary earlier. She bore a noticeable, youthful resemblance to Atalana. As she stood in the darkened doorway of our hut, with only the flicker of the oil lamp illuminating her features, I could see the resemblance again.

"Is he all right?" Ruia inquired anxiously.

"I hope so," I replied. "Thank you," and took the steaming cup from her hand and returned to the side of Catfish. "Drink this," I encouraged him. I looked up but the young woman had already left, her task complete.

The young prince took the cup and gulped it down wordlessly, handing the cup back to me.

"Heb, what did I see? Muttey…" he murmured, his head hanging almost to his chest. His eyes were glazed in shock and disbelief. He had been through a horrific trauma.

"Describe it to me," I encouraged.

Searching for words, in a halting manner, the Prince slowly outlined the same scenario as I myself had seen, the bloody vision.

"That is what I saw too," I replied gently. "I'm so sorry, Catfish. What a dreadful introduction into Second Sight."

"Heb, it was horrible!" and he wiped his moist forehead as though he could wipe out all memory of the tragic event he had witnessed in his vision.

"Beyond horrible," I agreed with him.

"Do you think it is true?"

"I think it is true, yes. I'm so sorry."

"How is it that I could see it so clearly then?"

"You inherited second sight from your Mother, the Queen. She was an ordained Maa Priestess of Het-Heru, an oracle."

"I don't like the… Gift." He grimaced.

"It isn't always pleasant to "see," but my visions are what saved your life and mine from Pharaoh's soldiers. We are lucky to have survived."

"We are lucky," he repeated dully. "But Nana and Udimu weren't."

"No," I agreed. I paused. "I don't know what your destiny is, Catfish, but you have been protected many times."

"Is that why you told us we needed to leave Waset?" the prince asked wearily.

"Yes, I had a vision on my way back to your home. I have had enough visions to trust them without question."

"It isn't my home anymore. I am all alone now. They're dead!" His head hung almost to his chest.

I didn't argue with Catfish. I knew Het-Heru was caring for him and had a bigger plan than I could discern. But to observe the loss of his foster parents, Muttey and Udimu, killed under such dreadful condition, was a devastating blow.

"How long must we stay here?" He sat up straighter, rubbing his sore neck. I was amazed at his inner strength and youthful resilience. He yawned widely.

"I don't know. Until the peril has passed."

"How will we know that?" He was having trouble keeping his eyes open and he yawned again.

"Perhaps we will be given another sign."

"Muttey gave her life to save mine, Heb," he mumbled somewhat incoherently.

"I know. She is, was, a courageous woman."

"I won't disappoint her, Heb." He looked at me for the first time since we had returned to the mud-brick hut, but his eyes were glassy and unfocused. "Her life will not have been taken in vain. I promise I will avenge her." He tried to smile valiantly, but the events of the last two days had taken their toll. All he could manage was a scowl. His eyelids were heavy and his head bobbed. "I think I will sleep now." He lay down upon the mat and was snoring almost immediately.

How could he go through the tumultuous last two days and be able to sleep? It was the herbal drink, of course. Catfish was a strong young man and I was genuinely impressed with him. If I had been in his place, I doubt I would be capable of rest, even with the help of sleeping herbs.

I picked up a rough linen bed cloth and covered him. Then I went through my satchel looking for the leather bag that contained the two amulets, and took out the talisman of Het-Heru, then closed the bag carefully, away from prying eyes. Finally I walked outside to feel the soft night air, the amulet clasped in my hand. Stars were twinkling in Nut's body. Every soul that died became a star, so it was said, living eternally in the vast starry body. Now Udimu and Muttey were there too. I wondered which stars were theirs? I sat upon the cool sandy ground and closed my eyes, rubbing the talisman, invoking the Beautiful One, Het-Heru to help me through this black night.

The next morning I awoke early. I was keeping vigil over Catfish in case he should awaken fearful or disoriented both from his vision and the sleeping draught. I could sense the whole Temple was awake and buzzing with gossip and speculation about our unfortunate mystical experience. Catfish, however, slept well into the morning. He had been awake for a while when Ruia came to fetch the alabaster goblet that contained the herbal potion. So I was there when the two young people saw each other in the fair morning light.

Catfish sat up on his sleeping mat, then stood, still a little dizzy and wavering on his feet. He walked over to the young woman and extended his hands. "I am Catfish," he introduced himself. "Thank you."

"Yes, I know," she replied, taking his hands in hers, all the while dimpling, her face tinged a faint pink. "I mean, I am very glad to meet you, Catfish. I was called Ruia at home. Here I am known as Ruia-Het."

The girl was a perfect image of feminine beauty. Ruia had a way of holding herself, regal yet approachable, that reminded me of Atalana. Her breasts were large, pressing against the fabric of her priestess robe, and I could tell she had wide, curving hips. I noticed again that Ruia displayed a few physical characteristics similar to Atalana. Her eyes were slanted, like Atalana's, but were a deeper brown than the Queen's. Both women's facial structures and high cheek bones were similar. Ruia was short, though, shorter than Atalana, and much shorter than Catfish. The extreme contrast of their two heights was unusual, yet somehow pleasing.

"Ruia. That is a very pretty name." Catfish stared at her as though he was still in a trance.

"How do you feel this morning?" she asked. As an Initiate, she was already well-trained. She must be learning herbal concoctions and remedies.

Catfish considered a moment. "I have a terrible headache. Here." He put his hand to his right temple in a quasi-dramatic gesture.

Ruia replied gently, grinning at the subterfuge. She coquettishly tilted her head toward her right shoulder, all the while staring demurely at the Prince. I noticed that she seemed innocent and naive. I imagine she had been sheltered first by her family and then by the temple. "I wouldn't doubt it. Shara-Het asked me to double the amount of herbs for the sleeping drink."

"Holy Neterw!" the Prince exclaimed. "It is no wonder I feel like this." Rather than being upset, he laughed heartily and Ruia laughed in reply. She reached up to feel his head and they bumped hands in so doing, and laughed again.

By Het-Heru. They were flirting with each other!

Over the next few weeks, the two teenagers were so obviously infatuated with each other, that we could hardly keep them apart. They stared at each other through meals. They blushed when they met each other in the daily comings and goings. They laughed at any remark.

I caught a glimpse of them early one evening before rituals, leaning on a column of Het-Heru. Their heads were close together, arms near their chests. Only the tips of their fingers were touching. I felt as though I was privileged to observe Atalana and Ankhamun's courtship through these two young people.

However, in the outside world, things were not so loving and harmonious.

We received first-hand reports from troops wounded by the King's military as they came seeking medical treatment from the Semu Priestesses at Enet-ta-Neter. Shara-Het and I questioned them at length. They told us that Waset had been overrun by several regiments. Many people had been murdered and a number of homes had been burnt to the ground. Soldiers were sent to interrogate those in the neighboring villages and farms as to the whereabouts of Catfish, but could get no satisfaction from anyone. A solid wall of silence was all they found.

The king suspected Waset's militia of fomenting civil war and planning to overthrow Pharaoh. Many people ran away after the local militia was disbanded. They left for other towns and cities, to organize new troops, and to escape from the King's long skinny hands of fury.

When soldiers found General Herusmatauy on his family's farm, the old gentleman behaved as though he was a doddering idiot, drooling and mumbling to himself. It was a brilliant act. The soldiers were thankful to leave him alone. However, for months we had no word from Wahankh and Wosret, the foster brothers of Catfish. We hoped they had escaped the wrath of King Serqet and were in hiding.

Soldiers were stationed in Waset, Abtu, and also Khemenu, where the townspeople had first rioted against the soldiers. Periodically the troops conducted forays to local Temples, interrogating Priests and Priestesses but without luck.

Soldiers did eventually come to Enet-ta-Neter. The Prince, Shara-Het and I remained in the sanctuary during the long, terrifying interrogation and search, chanting constantly to Het-Heru and burning myrrh for Her protection. Fortunately, Ruia and the other Priestesses, Initiates, and those in temporary service had no idea about Catfish, so they had nothing to reveal. Soldiers explored the entire temple compound, even ransacked the sleeping areas. My papyrus journal was safe, as none of the troops would be literate in translating hieroglyphics. I had the foresight to hide Atalana's fabulous necklace in the temple Naos along with the heqa and nekhekha, concealed out of sight behind the beautiful statue of Het-Heru.

When a team of soldiers investigated the Sanctuary, all they saw was a thick golden haze of incense and white-clad figures. They never "saw" us. I don't know what trick of light or shadow Het-Heru used, but it worked miraculously well. We had become impervious to ordinary sight. I shudder to think what might have happened if Her magick hadn't worked so well.

After a long, thorough search, the armed forces left, convinced the Prince was not hidden at Enet-ta-Neter. I wondered if the troops believed they were by now chasing a mirage.

The day after the military left, Catfish came to me, hand in hand with Ruia. "Heb, we love each other and want to marry. Will you give us your blessing?"

Ruia spoke up as well. "I have decided to forego further training here at Enet-ta-Neter. I want us to journey to Nekken, where I am from. I will introduce Catfish to my family. I believe they will also give us their blessing."

I could say I was shocked, but in truth I was not. Indeed, I was immensely pleased and happy for the young couple. "First, let me consult with Shara-Het," and we all marched over to the Temple. When we had conferred with the elderly Priestess, we found we were all in agreement, that marriage was a splendid idea.

"I speak for Het-Heru and She tells me that your meeting was arranged and your marriage is in accord with Divine Will," said Shara-Het. She hugged Catfish and then Ruia. "I couldn't be more pleased. I am only sad that I am too old and frail to make the trip with you, to see you wed. The Blessings of the Neter are upon you!"

Within the week Catfish, Ruia and I were traveling to Nekken in a loaned barge that was hung with banners of the likeness of Het-Heru. The banners were meant to indicate that the felluca clearly belonged to the Temple of that Neter. During our trip, we were not stopped nor boarded nor disturbed in any way.

The sailors lived in Nekken with their vessel, and returned home after tying up at the busy dock and helping us to disembark. Although king's soldiers roamed the city, they hardly gave us a second glance. We were merely three individuals in white robes, from the Temple of Het Heru.

When we arrived at Ruia's house, Catfish and I were brought by a woman servant into an immense outer room. I was surprised to discover that her family home was enormous and stately. They lived in a huge house with many rooms, plus extra houses outside for servants, officials, staff, a chapel, storerooms, with a thick mud-brick fence all around the perimeter, higher than two men, near the river but not too close to get flooded.

Her Father was seated on a backless wooden chair when we came in. He rose to his feet as soon as he saw his daughter. As he strode over to her, his eyes were gleaming with adoration.

"My darling girl, what brings you home to us?" He put his massive arms around her body and held her tightly.

Ruia hugged her father, then turned to Catfish, her arm still around her parent. "Father, I want you to meet Catfish. I met him at Enet-ta-Neter."

"I am pleased to meet you, Catfish."

"I am pleased to make your acquaintance, Sir," and they grasped each other's arms in greeting.

"Call me Osorkon."

Ruia continued with the formalities. "This is Heb, the guardian of Catfish."

Osorkon turned to greet me. He was an average sized man, but that was the only average thing about him. He had a huge barrel chest, muscular legs below his kilt, with a mass of curly hair at his throat peeking out beneath the elaborate collar he wore. His wide shoulders belied his height, seeming to indicate a much taller man. But the most arresting thing about the man was his eyes. As he leveled his gaze at me, I thought that I would not want to be in his displeasure. His piercing, enormous eyes were dark brown and looked directly into me, studying me for a moment's time. He must be a man chosen by Heru, with unblinking, far-seeing falcon eyes and a regal manner. Osorkon was undoubtedly a man of some power and prestige. Apparently he approved of what he saw in me. He smiled formally and said, "Welcome to our home, Heb."

"Thank you, Osorkon. I am indeed privileged to meet you." I bowed in response.

"Please sit and be comfortable," and Osorkon indicated other chairs.

Ruia moved hers closer to Catfish and held his hand. She got right to the point of their visit. "Father, we have something to ask you."

"Oh?" replied Osorkon. He tried to make his expression look severe, but failed. He could clearly see that his daughter was in love with Catfish.

Catfish cleared his throat, then spoke up. "Sir, I would like your blessings for us to be wed."

"My dear boy, this is my one and only daughter you are speaking of." His voice boomed with authority.

"Yes, sir, Ruia has told me."

"She is the jewel of our family." He raised his thick eyebrows to make his point.

"I promise to care for her to the depth of my being. I know we love each other very much. I have the permission and blessing of my guardian, my teacher at the Temple, and even the Neter Het-Heru to join in wedlock with your daughter." He straightened his back with pride.

"Well, who am I to argue with a Neter?" Osorkon joked, suddenly at ease.

Ruia jumped out of her chair and ran to her father's side. "Thank you so much, Father," she breathed, hugging him once again.

Catfish came and stood next to her, his arm around her waist.

"If you love him, which is obvious, why should I not give my permission? I have great respect for your intuition about people, my daughter. That is why your mother and I sent you to study at the Temple. Just like your cousin Atalana." Osorkon turned to me in explanation. "We belong to the House of the Southern Sycamore, dedicated to Het-Heru."

Now all was made clear in that one statement. Atalana. This was Atalana's family! No wonder Het-Heru had given Her blessing for the match. Indeed, She was instrumental in getting them together in the first place, arranging everything in advance, as usual.

Catfish looked at me meaningfully, clearing his throat to get my attention. "Heb." He nodded in Osorkon's direction.

Understanding his unspoken message, I interrupted the proceedings. "Lord Osorkon, may I speak to you in private? There are details that cannot be divulged at this moment except to your ears." I said in a hushed tone of voice. I could barely breathe from the knowledge that was flooding through my body."

"Of course, Heb. Ruia, why don't you find your dear Mother and let her know you are here. Then show Catfish around. Give him one of the special sleeping chambers."

"I will, Father." She eyed me with concern, but I shook my head, and smiled to reassure her.

The two young people left the room, hand in hand.

Osorkon led the way into another living area with two comfortable wooden chairs with backs to recline against and a pillow to sit upon. I picked up my bag and followed him into the luxurious room. Beautiful carpets lay on the floor, while sizeable alabaster pots of plants were dotted around the room. He motioned to one chair and sat in the other. I felt amazement that so many beautiful pieces of precious furniture could be owned by one family.

A serving girl had followed us into the room. "Not now, Tabes. My guest and I desire privacy."

"As you wish, lord." The girl Tabes left.

I sat in the chair my host had offered me. I adjusted my priest's robe, giving myself time to arrange my thoughts as well.

As I got comfortable, Osorkon pulled his chair closer, a quizzical look on his face. "What concerns you, dear Heb?" All traces of formality were gone.

I was not used to familiarities, but seeing that Ruia's Father was a benevolent man, I accepted it willingly. I asked, "You are related to Atalana?"

"Yes. We attended her coronation to King Ankhamun. Although we were not intimate with her family, we were devastated to hear about her death and that of the child. A terrible thing." He wiped his forehead, and several tears sparkled on his cheek.

I interrupted his reverie. "What I am about to tell you must remain between the two of us. Not your wife or even Ruia must know what I am about to tell you. Not until the time is right."

"You are being very mysterious, Heb," replied Osorkon.

"I must be cautious, Osorkon. For the benefit of the Pharaoh and our country."

"That devil!"

"Not the current Pharaoh. The future one."

"How do you mean?"

"Lord Osorkon, I served as Custodian of the Palace under Ankhamun and the Lady Atalana before I became a Kher Heb Priest of Het-Heru."

Osorkon nodded, listening. "We were distant cousins. As I said, we attended Atalana's coronation, along with her mother and siblings, as well as others of our family."

"Catfish is related to Atalana."

"He cannot be. I know all of her relatives."

"You do not know her son."

"Her son died when she did."

"No, sir, he did not. I was in attendance at the Queen's death."

"We heard she was bitten by serpents, so the rumors go. Our whole family, indeed all of Nekken, went into mourning for her. And later for Ankhamun."

"Yes, the story about the snakes is true. However, the snakes were not in her chamber by accident."

"What?" Osorkon sat up straighter and leaned towards me.

"I have reason to believe she was murdered. Someone went to great lengths to arrange to have the snakes put in her chamber, perhaps even bribing guards to accomplish the deed."

"That cannot be possible!" Osorkon exclaimed.

"I assure you most urgently it is. I was privy to inside knowledge directly from the King and Queen. Someone inside the Palace was trying to forcibly remove them from power. Pharaoh almost died from a camel accident years before. The camel was probably poisoned. Then later scorpions were found in the Royal Bed; Ankhamun and Atalana could have been stung to death."

Osorkon eyes were wide and his hand was held to his jaw in horror.

"Still later the Queen had gone on a retreat to Enet-ta-Neter. She returned to find the King ailing, almost ready for the Barque of Death. Apparently someone had been poisoning his food while she was away."

"Why would someone want to do that? Ankhamun was a good King; we all honored him."

"Perhaps someone wanted to take over the throne for himself." Before Osorkon could reply again, I continued. "The day that Atalana died, two serpents were found in her chamber. She had been bitten numerous times, apparently trying to protect her infant son, the Prince, from the poisonous snakes. I was in the room when she died," I added.

"This is unbelievable. An outrage!" he exclaimed.

"The King's health had been permanently afflicted by the poisons, and he believed he wouldn't live long either. He assumed the Prince was also in grave danger. Whoever was guilty of those crimes would try to murder the baby as well. Thus, Ankhamun asked me to hide the Prince until the boy was old enough to regain his rightful place. To prove that claim, Ankhamun gave me the heqa and nekhekha, as well as Atalana's royal necklace of Het-Heru. I have saved them for the day they would be necessary to declare the

Prince's heritage and legal right to the throne." With a dramatic flourish, I reached into my bag and produced the heqa, nekhekha, and the necklace of Het-Heru.

Osorkon gasped, then leaned over to inspect the necklace more closely. "I remember this," he murmured. "Atalana wore it the day of her Coronation. She looked so lovely."

"That is correct, my Lord," I affirmed, with a catch in my throat, swallowing hard. I remembered that day and Atalana's loveliness.

"The workmanship on these," the Lord held up the instruments of Royal Office, examining them closely, "is exquisite. I doubt that anyone other than a King would be in possession of such fine tools." He looked at me again, gleaning the truth from me. "You don't mean..."

"Yes, Catfish is the son of Queen Atalana."

Osorkon sat back heavily in his chair. I thought for a moment he would fall over. I allowed for the gravity of my information to sink in for a while. "So my daughter wants to marry Catfish..."

"...who is the son of King Ankhamun and Queen Atalana. The Prince and Heir to the Throne of Ta-Meir Res." I finished his statement for him.

"But then..." He stopped. "Does Catfish know?"

"Yes, he knows. But Ruia does not. It would be best if she was not told until the kingdom is safe once again. The knowledge could put her, and your family, in great danger."

"I agree. Oh, Divine Neters! How can we make the kingdom safe for him, for Atalana's son? For my future son-in-law?" Osorkon clapped me on the shoulder, beaming. "Yet, this is wonderful news!" he exclaimed. "We all thought the child had died."

"No, he has been alive and well." Then I told Osorkon about Udimu and Muttey, how Bashta and I had escaped to Waset and the couple had taken us in. How Muttey had raised the baby to manhood, lovingly and firmly. That only recently we had divulged his heritage to Catfish and had proceeded to train him for his Royal Duties. That somehow King Scorpion had found out and had sent soldiers to Waset, to capture or murder the Crown Prince. I explained how Muttey and Udimu had themselves been brutally murdered and how Catfish and I escaped once again, this time to the protection of Enet-ta-Neter. "He met your daughter at Het-Heru's Temple, and the rest of the story you know."

"We must do what we can to restore Catfish to his Throne."

"But the King…" I began.

"No, Heb, the man on the Throne of Ta-Meir Res is not the true King. If he were, he wouldn't murder to take over power, nor kill people he is ordained to protect! He is no true servant of Ma'at." Osorkon spoke with passion, not from emotion but with a tone of authority, coupled with family obligation and connection. "That assassin has sat upon the Throne for too long. He must be removed and soon, before he destroys the whole Kingdom with his madness! Catfish, with our help, can restore Ma'at, and dispel the darkness of Setekh, anarchy and chaos. But how?"

"I know that Het-Heru has been instrumental in every move and every event in Catfish' life. She has protected him, and others, more than once. So I surrender to Her Wisdom. She is responsible for everyone's safety and for the unveiling of all truth."

"Has Ruia told you anything about our family?" Osorkon asked.

"Only that she comes from a loving family, who lives in the city of Nekken."

"I am the governor, the Nomarche of Nekken. Not only am I wealthy, but I have many powerful political connections as well. I am the latest in a dynasty of wealth and power stretching back many generations. Therefore, I am in the perfect position to help Catfish. Help our country," he added with emphasis.

Once again Het-Heru, Mother of Pharaoh, Neter of Life, Mistress of Heaven, had arranged events perfectly. For the first time in many years, I felt the heavy weight of responsibility lessening. Perhaps I wouldn't have to hold the fate of Ta-Meir Res in my solitary hands much longer.

In a similar fashion to Waset, Osorkon's citadel, the House of the Southern Sycamore, had stored food for inhabitants of Nekken to safeguard for disasters. I later found out that Osorkon was a wise leader and the people of Nekken trusted him implicitly. He had an extensive web of political acquaintances and didn't hesitate to make use of them.

Soon after our conversation, Osorkon sent trusted members of his family as official envoys to Waset, Abtu, and Khemenu, ostensibly to trade food to local Nomarches in exchange for future promises. They were instructed to glean what they could about Pharaoh's plans and that of the military. Furthermore, those men visited other Noble families and obtained their assistance in raising an army to fight against the hated king. Unrest was brewing everywhere, while the famine continued unabated. Food riots continued to break out, even with soldiers everywhere. So it wasn't difficult to garner support to create armed forces of rebellion. The news of the massacre at Waset, when the soldiers went there looking for Catfish, spread throughout the Kingdom of Ta-Meir Res. The story was told and re-told, becoming more terrible with every retelling. With it grew widespread rage against those responsible, namely King Serqet and his personal army of scorpion-men—who were cruel, ruthless, and cold-hearted.

Osorkon held his secret weapon in abeyance—that of the Prince and his claim to the Throne of Ta-Meir Res. When all the proper pieces were in place for a successful rebellion, then he could let the Prince's identity be known. Meanwhile, the Nomarche continued to be cautious.

Catfish, on the other hand, had to restrain himself from starting a war of rebellion. He had vowed to avenge the murder of his parents, both his royal parents, as well as his foster parents who had raised him. Fortunately, his stay at Enet-ta-Neter had helped him become more patient, but that wouldn't last forever. General Herusmatauy was secretly brought to Nekken, to help with the planning of the war we contemplated. The retired General's back was stooped and now had to walk with a stick, but he was still in good mental health and high spirits. He was delighted to help with the war plans.

The two brothers, Wahankh and Wosret, sons of Udimu and Muttey, were discovered secreted in a small village outside Abtu and were brought to Nekken. They were elated when reunited with their brother Catfish, as ready to fight as he was. They played war games with Catfish, practicing their skills with bow, mace, spear, and dagger as they used to in the more peaceful days in Waset. They invited all the men of Nekken to join them, along with the city's security force and local militia. Other cities began their preparation, too. Soon Osorkon had an unofficial, but well-trained army in three cities as well as some smaller towns and villages, ready to fight at his command.

Catfish, his foster brothers Wosret and Wahankh, and I lived within the walls of the Noble House of the Southern Sycamore, guests of the Nomarche of Nekken, enjoying a palatial existence. Osorkon made sure we all had appropriate attire to wear, while servants waited on our every request. I could see that Catfish enjoyed it immensely, while I felt ill at ease, preferring to remain in my Priestly robes, living the simple life I was used to. However, I stayed within the mansion's walls, not wishing to put myself in harm's way. I had a wonderful chamber to sleep in, where I also conducted my morning and evening rituals to Het-Heru. Yet Catfish and his two foster brothers went to the city square to gleefully practice bashing heads, oblivious to or even courting danger.

Not only did Lord Osorkon have a huge home, but we discovered it was fortified as well. The walls had been constructed twice as thick as any normal home, with peep holes situated at regular intervals to detect if any enemy advanced upon it. Armed men were stationed at all the doorways day and night, to keep undesirable elements out, while Lord Osorkon had his own personal bodyguards. Food and water were stored inside, in case of a sudden siege. We were safe for the time being within its gloriously decorated mud brick-and-plaster enclosure. And we waited.

CHAPTER TWENTY-ONE

NEKKEN

King Serqet's frenzied anxiety grew daily, stimulated by intermittent riots of hungry citizens. With fury that Catfish had escaped his grasping hand, Shu-un-Atum ordered a military takeover of the southern Kingdom of Ta-Meir Res. Pharaoh enlisted all the men he could gather together, willing to fight against their own countrymen. Most men refused this service. Thus the King was forced to recruit those most unworthy. Prisoners were released to serve in his army regardless of their crimes. Drunkards were dragged bleary-eyed from their cups. Wife-beaters wrested from their unhappy homes. Unruly youngsters seeking excitement in any form were given weapons and authority with which to wreak further havoc. These uncaring men formed a ragtag army of misfits, which were sent to major cities and towns to declare martial law. Their orders were to wrest power from local Nomarches. Imprison or kill any who resisted, was the order—including the helpless—the infirm and elderly, women and children alike. Their unspeakable acts of ruthlessness aroused our Kingdom as nothing else had done. Bestiality and cruelty were the sparks which finally ignited the dry tinder of starvation, unrest and righteous anger, bursting into flames of rebellion everywhere. Citizens began to rise up against the King's troops.

Chanting and praying at my makeshift altar to Het-Heru, I asked that She alert me of any impending attack on our town. When I soon received the vision of massive troop deployment, setting sail for Nekken, I was both relieved and alarmed. The vision I received was not of the faces of men, but deadly, inhuman man-insects, wielding metallic and stone weapons, sailing from Abtu to Waset and Nekken to infest our towns with their filth, taking what they wanted—money, power, women and girls—with the intent to kill, maim, rape, and overpower. I notified Lord Osorkon and Catfish immediately of the coming horde.

Therefore, when Pharaoh's predatory troops arrived at Nekken, we were ready for them. Not only had all the men of the capital city been diligently practicing tactics and weaponry, we had the advantage of secrecy coupled with surprise. Different men who survived the battle told me what transpired.

Early in the day all the male citizens of Nekken, from young boys to elderly men, waited sweltering in the hot sun, anticipating the arrival of many boats. As an army they had no uniforms; most men wore only a belt and a small triangular loincloth. Others wore a short linen kilt, with two broad bands of leather tied across their chests. Most went barefoot, their feet tough as stone.

All our local vessels, large and small, had been moved further upriver from the main landing place then tied to rocks along the bank, to secure them from destruction or detection. Young boys hid near the dock, to discharge rocks from slingshots at the arriving enemy. Hurling stones demanded considerable practice in order to be effective, but these young men were skilled. A slingshot's main advantage was the easy availability of ammunition near the bank of the river. In the hands of these lightly armed skirmishers, stones from slingshots would be used to distract and harass the enemy.

Large papyrus crates were stacked around the dock, behind which our main fighting troops hid, quivers full of arrows on their backs, bows in hand. The bow-and-arrow was our most effective weapon. Each one was designed with a single curvature, made of wood, and strung with sinews or strings made of plant fiber. Bows were between five and ten hand spans in length, strengthened by binding the wooden rod with flax cord. These were used to fire strong reed arrows fletched with three feathers and tipped with flint or other sharpened stone, which was then tipped in camel or goat dung.

Our arrows were terrible, inhuman weapons, but we needed an overwhelming advantage over our enemy. Once lodged inside a body, an arrow began to fester immediately. The dung poisoned the bloodstream, creating infection and high fever, while the stone tip was impossible to remove without tearing delicate flesh, leaving a dreadful suppurating wound that was difficult to heal.

Our waiting bowmen were experts in the art of archery. They could send volleys of arrows from their quivers, inserting one arrow into the string, while they readied another between their fingers. Thus, arrows could fly almost without stop while the supply of arrows lasted. The bowmen prayed to Neith, Neter of the Hunt and Guardian of their weapons, for help, a steady hand, and a sure eye to their targets.

Still more of our forces were positioned on both sides of the wide river, ready to take down any of the enemy who tried to escape by land. Our warriors held sharp-edged spears with pointed blades made of copper or flint, and curved throwing sticks with which to fling at the opposing army. Others, expecting to fight at close quarters, were armed with clubs, maces, stone axes, and copper knives. They carried shields that were roughly rectangular and composed of a wooden frame covered with stiffened hide, to protect their bodies from similar weapons in the hands of their enemies.

However, our greatest advantage would be surprise.

Ra gave us yet further advantage. The soldiers arrived by boat around noontime, Ra's strongest hour. Sunlight glancing off the water diminished their vision; the troops squinted, needing to shield their eyes from the fierce light multiplied into stinging rays by the reflection of the water. Before the King's soldiers could disembark at the dock, the boys aimed their slingshots and easily found their marks, turning attention away from the dock and the hidden troops. After they had pelted the enemy for a while, our bowmen began shooting their arrows into the air. They eliminated enemy forces by the hundreds, while our forces remained protected behind the papyrus bundles. Then our warriors set fire to the approaching boats by attaching arrows soaked in oily rags, then lit them and shot into the enemy's midst. The billowing sails caught fire easily, until each boat had become a nightmarish, fiery inferno. Men could be heard screaming as the quickly-spreading fire burned their bodies; many jumped into the water to escape. Some drowned in the deep, fast-flowing river. If any were unlucky enough to climb up the river's bank, they were quickly dispatched by mace, club, or knife by the men of Nekken. Fallen enemies were mutilated and left in unholy lumps where they fell, their corpses exposed to vultures, crows, jackals, and other scavengers.

Although I did not leave the Noble House of the Sycamore until evening, in my mind's eye I could see some of the struggles that ensued that day, not only in Nekken but everywhere in Ta-Meir Res. As I chanted to Het-Heru and Her consort, the Warrior God of Kings, the Neter Heru, I became a falcon, soaring on the wind above the land of Ta-Meir Res. With the avenging Udjat Eye of Ra to guide me, I followed the wandering river's course, until I saw many places of battle. Mingled sounds of yelling and grunts of exertion, as one soldier fought with another, were accompanied by screams of wounded and dying men. Blood, red as Sekhmet's gown, poured upon the ground and splashed on garments, hands, and faces. Hands holding a dagger or a mace swiftly descended upon the heads or bodies of enemies, cracking open a skull here, slashing a neck or chest there. The bitter aroma of death was everywhere. Hungry vultures circled the bodies, waiting for their chance to feed on the carrion, rotting quickly in the blazing sun.

Before Ra-as-Atum could retire in the west that day, most of the King's soldiers had been killed in Nekken. The few of Pharaoh's soldiers that escaped by boat would surely bring reinforcements. Meanwhile our local military retreated to the town center, to regroup, wait, and rest. Fires had been lit here and there, illuminating the dirty and bloodied faces of the soldiers, while young girls brought clay basins and pitchers of water for them to wash themselves. Women of Nekken had been anxiously cooking and baking all day, while the sounds of battle echoed from the docks through the streets and their homes. They had no idea who they would be serving that night, family or foe, or which members of their families would lie bloody on the field of battle. Fortunately, our casualties were surprisingly light. Three men had been killed, and only a dozen wounded.

The women brought refreshment to the weary, hungry warriors, serving rich and poor, old and young, those had fought together and were now resting against the walls of buildings encircling the deserted marketplace. The reunion and embracing of loved ones was as nurturing as the food. The echoes of women crying in happy reunion or in desperate grief pierced my heart, and I struggled to overcome my own feelings as I listened.

Catfish walked through the evening encampment, embracing some, talking to others in a calm, strong voice. He was dressed in a fine linen kilt and tunic, a leather breastplate, the design of the Sacred Sycamore tree embossed on it, fastened over his chest, with sandals made of finely tooled leather tied on his large feet. He held a jeweled mace that Osorkon had crafted especially for him, his copper dagger tucked in his belt. I had seen him before he left the family home earlier that morning. He had cut a magnificent figure, striding confidently on his long legs through the entryway to face the enemy of his kinsmen and Ta-Meir Res. Now his kilt and tunic were stained with blood and dust, but he held his head proudly. The Prince had become a real soldier that day, impressing many with his skill, bravery and dedication. He had survived his first test as a warrior and had matured as a result.

General Herusmatauy hobbled along, using his walking stick. He and I accompanied the Prince as he walked among the troops of his homeland.

"Hurrah for the General!"

A victorious cheer went up as the old man appeared, and exhausted soldiers scrambled to their feet to greet him. Many clapped him on his back, while his free hand was grasped by many local warriors in appreciation. The first day of the General's brilliant plan had been well executed. We had few casualties and spirits were high.

I knew there would come a time when Catfish would be celebrated by his people as the true King. Until then, his secret needed to be protected, until we had triumphed over Serqet. Then Catfish could safely be placed upon the Throne of Ta-Meir Res.

Although none of us could know of the far-reaching events that transpired that day, later stories were told of the events that occurred throughout all the cities, towns, and villages. The citizens of Ta-Meir Res waged a ferocious battle against the Scorpion Army intended to enslave them. In the holy capital Abtu there had been fighting in every street, in the market place, even in various homes of the town. Apparently the rebellion had not yet gotten close to Abtu Palace, although the fiercest fighting took place on the road to the Royal structure. But Pharaoh and his troops held the Palace—for today.

CHAPTER TWENTY-TWO

KING SERQET

King Serqet huddled in a darkened room in the palace, listening to the shouts of angry men outside, dangerously near. Had they already made their way into the enclosure of the Palace? Who was winning? His troops? Or the citizens of Ta-Meir Res, waging a fierce battle to regain their freedom from his scorpion army? He could hear his own labored breathing, rasping in his ears. He was crouched, alone, in the dark, as he so often had experienced during his life. He cried in solitude, wiping bitter tears from his hardened thin cheeks. The King never had much of an appetite, and in the last few months had hardly eaten anything. His emaciated face already looked skeletal. His stomach complained with a distant growl, but to no avail. Food would not be coming today or ever.

He prayed to Ausar for forgiveness, for absolution, to save him from what could be a horrible destiny. He had never much believed in the Neters. If They were anything like his parents, They would not listen nor care for him. Yet, the King prayed fervently, hoping for a miracle. Hoping that at last Ausar, the King of Neters, would hear him and come to his rescue. Failing that, Ausar would at least put in a good word for him at the moment of his

Judgment, with Anpu in attendance, as Djehuti wrote down fateful words of judgment on His scroll. The image of the Destroyer loomed large and menacing. Shu-un-Atum closed his eyes and prayed ever more desperately.

Little did he know that at that moment his Captain of the Guard was racing for his life. Disguised in ragged clothing, the soldier was discovered riding atop a camel, loping through the palace yard heading towards the safety of the desert wilderness. However, citizens recognized and encircled him, wrenching him off the camel. He screamed as do all bullies and cowards when faced with their death.

Vengeful women fell upon the Captain of the Guard, who was now struggling on the ground, trying to get away from the many hands pulling at him. They began yanking out his hair, angrily slashing his cheeks with their fingernails, poking his eyes with sticks they carried. Meanwhile, men hacked at the hapless man with whatever was available. They used stones and copper hunting knives and fists and feet, kicking and smashing and swiping his body until the skin became a mass of bloody wounds, flesh flapping like pieces of cloth. The mob had become so enraged in their lust for vengeance that they didn't stop until all that was left was the white-hard bones and skull. A man in name only. The remains hardly resembled what had only moments ago had been a human being. He had been literally torn limb from limb, like a sacrificial lamb, by the super-human strength of the mob's anger. His arms and legs were thrown around like parts of rag dolls. Little bits of flesh stuck here and there to the bone. Hacked-off pieces of him were strewn on the ground. Organs had been ripped from the torso and chopped up with vicious whacks from sharp knives. His heart had been cut out, wrenched from his chest, dripping and squirting. Mummy-dry sand quickly absorbed the pooling blood. The ruin of his body mirrored his greedy, voracious appetite in the service of a cruelly insane Pharaoh. He and his soldiers had hacked up Ta-Meir Res, caring not about the cost of the ensuing carnage, without compassion for the starving population. Bloody justice had prevailed.

Panting, heads drooping with exertion, the citizens of Abtu finally stood up and surveyed the ruin—the Captain's destroyed physical body. Blood had spattered over a dozen of the closest people. They wiped their sweating foreheads with the back of their hands, many still holding reddened weapons. One man howled in victory, raising his knife in the air. Chunks of muscle and tendon, stinking like rotting garlic, and bone chips lie here and there on the glittering sand, making an interesting scarlet contrast to the whiteness of the blowing granules.

"To the King!" some woman yelled, her hands bloody as if she had just finished butchering a goat. The mob ran looking for Serqet in the bowels of the Palace.

The sound echoed throughout the Palace. Shu-un-Atum sucked in a breath of air and held it, listening to the captain's terminal agony. Cold gooseflesh rippled up his spine, making his hair stand on end, and he shivered uncontrollably in the hot room. He waited for another sound, but heard nothing more. His stomach knotted and he had an urgent desire to defecate.

Shu-un-Atum was sharpening a knife on a whetstone, when he heard the woman's battle cry. Without hesitation, he held it to his throat and sliced across, left to right, pulsing blood. He slid to the floor, spurting life in a pool. In moments, he had slipped into the oblivion of death, depriving others of the pleasure of his murder. Het-Heru and her Sister-Lioness-Self, Sekhmet, watched the end of his life with grim satisfaction.

How did I know all these things? Years of training coupled with the intensity of battle waging throughout the country had allowed me this knowledge. I could see battles in a bowl of soup. I envisioned the defeat of Serqet in the eyes of a dead fish I had for dinner. My own eyes had turned inward, seeing what should not have been looked upon by anyone. The misery I saw was too much for one man to bear. And yet I did bear it—somehow.

The people in Nekken celebrated when I informed them of the death of King Serqet. I did not want to spoil their victory and their happiness. But

I knew that more awful events were destined for Ta-Meir Res, my beloved country. Many more would die before peace could reign. Before Catfish could attain his rightful place as heir and Pharaoh. But tonight I let them celebrate. Soon enough war would come to every one's home and hearth.

CHAPTER TWENTY-THREE

PEACE AND UNIFICATION

The good people of Nekken had become my extended family. I loved them almost as much as I loved Catfish. Almost as much my beloved Atalana. Almost as much as my spiritual mother and source of strength, the Neter Het-Heru. Almost as much as my mentor Mukalia, the wise one. The townspeople were generous and friendly with me. Although I wasn't quite a stranger, being the guardian of Catfish, Osorkon's future son-in-law, they were unbelievably supportive. And I had become their oracle and visionary, to help and protect Nekken in return for their kindness.

The next day the town of Nekken prepared to hold a huge festival, not only in victory over the troops they had conquered, but also the death of a Pharaoh universally hated and reviled.

Cooking fires were lit and every home opened their food stores to prepare a great celebration feast. Boys snared wild ducks. Caged pigeons were slaughtered, then readied for cooking. Grain was pounded into flour, then rolled into loaves to bake. Beer vats were opened. Those not too injured helped clear the center of town for the gala.

As they celebrated the demise of King Serqet, I kept aloof from them, although Catfish intuited something was bothering me. I didn't want to ruin their happiness with what I sensed was coming. I could feel the changing fortunes and a disaster which could last years. The burden of knowledge weighed heavily upon my heart. I would get a chance to speak soon enough, though. I stood apart from the people of Nekken, staring into nothingness, my arms folded across my chest.

The young man who was becoming a warrior clapped me on the shoulder, startling me out of my reverie. "Why don't you come to the feast, Heb? You have worked hard and need to enjoy yourself," Catfish added, forthright as ever.

"Yes, do come with us, Heb," added Ruia, her face aglow from being close to her beloved Catfish.

"I'm tired," I apologized. "I think I will just go rest. But thank you both for asking." I veiled the knowledge in my eyes, not wishing to spoil the evening.

"As you wish," he replied, smiling at me. Then Catfish shrugged good-naturedly and returned to the festivities. The girl Ruia who would become his wife at his side, held tightly to his hand with both of hers. Did she also know? After all, she had been in training as a priestess.

I watched the two young people leave and went to Osorkon's great house. I heard the sound of voices coming from large hall, and went to inspect. I stood in the entryway. Osorkon was holding a meeting with battle leaders and envoys from the other nomarches. "We are victorious," he announced to all gathered in his beautiful, spacious home. A cheer erupted from everyone's lips.

"Hoorah!"

"We have won the day."

"The evil king will punish us no longer."

I had become so used to quiet Temple life that the noise and throng were wearying to me. I left his house and walked towards the Holy River. When I reached the banks, there was ghastly evidence of violence. Blood splashed upon the soil. Broken arrows. Abandoned slings. Even a few dead bodies of the enemy that had not been gathered up, while scavengers devoured the lifeless corpses greedily. This was no place to pray to Het-Heru.

So I trudged back to Osorkon's home and headed to my private chamber. There I could be at peace. I could still hear discussion in the hall. Otherwise all was still.

Several birds chirped and whistled outside the open space that looked down on the courtyard below. I sat cross-legged upon my straw mattress and closed my eyes. It was the first time of quiet in many weeks—or was it months? I sighed and tried to relax. My chest ached as it did so often and I rubbed it, hoping to relieve the pain.

Then suddenly my body stiffened as a vision appeared. A vulture flew over Abtu, then along the length of the river, holding a broken spear. I saw men, boats, and camels. The water ran red with blood. I saw men fighting one another, neighbor against neighbor. The people of Ta-Meir Res. Civil war that Catfish was afraid of and Ankhamun had strived to avoid was coming to our homeland.

How long would this last? I asked silently. But no answer was given. I hurried downstairs to inform the battle-weary men of the situation. They were gathered in the great hall, eating fruit and drinking barley beer.

"Osorkon, we cannot rest yet!" I exclaimed. They all looked up. "Another menace is on its way." I received looks of disbelief and disgust from the exhausted warriors.

Then Ruia's father came over to me. "What is it, Heb?" he asked grimly.

"I have received another vision, Osorkon," I replied. "I wish it were not true, but the vision is unmistakable. Many armed men, in boats, and on camels are heading towards Abtu, the holy city. I believe a Nomarche is trying to take power while our country is weak. This will be devastating to the country, to the people, bringing still more ruin and war into every village and town."

"We have finished fighting the battle Het-Heru told us was coming, which we won. We are all weary. How can there be another threat so soon?" answered the Nomarche.

"I know everyone is tired, Osorkon," I replied. "I don't know how to explain what is coming. I only know what I have been shown."

Another man spoke up. His eyes were narrowed with doubt. "How do you know this is a true vision?"

I shrugged. "I have received many visions from Het-Heru. All of them have come to pass. I assume this is no different."

"We will do what we must, Heb," the older man sighed. "Thank you for your sight. Without which, we might have found out too late to stop the events." Turning to the gathering, he continued, "Men, we must fight on."

"What about the feast, Osorkon?" asked one of the warriors.

"Let us celebrate tonight. Then tomorrow we must begin preparations to stop this Nomarche who thinks he can march into Abtu and assume the throne illegally."

The room began to buzz with ideas and plans.

I left to seek the solace of my room. I luxuriated in the softness of the clean straw bedding and smooth linen sheets. Osorkon was very wealthy and I enjoyed what that wealth could provide. Beyond the walls I could hear the festivity. The town celebrated in collective relief of having saved themselves from destruction by the army of horrific insect-men and the Scorpion King who had sent them. Let them enjoy themselves, I thought to myself. I turned to the wall and fell deeply asleep, the first restful slumber I enjoyed in a long time. And tonight I would have no bad dreams or visions. It would be my last peaceful slumber until the country was safe again.

When I awoke, I was stiff and sore. "I am getting old," I murmured to myself. I stretched and heard my bones snap in reply. I slipped on my kilt and went downstairs. All was quiet. But the servants had prepared some food for me. All I ate was some dried fruit and drank a goblet of cool water. Then I headed towards the town square, anticipating that the town members would be gathered there. I wasn't disappointed.

As I listened to their new war plans, I stretched again. I couldn't seem to get my back to relax. Between my shoulder blades was a stiffness and deep ache that no amount of movement could relieve.

I will skip quickly past the details of those dreadful years. Even the summary is hard enough for me to relate. After the suicide of Shu-un-Atum, King Serqet, the country celebrated for a short while. Then began a series of conflicts. A local Nomarche began to battle for the great prize, the throne of Southern Ta-Meir in Abtu.

Town fought village, village fought city, nome fought nome, while the southern kingdom was torn apart. What began in Abtu became a civil war, as the country of Ta-Meir Res tore itself apart. In the end, rivers of blood were spilt. To make matters worse, the famine continued as well. A terrible dark night had descended on the heart of Ta-Meir Res. Every soul within our country was weary with discord and mistrust.

Time passed as Ra repeatedly grew large and died. Full moons came and went. Then an inundation. Two. Three. I stayed in Osorkon's home, with Ruia and his family, while the Prince was fighting far away. Catfish declined to marry until the threat had passed and we were all safe once again. I prayed for his protection and the salvation of our country. I got thin and my hair turned white and still we were helpless against the needless slaughter of rebellion.

People fought fiercely for their homes, their towns, their farms, their lands. Everyone was involved: farmers, townspeople, royalty, common people, fishermen, young and old alike. If one was old enough to hold a weapon—sling, bow, or spear—then one was ready to fight.

During these battles, Catfish became a man, a general, a great leader. Catfish had not only become a legendary warrior by then, but had learned to use diplomacy as well. He was a wonderful blend of his fierce grandfather Menamen-Ra and his gentle father Ankhamun. I heard reports from time to time about his exploits. Sometimes they seemed almost miraculous, as he fought hand to hand with rebellious troops. Yet we did not reveal his noble status.

Why did we not reveal Catfish as king? We had proof that he was

Ankhamun's rightful heir. Because it wasn't time. That decision was the most difficult burden I ever carried.

Ruia often confessed to me her fear that Catfish would be killed before they could be married.

"We cannot be wed until the country is at peace," Catfish had confided in me.

I understood Ruia's fear very well. Even with the assurances of Het-Heru, I trembled in fear at every military dispatch that arrived in Nekken.

In my daily ritual to Het-Heru, She continued to remind me that civil war was necessary. Either in the quiet of my room in Osorkon's beautiful house, or by the bank of the river, I would stroke the smooth wooden amulet and call Her name. "Het-Heru, Lady of the Southern Sycamore, Mistress of Life, be with me now."

The golden glow I knew was Her presence appeared and my fears subsided, at least for the moment. "Why can't we stop the bloodshed and let everyone know that Catfish is our true King?" I asked her.

"Heb, I know you endure the agony of sorrow and war. But in order for the hearts of my people to be opened, they must experience the fiery cauldron of death and despair. They are being readied for a golden age that is coming. Without pain, birth would be an insignificant experience. Without suffering, they cannot appreciate peace."

So I counseled Osorkon to wait. I didn't know Catfish's revealing would be so dramatic.

The event that ended the civil war was the invasion of our Southern territory by the King of Hedje, the Northern territory, Deshret, the Red Crown. He took the initiative because our country had become greatly weakened. However, once that King had crossed over our boundary, a great "turning of the head" occurred. One moment each head in Ta-Meir Res was facing one other in bloody, civil strife. The next moment all heads faced north in protest, now aligned single-mindedly against the foreign invader from lower Ta-Meir.

More fighting ensued. Then at a battlefield not far from Abtu Temple, Catfish mortally wounded the King of Hedje. The remaining northern army surrendered their weapons and called a truce. They left soon after, journeying north to their homeland in the delta, leaving behind their injured king.

Torches were lit, although the night was filled by the full orb of Djehuti shining brightly down on the war-weary soldiers. The southern army opened jars of barley beer for the victorious celebration.

After all had been drinking for a while, Wosret made an impetuous pronouncement.

He walked over to Catfish, lifted the man's arm and shouted to the troops gathered nearby. "Here is my little brother, Catfish, who has helped us defeat the northern king. As you know, he has fought valiantly and with honor, sometimes without regard to his own safety. He has stood in the way of spears and daggers, saving many of us from death. We all owe our lives to him and his courage." He cleared his throat and waited until all drunken voices were stilled. "But that is not all." He looked around dramatically at the blood-stained, fierce faces of the troops. "Catfish came to live with my family when he was a baby."

A man shouted to him. "You're drunk, Wosret. Stop slobbering over him. We've all been brave. Have some more beer!"

Wahankh pushed his way through the crowd to stand with his brother and Catfish. The ferocious man's kilt was torn and filthy, and his chest and shoulders cut with still-healing battle wounds. "Listen to what Wosret says!"

Wosret continued, unabated. "He was brought to our home by my sister Bashta and Heb, whom many of you are acquainted with. What you don't know is that Catfish is Pharaoh's son. The one we all thought disappeared after the murder of his mother, Queen Atalana."

Members of the army gasped and exclaimed loudly.

"What?"

"That cannot be!"

"You're a liar, Wosret!"

"How do we know what you say is true?"

"Pharaoh's child died long ago."

Wosret shook his head mightily. "You are wrong! When we return to Nekken, I will show you the instruments of power that Pharaoh Ankhamun gave to Heb to hold in safe-keeping for just this day. The sacred heqa and nekhaka which my brother and I have seen for ourselves!"

"That is true!" added Wahankh. "He is the son of Pharaoh Ankhamun, and has been given to us as our next king!"

"This is the reason our parents were murdered by King Serqet. They were looking for Catfish, to murder him as they had murdered his royal parents. To prevent him from taking his rightful throne!" added Wosret.

"Is this true, Catfish?"

All eyes turned to the quiet warrior. He was older now, and still handsome. His muscular, tall figure stood out among the other warriors. His battle raiment, the gift from Osorkon, was falling to pieces, and he had scars from numerous battles all over his body.

He removed his arm from Wosret's grip and lowered it to his side. He spoke powerfully to the group, but simply. "My countrymen. What they say is correct." He put his arm around Wosret's shoulders and looked into the faces of the assembled men. "I have been guided by Het-Heru to become your rightful king. My lineage comes from my great-grandfather Horem, to Menamen-Ra and then to Ankhamun. I am the royal son of Queen Atalana and King Ankhamun." His eyes sparkled with emotion, while everyone present was affected as well.

"Hooray for Catfish!!"

The cheering didn't stop for quite a while.

With difficulty, he was able to interrupt the shouting. "Come with me to Nekken. I will show you my father's royal instruments, which have been saved for me. Also I will present to you the woman who will become First Royal Wife. At my coronation, she will wear the necklace of Het-Heru that once belonged to Queen Atalana." The excited troops celebrated until morning.

The King of Hedje died of battle wounds during the festivities that night, leaving both Northern and Southern Ta-Meir without a King. He would eventually be buried near the Temple of Ausar, where other kings had been laid to rest.

Then, disbanding, the army started the long trek back to their individual home towns.

Every one, both north and south, was glad for the long conflict to be finished. Everyone was war-weary, blood staining our minds and hearts. It seemed the holy Mother River herself had run red for too many inundations. Fields were worn out and needed to be planted. Villages and towns needed to be rebuilt. Amends needed to be made to neighbors. The bodies of loved ones needed to be put to rest, so they could be with Ausar.

Now neither country had a ruler. Catfish consulted with Osorkon and other nomarches, who decided that he was to be crowned Pharaoh of both territories, uniting the two kingdoms into one country to be named Kemetu. His true love, Ruia, would become his Primary Royal Wife. They had waited ten inundations to be married. Catfish would also marry Herneith, the only child of the dead Northern King, to settle all disputes with the Red Crown. She would become Narmer's Secondary Wife.

A new crown was designed. The Pshent would be placed upon his head, a combination of the Red Crown of the North and the White Crown of the South. Nekhebet (the vulture) and Wadjet (the cobra), Sisters of the Two Lands, would be co-joined in the new headdress. Both of them would perch over Pharaoh's forehead to bring wisdom to kings as well as to protect the new Pharaoh, his family dynasty, the citizens, and the land, which would henceforth be known as Kemetu. A new crown. A new nation. A new king. And a new beginning with peace for all.

CHAPTER TWENTY-FOUR

KING NARMER

I write this entry outside the remains of Abtu Palace. Today Catfish will be coronated as King Narmer, "Raging Catfish" because of his exploits as a brave and gallant warrior, the Avenging Eye of Ra. He will be ordained as the first Pharaoh of Kemetu, consisting of Upper and Lower Ta-Meir, joining the two lands together into one.

Abtu Palace had been almost demolished. But because of its long tradition and the fact it was his birthplace, Narmer wanted to hold his solemn investiture there. What had once been a beautiful and graceful palace built for royalty was now little more than broken mud bricks and rubble. Valuable items had been carted off by looters, either during the assault on Serqet or by the following civil war. Campfires had blacked the outside walls and inside chambers as well.

The lovely marble fountain in the royal suite had been removed piece by piece, and the elegant artwork on the wall had been hacked away. Nevertheless, Narmer set up his sleeping quarters there, with Ruia. "This was my home," he explained to her.

"I know my darling. I only wish you had a nicer homecoming," and she hugged him to her.

Narmer and Ruia asked me to be a part of the coronation, as Kher Heb priest but I declined. My body had become very frail. I didn't have the energy to be part of the long ceremony. I preferred to stay outside in the cooking area during the lengthy investiture formalities. However, the cooks laughingly chased me off, saying that I got in their way.

I had aged during the years of conflict and apprehension had weakened me. My chest pained me greatly. During inundations of turmoil and worry my heart felt as though it had been torn into tiny bits of papyrus and felt just as flimsy. My back had grown bent and all my hair had fallen out except for a fringe near my neck. Therefore, I was glad to sit outside in the warm evening air by myself. From there I could hear the chanting of priests, the tinkling sistrums, the beat of dunbeks, and the fragrant smell of sacred myrrh. Later there would be feasting, as the people celebrated the King's coronation as Pharaoh of Kemetu. Our beautiful land had merged into one—one river, one people, and one king. We would be at peace at last. Het-Heru's golden age.

I rubbed my aching, twisted fingers. So many inundations had passed since I had served Ankhamun. I smiled. Ankhamun, you would be pleased with your son. He has become a legendary figure, a great warrior, and now will become a great king. History will record this momentous day for all time.

I wandered into the garden and, lowering myself gingerly, sat on the ground by the old lotus pond, now dry and without flowers or papyrus shoots. I had brought my camel-hide bag with me, along with my journal. I smoothed out the scroll on my lap, so that I could reflect and write. The old sun disk Ra-as-Atum was setting, the red flame of the dying day illuminated the waterless pond with a strange scarlet glow.

I looked around me. I felt sick at the sight, remembering the beauty that had once flourished here.

Most of the trees and flowers in the garden had been trampled by the feet of many men, slashing and swiping at each other to survive, paying no heed to the plants around them. Vegetation had also died from lack of water. The grape vines were dead, as were all the fruit and nut trees. Without life-giving water, these exotic plants were unable to live. Sand blew through the stumps and blackened plants without ceasing, scouring the once-ornate marble benches, now lying in pieces around the pond. The desert was reclaiming the garden as its own.

The devastation of Abtu Palace was almost total. Most of the mud-brick walls had been knocked down with battering rams, in order for soldiers to storm the Palace and squeeze the life out of King Serqet, ironically already lying dead in his quarters. The Great Hall was a ruin of partial walls and columns; even the magnificent throne made of precious wood from a far-off land had been hacked to pieces by those furious with what it had stood for – the cruel annihilation of many innocent lives. Furniture was broken or had been carried away as souvenirs; the same with most of the household implements, cooking pots, mirrors, vases, and anything else that was of value.

We had only scraps of decoration to celebrate Narmer's investiture. Except for the sacred heqa and nekhekha, Implements of Rulership, none of this might have been possible. Without those tools, Catfish's claim to the throne could have been disputed without resolution and the throne would have been lost. I was proud that I had hoarded the royal tools throughout the chaos and upheaval that had swept through our land. Yet all through those terrible, dark days, I hoped that peace would come again, as surely as the Holy River flooded and ebbed, one inundation after another, in an endless cycle of death and rebirth.

Narmer's beloved Ruia would rule beside him, as First Royal Wife. For the investiture and marriage ceremony, Ruia wore the magnificent Het-Heru necklace that had once belonged to her distant cousin Atalana, a fitting gift from her husband as well as an heirloom of her own family. She had looked beautiful in her white coronation gown. She had the same shapely curves as her cousin, the slender oval face, and the slanted eyes. Ruia was a sweet, intelligent, intuitive woman and I silently thanked Het-Heru for bringing the two of them together.

Herneith, Princess of the Royal House of Lower Egypt, the Northern Territory, was to become Narmer's Secondary Wife.

Herneith was an important political link to seal the two royal houses into one. Without her, the northern kingdom might have rebelled against Narmer, making it impossible to merge the two kingdoms.

Herneith was a considerate woman, pleased to play her part in the creation of a new country, as well as to carry on her family's royal bloodline. She slept in a chamber separate from the royal couple, delighted with her new-found freedom and privacy she had never had before. Herneith was a slender woman with pale skin and green eyes. Her skin glowed like burnished gold, from coconut oil mixed with precious herbs applied to her body at least once a day by maid servants. Although she looked fragile, unlike Ruia, she was a strong woman and would live to see the birth of seven children and fifty inundations. With her marriage to Narmer, the north wholeheartedly joined their territory with the south, glad to be done with war.

After his coronation, Narmer would leave the devastated Palace at Abtu. This would be the last coronation ever to take place there. He planned to move all his retinue and goods, and relocate the capital at Ineb Hedj in the north. He and his engineers had drawn up plans to surround the area with dikes, damming up the reach of the holy river about five hundred hentis to the south, to convey the river through an artificial channel dug midway between the two mountain ranges. They excavated a lake around it to the north and west, fed by the river. Furthermore, workers had begun building a wall completely around the city and its outlying area, a magnificent wall which would be covered with gleaming white limestone. When finished, a traveler would be able to see these sparkling white walls of the new capital city from a long way off.

While these massive projects were proceeding, Narmer's engineers started construction, building a new palace and expanding the current village into a modern city, adjacent to the palace, complete with its own plumbing and reservoir system.

These substantial ventures had been blessed by Ptah, god of masons and craftsmen and his Ptah-priest workmen. Narmer also planned to expand Hwt-ka-Ptah, Temple of Ptah, to be in proper cosmic alignment with the large city structure. The new capital city was destined to become beautiful and fabulous.

For myself, I had no plans to move to the new city of Ineb Hedj. I was in poor health and my memories belonged in the Southern Kingdom. Perhaps I would spend my last days at Enet-ta-Neter. I fingered the amulet of Het-Heru, all color now completely gone from the small wooden amulet. I also examined the still-pristine, enigmatic carnelian seal in my hand, wondering yet again what it represented. My mother was the only one who could tell me and she journeyed with Ausar. I returned the two heirlooms to the hide bag and resumed my papyrus journal.

"Once when I sat on this bench I was a young man, but now I am old." I struggled to see in the fading light, trying to still my trembling hands, shaking from age. Periodically I wiped my watery old eyes, as I struggled to write, with gnarled fingers, the sacred and complex hieroglyphics that could express the magnitude of Het-Heru's accomplishments. My shaky hands made the symbols look squiggly and uneven.

I remembered what Abtu Palace had once looked like. The Palace, magnificently built and decorated, housed Pharaoh, Royal Servant of Ma'at, and Shepherd of the People of Ta-Meir Res. I thought of Atalana, the woman I had come to know and love, in this place "We have done well, my Beloved," I wrote. "He is a king to be proud of. Strong and wise, compassionate and caring, brave and respectful." I felt her gentle touch on my old wrinkled hand and I sighed with happiness, knowing her Ba was with me.

A man-servant brought a torch and fastened it to the low-hanging branch of a nearby devastated tree, so I could continue to write. "Thank you," I replied with gratitude at the small gesture of kindness. Then a cook brought me a steaming plate of food, which I picked at but ate little. My appetite was gone and my teeth rotten. I don't know how long I sat and wrote that night. No one came to disturb me, sitting at the far edge of the old pond. Sounds rose and fell around me, but I was too engrossed in my journal to pay much attention. One of the benefits of the elderly is that people leave you alone.

Suddenly I heard the sound of birds flocking in the desolated fruit trees nearby. There must have been hundreds of them, making a racket, cawing and chirping and whistling their individual bird songs. My brow wrinkled, as I puzzled over their behavior, unseemly at this time of day.

A lone falcon flew overhead, wheeling and circling. I could hear its scream.

Next I heard a throaty roar as two lionesses came to perch near the edge of the empty garden, while several sheep and goats joined them nearby. The she-lions made themselves comfortable, yawning and stretching in the near-darkness. I heard the strange laughing of a hyena.

"What is this? Has the world gone mad?" I got out the wooden amulet of Het-Heru and rubbed it. "What is happening, Het-Heru?" A golden light shone from somewhere above me. It couldn't be Djehuti's silvery orb since it had not yet risen in Nut's body and Ra-as-Atum had already set. I smelled myrrh, the fragrance of the Neter. A deep peace came upon me from that golden light, and I sighed in contentment.

I suddenly remembered the last morning of the Ancient One, Mukalia, that morning so long ago when she had quietly left her body. The morning after I had ecstatically joined with Atalana and we had conceived Catfish. Then I understood the significance of the animals. "Mukalia. Do you see this?" I smiled, put aside my journal, and laid my aching bones down upon the hard ground, curling up like a fetus. It was uncomfortable, but I knew the Barque of the Dead was coming. My last thoughts were of my beloved Atalana; Het-Heru, the Neter of Beauty; and the wise ancient one, Mukalia.

I yawned with great weariness. "Wait for me, Atalana. I'm coming."

Before I closed my eyes, the three most important women in my life merged together as one, a golden light leading me home…

HEB'S FATHER

Raging Catfish—Narmer—the newly-crowned Pharaoh, Unifier of the Two Lands of Ta-Meir into the new country of Kemetu, wearer of the Pshent, the Red and White Crown—dreamt of me. My Golden Shining Visage shimmered in his dream. Heb had often told him of my Visitations with joy and wonder. Except for the brief revelation of the massacre at Waset, this was the first time the King had experienced a vision of me for himself.

"Narmer," I spoke his King-Name softly and sweetly. "You have fulfilled your destiny. Your heritage is rich with kingship. Your father has brought you here for this moment. He has protected you, taught you, and saved you, for this important time. His love for your mother, for you, and for me, has been essential for the unification of your country."

"My father? But my father is long dead and lives in the Duat with Ausar."

"No, your father is here, Narmer. He has always been at your side and has taught you well."

"I don't understand."

"Heb is your father." My words were but a melodious whisper fluttering through his mind.

"But Heb is just a servant—and a Priest..." As Narmer spoke those words, the glow from me began to fade.

"He is much more than that. Search your heart and you will know. You have made him very proud." Saying that, my image faded.

The King woke from his dream at dawn. The light from Khepera, Neter of Morning and New Beginnings, shone on him as he lay on his sleeping roll with Ruia, in a small room of the destroyed Palace, musing about my words. "I must have drunk too much barley beer last night. It has made strange dreams." He got up quietly, to avoid disturbing Ruia, who was still sleeping. He stroked her smooth cheek and she uttered a soft crooning noise, without awakening.

Then he washed, dressed in his tunic and kilt, and asked his Viziers to join him. Rather than join the on-going celebration, he went to work. Years of discipline had trained him to tend to duties first, and pleasure second.

He was poring over the papyrus of the new city's plans placed on a heap of rugs when his Viziers arrived. He showed them the designs with growing pleasure.

They were interrupted by an announcement of an artist, a carver of stone, who was shown into his chamber, the same room once used by Ankhamun. The large desk was now gone, the slab smashed into hundreds of pieces. The curtains were torn and slashed and the beautifully decorated columns lay broken on the ground. This destruction had happened at the hands of the mobs, angry at King Serqet, taking out their rage on objects, since the Scorpion King was already dead by his own hand.

"Your gracious Majesty," the artist knelt on the floor, forehead touching the cold stone. An expensive linen robe, which reached to his knees, was draped around him. A collar made of delicate pieces of faience was around his neck. He wore a short black wig, but acted as though he was not completely comfortable with it. However, his graceful hands, with long, arched, powerful fingers were remarkable, as if they didn't belong to the man, but had a life of their own. Although he attempted to appear noble, his hands were raw from chiseling stone and marble. His cuticles were cut, several had dried blood on them, all his fingernails were broken and blunted, while his fingertips were heavily calloused. This indeed was a master carver.

"There is no need for that, sir," Narmer replied kindly. "Please get to your feet and state your business."

When the stone cutter had stood up, he continued. "Your Majesty, I am the most capable worker of stone in Ta-Meir," he started formally. "Ptah himself helps me guide my chisel." He flushed slightly with well-deserved pride. "Your father-in-law Osorkon has commissioned me to carve a ceremonial stone palette for the city of Nekken, chronicling your glorious history and the creation of our country."

"Is Osorkon well?" asked the King, interrupting him.

"Very well, your Majesty. I have just arrived by boat from his home. He sends his apologies for not attending your coronation."

"Tell him that I appreciate his good wishes, but he would have been most uncomfortable here. The palace is in ruins, and we have no facilities for visitors. When we have established our new capital, he can come for a long visit. Perhaps by then a royal prince will have arrived as well." He smiled and felt a warmth grow within him as he thought of his new wife and queen, his beloved Ruia.

"Yes, Sire. I will tell him so."

"Good. I have need of him and his family for a long time."

"I must sketch your likeness, your Majesty, for the palette."

"Yes, I understand and agree. Time is short, however, for tomorrow we leave to go north to the new capital. Can you sketch while we talk?" questioned Narmer.

"Yes, my Lord. It won't take very long, but I wanted to make sure to replicate your image suitably."

"Please do so then." The King turned back to the papyrus he had been studying and motioned to his Viziers to join him, while the artist made his sketches.

While Narmer was studying the document with his advisors, a guard found Heb's dead body, Pharaoh's most loyal servant, in the garden. The bones of Heb's gaunt, skinny body, barely covered with flesh, made him look much older than he was. Less than sixty inundations had passed since his birth in the slave quarters. Nevertheless he looked ancient. Next to him on the ground was a large soiled flaxen bag of rolled-up papyrus rolls. Grasped tightly in the lifeless hand was the pouch from Heb's mother. The hide was shiny from being handled. The guard pulled the pouch from the stiffened fingers and took it along with the bag of papyrus rolls to Pharaoh immediately.

Narmer was still talking with his new council, as the artist sketched him, when the guard asked for and was granted entry.

"Ankh. Uja. Senb." The guard bowed, then continued when given leave by Narmer. "Your Majesty. I regret to inform you that the Priest Heb is dead."

"Oh, no! Was it foul play, do you think?" Narmer asked quickly. He was used to murder; a knot of concern formed in his empty stomach. He had not yet eaten, wanting to tend to business first.

"No, your Majesty. I believe he died in his sleep, of old age."

"Oh."

"I found him with these." The guard held out the items he had found near the lifeless body.

Narmer's stomach growled loudly but he ignored it. Was it hunger or something else? He reached for the leather pouch and the flax bag, gripping them in his hand. He rocked back and forth on his heels, realizing how deeply he cared about his old guardian.

"Where did you find him?"

"In the garden, near the empty pond."

"Take me to him." Narmer turned. "But first. Master carver, are you finished with your sketches of me?"

"Yes, my Lord, I am. I will create a wonderful ceremonial piece. Osorkon plans to display it in Nekken, where the townspeople can honor you through its beauty and fine details."

"I hope to see it someday."

"It will be my honor, your Majesty." The artist left.

The guard then led Narmer to Heb's lifeless body. Narmer knelt next to the old man, picked up a stiffened hand and held it to his cheek for a few moments, brushing his lips with the dead fingers, then gently placed it on the old chest. He quickly brushed away tears that welled up. "This is a terrible blow. I will be lost without him," Narmer said. "Call some attendants to take him away, then wash and dress his body. We will need to make arrangements with priests of Anpu to begin the mummification process for him. That is all," added the King and dismissed the guard with a quick wave of his hand. He was too upset for subtle action today.

"Are you all right, my Lord?" asked one of the Viziers who had followed him outside.

"No, I'm not." Narmer replied. His mouth was drawn and a mournful crease formed between his eyes. "He was the last of those close to me. Like a father I never had. I can't believe he's gone."

He reverently untied the drawstrings and emptied the contents of the all-too-familiar leather bag onto the ground. How often had he glimpsed this bag in Heb's hand? But this was the first time he had ever seen what it contained.

Two items fell out of the bag. One was the faded amulet, all color having long since disappeared. Only the outline of the Neter remained and the King ran his fingers over the worn surface. The other was the carnelian signet. Pharaoh examined the carnelian rod, motioned to his new Viziers, standing quietly. "Have any of you ever observed a signet like this before?" he asked.

"No, sire," replied an older man from Waset. He came over, then minutely examining it. His robe was gleaming white and very new, probably sewn for the coronation ceremony of yesterday. His hair was thinning, mostly grey with a few black strands still remaining, and his face was clean-shaven. Like many older men, his black eyebrows were thick and bushy. Narmer had transactions with this nobleman for several years when he lived in Waset and trusted the quiet, practical man's words, which is why he had offered him the position of Vizier.

"It looks foreign, though," the Vizier continued, "Perhaps Sumer or Urak. And look here. One of the images is a lion. That usually indicates royalty."

"Isn't the Prince from Urak still in the palace?"

"Yes, sire."

"Please bring him to my chamber without delay." Narmer picked up the remaining items from the ground. He closed Heb's staring eyes gently, then stood, planning to return to the room he had just vacated.

As the Vizier turned to leave, he hobbled a little, his left knee swollen by inflammation.

"Mense," Narmer added, saying the man's name.

"Majesty." The older noble stopped, turned, and bowed stiffly. He had not slept in a proper bed in days and his back ached.

"Please tell me again that you are well enough to travel to Ineb Hedj and take on the duties I have outlined for you."

"Of course, Sire," he replied, a little bewildered. "Do I not please your Majesty?"

"You please me very well, Mense. I am only concerned for your health."

"Ah, that. Be not troubled. Since my wife died and my children are grown, I have nothing to occupy my time. I helped to restore you to your throne and am honored to be chosen as one of your Viziers in your new capital." His thumped his chest with his fist for emphasis. "This body has quite a few inundations left in it before I leave to travel with Ausar to the Duat." He looked down quickly at Heb's corpse and shuddered. "If the Neterw are willing, that is," he added.

"I am glad, Mense. You are a valuable man and a good friend as well."

"I can think of no greater purpose for the remainder of my life than to help you form a government for our country." Mense left, smiling.

He returned to the official room, accompanied by Yarikh, a stately Prince of Urak. The Prince was hurriedly fastening a long red robe edged with gold around his swarthy body. His normally regal appearance was much altered. His eyes were red and sunken from little sleep and having drunk too much barley beer during the festivities. His long, triangular, black beard was unkempt, while his head was missing his usual conical hat. His thick bristly hair stuck out wildly in many directions.

"Sire, you sent for me?" he asked, slurring his words both from being aroused from sleep and the after-effects of the beer.

"Yes," replied Narmer, more composed than he was a few minutes before. "I'm sorry to awaken you, but I have need of your wise counsel." He walked over to the Prince, clapping him on the shoulder in a friendly gesture. "What do you think, Yarikh?" the new monarch asked him, handing him the signet.

The Prince studied the signet closely, turning it over and peering at the engraving. He wiped off a smear with the corner of his robe. "This is the House of Urak's signet!" the Prince exclaimed finally. "It went missing many years ago, about the same time my great-grandmother's oldest sister disappeared, according to the stories I've heard. She was a young princess, on a holy pilgrimage to a sacred spring near Sumer with her ladies, priests, and guards. They all vanished without a trace. We never knew what happened to them. Where did you get this?"

"From a Kher Heb priest," King Narmer replied, not wishing to identify the man.

"Where did he get it?"

"I cannot tell you."

"Your Majesty, this is a Royal Signet, meant to be passed on to the first-born of each generation."

"I see." King Narmer gazed thoughtfully out the window at the distant rugged mountains. He pulled at his lower lip thoughtfully. His intelligent eyes suddenly burned and he rubbed them quickly, before his visitor could notice. The significance of the carved red stone from Heb's mother coupled with his dream came together as one. "Perhaps it was," he mused.

"I'm sorry. What did you say?" queried Yarikh.

"Would you mind if I kept this?" asked King Narmer quietly, not wishing to divulge more until the time was right.

"I don't see why not. We replaced it long ago."

"Thank you, Prince Yarikh," replied Narmer and turned away. He carefully put the two items back in Heb's bag and pulled the frayed leather drawstring shut.

"My pleasure, Sire. It is my desire that our countries will always be friends and be at peace." The Sumerian Prince bowed respectfully and left.

Narmer turned to his Viziers. "I need to be alone for a while," he dismissed them. Then he stopped them with a second thought. "Perhaps we should wait until we get to Ineb Hedj to finalize these plans. Why don't you have a hot meal and rest up for the long journey? Especially you, Mense. We have a great distance to travel. We will start tomorrow morning." The three viziers bowed courteously and left his chamber.

When they had gone, he laid out Heb's papyrus rolls. The King remembered his lessons when he was a boy, and with a little practice began to read the hieroglyphic journal. Heb's journal was a stunning chronicle. From his own inception in the stars of Nut's body, through the passionate vehicle of a loving man and woman, and building on lifelong support from many wonderful and generous people, he, Narmer, had become Master of Two Lands, Unifier of Upper and Lower Ta-Meir, bringer of Peace and Stability to the Red and Black Lands. The chaos of Setekh had been staved off, replaced by the order of Heru.

Separate threads that I, Het-Heru, wove on the complex loom of destiny which created a magnificent tapestry of Kingship. No thread was wasted; all were meaningful. Menamen-Ra helped to create a loving son Ankhamun and two unhappy sons. Childless, Ankhamun went to Enet-ta-Neter hoping to become potent, then bringing Atalana as a bride to Abtu Palace. Atalana, unable to heal her husband, and needing to have an heir, turned to a loving servant to conceive a royal child. The two unhappy brothers of Ankhamun created both murder and a reason for the child's survival in the world of battle and diplomacy. Bashta, Heb's other lover, took the royal child to her parent's home—Udimu and Muttey in Waset. While there the foster family and other citizens helped to forge the warrior. The River of Life failed its yearly floods, leading to famine and riots. King Serqet initiated the conflagration that would become civil war, ironically ending in his own downfall. Then came invasion by the Northern King, which led ultimately to unification. And finally his coronation as King of Two Lands united into one. Delete one thread and my tapestry would have fallen apart.

Narmer read on. As he did, uncharacteristic tears flowed unchecked, like rain drops on the papyrus in front of him, blurring some of the hieroglyphic images as he read.

In his diary, Heb humbly portrayed himself as a faithful, unflagging servant of Kings. The shy lover of a beautiful and powerful Queen. Becoming a Kher Heb Priest who was the loyal messenger and my oracle. A man who was a Prince in his own right but never knew it. A person who had sacrificed his own life so that a royal family could be protected and a country created. A father who had protected and cherished his son without asking for anything in return, not even recognition of parentage.

Narmer, Warrior King, Unifier of Upper and Lower Egypt, undisputed Ruler of Ta-Meir, Fertile Land of the River of Life, recipient of the love, nurturing, and wisdom of that great and modest man, clutched Heb's old leather bag tightly in his strong right hand and held it to his ab.

"Thank you for everything, my dearest father," he murmured lovingly. "I hope you are safely guided through the Duat, and that you meet my mother in the next world. You deserve to be together."

He smiled tenderly, wiped his damp face, and carefully put away the keepsakes and journal. He would bring these artifacts with him when he and his entourage moved north and save them for his own sons.

Then Narmer turned once again to the architectural plans for his new capital city painted on a large papyrus. With a sigh, he rolled up the papyrus carefully and put it safely in an old reed basket for the long trip to Ineb Hedj—where the future of upper and lower Ta-Meir, now known as Kemetu, waited.

Suddenly he understood that people were the only important treasures that one could have, and those treasures were fragile, ephemeral. His ab filled to overflowing with that realization. "Ruia!" he called. "My beloved, where are you?" With those words he ran from the ruined chamber, just as he would depart forever the smashed palace the next morning. He would leave death and destruction behind to create a hopeful white city, the new capital of a now-peaceful land. A golden glow surrounded him as he sought his love, his wife.

"You hold the destiny of Ta-Meir in your hands," I murmured to him, like a soft wind blowing a curtain aside, to reveal what is hidden behind.

THE END

GLOSSARY

ab: ancient Egyptian word for heart; in ancient Egyptian theology the heart was the seat of wisdom ankh: the Egyptian symbol - key of life and immortality; a loop-headed cross

apis: sacred bull

aten: sun disk

atmu: dusk

ba: one of the 9 souls (in ancient Egypt), connected to the body even after death, able to travel when body is dead, continuing to experience "life"

barque: large boat, usually manned by scores of oarsmen, often rigged with a square sail

canopic jars: four jars containing mummified remains of organs

       Lungs—Haapi (baboon)—north

       Stomach—Duamatef (dog or jackal)—south

       Liver—Imseti (human)—west

       Intestines—Qebehsnuf (falcon)—east

Cartouche: the oval ring surrounding and protecting a pharaoh's name written in hieroglyphics cherp: ancient Egyptian word for "first"

crook: a symbol of Pharaoh's power in the shape of a shepherd's crook; spiritual shepherd

cubit: measurement from elbow to finger, approximately eighteen to twenty-two inches

decans: the twenty-four hourly designations of night and day, charted by the stars; the decans of the night were each guarded by a Neter

djed pillar: "backbone of Ausar," painted wooden pillar representing stability and security, raised at death of old Pharaoh, coronation of new Pharaoh, and during periods of both crisis and celebration

dunbek: drum

electrum: a blend of gold and silver, used for plating statuary, walls and jewelry

felucca: a Nile River sailboat

Eosphoros: the planet Venus

Gold Light Temple: pyramidal-shaped temple originating in Mu, constructed of light energy

Great New Year: occurs every 2,160 years as the precession of the equinoxes marks the beginning of a new age

Hekau: sonics; mystical word-sounds that can move objects; Words of Power

Hem Neter: High Priestess of the Temple

Henti: Egyptian measurement of distance

heqa and nekhaka: crook and flail; hieroglyph for the word "rule" or "ruler"

Her Descher: the planet Mars, the "red one"

hieroglyphs: early form of writing using phonograms, logograms, and determinatives arranged in horizontal and vertical lines

hwr: Giza sphinx, also known as Horus of the Horizon; the hwr is directly aligned with the sun at dawn during the spring and fall equinox

imperishables: the fixed northern stars

inundation: yearly Nile flood commencing approximately every July 21st, corresponding roughly with the heliacal return of the star Sirius (Sopdit)

ka: a person's individual and spiritual power; usually an individual would have a statue or other likeness made of herself and kept in her mausoleum wherein the ka could reside, one of the nine souls

khabit: a non-corporeal spirit, a ghost, one of the nine souls

khamsim: a killing sandstorm that brings extreme heat and sometime tornadoes

khat: physical body; dead meat, one of the nine souls

khu: the highest and most spiritual of the nine souls

kapet: the most ancient formula—an oil, perfume, and/or incense made of wine, raisins, honey, myrrh, frankincense, cinnamon and other precious herbs and spices

kohl: a mixture of ground galena, sulphur, and animal fat used as eye make-up, alleviated eye inflammations and protected the eyes from the sun's glare

mastaba: burial chamber, shaped like a bench

menat: necklace of Hathor, symbolizes divine powers of healing

Meruti: beloved or dearest

mesd'emt: black eyeliner used to outline eyes, costlier than kohl

nemes: cloth headdress, such as the Giza sphinx wears; a piece of cloth pulled tight across the forehead and tied at the back, with two flaps hanging on the sides

Neter: designation for a god or goddess of Ancient Egypt; plural Neterw or Neteru; actual translation means "force of nature" or "energy source"

Nomarche: governor of an area

Nome: an area to be governed

Pharaoh: king, literal interpretation "royal house"

precession of the equinoxes: Earth's vernal equinox rises each year against the changing background of the twelve constellations of the zodiac. It takes 25,920 years to travel (backwards) through all twelve constellations, and 2,160 years to go through one sign, denoting the "change of an age" or the Great New Year according to the Ancient Egyptians.

rekkit: common people

ruha-et: evening

sacred geometry: perfect geometrical shapes and structures, including Phi (the golden section), pi and the square roots of two, three and five; an aspect of the spiritual, non-physical world. When used in construction, the results are visual and sensory harmony, power and energy.

sekhet Hetepet: field of peace; the late night hours

sentyt: Temple astrologer

shenti: a calf-length Egyptian kilt

sistrum: musical instrument used in worship, a type of rattle to bring protection and blessing through fertility and rebirth

Sopdit: the star Sirius – every year it disappears from view, then returns approximately mid July, heralding the beginning of the Nile flooding; star associated with Auset (Isis)

Sopdit New Year: occurs every 1,420 years in the ancient Egyptian calendar, corresponding to the movement of the star Sirius

Tenemos: mud-brick walls surrounding every temple complex, symbolizes sacred waters

udjat eye: right eye of Horus; protection from evil

waas scepter: a scepter favored by the Neterw

zep tepi: the first occasion when the world emerged from an infinite, lifeless sea and the sun rose for the first time

Crowns of Kings

Deshret—red crown of lower (northern) Egypt

Hedjet—white crown of upper (southern) Egypt

Pshent—double crown of Upper and Lower Egypt (2 crowns combined)

Ankh. Uja. Senb: A chant and a greeting—"life, health and happiness"

Nefer Nebet Hetepet Het-Heru: a temple chant—"Beautiful lady of pleasure, Het-Heru."

Khepera: (ra-as-khepera)—dawn phase of the sun

Ra: noontime phase of the sun

Atum: (ra-as-atum), evening phase of the sun

PLACES

Abtu Palace: ancient Egyptian name for Abydos, home of Pharaoh, situated in southern Egypt, located on high cliffs overlooking Nile River, north of Waset. Built of mud bricks. No remains exist.

Abtu Temple: ancient Egyptian name for Abydos, Shrine of Ausar, situated in southern Egypt – built of massive rectangular uncarved blocks; Ausar's skull is reputed to be buried there

Amentet: western land, the realm of Ausar and Shadow world of the earth

Bakhet: Sinai

Deshret: upper (southern) Egypt, people of the red land; desert

duat: a place where humans live after they die, heaven, netherworld, after-world, underworld, sky world, land of the gods, stars of the Milky Way; and land of the Neterw. Astronomically, the Duat is located in the sky between the constellations of Orion, Gemini (Twins), and Taurus (Bull).

Enet-ta-Neter: ancient Egyptian name for Dendera, Temple of Het-Heru (Hathor), situated in southern Egypt; Ausar's backbone is reputed to be buried there

Hwt-ka-Ptah: ancient Temple of Ptah at Memphis

Ineb Hedj: (also Noph), ancient Egyptian city of Memphis, situated in northern Egypt—about twelve miles south of present day Giza

Kemi: "Southern" country (Upper Egypt)

Kemet: ancient Egypt, also means People of the Black Land

Khemenu: Greek name Hermopolis; presently called Badari; a city on the border between Upper and Lower Egypt where the food riots first broke out

Kemetu: People of the Black Land (all Egyptian citizens of north and south)

Kush: ancient Nubia, northern Ethiopia

Mari: ancient city in Mesopotamia

Mu: mythical land situated in Pacific Ocean, destroyed by volcanic activity, earthquakes and tidal waves; (also known as Lemuria); preceded and was contemporary to Atlantis

Nubt: Temple of Sobek and Heru the Elder at modern Kom-Ombo

Nekken: now Hierakonpolis; ancient pre-dynastic capital of Egypt, a major metropolis, south of Waset

Per Auset: Philae, Temple of Auset (Isis), located on an island in southern Egypt

Res: the South (Upper Egypt)

Resu: Southern people (Upper Egyptians)

Rostau: necropolis between Giza and Memphis; a mystical location where Ausar lives

Ta-Meir: beloved land (all of Egypt); land of inundation

Ta-Meir Res: beloved Southern Land

Titania: mythical land originally situated in Atlantic Ocean, destroyed approximately 10,500 BC (also known as Atlantis) Urak: ancient city in Mesopotamia

Waset: modern Luxor, ancient Thebes, situated in southern Egypt

West bank of the Nile: the holy place where people were buried; cemeteries; the setting sun

GODS and GODDESSES

Amun: god of Waset, "Hidden or Unknowable One"

Anpu: (also known as Anubis)—jackal-headed god of the underworld; protector of travelers

Aten: god of the sun disk; the sun at noon

Atum: the great unknowable, unfathomable, omnipotent creator of the universe

Ausar: (also known as Osiris), "king of the gods," god of the dead and the afterlife, depicted as a green-skinned mummy; husband of Auset

Auset: (also known as Isis), wife of Ausar, royal mourner; goddess of magic and protectress of women, protected Ausar with her wings

Bast: (also known as Bastet), cat goddess, worshipped at Bubastis; goddess of celebration and play; guardian of children; goddess of felicity and family

Djehuti: (also known as Thoth), ibis-headed god of writing and knowledge; created hieroglyphics; ruler of the moon

Geb: god of the earth; father of Ausar, Auset, Nebt Het, Setekh and Heru the Elder

Hapi: god of the Nile, shown holding lotus flowers

Heh: god of millions of years; numerical designation for "million"

Heqet: frog goddess of fertility

Heru: (also known as Horus), falcon-headed god, son of Ausar and Auset, first pharaoh, protector of pharaohs

Het-Heru: (also known at Hathor), literally "house of Heru." Golden goddess of healing, love and joy, music and dancing, sensuality and sexuality, sometimes associated with Sekhmet. "Sekhmet went into Dendera as a Lion and came out as a cow." Sometimes depicted as a cow providing divine nourishment; considered goddess of time

Khepera: Ra in the form of a scarab beetle; the dawning sun; new beginnings

Ma'at: goddess of justice, harmony, truth and universal balance; the pharaoh's dead heart was weighed against her "feather of justice" at final judgment

Min: the god of sexual appetites; usually depicted with a huge phallus

Nebt Het: (also known as Nephthys), sister of Ausar, Auset, sister and wife of Setekh, goddess of underworld and psychic abilities

Nekhebet: vulture goddess depicted on crown and symbol of Upper Egypt (southern Egypt), protectress of Pharaoh and Egypt

Nut: goddess of the sky and heavens, swallows Ra at night, Ra passes through her body and she gives birth to him in the morning; wife of Geb

Ptah: mummiform god of craftsmen; god of temple at Noph; husband to Sekhmet

Ra: great sun god; the sun at noon

Sekhmet: primordial feminine force of creation, beginnings and endings, passion and desire; goddess of transformation; healer

Serqet: a scorpion goddess, patron of Pharaoh, dead souls and canopic jars; also an Egyptian king dating 3200 BC

Setekh: (also known as Seth or Set), murderer of Ausar; Heru's rival; god of storms and discord; chaos; primal energy; territory of Upper Egypt

Shu: god of air, son of Atum

Sons of Heru: Quebsnuf, Duamatef, Imseti and Haapi—guardians of the four cardinal directions; canopic jars with their images held mummified organs

Tauret: hippopotamus goddess of fertility, pregnancy and pregnant women

Tefnut: goddess of moisture, daughter of Atum

Wadjet: cobra goddess depicted on crown and symbol of Lower Egypt (northern Egypt); protectress of Pharaoh and Egypt

NAMES of INDIVIDUALS

Aapehty: youthful friend of Catfish who died as a boy

Nyla: Heb's mother

Ankhamun: (means Ankh, key of life and Amun, the hidden one); oldest beloved son of Menamen-Ra; Pharaoh

Atalana: priestess of Het-Heru; First Royal Wife and Queen of Pharaoh Ankhamun

Bashta: (her name is derived from Bast, goddess of hearth, home and family; guardian of children, felicity and loyalty); servant in Palace of Abtu; wet nurse to Catfish

Catfish: Pharaoh Ankhamun's only son

Heb: servant in Palace of Abtu, Custodian of the Household; Priest of Het-Heru

Herneith: secondary wife of Narmer, from the North

General Herusmatauy: retired general in Pharaoh's army, living in Waset (means in the service of Heru)

Horem: Menamen-Ra's father; Ankhamun's grandfather, builder of Abtu Palace

Menamen-Ra: (means hidden brightness); father of Ankhamun, Shu-un-Atum and Ptah-un-Atum Mense: Narmer's Vizier

Miw-sher: (means kitten); mother of Shu-un-Atum and Ptah-un-Atum

Mukalia: High Priestess of Het-Heru; Ancient One; last pure-blooded Muan in Ancient Egypt

Muttuy: (means motherly woman) mother of Bashta; foster mother of Catfish

Narmer: historical unifier of Upper and Lower Egypt—pre-dynastic or Dynasty 0; means "Raging Catfish"

Netikerty: (means she who is excellent); beloved first royal wife of Menamen-Ra

Ptah-un-Atum: (means Atum's builder) Grand Vizier, middle son of Menamen-Ra, obese half-brother to Ankhamun

Ruia: wife of Catfish, first royal wife of Narmer

Sebat: daughter of Heb and Bashta

Serqet: an historical Egyptian King from around 3200 BC (also known as King Scorpion)

Shara-Het: astrologer; High priestess of Het-Heru at Enet-ta-Neter after Mukalia dies

Shu-un-Atum: (means breath of Atum) Custodian of the Crown; youngest son of Menamen-Ra; half-brother to Ankhamun; also known as King Serqet/King Scorpion

Takharu: mother of Ruia

Tenti: husband of Bashta

Tietra-Het: priestess of Het-Heru at Enet-ta-Neter

Udimu: father of Bashta

Wahankh: soldier son of Muttuy and Udimu (means strong in life)

Wosret: soldier son of Muttuy and Udimu (means powerful one)

Yarikh: Prince of Urak from Mesopotamia

APPENDIX I

GODS AND GODDESSES OF ANCIENT EGYPT
(THE NETERW) AND HET-HERU

[I use the original ancient Egyptian (kemetic) names for the gods and goddesses and places both here and throughout the novel. Although you may be more familiar with the names of Osiris, Isis, Hathor, Anubis, Thoth, and Set, those are Greek names, which usage began in the Ptolemaic period. Although perhaps confusing at first, you can translate the names from the glossary as you read.]

THE NETERW

It is of utmost and critical importance that we understand the ancient Egyptians' spiritual life from their point of view. One cannot discuss ancient Egypt without including the Neterw. They are simply inseparable.

Who and what are the Neterw? Neter (plural Neterw) is the ancient Egyptian word and hieroglyph that we moderns translate to mean god or goddess. But the ancient Egyptians didn't consider them as gods. No, they thought of them, worked with them on a daily basis, lived their lives with the Neterw as elemental forces of the Universe—energy sources. These energy sources existed in all forms of nature, from the tiniest atom to the largest galaxy, plants, animals, stone, sand, and part of human beings as well.

The Neterw were also spiritual principles that reigned absolute in the universe. Unconditional love (represented as Auset); regeneration, rebirth, and resurrection (Ausar); spiritual guidance (Anpu); physical manifestation (Ptah); truth, harmony, justice, and balance (Ma'at); and so on, through the long litany of over 2,000 recorded Neterw.

Atum, the great unknowable, unfathomable, supreme creative force, governed as the chief Neter, from which the rest of the Neterw were individual emanations. Perhaps their system of individual Neterw came about in order for people to understand divine principles, to have a human-sized framework rather than an enormous, unknowable notion of existence.

They believed the Duat was a place where humans lived after they died; also known as heaven, netherworld, afterworld, underworld, sky world, land of the gods, stars of the Milky Way, and land of the Neterw. The Duat sky region is the place through which the Pharaohs thought that their souls would travel after death. It was the starting point of the Pharaoh's journey back to the stars from whence he came. Astronomically, the Duat is located in the sky between the constellations of Orion, Gemini (Twins), and Taurus (Bull). The ancient Egyptians called the region of the heavens of which Orion is a part, and which according to Robert Bauval, is the pattern for the ground at Giza (see Appendix II). The Duat was a very important place. They believed that the soul was taken there after death. But this Duat was not only as a region of the sky but also as a parallel universe where the soul had to undergo tests and judgment, a place where it could not escape the truth, where everything one had done and said in life was examined and judged.

The Duat was pictured on the ceilings of tombs and lids of sarcophagi as the star-spangled body of the Neter Nut (Nuit), the mother of Ausar and Auset. As the embodiment of the Duat, Nut is seen swallowing the sun in the west (at sunset) and giving birth to it in the east (at dawn). Her hands and feet rest on the western and eastern horizons.

Nothing was considered random in the Egyptian universe, everything was connected to a unified, cosmic world view. So in essence the ancient Egyptian priests believed the whole universe, from galaxies to the smallest crystal, as well as all lifeforms, contained emanations or manifestations of one ultimate divine principle—a unique form of monotheism!

Furthermore, to associate with a Neter was to develop that attribute within oneself and ultimately to "become" that Neter. A member of a priesthood of ancient Egypt was attempting to generate and expand her own spiritual development by the Neter she associated with, in the temple school she studied at. (A priestess was called a neter with a small n, thus emphasizing the capacity to grow into a Neter with a capital N) In fact, when performing rituals, a priestess was thought to become "possessed" of the Neter, through the means of divine magick or alchemy. To invite a Neter into oneself changes the vessel (person) who is occupied by the Neter. This idea is similar to Christianity, where sharing the bread and wine of Communion brings the Christ energy into oneself. Ultimately, the priestess' goal was to share that knowledge for growth in the community she served, a direct human representative of and stand-in for the Neter.

The idea of Neter may be a difficult conception to us westerners to grasp. However, from reading translations—such as the Book of the Dead with Pharaoh Ani becoming Ausar, it appears that the idea of becoming a Neter is the crux of the ancient Egyptian concept of scientific spirituality. The ancient Egyptians believed the entire universe was divine, from a person to a star to a grain of sand. Thus the Neterw were emanations of that universe; in turn, one could enhance one's own divinity through working with the Neterw.

The difference between an Egyptian Neter and a Greek god, or God, Christ, Jehovah, Yaweh, or Allah, is that for the latter the god is outside of him or herself, and the person prays for the god to intervene or improve one's life. In contrast, the Egyptian Neter is simultaneously inside and outside the individual. So as one asks for help or growth from a Neter, one can develop and expand that "goddess-like" characteristic within oneself.

From ancient times, even during the Middle Ages (saints), spiritual visions were commonplace, even encouraged, often through ritual initiations. Divine visits were frequent. Shamans, healers, and oracles in every ancient culture were highly regarded with respect and awe. Even Homer understood this phenomenon. Consider the goddess Athena visiting and working with Odysseus in *The Odyssey.*

Julian Jaynes, in his book *The Origin of Consciousness in the Breakdown of the Bi-Cameral Mind* theorizes that in the ancient world people thought they were getting messages directly from the gods because the two parts of the brain were still connected and working as one unit. Ancient people therefore couldn't make a distinction from a message heard in their own minds as opposed to coming from outside themselves. About 3,000 years ago, in the period of roughly 700 BC (two thousand years after Narmer), Jaynes posits that the brain separated. Impulses between the two spheres were then connected and transmitted through the corpus callosum to the now-separate and distinct sections. The bi-cameral brain divided into two parts as we know it today, left and right brain—logic, reason, and language (left) versus art and creativity (right). According to Jaynes, a significant shift of human consciousness consequently took place. Was that why over time gods were less credited with the personal authority they once had? Perhaps that is why we moderns seldom give credence or respect to mystical experiences.

Yet William Butler Yeats, the greatest modern poet, recorded a series of visions and messages taken from his wife when she was in a mediumistic trance in his most famous work called *The Vision.* Another poet and artist, William Blake, was a self-proclaimed mystic. In the 1960s and 70s this tendency to discount visions began to change and become more accepted within the New Age community.

Perhaps archaeologists won't find enough artifacts to verify the validity of these non-traditional theories and assumptions set forth. Not only that, but because of the different mind-set/consciousness in antiquity, it's possible modern Egyptologists may not be able to understand those people even if they had the proper artifacts to study. We may need to have our own experiences of the Neterw to truly appreciate the Egyptians' spiritual life.

THE NETER HET-HERU (Greek Name—Hathor)

Het-Heru was the consort of Heru. Her name literally means House of Heru. Het-Heru was a very ancient Egyptian Neter representing and embodying healing, romantic love and beauty, singing and dancing, sexuality and sensuality, spiritual nourishment and constructs of time. Consequently, those Priestesses who studied at the Temple of Het-Heru at Dendera were primarily interested in developing those characteristics within themselves and to serve others in that capacity. In the novel, these characteristics are most embodied by Atalana and Heb. She is depicted either as a beautiful woman or a cow. Het-Heru's symbols are the cow, the mirror, the menat necklace, and the ritual rattle (sistrum).

Het-Heru is a constant presence, representing the divine feminine principle, throughout the long history of Egypt and is among the most ancient of the Egyptian deities. Perhaps She is the next phase of the mother goddess religion in human consciousness. She figures prominently in the creation saga featuring Ra. Although Auset shared or adopted many of Het-Heru's attributes and would eventually eclipse Het-Heru in popularity, Het-Heru would remain an important deity for as long as worship of the traditional Egyptian Neterw was legal and permitted.

Het-Heru's demeanor glows with consistent confidence and sunny, good health. Het-Heru's temples, especially that at Enet-ta-Neter (Dendera) were centers for both healing (with a hospital/sanatorium on-site) and midwifery. Apparently Het-Heru was as intensely worshipped by women in childbirth or young girls desirous of husbands. Even today, she continues to be spiritually significant both for those Westerners who find spiritual inspiration in ancient Egyptian religion and also for local Egyptian women who still seek cures, fertility and protection at the remains of her shrines.

MIRROR OF HET-HERU

The mirror of Het-Heru was generally used by her priestesses for scrying, fortune-telling, explanation of dreams and other spiritual/psychic uses. Priestesses conducted oracles with Het-Heru in trance rituals held in crypts beneath the sanctuary in the temple of Enet-ta-Neter. Any person could spend the night sleeping on the temple roof and hope for a dream, which would be interpreted the next morning by a priestess. One can still see graffiti and game boards left behind by those pilgrims, carved into the stones of Enet-ta-Neter's roof.

Called Lady of Malachite and Lady of Turquoise [heart chakra colors], Het-Heru was also intimately connected to those minerals. Holding spiritual dominion over the Sinai Peninsula, She was responsible for the success and well-being of the mines in that area. Malachite was ground into eye make-up and applied liberally. Thus one not only worshipped Het-Heru by the act of embellishing the eyes, one also wore Her essence.

This practice is similar to devout Hindu women painting henna upon the body. The ritual ideally brings actual physical connection with the divine presence of the goddess Lakshmi (a Hindu goddess similar to Het-Heru), embodied in henna. Both Het-Heru and Lakshmi have dominion over joyousness, abundance, the beauty and vitality of women, and the gracious acceptance of the pleasures of life.

Het-Heru was the matron and embodiment of what were considered the pleasures of life and which remain so today: joy, love, romance, fecundity, dance, music, alcohol and perfume. A deity of women, she ruled anything having to do with the female gender. Yet although she was intrinsically connected to the female of the species, Het-Heru cannot be considered only a women's deity. She also had a large and devoted following among men. Both genders were able to recognize the sacred divinity within Her seductively-vibrant, joyous beauty. Hers is a warm, sensual beauty not aloof or remote. Although she ruled the perfumer's trade in general, Het-Heru was especially connected with the fragrance of myrrh, which was exceedingly precious to the ancient Egyptians and which on a spiritual level embodied the finest qualities of the divine feminine.

She is a questioner of the newly-dead soul on its way to the land of the west (Mistress of the Necropolis). Furthermore, Het-Heru was Mistress of Heaven, called the Duat. The Duat consisted of stars, most prominently Orion's Belt, located in the Milky Way. Was the "Milky Way" always called thus? Perhaps that's where the notion of a "cow goddess" and her "milk" came from. Orion was believed to be the divine origin-place of kings, who would return to that star system upon their death. One shaft in the Great Pyramid is aligned with Orion.

Het-Heru is seen in a multi-faceted way on three different levels. At the literal level she is the cow. At an allegorical level Het-Heru is a projection of the essential attributes of a cow—i.e. milk, a source of sustenance, placid, and peaceful. At the anagogical level Het-Heru is an emanation of the divine spirit, an energy source who contains all the elements above.

Hathor columns, Temple of Enet-ta-Neter (Dendera)

But why would I associate Narmer so closely to the romantic, sensuous Egyptian Neter Het-Heru in my story? Wouldn't it be more fitting for a warrior king to be influenced by Heru, or even Sekhmet, Neter of fire and war? I have an affinity for the Golden Goddess, but that is not reason for this in my novel. She was considered the "Mother" of Egyptian Kings and is thus responsible for the welfare of the country. In an ancient myth, Seven Het-Herus, disguised as seven young women, appear and announce the King's fate. Het-Heru is associated with Narmer in another important way. I found this obscure reference to Het-Heru and Narmer:

"The top of the [Narmer] palette is 'decorated' in a similar manner on both sides: the name of the king is inscribed in a so-called serekh [Narmer's name] between two bovine heads. The animal's heads are drawn from the front...In most publications, these heads have been described as cows' heads, which is interpreted as an early reference to the cult of a cow goddess, perhaps even Het-Heru [Hathor]."

http://www.ancient-egypt.org/kings/0101_narmer/palette.html

If you compare the beautiful face of Het-Heru from carvings at the Temple of Enet-ta-Neter to the Narmer Palette, you can see the similarities —the distinctly Asian shape of the face and eyes; highly stylized cow ears, and sensuous feminine lips.

In conclusion, the nurturing of the king-to-be (Narmer—also known as Catfish), who would grow up to nurture and develop the country-to-be (unified Egypt), was aided by the cow-goddess Het-Heru, feeding him the all-important, life-giving Spiritual Milk (protection, power and wisdom) of the universe.

There is one further interesting piece of information, which relates to this novel. The even-more ancient Neter, Sekhmet, the fierce lioness, is connected to Het-Heru. In an ancient myth, Sekhmet was commissioned by Ra to go find Egyptians who had strayed from the "faith" and punish them. Sekhmet got so involved in Her task that She began to kill people and drink their blood. Ra got upset and asked Djehuti to stop Sekhmet. Djehuti set out bowls of beer colored red like blood. After Sekhmet drank large quantities of this beer, She fell asleep and awoke as Het-Heru. The point of the story may be the "taming" of the uncontrolled feminine spirit. At Het-Heru's temple Enet-ta-Neter there are water spouts coming down from the roof carved in the image of lioness heads.

ANCIENT EGYPTIAN (KEMETIC) NAMES:
Het Heru, Het Heret, Het Hert, Het Her, Ht Hwr (meaning literally House of Horus the Elder)

GREEK NAMES: Hat Hor, Hathor, Athyr

VARIOUS TITLES/NAMES FOR HET-HERU
The Mistress of Heaven
Mistress of Life
The Mother of Pharaoh
Lady of Malachite
Lady of Turquoise
The Mistress of Turquoise
Neter of love, music and beauty
Neter of Love, Cheerfulness, Music, and Dance
Neter of love, beauty, and pleasure
Neter of Joy
Neter of women, fertility, children and childbirth
The Mother of Mothers
The Celestial Nurse
The Celestial Cow
Neter of the dead
Mistress of the Necropolis
Lady of the West
Lady of the Sky
Lady of the Stars
Lady of Gold

The Gold that is Het-Heru

The Golden One

Lady of Enet-ta-Neter

Lady to the Limit of the Universe

The Powerful One

Mistress of the Desert

Lady of the Southern Sycamore

The Great Wild Cow

Mother Cow Neter

Patroness of Women

The Lady of Drunkenness

Lady of Myrrh

Mistress of Dreams

Mistress of Time

Eye of Ra

The Vengeful Eye of Ra

FESTIVAL OF HET-HERU: DEDICATED TO HET-HERU— CELEBRATED ON NOVEMBER 2

Sistrum capitals atop the pillars throughout Egyptian temples show Het-Heru's full face with cow's ears atop a "naos"-style sistrum. Het-Heru was closely associated with Heru-Behdety (Horus the Younger) at Edfu, perhaps influencing the fact that She was a patroness of Kemet's queens (as Heru is to kings). Some queens are referred to by Het-Heru's titles of "Mistress of Heaven" and "Lady of Gold." Nefertari's spectacular temple at Abu Simbel depicts the Great Royal Wife as Het-Heru in many places; and her husband Ramses the Great is depicted in its sanctuary, suckling from the udder of Het-Heru, the divine cow.

Het-Heru's traditional votive offering was two mirrors, the better with which to see both her beauty and your own. Her image, specifically her head, was traditionally used to decorate sistrums and mirrors. Thus when gazing at one's own reflection in the mirror, one would see Het-Heru looking back, from underneath one's own face, serving as foundation and support, perhaps as role model and goal.

She is patroness of women, and professions given to Her priesthood include dancers, singers, actors and acrobats. The protector and sponsor of dancers, Het-Heru was associated with percussive music, in particular the sistrum. Even as late as the Greco-Roman era, the arts were under Het-Heru's dominion. Het-Heru's association with both cows and the sistrum may result from Her assimilation of the predynastic Neter Bat. Het-Heru was also considered the Protector of Queens, just as Heru, Her consort, was Protector of Kings.

HET-HERU'S TEMPLE AT ENET-TA-NETER (DENDERA)

The Temple of Het-Heru was built by the Ptolemies during the Greco-Roman period (332 BC – 395 AD) as a place of worship, a healing center, and a birthing hospital. Enet-ta-Neter was also called the Womb of Time and has a chapel dedicated to the creation of the universe. The temple expanse is built on dozens of acres with a mud-brick wall surrounding it.

Remains of Enet-ta-Neter Temple complex as it looks today

Yet according to an ancient myth, Enet-ta-Neter was simply re-built by the Ptolemies in the same manner as the original. Their design was based on an ancient architectural drawing allegedly found on a goatskin. So it is possible that the original structure and design of Enet-ta-Neter is far more ancient than is generally believed by traditional archaeologists. The ancient Egyptians, like the early Christians, built on very old, already-established sacred sites. Rituals and ceremonies conducted on sacred sites, an important part of most religions, developed into a high art in ancient Egypt. Even if the legend of the rebuilding of Enet-ta-Neter isn't factual, the site upon which the Ptolemies built Enet-ta-Neter could have already been holy and inhabited by a priesthood for ages.

The main temple at Enet-ta-Neter is built on three floors (including the crypts) and contains dozens of chambers, niches and underground passageways. In another chamber were carvings on all four walls showing the myth of Auset, Ausar, and the birth of their son Heru. There are two stairways leading to the roof and upper chambers. One stairway leading upwards has carvings of the Neterw of Time (decans) while the downward leading stairways has plain walls. Decans were protectors of each hour, both daylight and darkness. There is a sacred lake (now dry) on the Temple premises as well as other chapels and buildings.

In one chamber carvings on all four walls depict the myth of Auset, Ausar, and the birth of their son Heru.

In one of the second-floor chambers at Enet-ta-Neter is home to the famous Zodiac, an elaborate ceiling carving.

ZODIAC

The original artwork is considered to be the earliest zodiacal chart in history. The four corners are held up by Heru, while within the circle are many symbols including signs of the zodiac.

The original artwork was removed by Napoleon during his conquest of Egypt and is now exhibited in the Louvre Museum. A reproduction was later carved in modern times on the Enet-ta-Neter Ceiling.

Dendera Zodiac

Archeologists and astrologers each have their own brand of interpretation of the depictions on the Enet-ta-Neter Zodiac. One esoteric theory argues that the zodiac depicts a history of ancient Egypt, beginning at Zep Tepi—the FIRST TIME— when Auset and Ausar were living in Egypt—sometime during the age of Leo the Lion 10,500 BC. Because of the precession of the equinoxes, the constellation of Leo is no longer visible and is now below the horizon at Giza.

Incidentally, the same date, 10,500 BC, is given to the sinking of mythological Atlantis (*Atlantis: The Antediluvian World* by Ignatius Donnelly), coming at the end of the last ice age, as well as the date for the four stars in alignment with the four shafts in the Great Pyramid of Giza (*The Orion Mystery : Unlocking the Secrets of the Pyramids* by Robert Bauval). The leonine Giza Sphinx (Hwr, also known as Horus of the Horizon), which faces due east, points directly to the constellation of Leo as it would have been at dawn on the spring equinox in 10,500 BC. (*Fingerprints of the Gods* by Graham Hancock) If we believe John Anthony West's theory of water-weathering of the sphinx at 7,000 BC or earlier (see Appendix II), this date is entirely plausible. The fascinating award-winning documentary "Mystery of the Sphinx" is available on Youtube and Netflix.

SISTRUM

A ceremonial instrument, the sistrum, is a rattle that is often shaped like the ankh symbol. It is associated with Het-Heru, and its sound is thought to bring protection and divine blessing through fertility and rebirth.

MENAT NECKLACE

The menat necklace was a ceremonial object associated with the goddess Het-Heru whose priestesses are commonly shown holding the emblem. Queens and ladies of waiting, when officiating as priestesses, also wore or carried it. Het-Heru's priestesses are commonly shown holding the necklace. On rare occasions it was worn by men, particularly by priests of Het-Heru, and it was also worn by the god Khons. Originally it consisted of a necklace with small beads of numerous strands, the ends of which are caught into two strings of heavier beads, each ending in a counterweight. It was also worn by the goddess Hathor and symbolized the divine powers of healing. It also served as a medium to transfer the Neter's power to the pharaoh. The pharaoh's wife is sometimes depicted offering the necklace to her husband, since she is the earthly representative of Het-Heru.

Het-Heru's menat necklace is an object that also represents rebirth and divine powers of healing as well as favors of life, health, and rebirth. The menat was found in graves, where it was worn as an amulet to protect the deceased in their transition and rebirth in the afterlife.

Both the menat and the sistrum were believed to be infused with Het-Heru's Divine Spirit during purification and invocation rites and could thus transfer Her life-giving force.

APPENDIX II

HISTORY of EGYPT;
NARMER; NARMER PALETTE;
ABTU; WASET; The RIVER NILE

[I use the original ancient Egyptian (kemetic) words for all the names, places, various words, as well as members of the Neterw. I refer to various Neterw and cities by these original names, just as I do in the novel.]

HISTORY

The area of human habitation around Nekken (Hierakonpolis) in southern Egypt dates back tens of thousands of years to the Lower Paleolithic era, with an unbroken chain of habitation through to dynastic Egypt. Recorded history of ancient Egypt lasts from about 3200 B.C. to 525 A.D.

Thus, Egypt spanned more than 5,000 years of history and pre-history while scientists have only been examining evidence from this ancient civilization since the Napoleonic epoch. The pre-dynastic era (5,000 BC – 3,200 BC) is sketchy, with few artifacts to illuminate the times, a lack of hard evidence. Traditional archeologists and Egyptologists are working tirelessly to fill in the blanks, while a fascinating new contingent of Egyptologists, who disagree with some of the traditional consensus, are challenging old theories with their own.

At a conference I attended in 1998 in Cairo, Dr. Zahi Hawass, Director of Antiquities in Egypt, stated he believes that numerous ancient sites are still waiting to be discovered under expansive and isolated stretches of the Sahara desert. The Nile River has shifted course frequently during the millennia of Egypt's existence, so there are likely numerous structures still to be unearthed that once existed along the lush banks of the river.

Neolithic villagers along the Nile created irrigation projects to control and use the river. Thus, city states called nomes were formed. These nomes, ruled by chieftains (nomarches), were completely independent of one another. They fought frequent wars with each other for power and territory. These wars led to the formation of two kingdoms: Upper Egypt in the south and Lower Egypt in the north (c. 5,000 – 3,200 BC). There are references in carvings and papyrus that indicate the existence of separate northern and southern capitals of these kingdoms, perhaps Buto in the northern Delta and Nekken in Upper Egypt. The city of Nekken was a major urbanized center of the Naqada culture and a residence of powerful Upper Egyptian chiefs.

Northern (Lower) Egypt and southern (Upper) Egypt each developed its own method of farming and its own style of art and pottery. They blended together into one style after the unification, probably from the intensified contact with each other.

Each of these kingdoms had its own individual crown—White in the south, Red in the north. After Egypt was unified, the red and white crowns were combined to make one crown.

Furthermore, each kingdom had its own Neter protectress of Pharaoh —the vulture Nekhebet in the south and the cobra Wadjet (her sister) in the north. After unification, these two Neterw were depicted together on the crown of kings and queens, the most famous image being the cobra poised over the forehead of pharaohs.

Around 3,200 B.C. the northern and southern kingdoms were unified into one country, which begins the dynastic tradition. The Pharaoh Narmer is considered the chief architect of that formation. Traditionally, recorded history begins with the advent of dynastic Egypt. Three Pharaohs lived around that time—King Scorpion, King Narmer, and King Menes (also known as Aha). Some confusion occurred among Egyptologists as to the succession and identity of these Pharaohs. Artifacts dating the earliest pharaohs have been excavated at Abtu, Ineb Hedj , the Helwan cemeteries, Naqada, Saqqara, the eastern Delta region, Nekken, and as far away as Canaan and southern Palestine. These artifacts seem to substantiate the succession as:

> Scorpion (pre-dynastic),
>
> Narmer (first pharaoh of the 1st dynasty),
>
> and then Menes (2nd pharaoh of the 1st dynasty).

Necropolis seal impressions of the First Dynasty were recently found at Abtu Temple in the Umm el Qa'ab tombs of Den and Qa'a. (Preceding the names of the pharaohs was the epithet "Khentiamentyw," an early designation of Ausar [Osiris] indicating dead kings.) These seals corroborate that the succession of the 1st dynasty kings—Narmer, Menes (Aha), Djer, Djet, Merneith, Den, Adjib, Semerkhet, and Qaa.while omitting King Scorpion, who ruled before the advent of the dynastic system.

The unification of Egypt at the end of the pre-dynastic period took place in two areas:

a) the spread of a uniform material culture, as evidenced by the diffusion of products characteristic of the Naqada culture, centered around the city of Naqada, also called Nubt, and

b) the establishment of unified political control.

King Narmer is thought to have reigned c. 3,150 B.C. as the first king of the 1st dynasty of a unified Egypt. The name Narmer has been found all over Egypt including the local vicinities of Tarkhan to the south of Ineb Hdj

(Memphis), the Helwan cemeteries immediately to the East and in the sub-terranean eastern shaft of Djoser's Step pyramid complex at Saqqara. Narmer's name has been found on pottery vessels from the site of Minshat Abu Omar in the eastern Delta. Narmer's power in the region must have been extensive, since Egyptian potsherds inscribed with Narmer's name have also been found as far away as southern Palestine. Perhaps when the earliest site of the capital at Ineb Hedj is finally located, Narmer's role can be properly evaluated.

Narmer's importance as the probable unifier of Lower and Upper Egypt is generally indicated primarily by a palette and a mace head, which are attributed to him.

THE NARMER PALETTE

Palettes are key artifacts for data concerning the late pre-dynastic period. Much of what we know about King Narmer is derived from the world-famous Narmer Palette.

The Narmer Palette was excavated in southern Egypt, by the British archaeologist J.E. Quibell. He discovered it along with fragments of a ceremonial mace head, both inscribed with Narmer's name, in a deposit during the excavation season of 1897/98, along with other artifacts stemming from the early beginnings of the recorded history of ancient Egypt. He also found some mace head fragments inscribed with the name of Scorpion, Narmer's predecessor.

The Narmer Palette is a flat plate of schist, carved on both sides. Its size, weight and decoration suggest that it was a ceremonial palette, rather than a cosmetics palette for daily use. The two-sided Narmer palette has been interpreted as a thanks-offering for the successful victory of the southern over the northern kingdoms. Egyptologists believe that the palette was probably created sometime after the unification itself.

Today the Narmer Palette sits in a protected glass case on the main floor of the Cairo Museum. Roughly two feet tall and perhaps a foot wide, this small piece of beautifully decorated slate has shed as much light on ancient Egypt as the monumental Giza Sphinx or the immense Luxor Temple. The five thousand-year-old ceremonial artifact's symbols are thought to reveal the story of the unification of pre-dynastic Egypt, an event as significant as the Declaration of Independence, the Signing of the Magna Carta, the Russian Revolution, or the formation of the United Nations. With its intricately carved reliefs, the palette depicts Narmer, Unifier of Upper and Lower Egypt, a king who set in motion crucial and far-reaching historical events.

The palette is divided into three registers on both sides.

The top third of the palette is decorated in a similar manner on both sides: the name of the king is inscribed in a serekh (a forerunner of the cartouche) between two bovine heads. The animals' heads are drawn from the front, which is rather uncharacteristic of later Egyptian art. These heads have been described as cows' heads, interpreted as an early reference to the cult of a cow-goddess, perhaps even Het-Heru.

The serekh of his name as shown is thought to be read mr, above a catfish, thought to be read as n'r—Narmer, Raging Catfish. (Hieroglyphics contain no vowels.) The falcon in front of his name is the designation of Heru, first king, which became the title of every Pharaoh thereafter. King Narmer's totem animal, the catfish, was a Setekh animal. Thus King Narmer was the first of Setekh kings to reign during the next twenty dynasties.

The front side shows the king wearing the white crown of Upper Egypt, holding a mace. The clump of plants may indicate the northern Delta region, or could be representing southern oases. Narmer, as king of the South, is wielding his mace in a gesture of triumph over his Magan prisoner, whose name may be Wash. The victory is Narmer's alone. The king's stance is similar to Mesopotamian pictures of royalty and points to the influence Mesopotamia seems to have had on Egypt even in these early times.

Narmer is followed not by a symbol of state administration like a soldier or a scribe but by somebody carrying his sandals, a personal servant, maybe a high-ranking one as the rosette of seven petals seems to indicate. A bearers of sandals, being physically close to the pharaoh, often received a promotion to a higher rank. It has been suggested that being barefoot denotes the strong bond between the king and the land. Footwear certainly could have symbolic value. A pair of sandals, the soles of which were decorated with enemies of the pharaoh, was found in Tutankhamen's tomb.

The falcon Heru, the original divine ruler of Egypt from whom the pharaohs derived their legitimacy, holds on to a prisoner. The rope symbolizing bondage is a recurrent theme in a number of depictions. The falcon perches on six papyrus flowers, possibly denoting six thousand foes captured or killed, or just the fact that the prisoner comes from the papyrus-growing delta region.

Two bearded men, enemies of the king shown under his feet, are fleeing naked, possibly running or swimming, or are lying dead on the ground.

On the obverse side, Heru symbolizing Pharaoh is holding a tether attached to six papyrus plants, the symbol of Lower Egypt. The central figure is now wearing the red crown of Lower Egypt.

As king of Lower Egypt, Narmer marches forth, holding a mace or a scepter and the royal flagellum. He is preceded by Tjet, possibly his vizier or high priest, and four standard bearers who are carrying two falcon standards, a dog, wolf or jackal standard and what has been interpreted as a royal placenta.

Ten beheaded corpses are laid out as if for inspection, their heads placed between their legs. The fact that these bodies are bound suggests that they were executed after falling into Narmer's hands. A corpse with bound arms is also depicted. Mutilation of fallen enemies was commonplace in Pharaonic Egypt. During the New Kingdom cut-off hands and genitals were dedicated to Amun-Ra while their tally was kept by scribes.

Two long-necked chimaeras with bodies and heads of lionesses or panthers and snake-like necks are being held in check by two men sporting full beards, generally a hallmark of the enemies of Egyptian kings.

A bull, symbol for the victorious king, tramples a fallen enemy. Some later kings used the epithet Victorious Bull.

WARFARE

Then did unification of Egypt come through warfare, Narmer's southern kingdom conquering the northern, as the Narmer palette seems to indicate? Or was it created in a non-violent, political manner? Some suggest that Narmer married a Northern princess and thus the two kingdoms were unified politically. However, perhaps the marriage only legitimized the military conquest.

How often skirmishes truly occurred during this time period is disputed. However, tool evidences show that there was a gradual evolution in the production and advancement of weapons in the Nile valley. Weapons became more complex and elaborate. From simple stone-tipped arrows to more intricately assembled composite missiles, from wooden clubs to bejeweled and highly adorned mace-head clubs (such as Narmer's), weapons became more and more complex as time and civilizations progressed. In fact, this pattern clearly shows there is a direct correlation between warfare and the growth of civilizations. History demonstrates that as civilization advanced, so did warfare. There is strong evidence that King Scorpion (Narmer's predecessor) already had a well-developed war technology.

The Narmer Palette itself suggests violence or war:

- Narmer is shown holding a mace, while roughly holding a bunch of hair from a person kneeling at his feet.
- A bull (symbolizing the King) is shown trampling a man under his feet.
- Ten beheaded corpses are laid out in rows, their severed heads between their legs.
- Two men with beards (bearded men are usually depicted as enemies of Egypt)
- The falcon-shaped Heru, original divine King of Egypt, holds onto a prisoner with a rope, symbolizing bondage.

- The falcon perches on six papyrus flowers, possibly denoting six thousand prisoners captured or killed
- Two bearded men are fleeing or perhaps lying dead on the ground

INTERESTING THEORIES on the AGE of EGYPT

Since the earliest days of the 1st dynasty, Egypt emerged fully formed with art, hieroglyphics, sciences, medicine, mathematics, embalming, spiritual practices, astronomy, building, and technology intact. Indeed their history shows a slow devolution from the peak of their civilization from the early dynasties. How could this be possible? How could a civilization start at its zenith and slowly deteriorate? Only one other civilization followed suit – the Mayans of Mesoamerica.

One researcher alleges that Jean-Francois Champollion, who deciphered the Rosetta Stone, dated the unification of Upper and Lower Egypt to 5867 BC—almost three thousand years earlier than current traditional theory. By the same logic, the Narmer Palette could then be commemorating the dawn of the age of Taurus the Bull in 4468 BC—according to precession of the equinoxes. (Incidentally Ramses the Great of the 19th Dynasty reigned in the age of Aries the Ram and built the famous Avenue of the Rams at Karnak Temple.)

John Anthony West (author of *Serpent in the Sky: The High Wisdom of Ancient Egypt* and *A Traveler's Guide to Ancient Egypt*) helped in the creation of the Emmy-award winning documentary "The Mystery of the Sphinx," narrated by Charleton Heston. West, an independent Egyptologist, tour leader, writer, scholar and Pythagorean, has studied the teachings of Schwaller de Lubicz. De Lubicz, a mathematician who understood sacred geometry and researched Luxor Temple for over fifteen years, stated that he believed the age of the sphinx at the Giza plateau to be much older than archeologists believed. Following the trail of de Lubicz, West researched the ancient statue and, with the help of a noted geologist, Dr. Robert Schock, provided extensive evidence that the sphinx is weathered by rain and not by wind as is commonly thought. At a seminar of geologists, this new theory of rain weathering was embraced with enthusiasm. The problem is the last time Egypt had enough rainfall to account for the weathering pattern on the Sphinx occurred no earlier than 7,000 BC. Dr. Schock stated that 7,000 BC was a very conservative estimate; the sphinx could be much older! How old might Egypt actually be?

According to the ancient Egyptians themselves, taken from old Kings' Lists, Egypt had a period called Zep Tepi (the First

Time) when the Neterw were alive in Egypt. Zep Tepi lasted for 26,000 years. After Zep Tepi came the age of Shemsu Hor (Companions of Heru) which existed for another 10,000 years. These two epochs add up to a pre-historical period lasting at least 36,000 years. Re-dating the sphinx, indeed ancient Egypt itself, could put a whole new spin on the science of Egyptology, as well as revise the entire history of humankind.

Although the notion of re-dating the Unification of Upper and Lower Egypt much earlier is still hypothetical, the mystery schools teach that ancient occult Egypt aligned their temples, palaces, and much of Pharaoh's actions, indeed perhaps the character of Pharaoh himself, cosmically with the movement on the planets and positions of fixed stars, not to mention the precession of the equinoxes—a blend of astrology and astronomy. If indeed, the unification of Egypt and the life of Narmer came at the change of the ages, from Gemini the Twins to Taurus the Bull, it could have heralded a disruptive, but important, change in consciousness. This shift in consciousness might have been accompanied by civil strife, confusion, shifts of religious ideas and awareness, expansion of new ideas, a potent shift in the consciousness of kings and kingly duties, and so on.

Furthermore, the end of the age of Gemini (twins) might change other things also. Instead of having TWO kingdoms, Egypt became one united kingdom. The TWO royal crowns were incorporated into one crown. Rather than TWO protective goddesses, unified Egypt had the TWO goddess sisters Nekhebet and Wadjet working as one unit.

Later in history double Neterw like Shu and Tefnut, Geb and Nut were replaced by family units—Sekhmet, Ptah, and Nefertum; Amun-Ra, Mut and Khons; Heru, Het-Heru and Ithy; and the large family of Auset, Ausar, Nebethet, Setekh and Heru the Elder.

THE ENTITY of ANCIENT EGYPT

Which brings me to a question that has bothered me for years. Why and how did Egypt, as an identifiable civilization, last so long?

Generally invaders of a country overwhelm the culture and spiritual life of the country they invade, so that the invaded country takes on the characteristics of the invader. However, in ancient Egypt invaders were assimilated into the culture and spiritual life of Egypt and took these on as their own. For example, Alexander the Great changed his name and religious preferences, as did Ptolemy. Cleopatra VII (the last Ptolemaic ruler of Egypt) believed she was the Daughter of Auset, spoke Kemetic, and worshipped the old Egyptian Neterw, rather than practicing the Roman or Greek religions.

Egypt continued longer than any other civilization in history, although it shared some commonalities with other but shorter-lived civilizations like Assyria, Babylon, Greece and Rome. Was it because Egypt was isolated from the rest of the world? Artifacts as far back as Narmer have been found in other countries, suggesting trade and travel was brisk between them.

Was it because of a strong, unified government? The history of Egypt had times of breakdown in governments between kingdoms, known as intermediate periods, with ensuing chaos, strife, confusion, and even civil war. At various periods, the Hieksos, Nubians, Greeks or Romans ruled Egypt. Yet ancient Egypt—as an entity—regardless of who was ruling—can be recognized as Egypt throughout its long history until the fall of its civilization, sometime after the death of Cleopatra.

Furthermore, all the greatness identified with ancient Egypt was intact from the beginning—the religion (with all its complex rituals and ceremonies); science; medicine; mathematics; hieroglyphics; mummification processes; and the rulership of kings with all the ceremonial trappings. Ancient Egypt as we know it was complete from the beginning of their recorded history, then gradually degraded over time. Some artifacts found in ancient Egypt (i.e. the great pyramid, carved stone vases, precise geometrical architecture), cannot be duplicated today, even with modern technology.

Was it because of the spiritual, occult, astrological, and magickal strength of Egypt that it lasted for at least 3,200 years of recorded history? Was there an overall esoteric plan of Egypt which commenced in prehistory and continued unchanged throughout thousands of years? Who then were responsible as architects of that plan? How and by whom was that plan protected throughout the millennia? All these questions remain to be answered.

LEARNING and MAGICK

The famous Library of Alexandria contained innumerable scrolls of all the world's wisdom and knowledge. What a treasure trove of knowledge might be available to us if the Library had remained intact!

A long tradition of wisdom, knowledge and skill comes to us from Ancient Egypt. Although our schools teach that western civilization's learning is based on Greek thought, the foundation of learning and knowledge came from ancient Egypt. Herodotus, and other ancient Greek historians, wrote extensively of the schools in ancient Egypt, where most scholars from around the world went to learn the important knowledge of the day. Plato and Socrates (foremost philosophers), Hippocrates (Greek physician and father of modern medicine), Euclid (father of geometry), Archimedes and Pythagoras (Greek mathematicians) and countless others were reputed to have been admitted as students in the famous Temple Schools of Learning in ancient Egypt. At the very least, they studied and built their theories upon existing Egyptian knowledge.

The ancient Egyptians were possibly the first civilization to practice the science of mathematics, engineering, architecture, geometry, astronomy, timekeeping, philosophy, and medicine. Modern civilization still uses the ancient Egyptian method of timekeeping. The word chemistry is derived from the word alchemy which is the ancient name for Egypt (Kemet). The Egyptians excelled in medicine and applied mathematics. Although there is a large body of papyrus literature describing their achievements in medicine, there are no records to delineate how they reached their mathematical conclusions. Without a basis of advanced understanding, their astounding feats of engineering, astronomy and administration would not have been possible.

The Egyptians had a decimal system of 1's and 10's using seven different symbols:

> 1 is shown by a single stroke.
>
> 10 is shown by a drawing of a hobble for cattle.
>
> 100 is represented by a coil of rope.
>
> 1,000 is a drawing of a lotus plant.
>
> 10,000 is represented by a finger.
>
> 100,000 by a tadpole or frog
>
> 1,000,000 is the figure of the god Heh, with arms raised above his head.

The study of alchemy (magick), as created by the ancient Egyptians, and furthered by the later Mystery Schools have been well-documented in *The Emerald Tablets of Thoth* by Doreal; *The Mystery Schools* by Grace F. Knoche; *The Sacred Tradition in Ancient Egypt* and The Sacred Magic in Ancient Egypt by Rosemary Clark. Freemasons, Rosicrucians and others have passed on esoteric information found in ancient Egypt, not an easy task to achieve through centuries of neglect and religious/scientific/occult prejudice and punishment.

WASET/THEBES LUXOR

Modern-day Luxor is a bustling city, located along the Nile in southern Egypt, 3rd largest city after Cairo and Alexandria. One of its main industries is the cruise ships that travel up and down the river, bringing visitors to the well-known tourist attractions. Across the river, on the western side, are the Ramesseum and the Temple of Hatshepsut at Deir el-Bahari, and further inland, the Valley of the Kings and the Valley of the Queens and Nobles. The kings and queens didn't start using these valleys as cemeteries until the New Kingdom. The Ramesseum was created by Ramses the Great, while next to Hatshepsut's modern-looking temple is the ruins of a much older temple. Behind her temple are cliffs and the Sacred Mountain, the shape of which could be a prototype for the Giza Pyramids. On the other side of these cliffs, by the way, is the Valley of the Kings, with the Sacred Mountain facing the royal tombs.

In the time of Narmer, however, Luxor or Waset as it was then known, was a back-water town, while the cities of Abtu (Abydos) and Nekken (Hierakonpolis) were thriving metropolises. The two splendid temples in Luxor, Luxor Temple and the huge Karnak Temple complex, were built later in Egyptian history and didn't exist in Narmer's lifetime. However, spiritual dedication was probably practiced at those places by virtue of being sacred sites.

After the unification, Narmer built the grand city of Ineb Hedj (Memphis) as his capital in the northern part of Egypt. Only much later would Waset become the capital of ancient Egypt during the Greco-Roman rule and was renamed Thebes. The city reached its highest point of splendor and power in the Mycenaean period (1600-1100 BC).

ABTU (ABYDOS) TEMPLE

Abtu Temple (Abydos), one of the sites in my story, currently has three temples on its premises, but that wasn't always the case. Only the most ancient one existed in Narmer's time, called the Osireon, Temple to Ausar (Osiris) and resting place for his skull. This ancient temple is similar in style to the Giza sphinx enclosure and the smallest Mykere (Mycerinus) Pyramid Temple on the Giza plateau. Like them, it was constructed of gigantic, uncarved, unadorned, megalithic, rectangular blocks. (There is some artwork on these massive stones but are believed to be carved much later, during the reign of

Seti I). The Osireon is reputed to be the original Temple of Ausar, and was used extensively in earliest Egyptian times.

The other two temples in Abtu were built during the New Kingdom by Seti I and his son Ramses the Great. When one sees the styles of the old and new temples practically side by side in the same location, the vast difference between the two types of architecture is stunning.

ABTU (ABYDOS) PALACE

However, no archeological evidence exists of Abtu Palace (Abydos Palace) constructed across the river from Abtu Temple on the cliffs overlooking the Nile. I had written about the Palace and those cliffs before I ever traveled to Abydos, when I needed to see for myself what the area looked like. I was amazed when I finally saw it. The flat, mesa-like cliffs fit perfectly with the descriptions I had already written months before! I could easily imagine Abtu Palace perched on top of those cliffs, with a long hike down to the river Nile. Archeologists believe that a palace did stand there in ancient times, most likely predynastic. Since palaces were built of mud bricks, then plastered and painted (unlike temples that were built of granite in which to last for eternity). Thus the structure could have collapsed or been destroyed, or simply crumbled into dust after thousands of years. To my knowledge, no other royal palace has been discovered in Egypt, except for remnants of Cleopatra's palace located under the Mediterranean Sea at Alexandria.

MUMMIFICATION

One of the most perplexing, and perhaps misunderstood facets of ancient Egypt, was that of mummification. Generally mummification is seen as a fascinating, yet perhaps repulsive idea, with the jackal-headed Anpu (Anubis) representing a vast Religion of Death. However, the ancient Egyptians believed in resurrection (like some modern religions) and rebirth, perhaps even reincarnation. In the beginning only Pharaohs were mummified. Their bones were acknowledged to contain the wisdom that they had acquired in life and so their bodies were preserved in order for priests to commune with that knowledge. This idea of bones containing wisdom can also be illustrated at sacred Paleolithic sites in Great Britain (barrows), France (Carnac), and Ireland (Newgrange).

Later on, mummification became fashionable for everyone who could afford the lengthy, expensive process.

Furthermore, according to ancient documents written on papyrus and carved on stone, the ancient Egyptians believed their souls came from the stars and returned to the stars after the death of the body, in a process of renewal and restoration (reincarnation?). Fortunate souls (those succeeding in the Weighing of the Heart and answering questions similar to the ten commandments—I did not kill; I did not steal; etc.) would be guided through the netherworld of the Duat to return to their "home" in the stars.

> *A stairway to the sky is set up for me that I may ascend on it to the sky.*—Pyramid Text, Utterance 267, south wall of Unas Pyramid

Anpu was originally considered a spiritual guardian, guiding people along a spiritual path while they were still alive, "opening the doors" to higher wisdom. Only after the pre-dynastic age was he given the task of guiding souls of the dead through the Duat to the next life or afterlife.

ALONG the NILE—RIVER of LIFE

The Nile is the longest river in the world, flowing approximately 4,000 miles from East Africa to the Mediterranean. Studies have shown that the river gradually changed its location and size over millions of years. Unlike other rivers, the Nile flows from south to north. Hence, Upper Egypt is in the South, while Lower Egypt is in the North. Because the country would be a desert without the Nile, the ancient Greek historian Herodotus called Egypt "the gift of the Nile."

Without the life-giving Nile River, Egypt would probably have never become a great civilization. The narrow, but fertile, ribbon of land on either side of the Nile was used to feed its citizens and much of the world's population. Once a year floodwaters poured down from the south, overflowing its banks, and dumping nutrient-rich silt gathered from the rainfall of countries upstream. The flood corresponded with the return of the star Sirius in the constellation of Orion in the Egyptian sky on July 23rd. The actual date varies from year to year, signaling the rise of the river. Timekeeping was correlated to this flood and the Egyptian new year began.

Nowadays, because of the Aswan Dam, the Nile no longer floods its banks in annual inundation. However, current Egyptians have seen the importance of the fertile silt for their farms. So, the bottom of Lake Nasser is dredged by earth-movers while large trucks transport the rich black mud to dump on hungry fields.

The river was home to countless species of fish and provided much-needed protein to the masses living along its banks. Crocodiles and hippopotamuses were once in plentiful supply, but are only found now in greatly diminished numbers south of the Aswan Dam.

Today you can still see farmers with their water buffalo, irrigating and growing food along the Nile, as hundreds of generations have done before them. Millions of tourists cruise the Nile every year, bringing an important source of revenue to an otherwise impoverished country. In important ways, the Nile continues to be the giver of life.

But the Nile is also a symbol of time—of Egypt's generations, countless days and nights of human actions under the stars, measured by their movements.

So as Heb tells his story, it is also the story of the "birth" of Egypt in its earliest days, the dawn before recorded history—growing alongside Mother River, the mighty Nile.

ACKNOWLEDGMENTS

My love and gratitude to my partner of 23 years, Dr. Paul Obler, for his editing skills and endless encouragement. To Hierophant Peter Paddon for his valuable teaching skills, spiritual knowledge, and personal connection to Sekhmet. To Mohamed Nazmy, for his devotion to bringing pilgrims to the mystical sites of Ancient Egypt through his company, Quest Tours, and for his magic in getting me where I needed to go.

My deepest thanks to my friends Colin Wilson, Normandi Ellis, Karen Tate, and Charles Elliot for their kindness and graciousness to take time to read and comment on *Along the Nile.* To Karen Tate, my sister-in-Sekhmet, thank you for a brilliant introduction to my book.

I thank Karen Tate, Charles and Joanne Elliott, Chuck Schwartz, Vivianne Pulido-Price, May Salisbury, Normandi Ellis, Robert Bauval, John Anthony West, Robert Temple, Graham Hancock, Lady Olivia Robertson, Nicki Scully, Robert Masters, along with thousands of teachers, devotees and travelers, who bring ancient Egypt and its mysteries to life.

I wish Dr. Paul Obler, Colin Wilson, and Lady Olivia Robertson (a Grande Dame who founded the worldwide Fellowship of Isis), all of whom have departed this plane of existence in recent years, a blessed journey through the Duat.